I0831840

PLAYGROUND IN MY MIND

PLAYGROUND IN MY MIND

Juanita B. Tischendorf

Copyright Page

ISBN:978-1-928613-39-8

Printed in the United States of America

PLAYGROUND IN MY MIND

Dedication

To my loving and understanding husband, Mark

Epigraph

"Playground In My Mind"

(As recorded by Clint Holmes)
PAUL VANCE
LEE POCKRISS

When this old world gets me down and there's no love to be found.
I close my eyes and soon I find I'm in a playground in my mind.
Where the children laugh and the children play and we sing a song all day.

"My name is Michael, I got a nickel. I got a nickel, shiny and new.
I'm gonna buy me all kinds of candy. That's what I'm gonna do"

See the little children living in a world that I left behind.
Happy little children In the playground in my mind.

Oh, the wonders that I find in the playground in my mind.
In a world that used to be close your eyes and follow me.
Where the children laugh and the children play.
And we sing a song all day.

"My girl is Cindy when we get married, we're gonna have a baby or two.
We're gonna let them visit their grandma. That's what we're gonna do."

See the little children. See how they're playing so happy.
In the playground in my mind.

- SONG HITS, Summer 1974.

Preface

Have you ever felt pulled or twisted from the path you had chosen; as if forces beyond control were at the wheel and you were merely a passenger? If not, you are a lucky person and if so, don't think for a minute you are the only one who has felt as though the oars were being wield by others.

It appears all the important parts of life are controlled and we are merely pawns playing a role. One attempt to make sense of it all is to think that no matter how determined you are to follow the callings of your heart or aim to force yourself to do what is right, it is not your choice that guides you to the outcome. No, it is something called 'destiny' that sits in the driver's seat.

The story I am about to tell you will make a believer out of you or at least have you wondering if it could have been. Because one thing is sure, destiny can lead you into situations that are not as they seem to be.

PETER NEWMAN

Chapter 1

I stood beside the bed of my dying son, wishing there was something I could do to save him, but knew there was nothing. The doctors had made it perfectly clear that all they could do was being done already and that Max was now in God's hands. It hurt, it hurt so much to see my little boy laying there, possibly in pain, possibly beyond it and there was nothing I could do to save him. Each day that passed, Max was slipping further and further away and I felt like I was in a dream.

It was hard to accept Max as he is now. I close my eyes remembering the day my son was born. That day as soon as he made his entry, he was laid on Christine's chest and her eyes glowed with tears of joy. When the nurse retrieved him to take him across the room to clean his little body, my eyes followed his progress and I swear, my little man was looking all around, his head bobbing back and forth like a newborn, but his eyes alert as if taking this new world in.

When he was six weeks old, Christine and I took him to a shopping mall to have his picture taken and people would stop and say, "What an alert baby." And there was just something about him that went beyond the attraction of a newborn.

I force myself to look at my son again. His light brown hair dull and dishevel, his green eyes hidden behind his closed lids and his smile, gone made it hard to accept that this was Max. The Max I saw in my mind would be running and jumping, his hair unruly, but glowing with life and his green eyes glistening with mischievousness. And when he paused to breathe, Max's lips would draw up at the corners in a smile that would melt my heart.

The doctor had been honest with me. They explained that because the skin is so richly supplied with nerve endings, any serious burn will have pain and in addition to that pain would be the pain caused by the frequent dressing changes, wound cleansings and rehabilitation hydrotherapy. Max was intubated, and given intravenous opioids supplemented by benzodiazepines. The doctors would explain that there are several special problems that impact burn patients such as cardiac and respiratory instability so pain therapy must be tailored to avoid these problems and that can be challenging. A second problem is hypotension. I didn't care what it meant, I only wanted it all to go away and Max to come back to me. I knew that Max was acutely burned and though he whimpered now and again, I knew they were doing everything they could for him.

Max wore a mask over his mouth to help him breath and Max hadn't opened his eyes since coming to the hospital. I stare down at my son and feel the tears welding in my eyes. He is so like Christine. It is her hair, her eyes and her skin coloring that Max has inherited, though now he is so pale he blends into the white hospital sheet. But there is a little of me in him too. He has my smile and my eyebrows.

That thought causes a smile to play on my lips, but it is gone as quickly as it appears. This is not right. This is not how it should go. I was taught there was a reason for everything and thus, there was always a solution. A sob escapes and in a whisper, I say, "You need effective actions to deal with anger, not just simple platitudes. You need to take the time and trouble to seek the kind of guidance that will help you deal directly with your problems rather than to try and circumvent them."

I fight to hold back tears. This is my signature affirmation to calm the clients who came seeking my legal advice, one I found more useful than addressing whether they were guilty or innocent. Only now as I look at my son, I can find no comfort in these words.

I had just managed to get myself back in control when I am joined by a doctor. Out of habit, I look at my cell and see that it is now seven o'clock in the evening. It seems so much later.

"Hello, Mr. Newman. I'm Dr. Saio," he says before turning his attention to Max. "I understand you call this little guy, Max."

I do not respond.

"Mr. Newman?" the doctor says anxiously.

My mind is elsewhere. I feel my lips as they move into a smile, remembering that Max felt that time moved very slowly and I would tell him to enjoy it because soon it would feel as though time was speeding by too quickly. Max would just twist his head from side to side and press his lips together tightly. "Dad, he would say, time is time."

The smile is gone as I hear my name being worriedly called. And just like that I am back.

"What? Did you say something?"

"I asked if you call Maximillian; Max for short?"

"Yes. Sorry, who are you?"

"I'm Dr. Saio. I work with your son's doctor and I want to examine him now, if you don't mind."

As if I had a choice. "Yes, sure, go ahead," I said.

Dr. Saio smiles pleasantly and thanks me before leaning over the bed that held the pale listless body of my five-year-old son.

Dr. Saio has dark brown hair, neatly brushed back across the crown of his head, but as he leans over my son, a lock falls forward and rest on his forehead. He looks like he needs a shave, but on closer observation I am sure it is part of his style and it seems to fit his face. In any other situation, I thought to myself, I would like this guy. He was close to my age and we probably shared similar interests. He was pleasant, and had good bedside manners as he carefully examined Max, talking to him though he knew Max could not respond. That assures me that he will pay attention to make sure that Max is comfortable. But then comes the hard part.

"Max, can you hear me?" Dr. Saio spoke an octave louder than his normal voice. When there is no rely, I watch as the doctor leans closer to Max, his mouth closer to my son's ear. "Max, try and open your eyes." He pauses. "Tell me your name." When there is still no response, Peter watches as the doctor lifts one of Max's limp hands and places it in his own.

"Max if you hear me, move your fingers for me." I hold my breath, hoping for a miracle, but from the expression on the doctor's face, I know without being told that Max isn't responding.

I listlessly continue my observation as the doctor places Max's hand back on the white sheet and begins testing Max's reflexive eye movements.

As he works through the examination, Dr. Saio says, "He doesn't have a temperature, that's good." I think I respond, but can't be sure. Besides I think the question is rhetorical.

Dr. Saio continues his examination as I turn away, no longer able to watch. It is just too hard to be so helpless when my son is suffering.

"Mr. Newman." I turn back around to face the doctor. "Yes," I reply.

He has done this several times before, but somehow this time is harder. He sees the sadness in the father's eyes, and for a minute can't bear to cause him more pain. In his head, he repeats repeatedly, "I'm sorry, so sorry".

"Please have a seat," he says as he silently slides the empty chair on the linoleum floor until it is positioned directly across from the recliner. Then he waits.

I hesitate. This is not the actions of a man who is about to give good news, but I find myself walking over and siting in the recliner.

"You have been through so much."

Those are words I have heard repeatedly, but now I know it is going to be different. I brace myself for the worst. "Please, just tell me doctor." I can hear the anger in my voice, an anger that has been there waiting to bubble to the surface and explode.

"Max is not getting any better. He is in what we define as an irreversible coma and is now brain dead, yielding a flat electroencephalograph reading. We have taken two such readings, one a day and this diagnosis is confirmed by his unresponsiveness to all external stimuli and lack of any sign of the normal reflexes controlled by the brain stem or spinal cord."

I can feel my face distorting and cover it with my hands as I mumble, "Oh, no, no."

It is the only human sound in the room and I finally get hold of myself. I clear my throat and take a deep breath. Cautiously I look at the doctor. "Doctor Saio you must do something. I can't lose them both. I just can't."

Dr. Saio doesn't respond right away, but when he does it is not what I want to hear.

"Peter, may I call you Peter?"

I nod.

"Peter, I think it's time to let Max go. There isn't any medical measure we haven't already taken. We will still watch him closely, but we want to remove life support." Dr. Saio pauses, then says, "Peter"?

"I…"

"I know, I know," he says soothingly. "Max has been attached to life support to keep his heart functioning and to keep him breathing. Peter, your son has severe burns and if he were to wake up, he would not be able to sustain." Dr. Saio pauses to give me time to digest what he is saying.

"Peter, Max has only a 10 percent chance of surviving longer than a couple days and if he does do so, he will be in pain, physically and mentally disabled, and unable to move or swallow, requiring lifelong care." He again pauses to allow me to digest his words.

"This is your decision and yours alone. Whatever you want us to do, we will do."

I hear a strange sound and realize it is coming from me. It hurts to even think about it. I hear the words that Dr. Saio is saying, but cannot bring myself to accept them. Deep down inside me I know what the doctor says is true. That Max has been gone long before now and that the machines were extending his life. I know the doctors have moved swiftly, operating immediately to try and save Max, but… I can't finish that thought.

Images and sensations assault me. I feel Christine's hand as she gently touches my cheek as though consoling me. I hear her laughter and the way when she laughed her eyes would shine. Memories flood me as I recall how it felt to pick up Max and swing him around at shoulder height until he laughed so hard I had to stop for fear of him choking. I remember how it felt to take Max in my arms and hold him close as I planted a kiss on the top of his head or on his cheek.

Memories continue to flood my mind as Dr. Saio sits quietly in front of me. I remember how lost I felt when Christine had taken Max to visit her parents last summer. The house seemed to deflate a bit, settling quietly around me and no matter how I tried not to feel that way, it was like I was suspended, waiting for real life to begin again which would only happen at the moment my wife and son walked back through the door. The images pushed in and out of my head and I could not stop them, nor did I want to. These memories would have to last me now for the rest of my life.

I stood up and put my hands in my pockets and jiggled the change there. I felt light-headed and leaned against the wall and saw Dr. Saio start to get up, then sat back down.

I wondered what had I done that was so wrong? Why was it I was brought to this point? One day I had a lovely wife and a beautiful little boy. The next day my wife was gone and right now my son was struggling for life that the doctor felt would be a losing battle. We had been so happy. My family was my life and without them I could not fathom a reason for living. I had wanted to see Christine's youthful beauty deepen as she passed into her forties and then become even more precious as she entered her sixties. Now that would not happen.

And my son… Max, I would not see him grow and experience adolescence or his teenage dilemmas that I could help him through. Nor would I see him become a man and choose a wife to spend the rest of his life with, producing grandchildren for us to admire and spoil. All of that and more had been taken from me that day.

I am angry and the anger consumes me. There had been so much to look forward to and never could I have guessed it would end so quickly and in this state.

That was my last thought before losing consciousness.

The case had taken place on what was the cloudiest January, and the amount of calls coming into the precinct were drastically up. This was no surprise as depressive days lead to more police activity. The Rochester Police Department received a 911 call from Alexander Robinson saying that his wife, Emily Robinson was attempting to kill herself by drowning herself in the bathtub on the second floor of their home. Mr. Robinson repeated several times on the telephone saying, "She is killing herself."

Other lines were ringing with 911 calls with all kinds of reports that would keep the policemen busy until the following morning. It was all hands-on deck as officers responded to the Robinson residence, located at 20 Beaconsfield Road, in the suburb of Pittsford where those who were well off lived and where response time could be very impressive no matter what time of the day it was. Special Agent Don Worthington entered the residence with Officer Martin and from the minute they entered, the investigation began. Their eyes swept over the entrance area, noticing each piece of furnishing and any signs of a disturbance to the area. They walked around taking a closer look at the mahogany table that sat in the middle of the room, studying the door itself for any evidence of forced entry, a picture tilted or anything amiss. They were still surveying the room when Officer Martin looked up.

Walking toward them was a tall, slim man with a chiseled face and a stern expression. His face was long and well-tanned, his dark hair, perfectly coifed above his collar, with his tie pushed up close to his neck. His brown tweed suit with a five-button vest was obviously a tailored job, obvious by its fit on his lithe frame. Before he opened his mouth, his presence commanded attention. When he was directly in front of them, he said. "Follow me."

Don whispered to Martin, "I bet we're the only visitors who were not greeted first and then asked if he could take our coats". Martin knew that this could very well be true, but replied, "We are probably the only visitors greeted by Mr. Robinson himself."

Not saying another word, they followed Mr. Robinson upstairs to the master bedroom that was bigger than the whole second floor of either of their houses. The oversized room had a large California king bed and across from that was a sitting area, writing desk, dressing area, walk-in closet and a door leading to what must be a private terrace. Near the door entrance was a flat screen TV, hung over a Nespresso coffee machine sitting atop a marble table. With their mouths, agape they followed their host through a doorway and found themselves in the master marbled bathroom. There was an oversized trough sink in front of them with a padded stool and over on the far wall was a matching setup, only with a smaller trough sink. Along the side wall was the longest soaker tub they had ever seen and at the far end was a stone entrance that lead into a massive shower. There was recessed lights and wall sconces everywhere they looked. It was here that Emily Robinson was lying nude on the bathroom floor. Martin was in the process of stepping closer to the body when the paramedics entered the room.

While the paramedics did their job, Martin and Don walked around the bathroom, jotting down notes of what they saw until summoned by the paramedics to hear their findings. They report that the woman was cold to the touch, pale and non-responsive. They had administered CPR but the patient did not respond. Martin could see that now in what was a spotless bathroom there was all types of medical paraphernalia on the floor around her. Emily Robinson was declared dead at the scene. Knowing the drill, Martin didn't have to ask the first responders to try and not disturb the scene.

Now it was their time to act. Carefully the officers began the examination of the scene, putting on their plastic gloves and asking the homeowner to leave the room. They checked the bathtub which was full of water and when they put their hand in, the water was cold to the touch. It ran through Worthington's mind that Emily Robinson had apparently been moved from the bathtub by possibly her husband prior to the arrival of law enforcement and he had positioned her lying on her back on the bathroom floor. This was important.

On further observation Worthington noted that there was a bathtub caddie still in place across the center of the bathtub and the towels surrounding the bathtub were dry. Martin moved over to Emily's body and noted there were areas of bruising that had already turned purple in color and were located on her forehead and neck.

Once the investigation was complete at the scene Martin knew that the husband was the only one in the house and was the one who found the victim. The husband had openly admitted that he had moved the body. This information lead Martin to asking Alexander Robinson to come down to the precinct. When Mr. Robinson asked why, he replied that they needed to question him further.

Mr. Robinson complied. No one read him his rights before the questioning and Robinson tried to be as helpful as possible. He told officers that Emily had an addiction to prescription pills and explained that he believed that she must have overdosed. He would state multiple times during the interview that Emily had a drug addiction to pain pills as if he wasn't sure they had heard him. Worthington thought it strange that not once did Mr. Robinson repeat that his wife was "trying to kill herself" or explain why he stated that in his message to the 911 dispatcher. When asked if his wife had ever threatened suicide or attempt it in the past, Mr. Robinson replied, "No".

Detective Worthington asked Mr. Robinson where he was during the assumed suicide attempt and he replied that he was in the basement of the home with their three children. Emily had said she felt stressed after they finished dinner and wanted to just go upstairs and take a bath. They were alone in the house so Mr. Robinson decided to take the children downstairs to the basement to the playroom and give her some time alone. After going upstairs to get the kids a snack, Mr. Robinson thought he heard water running upstairs and went to check on Emily. On opening the bathroom door, he noticed that the floor was wet and then he saw Emily face down in the bath tub with her head submerged near the water facet. Not knowing what to do, Mr. Robinson pulled Emily out of the tub and phoned 911.

After a bit, Detective Worthington asked Mr. Robinson if he knew how Emily had sustained bruises on her body and he replied, he did not.

Later as the police investigated the scene, they did check the overflow valve in the tub and reported it was in working condition.

Their investigation turned up that the Pittsford Police had responded to the Robinson residence on another 911 call placed by Emily Robinson on a domestic matter. No one was arrested at that time as neither party reported any physical assault. But following the dispute report, Alexander had taken the children out of state without the knowledge or permission of Emily. He would bring them back in a few days after being served with a court order by

Emily Robinson's lawyer. Why would that be a legal matter?

The answer was forthcoming when it was learned that Emily Robinson had filed for divorce just the day before Alexander had taken the children. To retaliate the divorce filing, Alexander had filed for full custody of their three children. It was already proving to be a nasty divorce with both sides trying to discredit the other. Alexander Robinson went to the elementary school in Pittsford and told teachers that Emily was unfit as a mother and was addicted to prescription medication. Emily Robinson told her family and friends she was afraid to be alone in the house with Alexander and so her friends and family took turns staying at the Robinson house.

This was what had been told to them. If true, who was supposed to be staying at the residence on the evening of Emily's death, because they were alone with only the children on the premises.

The investigation revealed that Emily's cell phone records showed that she had called her father that very evening. When they interviewed him, he would say that his daughter had called to say she was scared to go home and be alone with Alexander. Her father would be the last person to speak with Emily.

The autopsy report performed on Emily Robinson found that there were several areas of trauma to the front, right and left side of the victim's head. In talking with family members, it was said that Emily Robinson did not have any type of injuries to her head or neck prior to that evening. The toxicology report on Emily did not show any signs of drug abuse and drug overdose was determined not to be the cause of death. The State Medical Examiner ruled Emily Robinson's death as undetermined.

Undetermined or not, the officers felt they had enough information. Alexander Robinson was taken into custody and charged with first degree murder in the death of his wife, Emily Robinson. The bail was set at one million dollars which Alexander could not raise.

At the preliminary hearing, the prosecutor would say that Robinson killed his wife because she wanted to divorce him. His defending attorney would say that Emily Robinson drowned in the bathtub after having a seizure brought on by alcohol withdrawal and they had proof to support this.

Robinson pleaded not guilty. A court case was scheduled. Several months prior to the date, Alexander asked to be released on his own recognizance and to have his trial delayed so he could be with his 5-year-old daughter during her recovery from a bone marrow transplant. The Robinson's daughter, Coco, had leukemia and was scheduled to undergo the transplant in two months. Court records say his trial was set to begin in two months. Robinson's attorney filed the request for a delay and it was denied.

As scheduled the case was taken to court. After reviewing the autopsy findings, a forensic pathology expert concluded Emily Robinson died of asphyxia due to neck compressions and/or drowning and said her death was a homicide.

Kept as a smoking gun, unsealed warrants disclosed that Alexander Robinson told investigators $200,000 was deposited into the couple's account and then withdrawn just a few days later and he didn't know where the money came from or where it went.

His attorney would go on record as saying neither he nor his client understood what had changed to lead to this arrest in the first place. The autopsy was consistent with her drowning and consistent with the fact that it was not a homicide. So, both were shocked when suddenly he'd been accused of first degree murder.

Just as they had a smoking gun, the prosecutor had one too. They would eventually learn of a new autopsy report that attempted to clarify the case as a homicide.

Per an affidavit, the findings of the autopsy and the investigative case file were reviewed by Dr. Thomas McMeekin, an expert in forensic pathology, who provided an opinion that Emily's death was "caused by asphyxia due to neck compression and/or drowning." He would suggest that the bruising found on her neck indicated there was a struggle before she died and concluded the manner of her death was homicide. Though medical records would report that Emily Robinson had been treated for seizures, this was not made part of the record or given any weight during the trial.

Alexander Robinson was convicted of first-degree murder and faced a sentence of life in prison.

Maybe he was guilty, but then, maybe not. As far as Peter was concerned, the man was not given a fair trial and there was room for reasonable doubt.

"Mr. Newman?"

I hear my name being called, but have trouble responding as the last images of the case finally free my mind and I jolt back to reality.

"What happened," I asked.

"You passed out."

"I'm sorry," I said as I tried to sit up on the bed next to Max's where someone had placed me.

"No reason to be sorry. We are just glad you are all right. But we would like you to rest a bit and think about allowing us to take your son off life support." Dr. Saio paused. "Max is right there," he said pointing over to my son's bed and we need you to make the decision when you are rested and you are ready.

Slowly the fog lifts and I am back in the room with my dying son. I realize that my unconscious mind has taken me away from all this and whether it is the right thing to do, or not, I am thankful for a few moments of peace. I can handle all kinds of cases and make all kinds of hard decisions without any personal feelings. Only now it is personal and so I need to assure myself I can make the right decision.

I manage to assure the doctor I will relax, but as soon as he leaves the room, I get up and go over to the side of Max's bed.

Nothing has changed. I stand there and I remember my dream. The Robinson case had been the first case that I tried as a lawyer and my father as a detective had worked the case. There would be other cases where our paths crossed, but that one was special.

My father began his career as a policeman, but moved quickly up the ranks to police detective, working mainly on murder cases. He could have gone all the way to chief of police, but what my father wanted and obtained was the position of captain which he said still gave him the power to have some control over his investigative cases.

Now as I remember this, I tell myself I know what needs to be done. My father always knew what he wanted and what to do at any given moment. Now as I stand looking at my son I call on him. "Dad, help me, please help me."

I sit down in the chair next to Max's bed overcome with grief and when Dr. Saio enters the room I didn't wait for him to ask. "Yes, I give you permission to take my son off life support."

Not wanting to, but unable to stop my eyes from travelling in that direction, I watch as the tubes and wires are disconnected and when it is done, the room emptied, leaving me alone with my son. I rose from my chair went over to look at Max and feel a pain in my heart that I know will never leave me. I lean over and kiss my son's cheek, wishing I could pick him up in my arms and hold him. Only that would cause him pain. So instead I drag the recliner closer to his bed.

This chair is becoming my whole world and as I sit back down my mind and body relax and I allow my mind to drift.

Chapter 2

The day we met was magical. I hurried out of the court room and stepped out into the bright sunlight on a cloudless June day in downtown Rochester. I was feeling good about the outcome of the trial. This was a big one and could skyrocket my career. So, with a smile on my face I blindly rushed down the courthouse steps and onto the sidewalk.

Moving at a fast clip too, Christine was unable to stop quick enough as she ran right into me, knocking my brief case from my grasp and almost sending us both toppling to the sidewalk.

"Sorry, sorry," she said as she stooped down to retrieve my brief case, only she did it at the same time as I and we bumped heads.

There was a moment. Christine and I reached up to rub our foreheads and at the same time our eyes met. I slowly managed to pull my eyes back into my head and gain a semblance of control as I reclaimed my brief case and straightened up slowly appreciating the tall thin figure and shapely legs in front of me. With my hand still massaging my forehead I finally stood erect taking in the figure clad in a bright green dress that was standing in front of me.

Suddenly I felt woozy, but not from the head butt I had received. It was from the captivating face with the glowing green eyes staring back at me. Her long light brown hair glistened in the sunlight as she attempted to push it back in place with one hand. She was beautiful and took my breath away, stunning me into silence.

Christine was silent too. We stood facing each other for some time; probably seconds but it seemed much longer, until I managed to say something. "Well, should we exchange insurance?"

And she smiled. And I was hooked. Until that moment, I felt that I had everything I wanted. I had a great life and loved what I did. I had lots of friends and business associates to spend time with and I couldn't be happier. Or so I thought. Lucky for me Christine was going through the same life assessment as she stood looking at me and before I finished my next sentence, "Would you like to go for a cup of coffee," she was already nodding her head, yes.

We walked side by side down the sidewalk, taking sideways glances at each other until we were seated across from one another at a local coffee shop. "This is not like me," Christine said.

Even though I knew I asked, "What do you mean."

"Well, we are strangers. We just met and here we are having a cup of coffee together and I don't even know your name."

"Well, my name is Peter Newman and I am a lawyer, not a serial killer."

"Good to know, Peter. So why did you become a lawyer?"

Peter didn't even have to think to answer the question. "Well, my father was in law enforcement. He would tell me, as much as my mom would allow him too, about the cases he went on. It made me feel as though he was doing something important and that's what I wanted to do." I paused and smiled at Christine. "Unlike my father, I saw more power in being a lawyer than a law officer."

"Your turn. What is your name and how do you make a living."

"Well, my name is Christine Pryor and I am a business analyst." She pauses and adds, "Now for the big question. Though I see you're not wearing a ring I need to ask; are you married? Are you engaged?"

Peter smiled and watched as Christine raised her brow in wonder. I let out a little laugh before finally replying, "No. Not married and not even close to being engaged to anyone."

"And you?"

"Same here. I am married to my job. I guess I want to be great and I want people to believe in me." She paused. "I suppose my colleagues would say that I come across as self-confident and independent, and I am, but I fight to be noticed and appreciated so how independent is that?"

As if aware of what she was saying, Christine looked up, her lids almost covering her eyes. "I'm so sorry. I don't know why I shared that." She looked directly into my eyes and said. "Don't feel you have to respond to such crazy talk."

"No. That's fine. I can say that people think I am courageous and value order and security in my life and they are right. I don't gravitate toward the unknown and tend to follow defined guidelines. I am uncomfortable with ambiguity and believe it or not, emotional impulsiveness is not in my nature." I smiled. "This is a first for me, too."

The honesty moved the relationship ahead and the conversation came easy as we sat talking, learning about each other. We found that we both liked spicy foods, living in a warm sunny place though that was far from what one would call Rochester, New York. We punctuated that with our reason for being here was work. And that brought us around to learning we worked in the same building.

"I can't believe we haven't met before," I said upon hearing this. "I'm in and out all day. I would think we would have met."

"It's a big building Peter and there are a lot of people working there." Christine glanced at her cell. "And speaking of working. I need to get back."

"What time is it?"

"After eleven o'clock. We've been here almost two hours."

They stood up together. "I was on my way to see a client so I better give him a call," I said, taking out my cell.

"I was on my way back to the office so I guess we aren't going in the same direction?"

"No, unfortunately not."

Slowly we walked out of the restaurant and paused on the sidewalk to exchange business cards. As she turned to go, my eyes never left her silhouette until she mingled in the crowd.

Not a day went by after that chance meeting that I and Christine were not in conversation or in each other's company. We shared long lunches and later even longer dinners together conversing on every topic under the sun. I learned that Christine had a normal childhood in a family of three children of which she was the youngest by quite a few years. Christine would tell me that being the youngest child in the family had its advantageous and disadvantageous. She got love, affection, support and all kinds of help from her parents and elder siblings, making it hard to step out beyond that comfortable environment and face the realities of the world. She laughed and added, "It was even more so since I was a late life baby and my brother and sister were almost old enough to be my parents."

I would tell her, "Well, I can relate. Being an only child, your parents put all their hopes and dreams into one basket, me. One thing I know for sure is I don't want to subject any child of mine to be put in that position."

"So, Peter," Christine asked shyly. "How many children would you like to have?"

Peter thought for a moment. "I want two; maybe three, but preferably two or four."

And Christine understood.

Everything changed for the two of us and anyone having any connection to either one knew something was going on. At dinner one night at her parents, her mother asked. "So, Christine, when are you going to tell us about him?"

Only mildly surprised, Christine looked across the table at her mother and slowly a smile covered her face. "I should have known you would figure something was up."

"Me," her mother said, "All of us can see it. Why just the other day I ran into your friend Sarah and she asked, What's up with Christine."

"Well, family, I met the man of my dreams. His name is Peter Newman and we have been seeing each other, and, I know this is crazy, but I think I fell in love with him the first day I met him."

"You think?" The family said in unison and as Christine looked from one family member to the next she could see them giggling and laughing.

Around the same time, I had made up my mind. Christine was the woman I wanted to marry so I shared this decision with my parents. There was silence and I was nervous, waiting.

"So, how long have you been dating?" asked my mother.

"Well, we've met for coffee, ate lunch together and had what you would call dating experience; dinner together for at least a couple months."

There is shock on my mother's face. "How many dinners," she asked cautiously.

"Hmm, maybe eight…somewhere around there."

"Eight!"

This is followed by an uncomfortable period of silence. "Son," my father finally said, "you have a good head on your shoulders so if you say you are going to ask this woman to marry you, she must be special."

"Yes, dad she is."

"Well," his mother said, it's time we met.

It was the happiest day of my life when I asked Christine if she would marry me and she said, "Yes". Then there was a whirlwind of activity as we prepared for that day when we would say, “I do.” I remember Christine looked pensive when I caught a glance of her in the floor-length white satin dress, with slim straps, a corseted waist and a full skirt. Her beautiful shiny hair was covered by a floor-length veil, but I could see her eyes shining as if she was going to cry. I knew how she felt at that moment because I felt it too. This was too much happiness for two people and we were afraid something would go wrong. But it didn’t and she looked like an angel standing there, waiting to become my wife.

There were many discussions with parents and family who wanted to help, but in our personal discussions, we agreed it was important to us that the day be relaxed and full of laughter. With that intent in mind we had our closest family and friends around us; those who we knew would add just what we wanted to our wedding day. The ceremony was held at the Irondequoit United Church of Christ which reflected our feelings of our day being a land mark experience and with a little over 200 guests it was everything we could hope for.

It was all going our way as we eased through four years of wedded bliss, moved into a home befitting a successful lawyer, and the one missing ingredient was soon achieved. We had Max.

Our life was perfect. I made partner in the law firm and was happy when Christine gave up her career to stay home to raise our son. Secretly I had hoped she would, but I would have been happy with whatever she chose to do. Yes, we had a wonderful, uncomplicated, life.

I am jarred awake and for a moment didn’t know where I was. I take the back of my hand and wipe tears from my cheeks; tears that have squeezed through my closed eyes. It takes a little longer for me to register why I have been crying and when reality returns, my world comes smashing down around me anew.

It is surreal. My life has been so wonderful without a hint that it would change so drastically. I can feel the tears starting so I stand and look up at the ceiling until I feel some control and then I go over and kiss Max's cheek. I think that maybe some fresh air will help so I allow myself to break the constant vigilance and with one more touch of his cheek, I force myself out of the room.

Outside his room where the hospital had been a bustling metropolis, all is quiet and serene. As I make my way down the empty corridor I hear my shoes echoing in the silence of the tiled hallway, but all that changes when I reach the lobby where the carpet masks the sound. I walk steadily up to the glass doors at the end of the lobby that slide open on my approach, allowing me access to the outside. I walk through the door, wait, then walk through the second set of doors as they allow me passage.

The frosty cold air greets me, waking every fiber of my being. Small, white specks float and blow with the wind, twirling and spinning until they ultimately land on top of the snow that has gathered on the ground. It comes back to me as I stand there, coatless in the freezing weather trying to keep my teeth from chattering that Rochester, has been staggered by a blizzard that hit on Thursday leaving thousands stranded on roadways. Seeing the frequency of the snow fall and the wind, I pull out my cell and click on the local news icon.

"*Rochester, staggered by a blizzard on Thursday that left thousands stranded on roadways, is being hit with a second storm today that continues into the night. Meteorologists predict that another foot of snow will be added to the two feet that has already fallen since Thursday. The severity of the issue has the authorities contacting the National Guard units in Buffalo and Binghamton to help*

Rochester crews assisting ambulances and clearing streets of snow and stranded cars.

"Right now, our top priority is to transport doctors and nurses during shift changes," said Capt. Walker of the National Guards in Rochester. 'Some haven't left the hospital for the past 36 hours."

I stand outside watching the flakes that increasingly gather tightly about me and fall to the grown, mingling with the two feet of snow already taking up space. But it doesn't matter. None of this matters to me because I am not a part of the world beyond this building. It is cold but I continue to stand there under the overhang watching the snow as it falls to the ground, my mind relieved from the pressure of what I must decide for Max. By now the cold has invaded my body causing me to shake uncontrollably, but I welcome the sensation because this is the only normal emotion I have had since the fire and just like that, my mind drifts back to the past.

Chapter 3

I woke up, my hair only slightly tousled and my mind already racing with activity. Today our son was turning five years old. It didn't seem possible that Max was turning five, which in my family was a very special event. It was for Christine and her family too, but not in the same way. Though I was as excited as Christine about Max's birthday, I couldn't quite understand the necessity to go overboard when Max would be just as happy going to McDonalds for hamburgers and fries.

I had to admit I understood Christine's motive. She loved wholeheartedly and generously and had a need to make the people she loved felt special. It was something she had to do and there was no talking her out of it. It had to be perfect. Christine had talked to Max, other parents of children his age and even his teacher, along with doing research months ahead of time to assure herself success. I didn't understand all the energy and money she expended, but I did understand her motive and I could not fault that.

A smile made its way to my face as I remembered her standing in the doorway of our living room with that deep look of concentration on her lovely face searching for the right words to defend her position for this special birthday celebration.

"Peter, this is a very special year. Max turning five means he is about to enter a whole new phase of life. Why turning five has so…"

While she searched for the right word, I interrupted saying, Okay Hon, but if you were to ask me, I think that a trip to the zoo would be as good as it gets for Max."

That should have been it and it was as far as words were exchanged, but each time Christine would present me with another idea for the party I tried to appear excited, but just couldn't pull it off. Christine would get that look on her face, the one that said that's okay honey, you can't be expected to understand and when she did that I felt like the only one in the room who didn't get the joke.

I looked over at the clock on the bed side table. It was time to wake the household. I leaned over and brushing my lips across my wife's cheek I whispered in her ear, "Wake up sleepy head."

Christine moaned as she turned over onto her back and I watched as she blinked, shut her eyes and blinked again, then focused on my face as she yawned and then fully opened her eyes. I smiled as she stretched, lifting her arms from under the cover and raising them above her head, then slowly placed a hand on either side of my face to bring me down for a morning kiss.

What time is it, she asked?

"Just after seven," I said. "I need to take a shower, but first I want to go say good morning to the birthday boy."

Christine is fully awake now. This was the day she had planned for during the past several months. Today Max would have his birthday party at FunScape. All the arrangements had been made, but she didn't feel comfortable leaving it totally in the hands of others to make it all happen as planned. To be certain of that she would get there early and see to matters herself. She put on her robe and slipped her small feet into her slippers, moving quickly across the bedroom and was in the doorway just as I returned from our son's room. A smile and a quick kiss and then she continues on her way to get Max up and dressed.

When Christine entered the room, Max was fully roused and in the process of jumping on his bed, his sturdy legs pumping his body to higher and higher heights. Christine grabbed her son in midair and tickled him. "Say you'll not jump on your bed again, Max or I'll tickle you to death." At first his reply was merely giggles, but finally he gave in and said, "Mama, I will, I will stop. I promise."

"Well, Max, what shall we wear today. Shall we put on your new Dockers and a pair of penny loafers?"

Even at five, Max knew that was not really a question his Mama was making. She was just talking out loud to herself. Max slid off the bed and started across to his bathroom. Christine looked at him and said, "Don't forget to brush your teeth Max. I'll be in to help you in a bit. And Max?"

"Yes."

"Happy Birthday Max." she said. "I love you Max."

"I love you too Mama."

There was a smile on her face as she laid out his clothes and began making his bed. On Max's bedside table, Christine picked up the picture that had fallen during the tickling session. Lovingly she wiped the glass and stared at the photo. It was of the three of us and like most pictures where they were united, the resemblance of Max to them both is obvious. He had my firm chin and eyebrows, but he had her cheekbones and eyes. In the picture, his light brown hair was tousled, giving into a slight wave to it, which she loved. Max had the best of each of us she thought. Christine set the picture back on the table, and began to quickly finish making the bed. When done she went to see how Max was coming along with his morning routines.

Max looked up his toothbrush moving quickly and haphazardly across his front teeth, then, looking beyond his mother, he started to giggle, a signal easily translated when Christine turned and caught me in the midst of lowering my arms. "Okay, mister, you aren't too old to tickle", Christine stated, as she moved closer to me and began tickling me. Max wanted in on this so he quickly jumped off the stool he used to bring him up to sink level, and ran over to tickle me until all three of us were on the rug laughing uncontrollably.

"Enough, we have got to get this show on the road," Christine said and we all unscrambled ourselves to finish getting ready. Christine checked Max's teeth and helped him wash his face and brush his hair. She then left him to finish dressing while she went to the kitchen. As she started downstairs she could hear the shower running in the master bathroom and knew her family was now on schedule.

In the kitchen, Christine poured the coffee that she had set up the night before with the automatic timer, then she went to get the orange juice to fill the glasses already on the table. By the time, she was joined by me and our son she had bagels, hot cereal and coffee all ready.

"Take a seat," she said as her family joined her and when they were all seated, Christine reminded me to be at FunScape by twelve noon for the party.

"If something comes up, please give me a call, hon."

"Don't worry, nothing will come up. I'll be there."

"When are you leaving for FunScape," I inquired.

"I plan on being there by eleven or half past to make a final check on the preparations prior to the other children arriving."

"Excuse me, please," Max said.

"Yes, what it is Max?"

"Mama are you going to wear the bracelet that we gave you?"

On Christine's birthday, I had taken Max out shopping and we had presented her with a charm bracelet. On the bracelet was a gold heart and a tiny photo holder in which she had placed a miniature copy of the picture that was on Max's night stand.

"You bet I'm wearing it, sweetie. It's my next favorite thing in the whole world after you and Papa."

That would be the last time the three of us would sit around that kitchen table. My wife, her face openly revealing her excitement and our son Max, his hair still tousled and his interest in breakfast waning at the mention of the party.

I left that morning wrestling my overcoat onto my shoulders, then accepting two sets of hugs and kisses before going down the hall to the mud room where I slipped my arms into my coat, put on my gloves and hat, then opened the door to the garage. I stepped out quickly trying not to let too much of the cold into the house and then went over to the furthest bay, pressing the remote door opener as I hurried over to my car.

In one motion, I slid into the driver's seat and turned on the ignition and then opened the garage door. Then I went about cranking up the blower and the heat, making sure the seat warmer was on high. With that done, I sat watching my breath, clearly visible while giving the car a chance to warm up. I could delay no longer so I backed the car out into the driveway, which thankfully had been plowed.

The snow was already high on either side of the driveway so I was careful to back up slowly and once I was sure the way was clear, I continued onto the street, shift gears and I was on my way. In that moment, my mindset turned to the agenda of my work day and as I eased my car down the street I was mentally removed from the cozy world inside my home.

The plows had been out early, so I had no problems getting downtown and soon was pulling into the parking garage next door to my office building. "Hello, Samuel, I said to the garage attendant."

"Hi, Mr. Newman. You're early today."

"Yes, I am early and I am going to leave early too. It's my son's birthday today and I have a party to attend."

"Tell him to have a happy birthday for me."

I nodded my head and parked in my assigned space. In a few minutes, I stood in the building lobby, saying hello to business acquaintances as I waited for the elevator. I managed to fit in the first car that made its way to the lobby, but just barely, my toes almost touching the elevator door. "Nineteen," I said when asked which floor, then stared into my reflection on the interior copper door. Occasionally I would wait for the next car but today I wanted to finish up early and didn't want to waste one minute.

The elevator stopped at each floor without failure. Each time I found himself stepping off so that those who needed could disembark until finally we arrived at the nineteenth floor. As I stepped off for the final time I took a deep breath, enjoying the unscented air in the hallway. The mixtures of perfumes, aftershave and colognes could be nauseating, I thought to himself. I smiled knowing I added to the fusion of scents too, and then, in a flash I was back thinking of work as I started down the hall to my office. I barely was inside when a voice spoke behind me.

"Mr. Newman, hello!" It was my secretary and out of habit I braced myself for what I knew came next. Linda was a walking talking miracle. She recited my appointments for the day, the calls that I need to make, and placed a cup of coffee on my desk before coming over to help me out of my overcoat.

"You really need to get yourself a new coat, Mr. Newman," she said. I smiled. I knew that was coming too and it was true only I just couldn't find the time or force myself to spend the money when this coat still could serve the purpose. I thanked Linda and assured her I was on top of my schedule.

As I expected, it was busy at the office. The Christmas season was upon us and it was a time for children, and what that meant was legal hassles. You had the divorced mothers who felt that the children should celebrate Christmas at their home even if the divorce degree gave the legal right for the holiday to be spent on alternate years with the father. Then there were those who felt that they deserved something in the store they did not have the funds to purchase. So, not knowing how else to satisfy their need they stole it and then they needed representation in court. Yes, I and the other partners in my law firm found the holiday season profitable as well as time consuming with urgent matters. For me there were murders and attempted murders filling my calendar and all the time, new ones coming in.

Anxious to get started, I allowed myself a quick sip of coffee before rushing into my day.

CHRISTINE NEWMAN

Chapter 4

On the other side of town, after a nourishing breakfast, Christine managed to get the kitchen back in order and herself and Max dressed and out the door by eleven. The party was set to start at 1:00 p.m. so she knew there was plenty of time, yet she was still anxious.

Christine took a moment to look out the side panels of the front door to see what it was like outside. She looked over at the driveway and noticed that it had been plowed. That was good, she thought to herself. Then she tried to look over the snow to see how the roads where, but couldn't get a good look. Besides, the side roads were always the worst and once you got on the main lines it was fine.

"Max, come on, we need to get on the road," she called. Max had run upstairs for something and didn't hear his mother calling. So, with no reaction, Christine went over to the bottom of the stairs and called him again

"I'm coming," Max trilled as he hurried down the landing. "Slow down, Max. You're going to fall," Christine lamented and Max pressed his lips tightly together as if concentrating on each step. When he reached the last step, Christine reached over and lifted him up and placed him gently on the foyer floor. Then taking his hand, they walked down the hall to the mud room.

Christine lifted Max again and sat him on the bench so that it was easier for him to get on his leggings and boots. She then reached up and took his coat off its hook and helped him put it on.

As Christine began wrapping a scarf around his neck, Max wiggled about. "That's too tight Mama. It's too high up to my mouth too."

"Okay," Christine said as she loosens the scarf a bit and pushed it down. "How's that?"

"Better."

She put on his hat and then helped him off the bench so that he stood beside her as she got into her outdoor gear and gathered her purse and the keys from the dish in the mudroom. They were ready.

Christine opened the garage door, pressing the car door remote opener several times as she shepherded Max to the back-seat car door and opened it. She patiently helped Max into his car seat and buckle him in. Making sure the car door was locked and closed she climbed into the driver's seat and just like her husband turned up the heat, waited and then opened the garage door and slowly backed out onto the road. They were on their way with Christine's mind going a mile a minute and happy to find the roads were clear.

"Mama, this is boring," Max said.

"Okay, Max, let's sing our song."

When I was a little boy, my Mom would sing and read to me and when I was older, she began to share with me how one song had been a part of our family history for years and years. We sang the song so often that I quickly learned it by heart and it was a part of me so I shared it with Christine and Max. Christine had thought the story and the song strange at first, but slowly it grew on her.

When I explained that this song and this story were family traditions and that traditions cultivate connection between immediate family members and their generations, Christine's heart went out to me. I knew that some traditions were simple like making snow ice cream at the first snowfall, but some families like mine have traditions that are different, that seem to hold deep meaning and so I was reluctant to not pass it on. I wasn't sure on the history since that had not been repeated often, but I think I had the gist of it. So, this became our tradition too, to sing this song and share the history with Max who would, like me, remember the song and botch the history part. Christine made sure that Max knew the song.

It was a special song and it wasn't until I was a grown man, did I learn the title. It was called, *Playground in My Mind*. Now as they made their way to FunScape, they began singing our song.

"When this old world gets me down, and there's no love to be found, I close my eyes and soon I find, I'm in a playground in my mind, Where the children laugh and the children play, and we sing a song all day. My name is Michael, I got a nickel, I got a nickel, shiny and new, I'm gonna buy me all kinds of candy, that's what I'm gonna do. See the little children, living in a world that I left behind, Happy little children, In the playground in my mind. Oh, the wonders that I find, In the playground in my mind, in a world that used to be, close your eyes and follow me, Where the children laugh and the children play, and we sing a song all day."

They sang all the versus and then repeated the tune, with Max missing a word or two as they drove to their destination.

The car was toasty warm with the heat and the sun shining through the windows. Outside it was still cold and the weatherman reported that we were in for another storm which meant we would have a white Christmas.

As they continued on their way, the roads this far out were still covered with snow and Christine had to concentrate on her driving, as they finished the last line of the song for the fifth time. Though the distance they had to go was no more than 22 miles, at her decrease in speed it was taking much longer. She seemed to catch every light driving painfully slow on the highway. Each time they had to stop, Christine had to hold tight to the steering wheel until the tires gripped the road. The roads were getting worse now as they got closer to their destination located just outside their county.

FunScape was on Route 96 in Victor, New York, a six-mile square township, in Ontario County. The children's party house was in the rear of the Eastview Mall in Victor. This was the party place for children and very popular among parents and the younger set which meant you had to make reservations early or else you might miss out. The downfall when it came to winter birthdays was that it was in a remote area so the plows didn't run as frequently as they did in the suburbs nearer to downtown. Considering how much snow had fallen over the past few weeks, it wasn't as bad as it could have been, Christine thought, but it was unpleasant for driving.

On a good day, it would have taken them twenty-five minutes, but today it had taken them almost twice that time before they turned into the Mall where the parking lot was in the process of being cleared, and the entrance was very slippery.

Christine was driving cautiously but the car still slid. In her head, she tried to remember to turn away from the direction of the slide and was doing just that when she heard a sound in front of her and looked up to see a plow in her path. At that instance, Christine put both her feet on the brake and turned the wheel sharply in the direction of the slide. The car swerved dangerously out of her control. Her heart pounded as she said a little prayer watching helplessly as the car missed the plow and ended up with its front end buried in a snow bank.

She was shaking, the car idling as she tried to calm herself. "Mama," Max said.

"We're okay, we're okay, baby." Max was silent and she turned around to look at him. "Max, baby, are you all right?"

"Yes, Mama, that was fun!"

Christine turned back around to stare out the windshield, wondering what to do now. Her heart skipped a beat when she heard a knock on the window and looked out to see a strange face peering in at her. She could tell by the way the man was dressed and the fact that the plow had now stopped, that he was the driver.

"Miss, are you all right?"

Christine rolled the window down slightly and said, "Yes, we're fine."

"I'm sorry. I didn't see you until it was too late. Try and back the car out now and I'll push if you need me to."

Christine nodded and waited for the snow plow driver to move out of the way, then backed out of the drift quite easily. She rolled the window back down and said, "Thank you. We'll be fine". She added, "It wasn't your fault. It was slippery."

The man gave her a smile and went back to the plow and climbed in. Then Christine eased the car a little further back and straightened her front wheels, so she could drive around to the rear of the mall where FunScape was located.

The lot was just about empty and she had her choice of parking spaces so she parked the car up close to the building hoping that if it started to snow again, the building would keep some of the snow from piling up on her car. She turned off the engine, picked up her purse and her briefcase that had all the important details for the party stored in it and then carefully stepped out of the car. Before she could help him, Max already had his seatbelt off and was anxiously waiting for the car door to open. Soon they were walking quickly toward the building.

"Mama, will Patrick be at my party," he asked.

"Yes, I think so Max. I talked to Patrick's mother and she said that he should be over his cold. If not, you know he wanted to be here, don't you?" Max nodded his head in reply as little kids will do even though this is not visible to the parent. Patrick was Max's best friend from pre-school. They had been best buddies since they were three years old and were practically inseparable. Patrick filled in as the brother Max wanted but that didn't stop Max from constantly asking them when would he have a brother of his own. Recently Max had added that request to his nighttime prayers, but though they were trying to reciprocate, they were having no luck. It would happen eventually, Christine was sure of that. They were both young and in good health, so it was just a matter of time, and there was plenty of that before they needed to worry about not being able to conceive.

Entering the lobby, they were greeted by Mrs. Murdock, the FunScape party planner. Mrs. Murdock was all smiles as she informed Christine not to worry everything was well in hand. "I think you," Mrs. Murdock said looking down at Max, "are going to have a wonderful; birthday".

Max who stood beside his mother while she spoke with Mrs. Murdock wanted to go exploring. He looked around the room all gaily decorated with streamers, balloons and papier-mâché cartoon characters. He knew this was all for him and tried to wiggle his hand free so that he could take a closer look.

"Be patient Max. Give Mama just a moment more," Christine said.

Max was a typical 5-year-old who could manage feelings and social situations with greater independence, and abounded with energy needing to be active most of the time. Since he could express himself verbally as well as with his body language, there was no doubt of what he wanted to do.

Max was still wearing his blue ski coat and a blue and white wool scarf around his neck that he tugged at now with his free hand, that held the hat he snatched off as soon as they entered the building. "Mama? he said though he tried to be still."

Christine smiled at Mrs. Murdock and then stooped down to help Max off with his coat, took his hat, scarf and gloves and placed them in one sleeve before patting his hair back in place. Mrs. Murdock commented. "My goodness, you look very handsome."

Max gave her his biggest smile. "Thank you, Mrs. Murdock".

"You're welcome", she said to Max, and then turning to Christine said, "I think that just about covers it, unless you have any more questions you want to ask."

"No, you seem to have everything under control", Max heard his mother say as he felt his hand being released. While they stood there a while longer, he was on his exploring expedition and heard nothing of their conversation as they discussed the gifts; especially one in particular. Max would get his first, two-wheel bicycle today. Since it was not wrapped, Christine had placed it in her trunk earlier that week. Now she discussed arrangements with Mrs. Murdock on having someone bring it in and putting it out of sight until it was close to the time for opening presents. With all the answers to her questions and a brief survey of the place as assurance, Christine relaxed. She spent the time snapping pictures with her cell phone and admiring the party room with its decorations knowing that once the children arrived it would not look quite the same.

Christine was so engrossed in checking out the room and taking pictures, she was unaware of time passing until Mrs. Murdock caught up with her. "Your guests are arriving," she said.

"Thank you, Mrs. Murdock."

Christine went to get Max and checked him over, then taking his hand, they walked over to the door to greet his friends. They stood side by side in the doorway. Christine spoke with the parent and Max giggled with his playmates as they began arriving in droves. Christine was secretly gratified that virtually everyone who had been sent an invitation was making an appearance. There were forty children ranging in ages from four to five and a matching set of adults with one of the last to arrive being Max's pal, Patrick.

Christine, seeing Patrick and his mother coming through the door, smiled and looked down in time to see the expression on Max's face when he too noticed Patrick. It was definitely going to be the most memorable day of Max's young life and Christine was sure she would enjoy it just as much as he did.

The room was alive with the laughter and sounds of happy children along with the sound of parents trying to keep their charges under control. Christine stepped aside and placed a call to Peter, but he was out of his office. He was going to miss the beginning.

She wanted to wait, but she had timed the party out and had to begin so at her signal, the party officially commenced with a parade of people dressed as Disney characters, dancing and singing to Max and his friends. The room filled with clapping and the laughter of children beside themselves with glee. Everyone was having a good time. When the parade ended, there were skits put on by the Disney characters and games for the children to play.

Christine again tried Peter's cell, but there was no answer. She figured he was either on his way or held up at work. In any case, she had to go on. Christine got volunteers to help her arrange the gifts at Max's chair before the children filed over to their seats for lunch. She stood behind Max waiting for everyone to settle down, and that's when it happened.

The whole building shook and suddenly the laughter in the room changed to screaming and pandemonium. Across the hall all work in the kitchen came to a halt. A hush of anticipation fell over the assembly of cooks and helpers as they set aside their whisks, ladles and spatulas leaning forward breathlessly asking, "What was that?"

Christine turned her head to look frightfully toward the doorway and saw a big chunk of the wall propelling toward the table where Max was seated. Quickly she snatched him from his seat, pushing him to the floor just before the debris hit her full in the face, breaking her nose and opening a wide gash on her cheek before she fell on top of him. Barely conscious Christine forced her eyes open and called out Max's name.

"Mama, I'm scared."

"It will be okay." But she was unable to finish her words to comfort Max. Just inches from where they laid, the floor buckled up and a blast of flames tore through the party room ripping apart walls and furniture and burning everything in its path. Christine urged herself to ignore the pain, but she could not. She knew her back was on fire and though her mind told her to roll over, she was unable to do anything about it. She could hear screams of terror and children crying where moments before there was laughter and gaiety. Someone moaned near her and she tried to console them, only she couldn't speak. Her lungs were filled with smoke, her throat burned by the intense heat. Debris and dust clouded the vision of those in the room. Someone would say later that it looked as though a volcano had erupted. Christine tried again to lift her body up, but there was no strength in her. She opened her mouth as if to speak but the flames and smoke silenced her.

There was fire and smoke everywhere. The smell of burning flesh filled the nostrils of the people who were able to flee the building looking shell-shocked and weeping. Once outside, parents rolled themselves and their children in the snow to extinguish the fire that licked at their clothes. They stared at the building watching it collapse into a huge cloud of smoke and fire, the gaiety of the party no longer imaginable.

In what seemed like hours to those waiting out in the cold the parking lot was filled with ambulances and fire engines trying to get the situation under control. Close on their heels came the news reporters, barely waiting for their cars to stop before rushing on the scene in search of anyone to tell them what had happened.

PETER NEWMAN

Chapter 5

Across town, I was finalizing my last appointment. I knew from the start that this case was not going to be easy. I was representing the parents who's twenty-four-year-old daughter had been murdered. The daughter, Marie Anderson was home for a visit and had gone out one evening with her friends to attend a party at a local hotel. The next morning, Mr. and Mrs. Anderson weren't too worried when they found their daughter hadn't returned home and it wasn't until trying to reach her on her cell to see if she would be home for dinner, that they became anxious because there was no answer. Their daughter always answered her cell.

The police were called and after interviewing the parents and determining that they didn't have anything to do with their daughter's disappearance, they began questioning her friends who were at the party. They checked out the surveillance tape from the hotel and found that Marie had never left the building so they began a room by room search of the hotel and checked fingerprints and took DNA of everyone they were able to trace down, who had been at the hotel that night. It had taken almost a year for the police to come up with a suspect. A Henry Randall who was around the same age as Marie, but had no connection that they could uncover to her which is what had made it so hard to connect him to the crime. From the information I had obtained, Mr. Randall had seen Marie at the party and had tried to approach her on several occasions. His reason for being there was as a server at the party and he had no connection to the hotel or its staff. He had managed to get her aside and when she fought off his advances, he had lost control and strangled her, then had taken her body down to the basement of the hotel and hid her body behind the furnace, amidst a pile of boxes.

We had all the evidence we needed to take the case to court and I was confident that the family would have closure. These kinds of cases were hard on the client and on me because I wanted justice for all.

I collected my files and soon was ready to leave the office. While putting on my overcoat I looked at my watch. The party was underway, but I was sure I would get there in time to see Max open his gifts. Quickly I put on my galoshes, coat and hat and headed toward the door, my briefcase swinging beside me. Linda was at her desk and looked at me as I exited my office and was in the process of locking the office door.

"Mr. Newman," she said.

"Linda, whatever it is, it will have to wait."

"No, I just wanted to ask you to tell Max happy birthday for me."

I smiled, "Sorry," I said, "sure and thanks Linda".

I was glad I had the office directly across from the entrance door as it was much easier to slip out without running into colleagues that way. In the hall, I waited for the elevator and even though it was late for people to be going to lunch, the elevator was slow in making its way to the nineteenth floor. When it arrived and the doors closed, I was already anxious. It seemed that the elevator could not have gone slower.

Finally, the doors opened and I was in the lobby of the main floor of the building. I headed toward the garage and just as I was about to open the door I remembered. In my office was Max's present. For one moment, I thought about just leaving it and swinging by the office on our way home to pick it up. But I wanted to give it to him at the party, so quickly I walked back across the lobby and pressed the elevator button. As if sensing I was in a hurry the doors opened immediately and I stepped over the threshold, and pressed the button for my floor.

My luck held out as the elevator made only two stops and I was joined by less than a dozen people before reaching my destination. Linda wasn't at her desk when I returned so

I was able to quickly slip in and get the present and back out without incident.

As I stood waiting for the elevator, I checked my watch. Christine had given me the time schedule for events at the party and I was sure I was still on schedule to make it in time to see Max open his presents. Besides I thought, trying to keep forty kids from age two to five on a tight schedule was not going to be easy for Christine and the FunScape employees.

When the elevator reached the lobby again, I got out and began making my way posthaste to the garage. I reached the double doors and pushed the lever and soon I was on my way across the garage floor, the sound of my footsteps muffled by my galoshes. As I headed toward my car, I reached into my pocket and took out my keys and pressed the car door opener and soon I was climbing into the driver's seat. Before fastening my seat belt, I started the engine, grateful the garage was covered so I didn't have to deal with brushing snow off my car.

While I waited for the engine to warm, I tried dialing Christine's cell phone. When she didn't answer, I assumed she probably couldn't hear it over the noise of the party, which was a good sign that all was going as planned.

I relaxed, thinking about the present I had purchased for Max. It had taken months to find that CD with the tune on it they loved so much, but it had been worth the effort. The song held so many memories for me and now for Max and Christine since I had introduced it to them.

When I decided to purchase this for Max, I realized I didn't know the title of the song, just the lyrics. I tried putting words from the song that I thought might be the title, but came up empty. Finally, I just put in a full line of the lyrics to see what would happen. Thank God for the internet, I thought. It worked. If it hadn't I would have gone from store to store singing the lyrics until someone recognizing the tune was able to tell me the title.

I pulled out of the parking lot and onto the street, humming the song, then absently adding the words.

"My name is Michael, and I've got a nickel, I've got a nickel all shiny and new. I'm going to buy me a lot of candy, that's what I'm going to do."

The traffic was heavy on the main streets, but once I got out of the city limits it began to thin and I could move at a good clip. Several traffic lights later, I flipped through the radio stations trying to find a news channel that was giving a weather report. As I searched through the channels, I paused as something caught my attention.

The announcer said, "It's a nightmarish scene, people on fire collapsing into the snow."

My eyes stared out the window and for the first time I noticed ambulances and fire engines screaming down the lane beside me and others going in the opposite direction. Not realizing what I was doing, I pushed down on the accelerator.

"At least two explosions were heard by those who were in FunScape...."

I pressed one hand to my throat, choking on the torrent of emotions welling up inside me. I bit down hard on my lower lip in an effort to hold back, my tears. I was overcome with emotion. "Stop it," I said to myself. "Stop it. They are okay. They are okay."

Finally, I was pulling into the driveway of Eastview Mall and heading toward FunScape at the back. The plows had done a good job of keeping the roadways clear and the salt had taken care of the rest as I sped through the parking lot, making my way to FunScape.

There was no way to get my car near FunScape. Police and firefighters had sealed-off all the areas leading to the back of the Mall, and here the roads and sidewalks where covered with snow, but that didn't stop me. I cut off the engine and exited the car running and slipping as I headed toward the smoke billowing behind the building. I could hear screaming and crying, see cops, firefighters and medical personnel running every which way and I wasn't so sure my family was all right.

Everywhere I looked it was pandemonium. I had never seen anything like it before, anywhere including television or the movies. Along the road in front of FunScape were parked cars and vans with their doors swung open and letters identifying various news media. Men and woman were running around with video cameras and microphones blocking possible eye witnesses from leaving before they had a chance to interview them. The reporters and cameramen were five deep around the entrance and the police who tried to control the mayhem were not having much luck. There were ambulances and rescue squad personnel parked randomly around what was left of the building that housed FunScape.

I stopped in my tracks not sure what to do, then finally started running again, forcing my way through the crowds, ignoring camera lenses and microphones being shoved in my direction and calling out, "Christine, Max, where are you?" But that was just the peeling, the barricades set up by the police to keep the onlookers from getting in the way was the real challenge. From that point on it was like a bad dream.

I pushed frantically, yelling out, "Christine, Max, its dad?" I dodged hands that tried to stop my progress until finally I yelled out that I needed to find my wife and son.

"Sir, sir, let me help you."

I looked in the direction of the voice and saw a uniformed policeman walking toward me. "Come on, I'll take you in."

This was a nightmare. It just couldn't be real, I thought as I walked with the officer, taking in the apperception around me. Everywhere I looked there were people crying hysterically some tugged at the officers clothing, desperate for information about friends and relatives who were in the building.

Though I tried not to, I was swallowed up by the hysteria going on all around me; so that I wasn't prepared for the sight that was now unfolding as we stepped out in front of the crowd. There before me was what use to be FunScape, I froze. There was nothing resembling the party place or the decorations that Christine had so lovingly put together. No steamers, no balloons, no colorful table clothes, gift bags or food. Nothing but a pile of rubble with smoke billowing from the charred debris and now and again a flame appearing only to be attacked viciously by a nearby firefighter. I was encapsulated by a roller-coaster of feelings of anger and grief whelming inside me, that formulated into a loud deep sound escaping from my lips My legs grew weak and I stumbled forward. The officer moved quickly, grabbing me under the arm and supporting me until I could stand on my own.

"Are you okay?" the officer inquired.

While struggling to compose myself, I mumbled, "Yes."

"Sir, look around and see if you can find your family."

Where we stood now it was obviously amongst those who had managed to escape the building because I could hear snatches of their conversations as they described their experience to reporters. I looked desperately about praying that Christine and Max would be among them. I rushed forward with the officer at my side when I thought that I saw my wife, only to be crestfallen to see that it was not her.

The officer could sense my pain. "Don't worry, we'll find them."

Severely straining the powers of endurance, I moved forward.

From close behind us someone was saying, "Windows shattered and glass was flying everywhere, along with pieces of the walls. Screams filled the room as people were diving for cover. But that wasn't the worse of it. It sounded like a huge thunderbolt and then everything was engulfed with fire. It was pandemonium with people trying to save themselves and their children."

I tried to block those words, my body shaking with my own sobs, my vision blurring from the tears. I tried to concentrate on the blue uniform and nothing else. One reporter managed to shove a mike in my face and I pushed it away, my tears of frustration and terror taking control as I screamed, "Get out of my way." As if they couldn't hear me they continued to block my progress. "My wife and child are in there. It was my son's birthday party…"

"Sir, sir, I need you to try to hold on. You must stay alert and look around you. There is still a chance they made it out. Focus man. Do you see them anywhere?"

"You're right. Sorry." I said as I scoured the area around me, listening to hear my wife's voice and then began calling out, "Christine, Christine can you hear me baby." My eyes swept over the area, my ears alert for the sound of her voice, but she wasn't anywhere.

I felt the officer tug at my arm and pull me forward to where bodies were being zipped into black plastic bags and I tried desperately to pull my arm out of the officer's grasp.

"No…I can't. Please, no."

The officer soothingly replied, "Listen sir, you don't have to check now. It makes it easier, but that's okay. It's your choice."

I knew they could use dental records and DNA to identify the victims and I didn't want to even think that Max or Christine could be amongst them. Not here.

The officer could see on my face that I wanted to know but couldn't bring myself to check so he tried another tactic. Maybe if they were here they could be identified by a picture and maybe, there was a chance, they had some ID from the victims.

"Sir, do you have a picture with you?"

"Yes,"

"May I have it."

While I shakily dug out my wallet, the officer asked, "What is the full name of your wife and your son?" I answered him and let out a sigh of relief, finding the pictures and handing them over to the officer.

Giving me encouragement, he said, "Maybe they have seen them. They may have been taken to the hospital."

There was hope. I tried to quiet my heart that was beating rapidly now. "No, I need to do this. I will do this."

For the first time, I looked directly at the officer, standing by my side and knew his compassion was real and his need to help me was real too. I had to be strong.

"I'm grateful to you, but I really need to do this, um…what is your name officer?

"It's Sam."

"Thank you, Sam. Please call me Peter."

"Well, Peter, I'll stay with you. Let's get this over with."

Together, now feeling like Sam was my friend, we viewed bodies of those who hadn't made it and others who were being transported to the hospital in various states. It was a sea of blood flowing over charred skin and gashes, clothing unrecognizable and hopes of finding any ID that hadn't been burned seemed improbable. I could hear whimpers from those who were fighting for their lives. They deserved to be identified and I knew that I could help with this too. Many of them were friends of mine and Christine. At that moment, I felt a responsibility and that gathered my strength.

Stiffly I walked down the long, thin path with the bodies arranged on either side. "Sam, do you have a pencil and paper?" I asked.

"Yes."

Intuitively he knew what I was doing. I waited for Sam and when he said, "Okay, I'm ready," I began rattling off the names of those I knew, confident that Sam would record their status. Some were so burned and covered with debris I couldn't identify them.

It made it easier to search for my wife and child now because I had turned my attention into hopefully giving someone else peace of mind knowing what had happened to their loved ones. Each time I peered into a face I could not recognize, I did my best to focus on what I could identify on that person. I had seen my share of dead people and those beaten beyond recognition, but I had never seen anyone badly burned or had the smell of burning flesh fill my nostrils. This was the most intense thing I had ever done. Each time I said a prayer when the person was not Christine or Max.

Finally, we moved over to the area where the injured were waiting to be transported to the hospital. Most of them had on oxygen masks and in some cases, their faces had been wiped off, making it much easier to identify them. When I could, I asked if they had seen my wife or son, but no one had an answer for me.

"Peter?"

It took a moment for the sound of someone calling my name to register. "Yes?" I replied.

"Peter, we are done here. If you want, I can take you into the building and we could look for her there." Seeing the stunned look on Peter's face Sam apologetically restated, "Where the building was."

"Yes, let's do that now," At this point I was barely able to function and I knew it. I took a couple of deep breaths knowing I had to stay in control as I walked beside the officer, stepping into the depths of the demolished building. All around us were people in official garb moving walls and debris off victims and calling out to each other when they recovered a body or found someone alive. Each time a person was found, Sam had to hold me back from running through the shambles to see if it was my wife or child. "Peter, you have to be careful or you might hurt someone or disturb the rubble."

His remark pulled me up short. “I’m so sorry.”

“It’s okay,” he replied, then seeing some of his comrades Sam yelled out, “Hey, men, I have Peter here who is looking for his wife and son. His wife put on the party so Peter, here may be able to help with identifying anyone you come across.”

“Thanks, we appreciate the help.”

And so, I was directed to each one of those unearthed in the remains of the building until I became so used to seeing burned bodies, it no longer affected me. Each time the person uncovered was dead, I would at first be taken aback, but forced myself to look and once I saw it wasn’t Christine or Max, I would let out my breath and try my best to identify them.

It was slow going. I kept alert hoping that they would find Christine or Max at any moment or that one of the other officers would. As we continued through the debris, the area we now entered was definitely the party room. Amongst the other debris was an occasional flick of red or green, or yellow—the remains from confetti, balloons and streamers. I looked at Officer Sam and said, “They would probably have been in here somewhere. This is the party room.”

“Okay, Sam said.

We stepped carefully forward, looking in front of us, and off to the side as we proceeded cautiously forward. We came across several bodies as we continued and even I could tell that this must be where it started, blocking the exiting of most of the occupants. My thoughts were interrupted as I noticed a flurry of activity on the far side of the room. Emergency personnel were trying to move something either out of the way or off someone. They seemed to be moving in slow motion as cautiously they worked to lift a large chunk of a pillar up and when they had managed to lift it there was a piercing scream of pain.

Officer Sam, took the lead to guide me over in that direction. By the time we arrived, first aid was already being administered to someone, but we could not get a good look because the officers held us back from the immediate area until they finished inspecting it for safety.

I stood helplessly by looking at other rescue crews administering first aid or digging through the rubble. All I could do was stare at them, watching those closer to us as they cleared an area and when a body was uncovered, check the neck and the wrist for a pulse and then first aid was rendered immediately to those who had managed to survive.

This area was now the focus of the paramedics and rescuers so I and Officer Sam were held back. Not knowing what else to do, I began yelling out, "Christine, Max, are you here." I yelled it over and over again.

Somewhere off to my left a voice yelled out at me. "Can you stop that, please, we need to hear each other."

I looked at Officer Sam who said, "They're right. You have to let them do their job."

Each victim was brought passed me and I would try to identify them before they were moved out. When the person was alive, it gave me hope that my family would be too. I needed that even more now because as I stood here amidst all the wreckage, it was hard to picture anyone making it out alive. For those who were lucky enough to have made it, they needed the quick actions of this team. They were in control and worked like a fine-tuned instrument, not missing a beat and I appreciated their actions. The paramedics were issuing orders to the firemen and police to help remove a body or signal for an ambulance to expedite the transport to hospitals.

Time had passed and the flurry of activity had died down as every inch of the area had been scrutinized. Still no one had found my wife or son. Where were they? Could they have been taken away already? I could feel the panic rising as the situation became more and more hopeless.

"Peter, we've seen it all. Come on we must go back now."

I wanted to resist, but I knew he was right. Maybe, I told myself, Max and Christine are now in the parking lot, searching for me as I searched for them. I had to keep my mind on that reunion as I cautiously reversed my steps back to the parking lot.

Back in the front area I noticed that there were covers over many of the bodies now. It was hard not to look as I followed Officer Sam. “Come on Peter, we need to move off to the side. They are using this area now.” I could see that and knew that they had obviously run out of body bags and were now just covering the bodies. Though I tried to keep my eyes straight ahead, it was hard. From the form of the sheets I could tell that most of them were covering the small bodies of children, making it even more unbearable. As I followed Officer Sam my eyes strayed and there it was. My worse fear was about to materialize.

My eyes stared over at a covered body where one arm was exposed as though reaching out to me. I turned in that direction, ignoring the tug on my arm because even at this distance I recognized the charm bracelet. Not knowing what I was saying, I repeated what Christine had said, “I will wear it always because on the bracelet dangles a gold heart and a tiny photo holder with a miniature copy of our family picture”.

Officer Sam couldn’t hear what I was saying, but tried to hold me back, only I was not about to be stopped.

“Peter, what is it, sir? What’s the matter?” I turned, a look of sheer rage covering my face silencing the officer.

It was coming. I could feel the scream working its way up from my stomach, closing off my air passage as it made it to my throat, then exploding from my lips. Stumbling forward I worked my way over to her, tears blinding me as I tried desperately to get to her. It was Christine, I knew it was her. Finally, I was there and reaching down to pull her up into my arms and rock her to and fro. The sheet slipped from her face allowing my tears to mingle with the dust and dirt all over her disguised features. And all I could do was call out her name repeatedly.

There was no need to ask Peter if this was his wife and there was no way to console him. The officer stood there, a witness of the tragic scene before him. The man was torn apart, suffering so deeply his torturous sobs filled the area, but Officer Sam knew that this was just the beginning. The man still had a son to find, but right now he needed to be with his wife. Officer Sam turned around taking in the devastation all around him while he gave Peter time to adjust to his loss. It was hard to envision the area as FunScape where children came to play video games or attend birthday parties. From the moment FunScape opened its doors almost fifteen years ago, they had been the favorite hot spot for young children who were celebrating a birthday or had earned the favor of a parent who treated them to a visit. Now, looking about it was impossible to not feel something inside knowing that the life of so many children had been ended or compromised in this disaster. He didn't want to even think about it as he waited patiently. To take his mind off the matter, he saw a fellow officer just across the way who was in the process of laying a sheet over another body.

"Martin, can I help you?"

"Oh, hi Sam. No, I'm all set..." Officer Martin paused without finishing his sentence and he seemed to be staring behind Sam. The expression on Martin's face was one of someone in deep thought as though trying to remember something.

"Martin, what is it?"

"Sam, that man over there. Did he come in with you?"

"Yes, that's his wife he's holding. I wanted to give him a little time alone. Why?"

"I'm not positive, but did the man mention a son?"

Officer Sam frowned slightly. "Yes, do you know anything?"

"I think so. We found a little boy under her. He was in bad shape, but was still alive. We took him to General Hospital."

Officer Sam was overcome with joy. "Thanks Martin," he said. "Thank you very much." He clapped Officer Martin on the back and then hurried as fast as he dared across the area until he stood looking down at Peter who was still clutching his wife and rocking her in his arms.

"Peter, sir, I think we found your son."

Chapter 6

The ride to the hospital seemed like an eternity for me since I was not sure what I would discover when we arrived at our destination. As for the Officer, he only knew that my son had been alive and taken to the hospital, along with several other victims. General Hospital was on the other side of the city and it would take about a half hour to get there from our current location. But we were going faster than the speed limit now as I watched the scenery whiz by the passenger side window of the patrol car.

Officer Sam was taking much the same route as I had in traveling to FunScape, on roads that were now pretty much dry and clear, but heavy with traffic. Not sure if it was a good idea or not, I asked Officer Sam to turn on the radio. I wanted to find out what had happened at FunScape. There had been a lot of media at the site so I figured there would be someone broadcasting the news of what had caused the devastation I had seen. I had to know.

After what we had gone through already, walking through the demolished building and seeing so many men, women and children dead or dying, nothing could be worse so Officer Sam turned on the radio. He flipped through a few stations and then stopped.

"In what is beginning to become one of the worst disasters here in Victor, at a little pass one o'clock today, a boiler located in the basement of the popular recreation building, called FunScape, exploded taking the lives of many children and adults, and injuring others. No death toll is immediately available but it is feared the number of victims could climb into the hundreds. Stay tuned for more updates."

Neither one of us spoke. So, they knew it had been a boiler in the basement exploding, but was it an accident or a malicious act. What caused that boiler to explode? I couldn't help myself as the lawyer in me questioned what I had heard. But who would do such a thing? Who would deliberately cause the death of so many innocent children? It had to be an accident.

Officer Sam broke the silence. "Sir, we should be there in five minutes."

Still in my head, I did not respond.

"Sir, did you hear me?"

"What? Oh, yes, I did. Sorry I was just thinking..." I replied. Then as an afterthought added, "Please call me Peter, Sam."

"Sorry, Peter."

"Sam, do you know anything more than what they said?"

"No, that is more than I knew. I was just informed that there had been an accident at FunScape and all available officers in the vicinity should go there immediately. Once we got there, we concentrated on finding survivors, not what happened."

Officer Sam knew a little more, but decided to keep that to himself.

They were pulling up in the loop in front of the emergency entrance and before Sam came to a complete stop, I swung my door open and jumped out.

Sam pulled the car up a little further in the circle, turned off the engine and reached across the seat to close the passenger door. He then got out and hurried to the entranceway. When he caught up to Peter he saw him desperately trying to make the receptionist understand him. Sam touched Peter's arm and proceeded to explain to the receptionist that they were looking for a little boy who had come by ambulance from the FunScape accident approximately a half hour ago, adding that Peter was the father and that they had learned the child had been transported to their hospital.

The receptionist spoke calmly, including me and the officer in her explanation as she told them several children had been admitted but they had not yet identified all of them. She inquired if I had a picture.

My hands shook so that I could not manage to do more than pull my wallet from my pocket. Without a word, Sam reached over and helped me open the wallet and locate the picture which he presented to the receptionist.

"Excuse me a moment," she said, taking the picture along with her and showing it to another hospital employee.

To me the person she was conversing with looked to be a doctor, but was possibly an intern. He was too far away to read the tag on his shirt. After a moment, the man turned and left. The receptionist walked back to her desk and handed me my photo. "Sir, we need some information for the file," she said. "We can take care of this while we wait to hear."

I did not feel like standing out here while my son could be somewhere in the boughs of the hospital, maybe even calling for me. But I knew there was nothing I could do so I stood responding to her questions, telling her Max's full name, our address and other details. When I gave her Max's birth day she looked up and then down quickly, hiding her face from my view.

It was painful having to deal with the formalities and waiting, especially knowing that my son was possibly clinging to life, but there was nothing I could do. The hospital was too big to go running around trying to find Max, so I had to wait.

The questions stopped and out of the corner of my eye, I saw a man approaching from behind the receptionist. It looked like the same man the receptionist spoke with earlier. As he came closer, I could feel my body shaking and when he was beside the receptionist I couldn't wait.

"Did you find him? Did you find Max?"

"Yes, I did."

Relief flooded through my body and I staggered backwards. Officer Sam reacted quickly, grabbing hold of me and forcing me over to a chair.

I resisted. I didn't want to sit. I wanted answers. Roughly I pushed Sam's hand away. "I'm all right, Sam. I'm fine."

I was not fine, Sam could see that, but I was not about to sit so Sam didn't force the issue. Instead he allowed me to move forward, keeping alert and standing close by me.

"How is he?"

"I don't know. The doctor will have to tell you that."

"So, what; you're not going to take me to him or tell me the room number?"

"No, sir, calm down. I don't have that information; only that he was brought here."

"But, … I began, then stopped. Coming down the corridor was a group of what appeared to be doctors and nurses. They were moving quickly, dispersing this way and that as they moved closer. Finally, one of them stepped out from the remaining group and stood in front of us and asked, "Are you Mr. Newman?" I took a step forward nodding my head.

"Hello, Mr. Newman, my name is Dr. Perkins and I remember your son. Dr. Martin is attending him and there should be some word soon."

It was as though a switch had been turned on. Suddenly my voice was stronger, my body no longer shaky as my role in this matter surfaced. "What do you mean there will be some word soon. I'm his father. Take me to his room!"

Dr. Perkins did not react to my outburst. He allowed me to vent.

"How is he? Is he awake?"

Instead of answering me, Dr. Perkins replied, "What is the name of your son's physician?"

I couldn't believe this. The doctor was totally ignoring what I asked and instead threw out another request of his own. I was frustrated and tired and only wanted one thing. I wanted to be with Max. I replied, "It's Dr. Boettrich. But what about my son?"

Could he not hear me? The doctor had to hear me, yet again, he did not respond to my question. Instead Dr. Perkins replied, "Officer, can you sit with Mr. Newman for a moment. I'll be right back."

Not waiting for a reply Dr. Perkins disappeared, leaving me in the care of Officer Sam who was as confused as I, but tried to keep me calm as we once again found ourselves waiting.

"Hello, Mr. Newman, my name is Dr. Martin.

Dr. Martin, Dr. Martin. I had heard that name before. Not only earlier today, but sometime back and I stood trying to remember and it finally came to me. Dr. Martin had been in the news last year. He was a prominent American emergency physician from Northern Illinois and pioneer in pre-hospital trauma systems. He had been interviewed about emergency care and had said that the care must begin immediately. He had seen cases where an hour after the accident, the patient died because the prehospital care came too late. If he was caring for Max, Max was in good hands.

"Mr. Newman, please be seated." I sat down and the doctor sat beside me. "How much do you want me to tell you?"

"All of it, please."

"Okay, your son has internal bleeding as a result of a torn pulmonary vein in his chest. He sustained blunt chest and probably head trauma. We had to act quickly. Suturing a hypertensive pulmonary artery is difficult in the best circumstances. Access in your son's case was less than ideal but we successfully repaired the tear. Your son was also admitted for severe second- and third-degree burns following his rescue and was unconscious on arrival. He had second-degree burns over 5% of his body and third-degree burns over 15% of his body -- both covering his thoracic and abdominal regions and his right elbow. His vital signs were quite unstable: blood pressure was 55 / 35; heart rate was 210 beats / min.; and respiratory rate was 40 breaths / min. He was quickly deteriorating from circulatory failure. Two IVs were inserted and fluids were administered through each. His vital signs stabilized and he has been transported to the pediatric intensive care unit (ICU)." Dr. Marlin paused. "I am telling you all of this so that you know why we couldn't wait to identify him or get permission to operate."

Peter had a vision of Max. He had seen all those bleeding and burned bodies while searching and he couldn't get the picture out of his head. There had to be a lot of pain involved, pain that he could not alleviate and that pain could take his life.

"Mr. Newman, do you understand what I told you and why we had to act before getting your permission to operate?"

"Yes, I do and I am grateful that you did act immediately. Doctor, does he have a chance?"

"There's always a chance. Right now, your son is unconscious and that is a good thing because he needs the rest and he is not feeling pain. I will check in on him periodically, but I know you are aware of how busy we all are right now. Is there anything else I can help you with?"

"No, I know your busy. I'm fine."

"Good, someone will come and get you when your son is able to be moved."

"Thanks," I said, holding back a sob as Dr. Martin touched my shoulder and then was gone. The rest was a blur. I was taken to a waiting room and Officer Sam was called back to the site, leaving me alone. I had no idea of the time, nor did it matter. Finally, from exhaustion or shock I dozed off.

I dreamed and in my dream, I saw Christine standing in the doorway of our home, wearing the dress I had bought her last Christmas. She loved the dress and I loved the way it looked on her as she moved, across the room toward me the material floating around her thin frame, making her look like an angel. She smiled with her lips and her eyes and at that moment I felt her love move all around me as she drew closer. She was there, within arm's reach, when I heard someone calling my name.

It was dark when I awoke. I had trouble remembering where I was and what had happened, but when I saw Dr. Marlin standing in front of me it all came back.

Dr. Marlin had witnessed reactions like these many times. He knew that this man had already gone through a lot and now needed time to catch up to where his life left off.

"Doctor," I said anxiously. "Is Max all right?"

Dr. Marlin cleared his throat. Sometimes it was hard to draw back the emotions; especially when a child was involved. He cleared his throat again. "Max is in our Trauma Unit. He is under critical watch and we can't move him to pediatrics, just yet."

"Can I see him?"

"In a bit, right now he's being settled in. I'll have someone come and get you soon, but we need you to be patient for a while longer."

I admittedly hated waiting. Our society breeds a "me-first" attitude but this was different. The surgical/procedural waiting room was an entirely different beast. Here, stress, anxiety, uncertainty and fear serve to make even the shortest of waits seem unbearable. I looked around at families sitting crouched forward in their uncomfortable chairs watching the door in hopes of seeing the smiling face of their surgeon with every turn of the doorknob. Here the wait may be rewarded by preservation of a life or, unfortunately, sometimes by a less desirable outcome.

Even the little rest I had gotten seemed to clear my head so that I could think. I reached into my pocket and pulled out my cell phone.

"Sir, Sir! A voice called out and I turned in the direction of the sound. It was the receptionist at the front desk.

I got up and went over to the counter.

"Yes," I said, expectedly.

The receptionist pointed to a sign on the wall, but before I even read it, I knew what it would say. Obviously, there was no cell phone use or smoking in this waiting area. So, I nodded my head and went over to the chair I had been sitting in. I put on my coat and went to the revolving doors leading to the outside.

It was now after midnight and the darkness hid everything from view. I pulled up the collar of my coat against the slight wind, blowing the chilly air against my cheek. I recalled a line from a movie, "Winter must be cold for those with no warm memories." I wasn't sure but I thought it might have been from the movie *An Affair to Remember*. How true those words were.

I buttoned my overcoat, and though my hands were stiff from the cold, I managed to dial the number of my in-laws who lived out of town and were unable to come for Max's birthday party. They had sent Max a remote-control car for his birthday, but Max would not get to see it now since Christine had taken it to FunScape, along with all the other presents. I choked up and hearing the voice of my mother-in-law on the line I quickly pulled myself together.

"Hello, Mom," I said wondering what I should say next.

"Hello, Peter. Is everything all right?"

That was all it took to make me crumble. Between sobs I managed to tell her what had happened, wishing that I had asked her first to put my father-in-law on the phone. But it was too late. I could hear her crying uncontrollably into the phone and then there was silence before the voice of my father-in-law was heard asking me to repeat what I had said. Somehow, I managed to pull away from my own pain and talk with my father-in-law trying to make it as easy as possible on him. I couldn't remember saying that Christine was dead, I hadn't even allowed myself to think it, yet somehow the message was received. They would be on the next plane.

For once I was thankful I didn't have to make the same call to my parents. My Papa had passed away two years ago, after a long bout with cancer. My mother was in a nursing home with advanced Alzheimer and no longer concerned with the matters of this world. There were other calls I should make, but I wasn't ready to make them just yet.

I suddenly was aware that I was cold so I turned and reentered the building.

Chapter 7

The next few weeks are a blur. Max was barely clinging to life as the doctors did hourly checks on his pulse and respiration. He had burns over seventy percent of his body and lay under a tent sheet, his body raw. I could not touch my son and the only means I had to comfort Max was my voice, so I spoke soothing words, hiding the horror of the situation and trying to remain positive.

Helplessly I sat by as they checked his pulse, respiration and observed them cleansing his burned skin. I was told there is pain involved in the treatment of huis burns, as the wounds must be cleansed and the dressings changed. All I could do was pray that Max would get better, but inside I could not fully believe it possible.

When Christine's parents arrived, I was glad to see them and without delay I shepherded them to Max's room, then went to find the doctor. He would be able to better tell them about Max's situation. I watched their faces as they heard what the Doctor Martin had to say and then when he left we talked trying to soothe each other. I was shocked at first when I noticed that Christine's parents seemed better able to cope than me and I later realized it was because they had confidence in Max's recovery.

I was glad for them, though I could not share the feeling. Later as we sat and talked about Christine, I left out a lot of detail, but they knew. Christine's father shared with me a newspaper story he had cut out of the paper. It covered the FunScape disaster.

At least nine are feared dead, 24 reportedly injured and 35 are said to be in serious condition when fire broke out at the Eastview Mall in Victor, NY. Doctors from the University of Rochester Children's center said they had received 20 injured children as of 3 pm. Several were in critical condition, most suffering from smoke inhalation.

Police sources said, the exact cause of the fire is yet to be ascertained and investigations are ongoing now, but signs point to the boiler after talking to several survivors who stated that before the fire there was an explosion.

More than 200 fire fighters and 79 fire engines were dispatched and the fire was put out by 5:30 pm. Although the fire was contained to the rear of the mall, smoke wafted through many areas and poured from windows broken by firefighters, and as a safety measure, forcing the police to evacuate the whole mall.

As scores of onlookers gathered on street corners in the chill air, Police closed several blocks of Route 96 South/Pittsford Victor Road on the west side of the complex to accommodate fire trucks, ambulances and other emergency vehicles. Scores of employees who had rushed from the building -- some without stopping to grab their coats -- huddled on the street to watch. Many are suffering frost bite and required medical attention.

Workers that use, maintain, and service boilers know that they can be potentially dangerous. The mall boilers are gas-fired vessels that heat water to generate steam. The steam is superheated under pressure and used for power, heating or other industrial purposes. Though the boilers are equipped with a pressure relief valve, the one that exploded, failed to contain the expansion pressure. The combination of exploding metal and superheated steam blew a cavern through the floor of FunScape and sent sparks and debris everywhere.

I spent my nights and my days in Max's hospital room. I had no idea of how much time passed or even when the day changed to night. I slept when I tired and I ate when my body called for nourishment. I was afraid to leave Max alone for any length of time so I never left the building until the day of my wife's funeral, all arranged by my in-laws.

I remember her parents coming to the hospital early that morning and taking me home to bathe and dress. I remember being shocked at the emptiness of our home. No sound of Max giggling or Christine opening her eyes to catch me staring at her. Everything was silent and in its place as I managed to ready myself. I stayed upstairs longer touching the clothes in her closet, visualizing her as she sat before the mirror in the bathroom. I could feel her here and I had to keep that feeling going if I could. I took one last look around before taking my suit jacket off the hanger and putting it on.

Something hard was in the pocket. I reached in and before pulling it out knew what it was. The gaily wrapped package taunted me as I slipped it back in its resting place. Finally, I was ready.

My in-laws sat at the table, looking lost and alone. When they heard my footsteps, they tried to look cheery. I stood watching as my mother-in-law rose and slowly walked across the kitchen to pour me a cup of coffee.

"Please sit down and rest, Peter, and drink this," she said. I did as she asked. My father-in-law reached across the table to touch my hand, saying, "It will be all right son. You need to remind yourself that Max needs you now and that you will always have Christine up here." He lifted his hand and touched his temple. Even though he tried, I detected the sob he was holding back. "Remember that son."

I went to the closet and grabbed my overcoat, even though it still smelt like smoke, I put it on. I took the gift out of suit jacket and put it in the pocket of my overcoat where it felt safe from harm. Then I followed my in-laws out to their car and soon we were on our way.

They had done a great job. The church that we attended faithfully every Sunday was filled with the aroma of fresh flowers. With her parents on either side of me, I managed to walk steadily to the coffin and look at my wife for the last time.

I let my mind pull forward the image of Christine as I looked down at her. She looked perfect, as if she was sleeping with her blonde hair flowing over the pillow and back from her smooth forehead. Her oval face and extraordinary long eyelashes concealed her entrancing green eyes as they cast shadows on her face. This was how I would remember her as I loved to watch her sleep.

Her hands were folded and gloved and the dress she wore covered her neck. I leaned over and kissed her gently on the cheek, ignoring the coldness when my lips made contact. As I straightened up I saw it. There on her left wrist was the charm bracelet the one she loved most after me and Max. Before the real vision penetrated my mind, I stepped away and returned to my seat.

After the service, I rode between my in-laws to the cemetery. We were all silent now dealing individually with our pain, trying to be supportive by not breaking down. Every now and then I saw my mother-in-law's lips quivering, but she managed to hold on. I was sure that both had allowed their tears and pain to run its course openly, long before this day.

And then she was gone. Her casket lowered gently into the chasm to remain for all eternity with the prayers to keep her safe. It had been hard for me to visualize my wife being in that closed coffin, or her body being lowered into the darkness of the grave, but I kept my father-in-law's words with me. She would always be there in my memory. For Christine was now resting in peace, but peace for me was yet to come.

Again, the days blended together in sameness. Christine's parents stayed at the house while I lived in Max's hospital room trying to be hopeful that I would be taking my son home again. I had to believe that. After saying goodbye to Christine, I could not face saying goodbye to Max.

I kept up my strength, by eating even though the food held no interest for me. I drank a lot of water to keep my throat moist so that that I could read and sing our song repeatedly, hoping to bring Max back to me. Sometimes I allowed Max's grandparents to take over while I left to stretch my legs and call my office, only to return sooner than expected.

I now slept on a cot that had been placed in the room and I managed to exercise by walking around the perimeter and using a wall to push against or the floor to do sit-ups. All of this added some normalcy to each day as the days continued to grow into weeks. Doctor Boettrich and sometimes Dr. Marlin examined Max. Nurses changed the sheets and kept Max's body clean. The grandparents came trying to hide their concern as they looked at their only grandchild. And most evenings, I had Max all to myself for long stretches of time. I was the one who spent the most time with Max, but as it turned out, I was the most ignorant about his condition, because I had to believe. That was until what I dreaded most, came to be.

"Mr. Newman, we need your permission to take Max off life support."

Truth and reality concerning impending death and necessary decisions I felt was something I would not have to deal with for a long time so I was not prepared. I had never been involved in a decision to remove someone from life support so I was still fairly horrified at the decisions being made, and how things went. Max was in a coma and had been for days. One thing in particular that the doctor said kept bothering me – he said that Max was currently suffering. To me the word "suffering" means pain and distress … and it seemed to me at the time that by keeping Max connected to the respirator, we were prolonging his pain. If I were in Max's place – what decision would I want made? Would I want to be let go of? Was my son going through a living hell … a personal torment … wanting or needing to be let go of, but having no way to communicate that to me?

Dr. Boettrich had taken over Max's care several weeks earlier while Dr. Marlin still continued to check on Max. They were both in agreement.

"What? What are you trying to tell me?"

"I know it's hard to accept, but Mr. Newman your son is brain dead."

"That's not true, Max is breathing. I can see him breathing."

"No, he's not breathing. The machines are doing that for him. The last test showed there is no brain activity. Max can go on forever on the machines, but it is not going to bring him back to you; not the Max you know. But it is your decision."

Somewhere deep inside I knew they were right, but I wasn't ready to let him go so I asked for more time.

I could see the disappointment on the doctor's face as he left me alone with Max, but I didn't care. All I cared about now was Max and I was afraid that if they took him off life support he would be gone; gone just like Christine and I couldn't handle that.

I looked down at my son, motionless on the bed. He couldn't open his eyes and he couldn't smile, but this was still Max. I walked around the room in agony, calling out to Christine to help me make the right decision. I knew that the real Max had left a long time ago.

But I would not think that way. I just couldn't because if there was even a tiny chance that Max could make it on his own, I would hang on to that hope. Only to prove he could, I had to let him go.

Finally, I sat down in the chair, knocking my suit jacket to the floor and seeing the gaily wrapped gift fall from the pocket. I picked up the gift saying, "This is a sign. It has to be a sign."

Tears streamed down my face as I went over to Max's bed.

"Guess what I found, Max? I found our song in a music store. Yes, son, it's "Playground in my mind," I laughed. "The song's name is "Playground in my mind. I didn't know that until I began looking for this for your birthday. Want to hear it?"

I didn't care that he didn't answer as I went out in the hallway to see if anyone had a CD player I could borrow. I was in luck. I took the player to Max's room, put in the CD and somehow, I managed to sing along, thinking that if anything could bring him back to me, maybe this would.

"*When this whole world gets me down and there's no love to be found I close my eyes and soon I find, I'm in a playground in my mind. Where the children laugh and the children play and they sing a song all day. My name is Michael I've got a nickel, I've got a nickel shiny and new. I'm gonna buy me all kinds of candy, that's what I'm gonna do. Oh, the wonders that I find in the playground in my mind. In a world that use to be. Close your eyes and follow me. Where the children laugh and the children play. And we sing a song all day. My girl is Cindy when we get married we're gonna have a baby or two we're gonna let them visit their grandma that's what we're gonna do. See the little children living in a world that I left behind. Happy little children in the playground in my mind. See the little children, see how they play so happy in the playground in my mind.*"

I played the song repeatedly that night, suddenly realizing why I loved it so. No one could listen to this song and be sad. There was something about the words and the tune that lifted my spirits and I began to feel much better. I now could place Max's life in the hands of the creator. I drifted off to sleep.

The next day I sat down with Christine's parents and explained what the doctor had said. It was easy to see that just like the doctors, Max's grandparents knew it was time to let him go. I was the only one left behind.

The ceremony took place at eleven fifteen on December tenth. I watched the tubes being removed one by one until Max lay on the bed separated from the machines that had sustained him and I closed my eyes and prayed. When I opened them my eyes immediately fell on my son's chest. It was going up and down. Max was breathing on his own. There was still room to hope. After his in-laws left, I spent the night fully awake talking to Max, asking him to not give up and to hang on. I played our song repeatedly. Finally, totally exhausted I laid down on the cot. I must have fallen asleep because what I could remember when I woke had to be a dream.

The lights were out in the room and I had shut the door before lying down on the cot. I felt serene which was strange knowing that Max was going it alone now and anything could happen, but that was how I felt. So, it didn't surprise me to think I drifted off immediately. I remember sometime during the night the door to Max's room opened and I had glanced at the doorway figuring it was a nurse or a doctor coming to check on Max. But there was something odd that made me fixate on the doorway. It was the bright white light pulsating until it faded away, leaving only the dimmed light of the hallway to illuminate the form standing there still and silent.

What occurred had me questioning my sanity. If I had to ascribe the experience to something it would be to what it must feel like to be possessed. First, I experienced a transient inability to move or speak as I transitioned from sleep to wakefulness. I felt absolutely frozen in place. Eye movements and breathing were preserved, and I experienced a sense of breathlessness. This paralysis was accompanied by frightening hallucinations and I was seeing, hearing, smelling, and feeling things that could not be there.

I saw a presence of a human figure at the bedside, that I could only describe as dark, like a ghost or a shadow. It was just beyond the periphery of vision, and it was menacing.

I fought to get up and felt a sensation of being held down and I was downright terrified.

I tried to call out, but I couldn't get my voice to work so I tried to get up, but my body wouldn't cooperate. All I could do was stare silently at the image and that frightened me the most. As I watched, what had appeared to be the form of a grown person, now was the form of a mere child who looked to be close to Max's age. The child seemed to be trying to get his bearings and once he did, he saw Max laying in the bed. Slowly he moved across the room until he stood beside Max's bed. I now could see him clearly.

He wore old fashion clothes that even with all the wild styles of the day, I could not remember seeing anyone else wearing clothes from that era. He had on a loose, belted, single-breasted jacket with box pleats on the back and front, with a belt or half-belt. He had long black stockings and it looked like his wide pants tucked into the top of them. On his feet were oxford shoes.

The boy started climbing up on Max's bed and I struggled to put my body in motion. The chance of Max being infected was very high and any contact directly to his body would be extremely dangerous. But I couldn't move. All I could do was watch the boy as he finally made it up on the bed where he looked down at Max with a serious expression on his young face. He stayed perched beside him for quite a while, just staring and then he looked over at me. There was something peaceful and calming in the expression on his face displacing, temporarily my feeling of helplessness. It was but a moment that our eyes made contact, and then the boy seemed to float over Max's body before he disappeared.

Suddenly the effort to speak and move returned to me and I started gasping for breath. At that instance, I thought I was having a stroke.

Someone touched my shoulder, sending a chill through me and I jumped off the cot, almost knocking over the doctor who stood behind me.

"I'm sorry, Mr. Newman. You must have been having a nightmare. The nurse who came in to check on your son called me. Are you, all right?"

"Yes, I'm fine. Did you say a nurse was in here?"

"Yes, she came to check on Max. Mr. Newman, your son passed away last night."

I experienced a rush of remembrance, the full force of my dream returning making my body sway. The doctor grabbed my shoulders and then pushed me gently down to the cot in a sitting position. There was suddenly a flurry of activity in the room, but I was unable to play an active role. Someone was forcing a glass to my lips and holding it while I drank the water. I could hear them talking as I sat silently until finally I could speak.

"I'm all right now. Really, I'm all right."

TAYLOR BOUCHAND

Chapter 8

What in the world am I doing. This is stupid. I could ruin my reputation if anyone found out about this. I don't think there is a big market for crazy artists out there. That made me laugh because to be artistic it takes being sensitive to color, form, and feelings and to be somewhat of a visionary which then makes this all 'normal'.

Yes, what I am feeling and seeing may be normal for me. I am a true artistic personality. My livelihood depends on using my hands and mind to create new things. At least this is what I'm saying and this is what I am sticking too. I smile.

That is my mind set as I start out that day but it only last for a few minutes. Soon I am thinking, it isn't too late to just turn around and go back home. Yes, I could just turn around and go back to the parking garage and get into my car. Only that would solve nothing and I needed to know what was happening to me.

Okay, just take it one step at a time. Push the button. I do. The elevator arrived. Climb in. I do. Now push the button for the floor. I do that too. I take a deep breath proud of myself for making it this far, but then the elevator stops and the doors open and I have another panic attack.

At first, I stand, staring at the open elevator door, frozen. I shake my head trying to shake some common sense to the forefront and manage to step out of the elevator before the doors close again with me still in it.

"Deep breaths, deep breaths." There is silly I say in a whisper and my feet move on their own volition until I am at front door of the office. There I freeze and breathe deeply, sucking in all the air my lungs can hold and pushed the door open.

Inside I wait at the threshold for my eyes to adjust to the light entering the room from the panels of floor to ceiling windows on my left. Then gingerly I take a step forward until I reach the desk of the receptionist.

"You must be Ms. Bouchard," she said. "My name is Amy. Dr. Paulson is expecting you."

The woman seemed to be about my age and had a pleasant voice and smile. I watch as she slowly comes from around her desk and stands beside me. I notice we are about the same height and size, but for some reason I feel shorter. I manage to take the hand she offers.

"Please take a seat."

I can't find my words just yet and try smiling, hoping it doesn't look as fake as it feels. She must think I am an idiot I whisper under my breath as I make my way to the chair she has pointed out and lower myself until I feel my body make contact with the seat.

I cannot believe I am doing this. I wasn't even sure who I should see; a psychologist or a psychiatrist so I looked it up and decided a psychiatrist might be more accepting of what I had to share. After that I went on the internet and searched for psychiatrists, reading their bios and details until I settled on one. It would have been easier if I could have asked for a referral from a friend or comrade, but I couldn't. I didn't want anyone to know. Hopefully I made the right choice.

My thoughts are interrupted as Amy comes toward me. I wonder what crazy thing I've done now, but she says, "Ms. Bouchand, we need to have you fill out this personal and family history." Amy holds the paper out and I take it from her hands. "Also," she adds as she presents another form, "this is a mood assessment. It will help us understand what brings you here."

I take the form and look at the first question. Are you basically satisfied with your life? I look down further and it asks, are you bothered by thoughts you can't get out of your head? I almost laugh out loud, thinking, they have got to be kidding. Boy are they in for a shocker.

Amy has been staring at me and obviously reads my expression, but not really. She says, "Not to worry, the mood assessment is a questionnaire which asks you to rate how you are doing in a variety of areas. It asks about things like your interest levels, your sleep habits, and your mood."

I decide to humor her. "Anything else?"

"Well, it also asks you to list specific concerns and the reasons why you are seeking treatment."

"So, it's like a starting point?"

"Yes, Dr. Paulson will go over this with you and between the two of you discuss how to proceed from this point forward."

I thank Amy and start filling in the information.

Amy goes back behind her desk. Whenever I look up, she smiles at me and I smile back. It wasn't hard to answer the questions or fill in the other form's details so I feel myself relaxing. Once I have supplied all the personal data, I take a minute and review the form then turn to the mood assessment and begin answering the questions. Just when I am feeling as though I am quite normal, I come to the question asking why I am here.

I pause, wondering what I should say and then decide that if I want to get help, I must be honest. "Here goes," I whisper and when I am done I gather all the papers together and carry them over to Amy. Not knowing what to do, I stand in front of her desk waiting for a command.

"Thank you," Amy said. Please have a seat. I am going to give this to Dr. Paulson. I'll only be a minute."

What control, I think. She doesn't even glance at the mood assessment. I would have gone right to that page first.

I don't want to sit any more so I just walk around looking at the room with a critical eye. The waiting room is a showcase of interior design skills with an excellent choice of soft music coming through the speakers. As I walk around I can tell it's been well thought out to be more than a room to wait in. It's the emotional airlock between the chaos of the outside world and the sanctuary of the psychiatrist's inner office. The soft muted colors relax me and I find the room to be very pleasant.

"Ms. Bouchand". It is Amy. She stands behind me. I rotate and see her outstretched arm and watch as she turns her hand over so that the palm faces up. "This way, Ms. Bouchard."

Without a word, I walk silently beside her as she guides me toward a door on the far side of the reception area. Before I have a chance to panic, she opens the door and steps aside, saying, "Please, go in."

"Thank you." I can't believe I said, 'thank you' when I feel as though she has just lead me to the slaughter.

All my doubts and dreads vanish as I step inside. In the immediate area, close to the doorway through which I came I note that the walls are of a muted gray, bare except for a portrait that even from this angle I recognize as 'Blue Boy' a full-length portrait in oil by Thomas Gainsborough, dating back to 1770, and considered to be Gainsborough's most famous work. It is thought to be a portrait of the son of a wealthy hardware merchant, although this has never been proven. For artists like myself it is a historical costume study as well as a portrait: as the youth is in dress of the 17th century period. I had studied so many portraits that though I couldn't exactly remember the details of the painting itself, I did remember the artist and facts. This was of course, a print, but from what I see, a very good one. I made a mental note to later take a closer look at it.

Tearing my eyes away I look around. The office, done in soft grays and maroon with touches of yellow, convey that this is a place where I can be comfortable and say what I feel, that I am here and I'm a human being. Over to the right is a tankful of tropical fish which I watch for a minute before continuing my survey. The psychiatrist's personal taste is evident with its fireplace, period furniture, cream-colored carpeting and collection of artworks, including an early-19th century seascape. As I allow my eyes to roam, they fall on a wood carving of a Cyclops, startling me at first, but then I see the beauty of it and relax. Someone has designed this room well.

My eyes travel to the only other person in the room. Dr. Paulson sits behind a massive mahogany desk in a high back chair. I look at his desktop and see a tiffany lamp on one corner and next to it, the back of a picture frame. Beyond that there is little to be found on the surface.

I smile as Dr. Paulson raises from his chair and comes over to me, offering his hand. He is a man of no age, but his grey hair and close chopped beard leads me to guess his age to be somewhere in the late forties or early fifties. There is not a visible wrinkle on his caramel colored skin. As he draws closer, I stare into his brown twinkling eyes and I immediately feel comforted. Befitting a man of his stature he is richly dressed in the finest of suits and the whitest of linen shirt. He wears a tie, blue and speckled with dots and when our hands meet, his handshake is firm. I like him.

"Hello, Ms. Bouchard," he said, "I have been looking forward to our meeting. I so admire your work and I even have a few cherished pieces myself." There was a slight pause before he finished. "Please, do come in and have a seat."

I sound confident when I say, "Thank you." As I walk beside him I wonder what area of the room we will occupy and I am happy the seat he offers is the one in front of his desk.

"Ms. Bouchard… or can I call you Taylor?"

I manage to reply appropriately. "Taylor will be fine, doctor."

Dr. Paulson sits and looks over the papers on his desk. "I know something must be troubling you or else you wouldn't be here today. I want to help with that, but to do so I need to know more about you." He paused then added, "Is that all right with you Taylor?"

"Yes, of course," I reply and unsure where to begin I start by saying I am here because my friends are worried about me.

Dr. Paulson nods his head, but says nothing.

"Before we begin, I want you to remember one thing, doctor."

"Yes, Taylor, what would you like me to remember?"

"That I came to you. I wasn't sent to you, so in all probability the fact of whether I am insane or not should lean in my favor. I mean, if I were insane, I would not have chosen to come here today. Correct?"

Dr. Paulson is silent.

What must I do to get him to speak because I need verbal confirmation. I wonder if this outburst will have him wondering about my emotional health so I think I will try another tactic.

Just as I am about to break the silence, Dr. Paulson speaks, saying first that I am not to worry how to answer the questions he needs to ask and assures me that he will not be jumping to any conclusions until he has heard what I need to say and has the background details to formulate a diagnosis.

So, I find myself responding to his questions on my physical health and mental state. Then his questions become more personal.

"Tell me about your childhood."

"I am an only child and grew up in a loving household. My father was a doctor and my mother a writer."

"What was your relationship to each of them?"

I thought for a moment. "Well my father was the disciplinary in our home and my mother was the one who helped me with my homework." I looked at Dr. Paulson and asked, "Is that what you meant?"

"It's what you want to say, Taylor. I want you to answer as you see fit. "Is there any moment in your childhood that stands out?"

"Yes, now that you mention it, there is. I do remember one time when my father was really mad and punished me."

Dr. Paulson remained silent so I continued.

"It was the time when I took my mother's pendant. My father had given my mother this pendant and she wore it all the time, except when they were going out for the evening and she wore other jewelry. On those times, the pendant was put into a velvet lined case and stored in the top drawer of her dresser. I had seen her put it there so many times and I don't know why I decided that day I wanted it. In any case, one evening when they were going out, I kissed them goodbye and that pendant popped into my mind. At first, I went up into their room and opened the bureau drawer and took out the box just to look at it. I opened the case and there it was all nestled prettily into the velvet lining and before I knew what I was doing, I had taken it out and put it around my neck.

I went to the mirror and pranced around with it on, then went to my room to play. When I heard my parent's voices downstairs I quickly left my bedroom and ran downstairs. At first they acted as though they were glad to see me, but then, first my father and then my mother backed away from me. I asked them what was wrong and then I knew. The pendant was around my neck hanging outside my pajama top. I started apologizing but they weren't accepting any explanation."

"My father grabbed me by my upper arms and moving down to my height stared into my eyes and said, "You know better. You are not to touch this, ever." Then my mother undid the clasp at the back and went up to their bedroom. Shortly afterwards my father followed her, leaving me to think about what I had done. I never touched it again."

"How old were you when this happened?"

"I think I was around ten or twelve." I pause. "I was sixteen when my mother died of breast cancer. It would not be until I left for college that dad would sell the house and move into a condo and it was on my graduation day from college that he gave me the pendant, saying that I must keep it safe and so I wear it every day, just like my mother did."

Dr. Paulson was taking notes while I spoke and when I stopped speaking he said, "Did you ever wish for a brother or a sister?"

"I guess I never needed anyone more than my parents and my friends so I never missed having a sibling. I did have a best friend too. Annie and I were inseparable from the age of three until we left home for college. We saw less and less of each other then, but that normally happens."

"Are you still in touch?"

"Yes, but we don't get to see each other often. It's mostly an electronic friendship now," I add with a grin.

"I know you're not married, but do you have a special man in your life?"

I was in the midst of taking a drink of water and almost choked. I cleared my throat and said, "Sorry."

"In college, I met Adam who I really thought was my soul mate, but it didn't work out. I think it was my fault as I was so into my studies I just didn't allow myself to have fun. Wish I did, but I didn't. Now that I think about it, I did myself an injustice because most of my friends are married now and I am still looking for that certain one."

"Was that your only serious relationship?"

"You can say that. There was Thomas, but Thomas was studying to be a doctor so he had little spare time too. That made him perfect for me until I graduated."

"So, I don't have to ask if you are successful in your career because I know that is true," said Dr. Paulson.

"It was hard going at first. Trying to find my notch but I knew I was good at what I did and eventually others recognized it too. Of course, I had to get an agent. You need to if you plan on becoming known. Agents can get in the door where it would be impossible for me to get in. I guess there is something about having someone else toot your horn to drum up interest," I add.

"So that's what you do for work. What do you do for fun?"

"Hm," I said. "Well, I have a few close friends that I get together with now and then and I spend a lot of time boating, traveling and going for long walks. I do some activities just to free my mind and yes, to get new ideas from what I see." I pause. That doctor, is me in a nutshell."

I watch as Dr. Paulson looks at his watch. "We are out of time Taylor, but I think we covered a lot in this session."

I can't believe it has been an hour. Following Dr. Paulson's lead, I stand. "Thank you, doctor."

I walk beside him to the door and then turn to face him. We shake hands.

I walk alone into the reception area, feeling at peace. I even have a genuine smile on my face when Amy greets me. "Would you like to make your next appointment now," she asks.

No reason not to. I already know I want to come back so we settle on a date and time.

Chapter 9

I remember that night so well. It was the day after the blizzard last year and I had managed to put the time to good use catching up on some of my unfinished works. There is a difference between wanting to stay indoors and being forced to, so I imagine I was primed to venture out at the first opportunity that presented itself. That desire may have been brought about by a new client, Mr. Masterson.

Several days earlier I had visited Mr. Masterson at his home. He was commissioning me to do a sculpture and I had informed him that this meeting was an important part of my work since I created my sculptures to match the people who were to enjoy them. This I felt was what set me apart from my peers who generally created their pictures and sculptors by verbal request or looking at drawings.

In any event, I decided to venture out. This wasn't odd for me as I walk a lot and find the cold refreshing to an overworked mind. And it was indeed cold. The damp mist from Lake Ontario drifted around me, it drifted down across the boardwalk and through the gazebo that set in the distance, empty and quiet at that hour. The children who usually played there had gone home, leaving the evidence of their arrival and departure clued into the deep snow that I now added my boot impressions to.

The ice-covered tree branches glistened in the dark and the long rows of benches that lined what was the walkway had icicles clinging to them making everything seem part of a wonderful fairy tale.

It was kind of awkward walking as I carried a large sketching pad, making it harder to stay upright with my legs sinking far from view as I took each step. I kept shifting the pad from one arm to the other and several times held it up over my head to keep it dry until I could step on to the plowed surface of the sidewalk leading to the gazebo.

In front of me the halogen street lights shone yellow in the shadowy air and I could hear the crisp sound of my own footsteps on the snow-covered sidewalk as I continued. Behind me only the sounds of the snow plows were audible.

I can't say exactly when it happened, but the sound of the snow plows eventually ceased and were replaced with sounds filling the night air that were strange to my ears as though they were from another time. I can't explain it any better than that.

Anyway, I continued and it was as though I had passed through a portal, by body seemed light, without weight as I traversed further along the path, suddenly aware that the snow wasn't as thick along the path as it had been and the cold wasn't as biting as it had been earlier.

The little boy playing by himself in the middle of the gazebo made no sound. He was sitting on the cold wooden floor, playing a game and every now and then I could see a small ball bounce in the air and his hand reaching out to collect something he had splayed out in front of him. The movements continued as I advanced with him paying me no heed. Finally, I was so close I could see the jacks that laid on the floor of the gazebo.

I stood there and watched him as he repeatedly bounced the ball and tried to grab up a handful of jacks, singing a song as he did so.

There was something odd about him, I kept thinking, unable to put my finger on exactly what it was beyond it being odd for a child so young to be in the park alone. No other children were in sight. There was the mist and there was something else odd. I couldn't remember there being a row of streetlights stretching from the boardwalk to the gazebo. As I looked about for his mother she was nowhere to be seen. I moved closer to see if she was maybe seated inside the gazebo, but it was empty except for the little boy.

"It's getting pretty dark," I said. "You should be going home." I wasn't sure if this was what I should say to a child, but it was all I could think of.

At first, he said nothing, nor showed any signs of hearing my voice interrupting the silence of the small world in the gazebo. The child continued to throw the ball up in the air and grab another handful of jacks. Before he repeated the action for a second time in my presence, he looked up in my direction, showing the first sign that he knew I was there.

"Is it late?" he asked. "I don't know time very well."

I couldn't help from smiling at him. "Yes," I said, "it's quite late."

It seemed that for the first time the child looked around and became aware that it had grown dark outside. Yet he made no move to leave, so I again tried to make him understand that it was very late and that is when he said, "Nobody's ready for me."

I didn't know quite how to respond to this so I turned away. He wasn't my child, or one that I knew so it really was none of my business. While I was thinking these thoughts, I found myself turning to face him again. I watched as the little boy straightened up and stood. I stared at him as he pushed his hair away from his face, tucking it under the edge of his hat. As I watched him, I noticed that even under his ill-fitting clothes I could tell he was very thin.

"Can I walk with you?" he asked. It is dark and I have no one to play with."

I wondered what to do, but then decided maybe I could take him home.

"Come on then."

I kept looking around for someone he might belong to, but there was nobody but the little boy and me.

"You are alone. Isn't anybody with you?"

"No," he said. "Who would be with me?"

Again, I found myself wondering what an odd thing to say. And again, I couldn't think of any response.

"Anyway," he said. "You're with me."

We continued down the path together. Finally, he asked me, "Why are you carrying that pad?"

"Well, I use it to draw what I see."

"What do you see?"

"Well, lots of things, like trees, birds, people. I make a sketch and then a drawing or even a sculpture."

"What's a sculpture?"

I thought for a moment and then replied, "Do you know what a statute is?"

"Yes."

"Well, a sculpture is another word for statute."

I looked down and saw as he nodded his head. "I knew that you made sculptures," he said shyly.

"How could you know that?"

"Oh, I just knew."

It was an innocent lie so I didn't probe him further as we continued on our way. The frigid air drifted around us, chilling me to the bones. Here I was walking down the boardwalk with a little boy no higher than my elbow and we didn't even know each other, in fact hadn't really met. Suddenly I began to worry. Could I be arrested for what I was doing, even if all I was doing was trying to help. This was crazy.

I looked down at my companion who seemed to be involved in counting the benches that we passed and as if sensing what was running through my mind, I felt his little hand reach for mine and give it a squeeze. Then he looked up at me and said, "It's Michael. My name is Michael."

"Michael," I repeated. "Michael, what?"

"Michael Roman. My name is Michael and I live with my parents in a hotel near here." There was a sadness in his tone as he added. "I don't see my parents very often. They are musicians," he declared sadly.

"Ah, how nice. What do they play?"

"They are concert pianists, which came out sounding more like 'penniless'. "They're playing at the Hallow Theater." He smiled and then released my hand and began to try and skip along the path, then suddenly turned around and came back to me, putting his hand in mine once again and saying, "They're not home very much.

I could feel my heart going out to him. He was such a sweet child I was thinking when it dawned on me what he had said.

"Michael, where did you say they were playing?"

"The Hallow Theater."

"Do you mean the Halstein Theater?"

"Yes. That's what I said."

That was impossible. He must have gotten it wrong. The Halstein Theater had been torn down years ago. I was just a child myself when they took the theater down. Yes, he must have it wrong. He had said they travelled a lot and there could be a Halstein Theater somewhere and he may have just made a mistake.

"I go to school," Michael was saying, "but only in the mornings. I'm too little to go all day yet."

"What are you learning in school?"

Michael sighed and said, "I don't have very fun stuff to learn. I count and say my ABCs. I do like to read though."

Surprised I ask, "You can read?"

"No, silly, the teacher reads to us. When I am bigger, I will learn geography and history and even how to read by myself."

"Yes, you will. And I think you will have no trouble with your lessons either. You seem to be a very smart little boy."

"Yes, I am, but that's because…"

"Yes," I prodded.

"Because I knew it before," he replied.

Again, a weird sensation came over me at his words. This was an odd thing to say. He was full of odd replies. I looked at him, but he didn't seem to notice I was confused.

"I know Christopher Rodan."

“Who’s Christopher Rodan,” I asked getting use to his topic jumping.

"Christopher Rodan is in my class," he said. "I like him, but he is not as smart as I am. He's just a little boy."

"Oh, I see," I said with my mind elsewhere.

We continued along the boardwalk with Michael skipping beside me. We walked for some time in silence and then he spoke again. "It's fun having somebody to play with," he said.

I looked down at him and for the first time noticed his clothes. He was dressed in a style of clothing I hadn't seen in some time. The little boy had on a tweed pair of wide shorts that met up with heavy wool socks at his knee. On his head was a tweed cap that had ear covers and around his neck was a scotch print scarf that matched his wool jacket that buttoned up the front. Amongst all this material was a shock of brown hair and exquisite eyes. He looked to be outfitted in clothing from the 1920s, but then I wasn’t up on the latest in fashions for children. As I looked at him I couldn't help thinking what a lovely model he would make for a sculpture.

"Don't you have anyone to play with?" he asked.

"No," I said smiling.

I had a feeling that he felt sorry for me, and at the same time was happy that I had nobody else but him to play with. The idea of it all made me want to laugh. A child's games are so real, I thought, for children believe everything.

I felt I was ready to find out where he was from. I was ready to hear his reply which somehow, I knew I should prepare myself for.

"Michael. You said that you were staying at a hotel here. Where are you from."

"I told you I was from the hotel but I don't know its name?"

"Oh, I understand that. Can you tell me where you live when you are not at the hotel?"

I felt as though I could hear his mind working on my question as we stood side by side on the snow-covered boardwalk. Finally, he had an answer.

"I know a song," he said. "Would you like to hear it?"

He didn't need a reply from me as he looked up and began to recite these words.

"Now I lay me down to sleep. I pray the lord my soul to keep If I should die before I wake, I pray the lord my soul will take."

The words caught me off guard. It was not what I had expected, but then I didn't know what I anticipated anyway. Maybe I thought he would sing a nursery rhyme or a song he learned at school. Maybe even whatever he had been singing when I first saw him.

This was a prayer you say at night and though I knew it too, it just was so strange a response to my question.

"Who taught you that? " I asked trying to keep the surprise out of my voice.

The child shook his head as he continued to look up at me.

"Nobody taught me," he said. "It's just a song."

I smiled at him and he smiled back. This wasn't a song, at least I hadn't learned it as such. But he was the child of musicians and they may have taught him this bedtime prayer as a song. Why not?

We were walking again and had reached the end of the boardwalk where we stepped down to find the snow on the beach was deeper, much deeper than the child's boots. I would continue down the beach to my house from this point on and I thought it was best I were alone.

We stood there in solitude and silence while I looked out at the frozen water, my eyes reaching out further where the lake was not frozen. I was beginning to feel the chill of the evening air as it blew across Lake Ontario, then up the beach until it reached the boardwalk before warming ever so slightly. I looked down at my little companion thinking that he must be quite cold, but it was not apparent. He stood there so quiet and peaceful looking in front of him, not shivering or complaining of the cold as I thought to myself it was time to go home.

I continued my vigilance trying to determine what I should do. I could call the police and tell them there was a little boy on the beach who was lost and unable to tell me where he lived, or I could walk with him and see if he knew how to find his way, though he did not know the name of where he was going. But none of that seemed to be the right thing to do in Michael's case. My mind told me that I didn't know where Michael lived and didn't want to leave him alone, but what was I to do. He couldn't tell me the name of the hotel and .... Suddenly I knew what I should do.

Michael would be all right and I must not do anything to interfere. I must go my own way. It sounded crazy even to me, but though I didn't know why I thought this was best, I knew that I had to leave Michael alone and let him do what he must do, I knew it was right.

"Well, I have to go now" I said, "goodbye".

Our hands had been clasped and I moved his over in front of me and as though parting company with an adult I smiled politely and shook his hand.

"Do you know the game I like to play best?" he asked.

"No," I said, only slightly surprised he was ignoring

the fact that I needed to go. That was not odd as most people who are lonely tend to ignore a spoken goodbye, and I had a feeling that Michael was lonely.

"The wishing game."

"I don't think I know that game Michael. How do you play it?"

"It's easy, really, you just say what you wish." He paused for a moment and looked directly up into my eyes. "Want to know what I wish for?"

"Sure, tell me what you wish for."

"I wish you'd wait for me to grow up," he said.

Then as though not expecting any reply or even a look at my face or some reaction, little Michael turned and was walking quietly back down the boardwalk. I could only stand there looking after him; until I couldn't see him anymore. Then, I continued on my way.

When I arrived home, I was chilled to the bone and decided a hot shower would warm me, so I took off my coat, and neck scarf and hung them up before sitting on the bench to pull off my wet boots. I checked to make sure the door was locked and then headed upstairs.

I went into my bedroom and got out a night gown before going into the bathroom. I was tired; too tired for a bath so I turned on the shower and adjusted the temperature. I opened the cabinet drawer and got out a hair clip then twisted my hair up on top of my head. I paused, peering into the mirror. I looked the same as I had earlier that day, but somehow, I had expected a change because I felt different.

Finally, I stepped out of my clothing and climbed into the shower.

The feel of the warm water flowing over my body relaxed me and cleared my mind and by the time I stepped out, I felt like a new person. I dried myself and put on a big fluffy robe before heading down to the kitchen. I was suddenly hungry.

There was a note on the counter from my housekeeper, Mildred informing me she had left my dinner in the oven and all I needed to do was zap it for three minutes in the microwave. I did just that. While I waited, I checked the refrigerator and found a salad already prepared for me, which I took out and placed on the table, before going about getting out silverware and filling a glass with water. By then the microwave buzzer went off and I was ready to sit down to eat, alone at the kitchen table, my only companion was the evening paper that I browsed until I finished. I tidied up placing the dishes in the dishwasher and wiping away any telltale signs of the meal, then went into the den to watch a little television before turning in for the evening.

As I moved across the floor in the foyer it dawned on me that I hadn't made one drawing or even given thought to the Masterson's commission. Usually, I would have had two or three ideas generated during such a long walk, but then, I thought, I would have been alone.

I walked up close to the sliding glass doors in the den, looking out into the shadows beyond though there wasn't much to see this time of the year except for the beach and barren lake that reached up to the sky on the horizon.

Eventually, I reflected on the child I had met on the boardwalk. I recalled the bedtime rhyme he had song in a tuneless way only repeating the words and not putting any feeling into them. I would have thought his parents would have taught him how to sing, but quite obviously, they had not. I wondered why I even thought that. Yet, I had to admit the tonelessness is the very thing that made his song hard to forget, that and the fact that it was really a bedtime prayer. Then there was the song he was singing in the gazebo, but I didn't know the tune, or just hadn't recognized it.

I allowed judgments of the child to freely fill my head. I remembered the last thing he had said to me, before he turned and walked away, and I thought the truth was grownups couldn't wait for children to grow up. Children grew up with other children. The grownups didn't wait for the child to mature and the child didn't hope that the adult would wait for them to reach adulthood. At least not when the child was five and the adult was thirty-five. The cycle of life was to be children together, then adults together and finally senior citizens together. At the end of the cycle all would go together or separately into whatever was the "hereafter".

Chapter 10

I am in a tunnel, passing through light and motion quickly as I become conscious of sound. I am gaining consciousness and can't see Michael anymore so I struggle to close out the sound that is forcing me back. Someone is calling my name, but I don't recognize the voice or feel ready to come back yet, only the voice is persistent.

It is a voice that seems somehow familiar and I feel as though I should answer the owner whose tone shows no signs of relenting. The voice calls out again and again and I realize it is now coming from nearby. It feels as though I am traveling at kaleidoscope speed up a brilliant tunnel of light until the voice becomes totally identifiable. It is Dr. Paulson.

"Taylor, can you hear me?"

At first, I can't find my voice, but then I manage to squeeze out, "Yes?" through my dry parched throat.

"Yes?" I say again. "I'm sorry doctor."

"It's okay. It's normal to get caught up in your memories."

I sit up slowly and Dr. Paulson hands me a glass of water. I smile my thanks and take a sip as I try to remember what I said to him. I couldn't remember.

"Doctor, did you hypnotize me?" I ask worriedly.

Dr. Paulson looks calmly at me and says, "No, Taylor."

"Well how come I can't remember anything?"

"You will. How are you feeling now?"

"It is a bizarre feeling. I am here, but confused as to whether I am really thinking the thoughts that I am thinking. I know how crazy I sound saying this, but it is the only way I can explain it.

“It’s because you were part of what you were sharing with me. It happens when we really keep concentrating on something that has been bothering us, or are worrying about things that are not happening now, we tend to suddenly slip into this mode.”

“But why can’t I remember what I said?”

“When you are so engrossed in what you are saying, it becomes real and it will take a moment to reorient yourself. You were a million miles away. I could see that."

I am quiet as I gather up my courage to ask the question that I want answered. “So, what do you think? Am I going crazy?”

Dr. Paulson does not react right away as he contemplates my question. "I really can't say what I think yet Taylor since I haven't heard the whole story. I will wait until we have a chance to go over all that you can remember, then, who knows ...”

"Yes, who knows. I just might be going insane, right?"

"Taylor, I have no reason to believe you are going insane. Most people have dreams that seem so real they can't place them as a dream. Or others may have premonitions that seem absolutely to predict that something is going to take place. I can’t, judge them either. I cannot establish that all the events related to me have occurred exactly as they have been recounted; human beings are fallible, excitable, and prone to exaggeration. But I can document every detail as it is being told to me and then measure the credibility always keeping in mind that there may be shortcomings in our commonsense notions of what is, and what is not possible.”

I nod my head even though I don’t fully understand.

“To help you I need to hear it all.” Dr. Paulson pauses. “I do believe that you are a level-headed individual who is experiencing some type of phenomenon and if I am to help, I must wait until I am able to better understand before I present you with any theory."

This is not what I want to hear. I want some explanation that will give credence to my experience. Yet, I wonder, what would I think of the doctor if he were to decide without hearing the whole story. Would I feel confident in his decision?

"I can see your point," I reply solemnly.

"Our time is up for today so we will continue where we left off at our next session. "

Dr. Paulson walks with me to the door and we shake hands. In the reception area, I set up my next appointment with Amy and then leave his office grateful for the opportunity to finally be able to share this with someone.

I chuckle. The doctor will find some explanation for all of this. I feel confident that he will. By the time, I climb into my car, I am feeling much better. It is like the act of placing this in the hands of the doctor, takes the worry away from me and I like that feeling.

As I drive toward home I begin to take back some of the burden of trying to understand what is happening to me. I can't accept that it is real, yet the past, the present and the future is connected in ways we can't know. Maybe I am remembering something that happened and twisting it into the present.

I didn't like this train of thought and turning the wheel, I change my mind about going straight home. I drive to the mall instead where I do a little impulse buying and then feeling hungry go to the food court to buy a soft pretzel and something to drink.

It is growing dark outside when I finally leave the mall and head toward home. There are quite a few cars on the roadways, but it doesn't bother me as I am not in any hurry. I turn on the radio and relaxing music fills the car.

I feel light and gay until I pull into my driveway and

get out of my car. I am suddenly overcome with a wave of loneliness. I stand looking at my hands, recalling the young, confident face that had smiled up at me in now what has become more like a dream and in my head, pops the words of Bill Monroe's song, *Beyond the walls of time*.

I manage to close the car door and quickly enter the house, rushing through the foyer. It is only when I feel a sharp stab at my ankle do I stop. Looking down I see the porcelain vase on the table beside me has fallen to the floor. Confused I reach down to pick it up and put it back on the table when I hear a concerned voice coming from behind me.

"Miss, are you, all right?"

It is my housekeeper, Mildred.

"Sure, I'm fine," I reply, happy the vase hadn't broken, though it isn't of any significant value except that I tend to like it. I look up at Mildred who is still standing in the foyer. 'Was there something you wanted, Mildred?"

"Yes, Ms. Bouchard. I came to ask you when you would like me to have dinner on the table."

"Anytime will be fine," I respond. I look at the vase making sure it is sitting securely, then realize Mildred hasn't moved from her spot. "Anything else?"

"If you don't need me, Ms. Bouchard, I would appreciate being able to leave early. Dinner is ready and I only need to serve it to you."

"Don't worry about that. I can do it myself. You just go ahead home and I'll see you tomorrow, Mildred. "

"Thank you, Ms. Bouchard," she says.

I wait in the foyer as Mildred gathers her things and prepare to leave, then walk beside her as she rattles off last-minute instructions before stepping out the door. I close and lock the door behind her, then coming to my senses, start to open the door and yell out at her. I hadn't asked if anything was wrong. I was so wrapped up in my own self I wasn't thinking straight.

I make a note to ask her when she returns. Mildred did not have an easy life and I try to help her whenever she lets me. She had told me that the unexpected death of her husband had required that she seek employment since she had seven children that were between the ages of two and fourteen to feed. That was when she first came to work for me. I remember this proud woman was in such an emotional turmoil and facing a financial crisis that she was forced to ask for an advancement on her pay which I willingly gave her and have never regretted it.

As I close and lock the front door, I remember Mildred mentioning earlier something about a school play that was coming up so maybe that was why she needed to leave early.

I head toward the kitchen, planning to fix my plate, but I'm not hungry. Instead I wander around making sure everything is turned off before going to the living room and turning on the stereo. Soon the sounds of Mozart's "A Little Night Music" Serenade No. 13 in G major fill the emptiness and the upbeat chords lift my spirits with melodious harmony.

Somewhere I had read that exercise clears the head and sharpens the mind so I listen to the music and give into the urge to dance around the room, twirling until becoming dizzy, then falling into a chair laughing at myself. It is just what I need to get the adrenaline flowing so that my creative juices are activated.

It is time to work on the sculptor for my newest client, Mr. Masterson so I go to get my briefcase and review the pictures I had taken on my visit to his home. Sitting in front of the fireplace in the den I concentrate on my notes expressing my opinions of the couple and their home, then view the photos through the viewfinder.

I lean back on the sofa and stare into the flames of the fireplace and I see it. I see exactly what I want for him. Quickly I take my pencil and draw a couple dancing with great delight to celebrate their bond of love. Arnie and Vivian Masterson are a beautiful, highly successful couple who exude sexiness, but are family oriented. This sculpture would be from metal with a rich, dark gray surface. Simple yet evocative, it would have flowing lines and an open, airy composition to convey a sense of joyful companionship.

My hand works freely designing this new creation and I can feel the joy build within me. As my hand moves across the blank page, the lines seem to form on their own what I conceive to be the perfect piece. I am well into it, unaware of the music, time or space until I set aside the sketch and rub my strained eyes. I have been seated in one position for some time now and my leg is cramping from lack of movement. I try to stand, but fall back in the chair, rubbing the leg while I glance at the sketch.

I like it, but I feel the need to continue so I set aside this sketch and start another that comes to me; even easier than the one before. I am only slightly surprised when I recognize the figure staring up at me from the pad. It is the face of a child, the face of Michael.

I sit for a long time looking at the sketch and then before I am aware of what I am doing, I begin making more sketches of Michael in different poses. There is one of him sitting on the ground playing jacks, another of him looking quizzically up and one as he stands gazing forward as if seeing something no one else can see. Each one seems to have that quality of the child being of another time and even as I depict it I could not explain it. These were for me, though I didn't need anything to help me remember Michael. I put all the sketches into my briefcase.

I need to get my mind off Michael so I go over to the wine cooler and got out a bottle of wine and stand pouring myself a glass that I take with me over to sit in front of the fire. Slowly I sip my wine.

It is getting late now and I decide to call it a day, knowing that when my head rests on the pillow I will no longer oversee my mind, but it doesn't it matter. Awake or asleep I keep thinking of Michael.

What is it about this child that has captured me? He is but a little boy and of no concern of mine and I might never see him again. Yet, deep down I know that to be wrong. I will see Michael again and I am sure that he is to play a major role in my life. I know this because I can't forget him. That night I sleep, but if I dreamt I can't remember. I wake up refreshed and ready to greet the day.

Funny thing about creative people, they are very particular. Not only am I fastidious about my sculptures, I am meticulous about my clothing. It must project the image that I want on any day and in any situation. This morning I am to meet with Mr. Masterson and show him the sketches I have done for his mantel piece. I feel sure he will like the renditions, but it does help to look like I know what I am doing. It gives the client permission to have confidence in my opinion and thus aids in getting their approval.

So, I take pains in preparing myself for the meeting and then add some finishing touches to the sketches. When I am done, I give myself and the sketches a final once over and am satisfied.

I carry my briefcase to the foyer and place it on the table. As I stand there, I hear the key turning in the lock and when it opens, Mildred stands in the doorway.

"You gave me a fright," she says jumping back.

"Sorry, Mildred. I was just putting my briefcase on the table to take with me this morning. How was your evening?"

"Oh, thank you for the time. It was very enjoyable. Thank you for asking."

Mildred hangs up her coat and sits on the hall bench to take off her boots before walking with me to the kitchen.

I notice she has a bag in her hand and I watch as she moves deftly about the kitchen, taking out cups for coffee, a glass and the orange juice from the refrigerator. That done she opens the bag and takes out fresh bagels before turning on the coffee maker.

"Sit down. It will be ready in a minute," Mildred says.

"No, but thank you Mildred."

"But Ms. Bouchard, you didn't eat your dinner last night so you must be hungry. Just sit down and have a glass of juice and a bagel before you go."

There would be no use arguing with her because Mildred was determined to not let me out of the house until I had put something in my stomach. It was my reason for hiring her in the first place. I had someone who came in to clean before Mildred, but that was the extent of what was done. I hired Mildred after interviewing her and realizing that she was indeed a treasure. She was the type of person who cared about others and that was what I needed. Mildred had never let me down. She handled the cleaning crew and took care of me, making sure I got my proper rest and proper nutrition. There was nothing she considered beneath her to do. She would answer the phone, the door, prepare food for a visitor without having to be asked, and always made sure that there was food in the refrigerator. Giving in to her demands was the least I could do.

I didn't realize how anxious I was until I finally am

on my way, wondering which of the sketches would be the one chosen by Mr. Masterson. Which would he determine would sit on his mantle. I liked them all, but I couldn't let go of the need to know the one he would like the most; the one that would become three dimensional.

It is freezing outside and the snow has accumulated several inches since last night. The cold clears my head and makes my body want to move faster as I trudge through the almost knee-deep drifts to my car, wishing I had put it in the garage last night. Finally, I am behind the wheel and begin the journey to the Masterson's home.

On the snow-covered roads, it is almost a thirty-minute drive, but I arrive on time and scale the slippery stone steps to their massive front door. I ring the door bell and in minutes the door is opened by a man who invites me in and asks to take my coat and hat. While he takes care of my coat, I sit and remove my boots, then stand and smooth my hair in front of the hallway mirror.

“Are you ready, Miss?”

“Yes.”

I follow him to what appears to be the study and standing in the doorway is Mr. Masterson.

“Can I get you a cup of coffee,” he asks.

“Yes, please. I take it black.”

Mr. Masterson nods his head toward the door and a few minutes later we are presented with a cup of coffee for each of us and a plate of pastries.

“Please, take a seat, Ms. Bouchand.”

“Taylor, please.” I say.

I walk over to a chair near the fire place and Mr. Masterson takes a seat across from me. I take a few sips of the coffee and decline a pastry.

Mr. Masterson asks. "What do you have to show me

Taylor."

"Well, sir, I have several sketches to show you." I open my brief case and pull out the sketches. "I think you will like what I have come up with."

"I'm sure I will", Mr. Masterson replied.

I stand and place the sketches on the table between us and he rises so that we stand side by side, looking at the first one, then I step back and allow him privacy in acquainting himself with my art.

Suddenly, the silence is broken as he reaches down and picks up one of the sketches. "Here," he cries out; "that's it!"

I lean over his shoulder and see it is the one of the dancers stretched out from each other as if in the midst of a dance.

"It's perfection. I love how you have them, sort of flat instead of rounded out as full figure people. It makes them more exciting to look at. And the arms blending into one is perfect."

I reach down to gather up the other sketches and the ones of Michael fall to the floor. I am picking them up when Mr. Masterson says, "Who's the subject for these?"

"It's just a little boy I met on the boardwalk at Lake Ontario.

"Ah," said Mr. Masterson happily; "This is different. It's good, it has charisma; it's very good. Do you know why I like it? I can see the past in it and I feel as though I've seen that little boy before, somewhere; and yet I couldn't tell you where."

I watch as he holds it out in front of him; then he puts it down, walks away, and comes back to it again. He seems to be concentrating, but not on the sketch so much as on the little boy. It is as though he thought it was important he remember where he had seen him.

My heartbeat quickens, and I feel my hands trembling only I didn’t know why. I should just be happy he likes the sketch. I hadn't broken any laws in drafting a picture of this strange, captivating little boy. Of that I am sure. But I still felt uneasy. I kind of hope he will remember where he has seen him, but then again, I am afraid of what he would say. Finally, Mr. Masterson speaks.

"Yes," he said, "There is something about the child that makes me sure I have seen him before. Wait a minute. I think I know. I've seen a portrait of him before at the Memorial Art Gallery"

I draw in my breath sharply; and I feel again the dream-like quality of that walk along the Boardwalk with Michael.

"Not that it's a copy," Mr. Masterson says hastily, "I'm not even saying it is the same child; and the style is very much your own. There’s just something in each that reminds me of the other."

Mr. Masterson continues to stare at this one sketch as I stand nervously by wanting to leave, but not knowing why I feel that way. He straightens up. "I want to commission you to do a painting of this one for the library. That is if this isn’t something you are doing for someone else."

"No,” I say hesitantly, “It isn’t.”

“Great. Then it’s settled.”

“Do you have a size in mind,” I ask.

“Come with me, “he says.

I follow him into their library where there is lots of wood and shadows. He takes me over to the fireplace and points above it. “That’s where I would like it.”

As I stand wondering how to get the dimensions, Mr. Masterson leaves and returns with a man in tow who climbs on the library ladder and works it over to the area where he begins taking the measurements. As he supplies them, I write them down on my pad. “Thank you,” I say as the man prepares to leave.

I follow Mr. Masterson out of the library and back into the study where we talk for a bit more and I finally say, “I think I have all I need so I will say goodbye."

"Taylor, I am very pleased with what you have presented me with today and look forward to seeing the end results.”

“Thank you so much. I appreciate your confidence in me.”

He walks with me to the door and we shake hands. I then began putting on my coat, boots, hat and gloves thinking how much I want this winter to end. Finally, I am on my way. I walk carefully down the sidewalk to climb into my car and once inside I immediately turn on the engine. I wish I could wait until it warmed a little but when I look at the clock I see I am running late for my next doctor’s appointment.

Chapter 11

I like my time with Dr. Paulson. If someone had asked me earlier what I thought about seeing a psychiatrist, I would have said it was a waste of time. It is not. Opening up about the things I tend to keep to myself is always scary. But since that first visit when I wanted to turn around and leave I am so glad I didn't. Now as I hurry to my appointment, anxious to get started, I wonder what he will have me talk about, or is it my turn to bring up the topics.

I smile at the familiar face of Amy as she walks with me to the cloak closet and chats while I slip out of my coat and hat, then sit on the bench to take off my boots. "Boy,' I say, "I can't wait for summer."

Amy smiles and gives me a minute to primp before we walk to the door of Dr. Paulson's office. I take a deep breath, smile and enter the room.

Dr. Paulson is waiting for me and waits until I choose a seat. "So, Taylor, let's begin. I'd like to hear more about your childhood if that's okay with you."

"Well, there's not much to tell, really. I am an only child; no brothers, no sisters."

"Did you miss not having a brother or a sister?"

"No, not really. There were times when I thought it would be fun, but my parents were very attentive to me and I liked getting all the attention."

I look around the office trying to think of what else to say.

"I was adopted when I was a baby."

Dr. Paulson was taking notes and I waited, wondering what he had written down.

"How would you describe yourself Taylor."

"Well, hm, I think I can say I am accomplished and people who know me say that I am delightful and kindhearted."

"How do you see yourself?"

"I am proud and intensely individual. My desire is to be the very best I can be and that takes dedication to myself and to my art."

"Have you ever been in love…I mean romantically?"

I thought about this and though it felt right to bend the truth a little, I came out with it. "No, I have not been romantically involved with anyone for a long time."

"Why is that, do you think?"

"I don't have to think. I know it is because I am so into my work."

Dr. Paulson keeps his head down so I can't see his expression. When he does look at me, I can't tell what he is thinking.

"Have you ever tried to find out who your real parents are? Aren't you a bit curious about them."

"No, I can say that I honestly haven't thought much about them. I know that they gave me up when I was a baby. They have never contacted me so I must assume they had no interest in knowing about me."

I sense my answer might be troubling, but it is the truth.

"Taylor, this may sound odd to ask, but did you have an imaginary friend when you were little?"

"No, no." I pause thinking. "No, I say hesitantly, not that I recall."

"What type of friendships do you have."

"What do you mean."

"Well, I mean people who you have a strong

interpersonal bond with."

I think a moment and then say, "I'm not sure what you are driving at."

"I simply want to know if you have people in your life who you show affection, and feel sympathy for. Individuals who you share a mutual understanding and compassion and you enjoy their company."

"Sure, I do. There's Samuel and there's Annie."

"Tell me about Samuel."

"Samuel is a freelancer like myself. He is an agent to many individuals trying to make it as an artist and we have become friends. We get together and talk about ourselves and people we know." I pause. "Samuel's career was interrupted when he joined the Navy. He was a Navy Seal and the training he received had him interested in working as a private detective at first, and somehow he decided to switch gears and become an agent."

"So, you two get together socially?"

"Yes, we do. It's casual like. We might run into each other and then decide to have a drink." I know I'm not hiding the defensiveness I am feeling because even as I talk, I realize this is not a typical friendship.

"Don't take this the wrong way, Taylor, these are only questions and there are no wrong or right answers. I need to know you and this is how I can do that.

"I'm sorry. I am not one to tell people about my personal life so this is hard for me. Rest assure I do have friends. Take Annie. Annie and I go way back and we get together whenever she is in town. She lives in Houston, Texas and she is an artist too."

Dr. Paulson writes something down and then looks at me. "Okay, then."

"Okay, what." I ask.

"I mean, can you tell me about Annie?"

I talk about Annie and I can see by his expression that this is more in line with describing a friend. I can hear the joy in my voice as I talk about her and the fun we had as children and later as adults. When I finish sharing, I look at the doctor.

"Can I ask you a question, Doctor?"

"Sure."

"Do you think that our childhood is a major part of who and what we become?"

"It's not childhood, Taylor. It is family. It is here that we experience our first, deepest, most complex, and sometimes most painful interactions. Despite the inevitable dysfunction that exists in all families, they generate a certain intimacy and honesty that we rarely encounter elsewhere. As we grow from child to adult, spouse to parent, who we are is characterized by our place in the family."

Dr. Paulson stands up. "Does that answer your question?"

"Yes, it does. Thank you."

"I think that is enough for today, Taylor.

I stand up and reach out to shake his hand. "Thank you, Doctor. I apologize for getting offensive. I think I understand why you had to be so personal."

"Good. We need to trust and feel comfortable with each other if we are to understand what is happening to you."

"So, when should I see you again?"

"Let's say, two weeks from now. But if something happens and you need to see me sooner, just call."

I follow him to the door and I hesitate a minute

wanting to say something more, but change my mind. Instead I smile and enter the reception area where I schedule the next appointment.

Chapter 12

Life goes on as usual for me as I work and finally finish a figurine that is of long stem calla lilies done in bronze for Mr. and Mrs. Mathews, clients who live in Mendon. My clients, the Matthews are very open, nature loving individuals and I have known them for some time, so I can imagine that they will love what I have sculpted.

This is the third piece I have done for them over a period of a couple years, and I am used to the high praise they show when I unveil the latest creation, but I never get tired of it. This figurine is for the mantle over the huge stone fireplace and I am as anxious to see it in place as they are. We stand admiring it and I am not surprised when they commission me to do another of the same piece since I am rather proud of the results and see the huge mantle would look magnificent with one at each end.

Not all my work is met with such praise. Every now and then I will have a misinterpretation of what a client favors. It happens and did with the Monroe's.

Mrs. Monroe and her husband were an older couple. If I had to guess I would say they were in their late seventies. It was Mrs. Monroe who hired me to make a sculpture for her husband and it is to be a surprise so I do not get the chance to meet her husband during the whole process.

On the day I deliver the sculptor, is the first time I meet Mr. Monroe; a large man with a stern disposition. The minute I see him I know the sculptor is not right for him, but at his wife's request, I present it, watching as he undoes the protective packaging to reveal my creation.

Mr. Monroe groans when he sees what his wife has commissioned me to create for his office and not holding back bellows his disproval. I try to apologize only he won't allow it. It is his wife who calms him and what could have been a disaster is rectified by her purchasing the sculpture of gladiolas and her husband commissioning me to do another sculptor for him.

Though most of my projects are three dimensional, I haven't totally given up on painting. It is just that I find sculpturing to be more to my liking. There is an incredible feeling I. experience when molding clay or melted metal into something beautiful and graceful. The three-dimensional effect is a reality in sculpturing, but only an illusion in painting. Yet now and again I take a commission for a painting to keep my hand in it. I do so for a man named Mr. Clayton who has asked for something a little different that would only work on canvas.

After a day of making deliveries I am in the studio the next day preparing a five-foot canvas. I stretch and mount it, wet one side of it with water, and work in a light surface of white lead with my palette knife. Then I set it aside to dry. After that there is nothing to do but wait before I can begin the painting, so I start working on my new commissions, my head filling with thoughts of Michael until I can't concentrate on what I am doing.

Finally, I decide to do some research but when I do a Google search on the Romans, not knowing their first names I come up with a lot of choices. I search again on what I know and that is they are concert pianist. I find something, and lean back against my chair, thinking that this can't be them. But even as I think it, somehow, I know it's true.

Michael comes at the end of the week. Before Mildred can respond, I answer the door myself. I have been sitting in my studio staring out the window and see Michael as he walks slowly to the door. I realize that I am breathless, my heart in overtime as I stand there in the foyer. When I do not open the door, there is a light tap and I take a deep breath then swing the door open.

He stands on the steps before me, pale and silent, dressed in dark clothing and I can sense something is wrong. I peer into his dear face and I want to ask what is it, but I am afraid of what he may say so I remain silent, wondering all the time why do I feel like this.

Michael raises his head, his brown eyes seeming to stare straight through to my very soul and after a bit I find my voice. "What is it Michael,"

Even I hear the panic in my voice as I try to hide it. "Please, Michael, tell me what is wrong."

For a moment, I am afraid he is not going to answer me and then he says chokingly, "It's father and mother." He takes a deep breath before continuing. "They had an accident." I stand there with tears filling my eyes though I have never met his parents. Michael sees this and tries to smile consolingly, but his eyes betray his pain. Before the words come out of his mouth, I am aware of what he will say and I dread hearing it. "They're dead, Taylor," he cries out in pain. "My parents are dead."

"Oh, my god, Michael." And I surprise myself when I say, "I know. Come in, please."

Michael steps inside and I help him into the den, lowering him into a chair. I take a Kleenex and hand it to him. I take another and wipe my eyes. I clear my throat and say, "Stay here Michael. I'll get you a glass of water."

I hurry into the kitchen and pour a glass of water and not seeing Mildred, I fill the teapot and put it on the stove. When I return to Michael, he breaks down totally.

I stand beside his chair and lean down to hug him tightly, telling him it is okay to cry. And he cries, the sound coming deeply from within him. I release him when the tea kettle whistles and hurry into the kitchen. Still no Mildred in sight, I quickly setup a tray to take back with me. When

I enter the room, I see Michael seems more in control and he looks at me repeating, "They're dead, Taylor."

"I know," I answer back, not thinking; then biting my lip and taking his hand in mine I realize he has heard what I have said and that I must explain myself. What will I say if he asks how I know. It may have slipped by once, but not twice and then it comes to me. Even though he hasn't recovered enough to ask, I offer an explanation. "I read about it," I tell him. "In the paper."

"Oh," he says distantly, yes." But he isn't thinking about me as he tries to accept what he is saying. I see the pain and confusion as I help him out of his coat and drape it over the sofa. I am confused as to what I should do next. Should I comfort him or should I allow him to adjust without outside input.

"I'm sorry, Michael," I say again with meaning. "Truly, sorry for your lost." He draws a deep breath. "I loved them so," he replies in a voice quivering with emotion. "I didn't see them very much, but I miss them terribly. The way they died."

I can't stand to see him hurting so much as I stand by idly unable to console him nor could I block the visions that entered my head.

They were there, Robert and Clara, stepping out of the concert hall holding onto their child as they looked up and saw a faint glow appear above the trees. It must have puzzled them at first as they watched it, seeing it as it grew brighter and brighter until the flames shot higher and higher and widened rapidly until they were everywhere. They ran then as though demons were chasing them screaming in their eyes and confusion and panic swirling in their brain. There was no time and they knew but they had to try. So, they ran making the child keep up with them and then came the deafening explosion that bust in their ears followed by flames and the trembling earth beneath their feet. They lost their footing then and one by one they fell into the sparks descending slowly, lazily and landing on their clothing igniting it until there was-nothing-left to identify.

I must get a hold of myself. This is not the way I can help Michael and I shake the vision from my mind.

"Oh Taylor," he cried and hid his face, weeping uncontrollably almost as though he had read my thoughts and seen the horrible picture I painted. in my mind, or was it only a picture? I can't go there.

I want to comfort him; but I think it is best that I let him cry himself out so I force myself to turn around and walk over to the window.

I stare out at the deep blue sky meshing seamlessly with the water on the horizon and try desperately to block out the crying behind me. I strain forward trying to not hear and soon I find my muscles aching from the tension. More than anything in the world I want to be the one to help him through his sorrow.

I walk over and pick up my cup of tea taking it with me to the window and again stare out, waiting, I guess for an indicator that he wants to talk. Then I hear him say, "Darling Taylor, don't let's talk about distressing things any more. Let's forget about it and talk of pleasant things." His choice of words is only slightly surprising to me. Why is that, I wonder.

In the light of the den I turn with tears clinging to my eyelid and I brighten at the change I see in Michael, no quivering and no tears now. I sense he has accepted this loss and has no concept of all that happened that day.

"Have some tea, Michael."

"Thank you, I will," he says. He looks bright and cheerful again in contrast with the sorrow and worry that appeared on his face earlier. I hear him clear his throat and then he smiles, a nervous timid smile that tugs at my heart.

It does seem strange to me, but only for a few minutes because without him saying it, I know that he has been reliving the episode and realizes it is not just happening now. I know this and it scares me to know this.

I sit beside him and we sip our tea silently. “Taylor, do you still want to paint me?”

“Yes, I do, but Michael" I say; "you can't feel up to posing for me now, do you? I mean-after this?"

I am staring at him, watching as he blows his nose. "I wanted to come," he said erratically. "I wanted to see you and I wanted to be here." He gives a little hiccup as he sucks air into his lungs, then after a shaky sigh, begins. "I might as well pose, I don't look my best, though."

I am glad to hear him say this and I think that if anything, he looks more handsome than before. And, I pause, trying not to say what comes immediately to my lips.

The tears have left no mark on his young face, but instead they leave their mark by making his eyes dark and dreamy. I want to paint him more than ever and so I decide I will.

I will sketch him for a sculptor and do my portrait of him from the sketch or maybe I will make the portrait and create the sculptor from the finish work. I am so scatterbrained around him and I wonder why that is. He is but a child. I am still somewhat undecided as I walk with Michael across the foyer to the studio. I place him in a chair that sits against the wall at the end of the room then go about moving a room divider behind the chair and to add color to the background, drape a pale blue silk cloth over the divider to provide just the right backdrop. The positioning is perfect, especially when the light from the window provides an almost ethereal glow around his head, an image I find most appropriate and am anxious to capture before it disappears. I set up my easel at the right angle; and feel his dark eyes on me, catching an expression which startles and puzzles me at first, and then makes me smile. I know that the real reason for his visit is not to tell me bad news, but to make sure I get started on the portrait. Not a word does he speak, not a muscle does he move. When I am satisfied that I have everything the way I want it, I set my canvas up and begin to work in earnest. Sometime during my staging I have made my decision.

The portrait I start that day needs no description, for most have seen it in the Metropolitan Museum, in New York. It is the portrait of a boy somewhere in his early teens, seated in front of a blue screen. The Museum calls it Blue Boy, but to me it has always been simply Michael.

It has been some time since something has inspired me so deeply that I want to paint. I work wrapped in silence, almost as though in a dream. And as I work, I am filled with a strange excitement. So, rapt am I in painting, that I fail to keep track of the time; I must have been painting for hours, when I suddenly see Michael sag forward in his chair, and start to slide to the floor. I drop my brush and run to him, with my heart in my mouth, grasping him under his shoulders and lifting him up in the seat. "Are you all right Michael? I'm so sorry!"

Michael opens his eyes, and smiles timidly at me. "I'm tired Taylor," was all he said.

He seems to me to be quite frail for a boy of his age, seeming to weight almost nothing as I help him over to the sofa and lay him down. I pour him a fresh cup of tea with lemon and honey. When it is ready, I make him drink it, and a little color comes back into his cheeks. "I'm better now," he says. "I'm not so cold."

I begin pouring myself a cup as well and turn quickly back around. "Are you cold, Michael?"

"Yes, but not as much as before." I have been thinking it is quite warm in the room. How can he be cold, I wonder. Maybe it's because Michael's suffering has wrapped him in a chill that no amount of heat can shake.

"I can sit there again, if you want me to," he adds.

But of course, I don't want him to. "No," I affirm, "it's

time for you to rest. You did a great job of posing for me and I have accomplished much more than I expected. I think that right now the best thing for you is to get some sleep and we can start up again in the morning. Besides we have plenty of time to complete it."

There is another little sigh from Michael that is almost like a whisper. "No," he says, "there isn't. But I'll do as you say; I'll rest, if you say so."

Shivering a little, he lays back down and I take the throw on the back of the sofa and wrap it around his body. I carefully lift his head and place one of the large pillows under it. Michael then closes his eyes, his hair seemingly darker stands out on the white pillow, his hand cold as death as he reaches up to grab mine.

I lean over looking down at him, the curve of the young brow, the long dark lashes which rest so gently on his cheek; and I feel my heart tighten with a sort of fear, and yet at the same time with pleasure. Who are you? I think; and what has brought you here to me? He is a child and a stranger so lost and lonely as though he has stepped out of some story in the past?

My hands must have shaken a little, for Michael opens his eyes and looks gravely up at me. "You're all I have now, Taylor, he says.

My startled expression of surprise, and dismay, has him releasing my hand, and he sits back up still huddled under the throw, his thin arms appear from under the cover and wrap around his knees. "Except for my uncle," he says, to reassure me. "Only I don't know him very well. He's going to take care of me from now on."

A little surprised by his announcement I am not sure what this means. "Well," I say awkwardly, "that's all right, then, isn't it?"

He looks at me with an overwhelming expression and it is his turn to ask for reassurance. "It's still all right if I come," he asks uncertainly, "I can come to see you? To pose,

I mean?"

When I do not respond, he adds, "You don't want me never to come again?"

I can't speak, but he must have seen in my face my answer for he smiles, and brushes the hair back from his face with the same gesture I saw him use that first evening I laid eyes on him. That was how many years ago? Or was it years. All I am sure of is that we met on the Boardwalk and that some time must have passed because he is much older than he was then

"I'll come back as soon as I can," he says responding to an unasked question.

"Michael," I begin softly.

"Yes, Taylor? "

I hesitate, wondering exactly what there is that I can say. Yet I continue, "Where does your uncle live?" I ask and already I am afraid to hear his answer. I tell myself that I need to know where he will be in case I need to find him again, but even I know that isn't the real reason. I want to hear what he will say and I can't feign shock at his reply.

Michael shakes his head. "What does it matter where I live?" he says. "You can't come to me. "I can only come to you."

He speaks sadly, with kindheartedness, but with infinite finality and I look deeply at him and he looks deeply back at me. Though we now stand together in the same room it appears we are looking at each other across a vast expanse that is barren and forbidding. It is a space between now and then, an expanse that no soul has ever traveled before. I can feel this and I know deep down it is real. I also know that there is no passing either to go or to return.

I am frightened and the whole concept chills me to the very soul. Michael makes a little, helpless gesture, as though to reach out to me. And then the moment is gone, and he withdraws once more into himself, a stranger, dreaming of something I cannot see.

After a while Michael gets up and without a word passing between us, we walk to the foyer. I help him put on his coat suppressing an urge to ask him to stay.

“Goodbye, Taylor," he says as we stand at the door. "I'll come back as soon as I can. I'll try to hurry back, I promise."

He looks up at me with dark eyes wide and earnest. "I didn't want you to know," he said, “But I think you do know, huh?”

Not sure how to respond I pause before saying, "I know you didn't want me to know Michael, but you had to know I'd figure it out sooner or later." I pause again. “I’m not exactly sure what is happening, but I know it is not natural.”

“Don’t be scared Taylor. Please, don’t be scared.” It is over in a few minutes. Michael turns only to look back once before going on his way and when he does he says, "Try to wait," he whispers, "please, try to wait for me."

Dr. Paulson's voice is finally audible to me as I work my way back to the present. It is indeed getting harder to do that and I wonder if the doctor knows.

"Taylor, how do you feel?"

"How do you think I feel. I am yearning for something that is clearly becoming impossible to grasp.”

Dr. Paulson looks at me with a blank expression on his face and I ask, “so, tell me what you think? What is the significance of Michael coming to tell me of his parent’s death.”

I am seated in front of Dr. Paulson's desk, showing him the sketches I have made on the second meeting with

Michael. Hoping this gives truth to all I am saying.

Dr. Paulson continues staring at the sketches. Finally, he speaks. "Taylor, I thought he would be much younger. From what you have told me, I thought he would be around five years of age."

I let out a sign of relief. I wasn't crazy... Dr. Paulson saw the age difference too. Michael was indeed much older than it was possible to age since the last time I saw him. I didn't reply, instead looked off in space, waiting ...

Dr. Paulson clears his throat, "Well, these are very good, very good indeed."

"No, not just good. They prove that I am not going crazy, this is really happening to me."

Dr. Paulson is quietly gazing at me then says, "Our time is up Taylor. We'll pick up here during our next session."

"But doctor…"

"Taylor, I understand, but you need to think about our session as much as I do."

Sadly, I give in, pacifying myself by knowing I will be back.

It is on a Sunday morning that I see Michael again. There had been a couple weeks of frigid weather, and the rink at Xerox square is good for skating so I take out my old pair of Bauer Ice Skates, and drive downtown. I am glad for the skating lessons I had taken as a child and enjoy being able to master feats on the frozen tundra. It is probably the reason that I purchased these skates that were NHL Approved. Don't get me wrong, I am not of ice hockey caliber, but I can hold my own.

The ice is crowded with skaters as I sit down on a

bench by the theater entrance to put on my skates, and strap my shoes to my belt. I step down on to the ice taking a wide glide, maneuvering myself along the edges of the oval rink. Once I am feeling in tune with my skates I do an axle and a sit spin, then return to just gliding on the ice feeling the sun on my face and watching the other skaters that pass by me. Couples with linked hands and red cheeks glide effortlessly as they smile, giggle or laugh at each other and schoolboys skate past, as if chasing a hockey puck, bent forward on racing skates as they cut through the ice. A young man, quite the executive type is doing fancy figures by himself; dressed in brown, with a red woolen scarf, he swings forward, turns, jumps, and circles backward, his skates together in a straight line, knees bent, exuding intent pride. I stop and watch him for a moment, and then glide out into the sun. All around me the skaters pass by, most moving effortlessly and the scene provides a sense of peace and tranquility, knowing I am not alone.

It is accentuated by the fact it is one of those days of stunning weather such as we get in New York in winter, with a blue sky, and fluffy clouds going slowly across the sun, then float away allowing the sunshine to return. Each time the sun reappears it sparkles like diamonds across the ice surface and in the distance, the city shines in the sunlight, making everything look clean and inviting.

I skate around the ice slowly then taking advantage of the space before me, I take long strides, breathing deeply and feeling young and strong, with blood rushing through my veins keeping my body warm while the cold air feels great on my face.

I don't recognize him at first as he seems to me to be taller than I remember him to be. When he turns around and sees me, I think, he seems a lot older, too. He has been doing a pretty bad figure eight in a dated outfit that makes him stand out from the other skaters. He is on the far corner of the rink that I had passed by several times, but until now hadn't seen him there.

I am not even sure that it is him, until that moment he looks up and sees me.

"Hello, Ms. Bouchard," he says.

I watch as he coasts over to me, and puts out his hands to stop himself. There is something very different about my little friend as he comes closer and it has nothing to do with the clothing. I can't believe it, but it is quite apparent as he moves even closer.

"I wasn't sure it was you. You look much older. It doesn't seem as though it has been that long since I last saw you."

Michael smiles and presses the toe of one skate down into the ice, to hold himself. "Oh well," he says; "maybe you didn't see me very good."

We stand there facing each other for some time. I don't know how long we are like that, smiling at each other until Michael puts his arm in mine. "Come along," he said. "Let's skate."

We start off together arm in arm; and once again the world around me grows hazy and unreal. Skaters swing by us, their steel blades flashing in the sun until suddenly it appears we are alone.

The forms moved around us for a moment and then are gone. I feel as though we have our own quiet space in the universe and it all serves to bring back to me a feeling I had had once before. It is a feeling of being in a dream and yet being fully awake. How strange, I think as I look at the slender figure at my side, the quiet and gentle motion around us growing more distant and I know there is no question about it, he is taller than I have remembered.

"It seems to me," I said, "that you've grown a lot since I last saw you."

"I know," he replied.

I could only look at him and wonder if his reply is normal for a boy or as odd as I felt it to be. Michael was staring at me, but I said nothing, only smiled uncertainly.

After a while, Michael adds seriously, "I'm hurrying."

He seems as light as a feather beside me, but I can feel his arm in mine as we skate. Aside from the terrible figure eights he attempted, Michael is skating smoothly beside me. We hold hands and do a small turn which he maneuvers appreciatively and I relax and enjoy the moment.

"How is your uncle? "

“He’s in California now."

I can’t detect any sadness in his voice at being left alone. Though he has grown, he is still a child with what seems to be no adult supervision. I would have thought being left alone would bother him but I could see nothing but joy in his face.

"I did some sketches of you," I tell him, "

"I know.”

“No, I mean I did some earlier.”

“You did?" he responds. "What are you going to do with them.”

I proceed to tell him I have a client who wished to have a sculpture made and when I showed him what I came up with, the sketches of him I had made on the boardwalk had fallen from my briefcase.

“He liked them very much and has asked me to go ahead with one of them. He is quite taken with you. He even thinks he knew you or someone like you."

"I'm glad for you," Michael said.

“Yes, thank you.” He wants me to think about trying to capture your face, but older. Not sure how that will work.”

I glance at Michael after saying that and I can swear that a light seemed to illuminate his features and I see an expression that I can only translate as him knowing something that I do not.

I feel him grip my arm tighter as he gives me a wide grin, then he makes a wild swing to the right, almost taking us both down to the ice, before he frees me and takes off shakily on his own. "Hooray," he cries, "I'm going to have a sculpture of me!

I couldn't help laughing at his antics on the icy surface of the rink and then I squeal in surprise as he skates toward me, his progress none to steady as I envision the impact, but he swings to the left grabs my arm and slows down. He is at my side and says, "Won't Thornton be jealous."

"Thornton? " I ask, "who is Thornton?"

"Thornton is my best friend," he explains. "His father is a painter and Thornton says he is quite famous. Anyway, he was bragging that his father made a portrait of him. Now, he will be jealous when I tell him that you are going to do a sculpture of me." Michael is so excited now as he continues. "I am going to go up and tell him as soon as I see him and make him eat his words."

"What words," I ask.

"He said that his father hadn't heard of you before and so you must not be a real artist. He made me so mad that I slapped him, and we quarreled. "

"That isn't a nice thing to do, Michael. You should apologize to him."

"I did, really I did, and I meant it too," he said despondently.

"Well," I said, changing the subject. "I thought it was Christopher who was your best friend."

Michael looks away suddenly and I feel his hand

tremble on my arm. "Christopher died," he said in a whisper. "He had pneumonia. Now my best friend is Thornton. I thought you'd know."

That was strange. Why would Michael think I knew? "How would I know?" I ask.

He stumbled suddenly. "My skate came untied" he said. "I've got to stop."

I hold his arm firmly and help him to the side of the rink where the benches are and wait until he is seated. I then kneel to tie his skate lace. Kneeling there in front of him I look up into his flushed face. It is the face of a child, framed in his dark hair. He is calm as he looks far away, lost somewhere in time, not here and now. I want to ask more about Christopher, but I am afraid of what Michael might say. I still hadn't asked about his parents which I intended to do, but not just yet.

Michael smiles at me and silently I think he is a little boy with a lot of secrets and at some point I am going to hear them all, and then ... Just thinking about that rattles, me.

"There," I said, "all fixed."

I help him up from the bench and we glide over to the refreshment stand window that offers a variety of snacks for the skaters and onlookers. I turn and ask Michael if he would care to go in and rest for a while, and if he would like a cup of hot chocolate.

"Oh yes," he cried. "I love hot chocolate."

"Well then, we shall have some."

Inside, Michael takes a seat and I go to the counter and order our hot chocolate. Later we sit at a table, warmed by the sun shining through the window and the hot drink.

“How is school?”

"It's all right," he says, but without much enthusiasm. "I'm taking French."

"French?" I ask; startled, wondering about this since I didn't think they would be teaching French in his grade. Why the last time he had been just beginning to learn his alphabet. He must be mistaken.

"Yes," he said. "I can say colors, and I can count to ten in French.

Un, deux, trois, quatre ...

"That's pretty good," I reply questioningly,

"I can say the war, in French. C'est la guerre."

I wasn't sure of the war he was talking about so I ask, ""The war?" "What war?"

Michael only shook his head. "I don't know," he said. "It's just the war."

I could see his mind working and then his eyes grew wide, and he looks at me in fright. "They won't hurt children like me," he asks. "will they?"

"No," I said. "No."

He takes a deep breath. "That's good," he said. "I don't like being hurt."

That ended the conversation and Michael picked up his hot chocolate and his face disappeared. When he looked up I could see the same happy face of before, no longer worried about any silly war.

"This is lots of fun", Michael said.

"I totally agree with you. This is lots of fun."

Our chocolate was gone and we clump our way to the door. "Come along," I said; "we've time for one more skate around the rink."

Michael took my arm, going down the steps to the ice. Though I should have been used to his odd sayings, I was taken aback when he said, "I hate it to stop, because when will we ever have it again?"

As usual, I was unable to think of what I should say in reply, so I remain silent as we set off together hand in hand, and made a final spin around the rink. It is getting late and I know it is time for me to be thinking about getting back home, so I regretfully guide us toward the edge of the rink where I had first seen Michael. I stand in front of him and smile, watching as he smiles back. It isn't easy to say goodbye to him. There is something still pressing on my mind and I must ask this one question before we part.

"Michael, tell me-when did Christopher die?"

He looks away as though he wants to hide his pain.

"Two years ago," he said.

"Well, Taylor, I would like to hear more, but our time is up and there is another client waiting. I must say that your experience has indeed perked my interest, but the more you tell me, the more I am convinced that there is more to this than meets the eye. I must admit I am puzzled but we are getting somewhere. It is indeed intriguing."

"Yes?", I said with little surprise. "I thought you might feel that way. I reluctantly rose and allow myself to be guided to the door wishing that I could stay and tell him more. There was so much still unspoken. I had only cracked the surface.

I shook Dr. Paulson's hand then turned to leave. As I cross the lobby I couldn't help wondering what he wasn't saying. Here was a tall, reasonably handsome grey-haired man who had a medical degree. Did he think that I was going insane or was I still a rational woman in his eyes? I just couldn't tell and it was probably since even I was having problems believing what I had experienced. How did a child grow up so fast? Even as I walked out of his office I knew that when I returned to tell him of the changes that came next, he would not easily accept it. I was aware of how crazy it would sound and I wondered why it hadn't unraveled me yet.

It wasn't so much that I wanted an explanation, I just needed someone bias to hear me out. As I began my trip homeward I wondered about Michael. Like a mischievous child, his memory taunts me from day to day. He is the one captured in the deepness of the past that is now dappling into the future and I am sure he knows that he didn't quite fit in to the "now". Michael is not merely a neutral observer, not merely a child this time as he must have been before. He is the central point of my life now and the truth be known, I think that we are both unsure of where this journey will take us.

Chapter 13

I was showing Mr. Masterson some sketches I had made of Michael in his skating costume, pictures of the child in motion, doing an inner edge, or poised on his toes as though to run. Mrs. Masterson is there, too, looking over his shoulder. It is my first meeting with her and I find I like her soft voice, her intense, dark brown eyes fitting perfectly in her heart shaped face. There is a pleasant expression on her face as she considers each sketch as though seeking something beyond the paper itself.

I am to learn later that when it came to sculpture and sculptors, there is no getting around Mrs. Masterson. Most of her life she has spent admiring art and artist. She can tell you immediately who had created a portrait or a sculpture without glancing at the signature and she can identify them beyond just those of the famous. It is like a hobby of hers, this in-depth knowledge and it goes even further in that she can feel the mood of the artist when they were creating the piece. She judges a man or woman by their work, and nothing else; she either wants it, or she doesn't want it and she will not sway in her decision.

Mr. Masterson holds the sketches out at arm's length, with his head tilted back, looking at them down his nose.

"This boy looks older to me than the first one," he says. "I see the same face though and I like it, on the whole. He was, perhaps, a little young, before. He is silent as he continues to stare. " Yes," he adds; " they aren't bad," then turning to face his wife says, "are they, Mrs. Masterson? "

"Is that all you can say?" remarks Mrs. Masterson. "That they aren't bad?"

Mr. Masterson tilts his head a little to one side thinking that his wife wants him to express the feeling of the painting. "The thing I like about them, is the way you've managed, to catch that look of not belonging…how was it you said; not altogether fitting into the present. For some unknown reason man is considered to always be more present-minded so that is how he is depicted in most paintings."

"You can have the present," said Mrs. Masterson. "And you know what you can do with it, she said with joviality in her voice." Then turning towards me she adds, "What my husband is trying to say, is that you have captured the quality of something eternal. And, these sketches are wonderful."

Mrs. Masterson pauses and places a finger on her chin, as she studies the sketch her husband holds. "You can see it in all the great sculpturing of Rodan. The quality of agelessness takes the sculptors vision and turns it into something that is of the past and considered dead yet, though the rendition is motionless it has one wondering if it is alive, if it does still exist."

"Thank you. You are very insightful. That is exactly what I tried to capture." I pause. "I am glad you are pleased with the sketches and I will do my best to meet your expectations. "

After a while, Mrs. Masterson excuses herself and shortly after her departure, a decanter of brandy is brought into the study. Mr. Masterson offers me a seat.

"You made a hit with my wife and I assure you that she doesn't give idle praise to anyone."

"Your wife knows her art."

Mr. Masterson didn't hide his delight in my observation of his spouse.

"Would you like a brandy Ms. Bouchard?"

"Mr. Masterson, please call me Taylor, and yes, thank you."

"Taylor, it is. And, please call me Arnie," he says pouring us each a glass.

We sit silently for a moment before Arnie again speaks. "Taylor, I want to share something with you, if you don't mind."

"I am interested in anything you have to say, Arnie, please go on."

“Your work reminds me of August Rodan, too. I’m sure you know his work?"

"Yes, The Thinker, The Kiss, The Prodigal Son. "

"So, what do you think of his work?"

"I think his work is what inspired me? That is probably why you can see similarities in the style. I think every artist relates to one or more of the artist they study and I know that I related to Rodan. It stands to reason I would then use some of his style of creation in my paintings."

I can tell by the way Mr. Masterson rubs his chin that he wants to say more so I remain silent.

"Like my wife, I consider Rodan to be one of the greatest and most prolific sculptors of the 19th century. He is the one artist that I know as much about as my wife, Vivian does. You know, he is often credited with bringing new life and direction to a dying art. But he had to work his way up. He was the son of a minor employee of the Parisian police department and enrolled at the age of 14 in a school that trained craftsmen and decorative artists. He started out earning his living as a studio helper on ornamental detail for other sculptors while working at home on his own. It wasn’t until he was thirty-five that he completed his first masterpiece and that was because of an exhilarating trip to Italy providing him with firsthand knowledge of the sculptures of Michelangelo, His first masterpiece was ... "

"Yes, I know, it was *The Vanquished,* a young male nude later called *The Age* of *Bronze."*

"That's correct, Taylor. Like your sketches that manage to capture the present and mingle it with the past. I think Rodan would be proud of what you have accomplished."

I am listening but know a lot of what Arnie is saying about Rodan, but I didn't want to stop him as he seemed to enjoy sharing it all with me.

As I continue to listen I sense something drawing me in, but it has nothing to do with the artist. At first, I can't understand why I am feeling this way, then it hits me.

"Arnie, do you know when Rodan died?"

"Yes, I believe it was in 1917."

I sit there quietly estimating. "Yes, that would make him somewhere in his late seventies when he died."

"If I remember correctly, Rodan was in bad health and suffered a mental deficiency around the outbreak of World War I in 1914." He paused to concentrate and then adds, "Yes, I believe that is correct. His healthy and mental stability gave way rapidly before his death in 1917."

The war. I was now thinking about the war. I had to leave. Trying to compose myself I planned for my departure.

"Well, Arnie, this has been interesting and I have taken up enough of your time. Besides, I have work to do, so if you will excuse me I'll be on my way."

"I have enjoyed our talk Taylor, almost as much as I enjoy your work."

"Thank you." I am about to ask him to please say my good byes to Mrs. Masterson, when I realize she has joined us.

Mr. Masterson and his wife walk me to the door and before departing I shake hands with each of them.

"Goodbye," I say; and to Mrs. Masterson add, "I'm very glad to have met you."

She looks at me for a moment with those deep brown eyes and, all at once, to my surprise, she says. "Please, can I see the sketches one more time before you go?"

“Sure.” I move to the table in the foyer and open the portfolio, handing the sketches to Mrs. Masterson. She seems to not just take the sketches from my hand, but more as though she possesses them, making them her own. I like the way she seems totally absorbed and Arnie walks over behind her to look again.

"I' suppose it could be the clothes," Arnie says, "that make him look a little older in these sketches than the ones earlier."

I didn't think so, but I didn't know how to say what I thought; I stood there feeling uneasy, aware of my heart beating a little fast, and wondering what Mrs. Masterson would say. She put the sketches down at last, and gave me a wink and a smile. "I have to tell you Ms. Bouchard, I usually like sculptors done by men, but you have surpassed anything that a male sculptor has shown us in the past.

"That is a nice compliment and I appreciate it. It is hard for women to break into any field, but we seem to be managing to do it."

"Ms. Bouchard," she adds; "you're nice and you know the art business. I know you can sculpt; and because we aren't big collectors, we don’t buy things we like just for the fun of sitting around and looking at them the rest of our lives. If we buy you can be sure we will appreciate the statues for a very long time and consider them to be priceless works of art."

"Yes," said Mr. Masterson agreeably; "that's exactly what I would say."

I take a deep breath, my throat choking up on me from the extent of her praise. Finally, I can squeeze out a thank you.

I again state that I must go. And with a last goodbye, I leave.

I don't remember my drive home as my mind was far away thinking about the light Mr. Masterson shed. I felt as though he was feeding me details, knowing what I needed, but that would be ridiculous because he didn't know about Michael. My head spins with so many questions that only Michael can answer.

I can't believe that Mr. Masterson instantly noticed the age difference. How I wanted to tell him my story, but that would be crazy. It was enough that I was dealing with this, this child who is rapidly aging before my very eyes. I don't want to deal with convincing a client I'm not insane. I chuckle, though it isn't funny.

I need to see Michael. There are so many answers I need. Recently even the song I heard him singing in the gazebo plagues me because I don't know its name and it might also be a clue.

By the time, I pull into my driveway, I find myself rushing to the door. I am barely inside before I drop my briefcase and portfolio in the foyer and dig through my purse for my cell phone. Urgently I press the numbers and the call is answered immediately. In a few minutes, I am heading out the door and on my way to Captain's Cove.

Chapter 14

"Calm down Taylor and let me see if I have this right," says Samuel, "What you want is for me to find a little boy whose name is Michael, who may or may not be a little boy anymore. You don't know where he lives, nor anything about him." He pauses and adds, "So, you've got a good start."

I can hear the sarcasm in his voice even though we both know he will try to do as I ask. "Come on Taylor, you must tell me more."

Samuel and I have been friends for a long time and during those years he has dappled in many careers. It is this background that will help him to help me. He knows many people in many walks of life and that should help immensely in tracking down Michael.

I know how powerful his memory and connections are. Back when I was starting out I was selling my creations at the local fairs and it was at the Corn Hill Festival that Samuel and I chanced to meet. Over the years he introduced me to many influential people who remain clients. That was almost fifteen years ago and we have been friends since that time.

"His parents are concert pianists," I add humbly. At the Eastman Theater, I think."

"That makes it a little easier. Are they on the circuit?"

I hold back a laugh that tries to escape thinking, yes, but not what you are thinking. So instead I tell him that their last name is Roman.

"Roman," he repeats; "Roman." I could see the

wheels turning in his head. “Wait a moment there used to be a couple by the name of Roman." he declares. "Down at the old Halstein Theater."

"That's right. That's where they were, I mean, that’s where they did play."

Samuel looks at me strangely. "Well, then, Taylor, they'd be dead or if by a miracle, they are alive they would be the oldest ever in the old folks' home. No, that can't be the same ones you are looking for now. It must be some other people."

I know it is them and I know it is crazy, but I need to take the chance of Samuel thinking I have gone mad.

"Samuel, how well did you know them?"

"It wasn't first hand, Taylor. I am not that old. No, I heard about them from others who knew someone that knew them."

"Please tell me what you’ve heard. It may help to ring a bell." I ignore the look on Samuel’s face. I can’t blame him for thinking I’m out of my mind because I’m beginning to doubt my sanity too.

Samuel takes out his cell and in a few minutes, he finds what he is looking for. "Sure. Now let’s see. Their names were Clara and Robert Roman and I would have to say they played a large if not vital role in 19th-century music. They were both virtuoso pianists, Robert as a major composer and critic and champion of Brahms, Chopin and others. Clara was a celebrated pianist and the wife of Robert Roman. Friedrich Tormaine was her father and he trained Clara and taught Roman. Clara made her debut around 1828 and went on several tours in the following years. Her marriage to Roman was bitterly opposed by her father, but no one could have stopped her. During the marriage, she basically abandoned touring, except for the last two years of their life. As I recall they had one or two children, but I wouldn’t know names or sex. It wasn't until long into their marriage that Clara would perform again."

"Did you say the 19th century?"

"Yes, I did. Clara and Robert Roman lived and died in the 19th century." Samuel pauses as he does another search. "It was November 15, 1864 when they died, to be exact. Any children they had would be; ah, let me see, over a hundred for sure. No, this can't be the same family, but that isn't to say that some later generation of offspring became pianist, and they carried the same name of their past relatives. And, if by fate an offspring married a pianist, then the Romans you speak of may be two to four generation off springs of the famous pair."

He was making fun and I knew it, but I ignored that because I had a question to ask. "Samuel, they died on the same day?"

"Oh, yes, I know it sounds strange, but it isn't," he says as he searches further. "They only had one child," he adds off handedly as he reads through information on the screen.

Samuel pauses. Yes, this is it. Looking over Samuel's shoulder I read the article for myself.

The Halstein Theater fire happened on November 15, 1864, in Rochester, New York. It was the deadliest theater fire and the deadliest single-building fire in United States history. At least 602 people died because of the fire, but not all the deaths were reported, as some of the bodies were removed from the scene. The theater opened officially on November 1, 1864 after numerous delays and was lauded by drama critics as the most beautiful.

The Halstein had a capacity of 1,602 with three audience levels. The main floor, known as the orchestra or parquet, had approximately 700 seats on the same level as the foyer and Grand Stair Hall. The second level, the dress circle or [first] balcony, had more than 400 seats. The third level, the gallery, had about 500 seats. There were four boxes on the first level and two above.

The theater had only one entrance. A broad stairway which led from the foyer to the balcony level was also used to reach the stairs to the gallery level. Theater designers claimed this allowed patrons to "see and be seen" regardless of the price of their seats. However, the common stairway ignored Rochester fire ordinances that required separate stairways and exits for each balcony. The design proved disastrous: people exiting the gallery encountered a crowd leaving the balcony level, and people descending from the upper levels met the orchestra level patrons in the foyer.

Despite being billed as "Absolutely Fireproof" in advertisements and playbills, numerous deficiencies in fire readiness were apparent:

On November 15, 1864, a Tuesday, the Halstein presented a piano concert, with Robert and Clara Roman performing Ludwig van Beethoven's popular Symphony No 1 in C and Symphony No 9 in D minor. The pianists drew a sellout audience. Tickets were sold for every seat in the house, plus hundreds more for the "standing room" areas at the back of the theater. The standing room areas were so crowded that some patrons instead sat in the aisles, blocking the exits.

At about 8:15 sparks from an arc light ignited a muslin curtain, probably as a result of an electrical short circuit. A stagehand tried to douse the fire with the Kilfyre canisters provided, but it quickly spread to the fly gallery high above the stage. The stage manager tried to lower the asbestos fire curtain, but it snagged. A chemist who later tested part of the curtain stated that it was mainly wood pulp mixed with asbestos, and would have been "of no value in a fire".

Robert Roman, who was preparing to go on stage at the time, ran out and attempted to calm the crowd, first making sure that his young son was in the care of a stagehand. By this time, many of the patrons on all levels were quickly attempting to flee the theater. Some had found the fire exits hidden behind draperies on the north side of the building, but found that they could not open the unfamiliar bascule locks. A third door was opened either by brute force or by a blast of air, but most of the other doors could not be opened. Some patrons panicked, crushing or trampling others in a desperate attempt to escape from the fire. Many were killed while trapped in dead ends or while trying to open what looked like doors with windows in them but were only windows.

Someone opened the massive double freight doors in the north wall, normally used for scenery, allowing "a cyclonic blast" of cold air to rush into the building and create an enormous fireball. As the vents above the stage were nailed or wired shut, the fireball instead traveled outwards, ducking under the stuck asbestos curtain and streaking toward the vents behind the dress circle and gallery 50 feet away. The hot gases and flames passed over the heads of those in the orchestra seats and incinerated everything flammable in the gallery and dress circle levels, including patrons still trapped in those areas.

Those in the orchestra section exited into the foyer and out of the front door, but those in the dress circle and gallery who escaped the fireball could not reach the foyer because the iron grates that barred the stairways were still in place. The largest death toll was at the base of these stairways, where hundreds of people were trampled, crushed, or asphyxiated.

"Oh, my God. What happened to the child."

Samuel looks further down in the article and says, there is nothing here. Now, caught up in the drama of the moment, Samuel continues going through records online and says, "His name was Michael and he was back stage at the time of the fire."

"And?"

“And, nothing. That is all I can find. He mumbles something?”

“This has to be him, Samuel. How else can I explain this?"

"Come on Taylor. I can't believe it. It is impossible."

"Well, don't you think I know that. It’s crazy but until I can find something to prove it is not so, I have to believe that this is Michael.

“Taylor, please. You are scaring me.”

To take his mind off this train of thought, I ask, “what else can you tell me about Clara Roman?"

"Not much right now. Oh, yes, she also edited her husband's compositions."

"Okay, what more can you find out about Robert Roman."

Samuel knows all the right words and has log ins to all the news archives to get to the information he wants.

"He was a German romantic composer and pianist. He studied the piano at an early age and wrote his first compositions when still a young boy. It was a known fact that second to his love of music was his enthusiasm for literature. It served him well in his later career, for he became one of the outstanding composer-critics of his day and remained highly sensitive to the relationship between words and music throughout his life. Even though taught by Friedrich Tormaine, in composition, Roman was virtually self-taught, his formal instruction in theoretical subjects being limited to a few months of harmony lessons and a few weeks studying orchestration."

"Is that all?"

"Yes, I'm sorry Taylor, that is all I can find right now. Cara and Robert Roman were gifted individuals and their gift was so extensive I wouldn’t doubt it still lives on in their offspring. Now, Taylor can I ask you something?"

"Yes, I think you have earned that right. What is it?"

"Do you hear what you are saying? You are sure you saw this boy?"

"Yes," I said. "I made some sketches of him."

He shakes his head uncertainly. "That doesn't signify a certainty," he remarks. "I am thinking maybe you made him up in your mind from something you read or saw."

"No, I didn't make him up."

"Okay, don't get excited. I'll ask around if you want," he said, "but listen, Taylor," his voice sank to a low and urgent level. "'don't go getting into any trouble with the police. If you see the boy again, be careful. These days you never know. He could be living on the street for all you know."

"I don't want any trouble and I hear you loud and clear, but I don't think this child would be up to something like that. I can't turn my back on him because I want to sculpt him."

And I thought that is all there is to it. I would have sworn that is all I wanted.

I see the look on Samuel's face. "Don't worry Samuel. He's a little boy and I know how to handle myself."

As I drive away I know I can trust Samuel and that he cares about me enough to believe that there is something here and he will try and find out what it is.

The next day in my studio I try to work. I am doing a sculpture of the lake with the skaters on it, from memory and from some sketches, but it is hard to concentrate. My heart isn't in it. My mind flies off in a dozen directions at once. I wonder whether I should work on the sculpture for Mr. Masterson's, and whether Samuel will be able to find out anything more about the Romans. I look around my studio and see the starting of a sculpture of a ballerina, yet to be finished. So many projects left in limbo since Michael appeared.

I need to get to work and I do, for a short time but a sense of restlessness causing me to finally give up. I get myself a cup of tea and return to the studio only to stand and stare until it grows dark and I gladly go up to bed.

The next morning, I waste no time getting myself in order and into the studio and I do well for a period until I receive a call from Samuel. That interruption has me keeping an eye on the time and as soon as it is suitable for lunch, I leave for the Captain's Cove.

Samuel isn't at the restaurant when I get there so I order and eat alone. Still no Samuel, I pull out my pad and sketch, looking around often until finally I see Samuel over at the bar. I watch as he comes over and sits at my table.

"No luck, Taylor," he says. "I'm sorry."

"Didn't you find out anything at all?" I ask.

Samuel shakes his head and when the waitress delivers his beer he takes a long drink, and, leaning back, gazes solemnly around the room then at my sketch. He reaches across the table and lifts the pad for a closer look. "This is nice," he says.

I had sketched the carousel on the beach full of laughing children with the boardwalk behind them and the lake on the horizon. The children were playing and smiling with their heads going every which way. They were innocent figures, and I knew that Samuel really liked it.

"Yes, sir," he declared; "when I see things like this, I think I've been wasting my time not staying in one place longer. I see things in my trips, but you know, I glimpse them and that is not enough to get the real feel of what goes on."

A couple walks by our table on their way out and looking at the sketch, smile. "It's very nice."

I thank them and then turn back to Samuel. "Maybe I'll sketch you standing on the beach."

"All right," says Samuel; calling my bluff. "That'll be nice for me. Only make it look good, and don't drown me."

We part ways. The snow is falling as I head toward home, small flakes coming down slowly, through the gray sky, but there is a threat of a real nor easterner announced by the weatherman. Right now, what I want is a little fire and tomorrow's sun, rising and warming me. In my head Samuel's words keep repeating, "Don't drown me. Don't drown me," I say out loud, wondering why I keep thinking about that and wonder if it means something. Finally, I shake it off as just recalling the last thing he said.

I am not thinking clearly and who would blame me. I find myself wondering, what if tomorrow vanished in the storm? What if time stood still? I try to laugh at myself but it's not funny. I ask myself would we find yesterday again ahead of us, where we had thought tomorrow's sun would rise?

I begin to seriously doubt my sanity. Luckily, I pull into my driveway and I let myself into the house, brushing the snow from my coat on the doorstep before entering. As I stand in the foyer ignoring the blast of cold air coming from outdoors, I don't rush to close it. Instead I look at Mildred standing in front of me and I can see the worry in her eyes.

"Hi Mildred."

"Hi miss. I was worried. It is starting to really come down."

"I know."

Mildred asks if she can get me anything and I tell her I just want to get some work done. I watch as she heads toward the kitchen. I turn and start to close the door and then I see him. There on the sidewalk, heading in my direction is a man, his head down against the wind so that I can't see his face. When he steps through the doorway I move over and let him in.

What am I doing, I ask myself? I move behind him and close the door.

I stand in the foyer with him as he takes off his hat and coat and hangs them in the closet. Then together we walk to the studio.

In the studio, I watch as he walks over to sit in the leather chair near the easel, his hands grasping the arms of the chair and his feet just touching the floor. I move slowly behind him and lean against the side of the doorway, looking at him, feeling weak with happiness.

"I thought maybe you wanted me to come, Taylor," he said.

Chapter 15

He sat quietly in the big chair while I put away my brushes and stood wondering what I should do next. His gaze, moved about, lingering on everything; the brocade furniture, the brightly painted walls, the sculptures and figurines in all states of completion, and the other odds and ends scattered about for my artistic pleasure. He looked about as if seeing it all for the first time, but that was not so. Maybe he now saw it through different eyes and I wondered what was his opinion.

I find myself gazing at areas of the room and realize that it feels as though I am seeing it for the first too. I allow my gaze to fall on Michael, wondering what spell he has put on me and I see his eyes widen and his chest raise as he takes a deep breath.

It must have been my imagination for sure because this is my studio and it is exactly as it should be.

"I've never been in a studio before. It's quite interesting." I am about to correct him when Mildred taps lightly on the door. Before I have a chance to answer she pushes the door open and enters. “Can I get you anything?”

“No, I’m fine Mildred.”

Mildred nods and leaves the room, closing the door behind her.

Michael gets up from the chair and begins walking around the studio and stopping in front of one sculpture, he turns and said, "do you mind"?

"No, touch it, it's okay. Half of the beauty is in the touch. It you want to get the full appreciation of them, you must touch."

I stood observing as Michael moves about running his hands along the sides of the figurines, picking them up, studying them at close range before setting them gently back in place. It fascinates me ... no, it pleases me 'to see him getting so much joy out of my creations.

Michael pauses at one of the easels in the room where rests several sketches. He turns to me and I nod approval, then watch as he carefully picks them up. His dark eyes dance as he views each one separately, gazing around the room before putting it aside to look at the next. “They're great," he says. They are exact matches and they are wonderful.”

He continues his survey. "I don’t know who they are, but they look like people I would like to meet and things I would like to see." He leans down and comes up with another sketch, “And this…Taylor I would like to see this.”

I glance over his shoulder to see the one he is holding and my gaze follows his to the figurine. I had done this bronze of the skyscrapers at Radio City. It wasn’t that he didn’t see the figurine in the room, it was that he wanted to see the real thing. "Yes," I said; "well ... they're not really that far away so you may get to see them.”

Michael continues to look at the sketch in his hand for some time. Finally, he raises his head and his eyes stare in front of him. I have been so engrossed in watching him I am surprise when I look out the window to see it is growing dark. The snow is falling heavily now and when I look back inside the room, I see shadows in the corners. I walk across the room and press the light switch into the "on" position and the room sprang into a glow of artificial creation touching every corner of the four walls and holding the present in a cube of unmoving light.

Michael seems to be gazing through the shadows into some other place, far off and strange. I see his lips part, and hear a long sigh escape him while outside, the snow, catches a sudden rift of wind, and it makes a soft, spitting sound as it hits the front the window. I jump before I realize what caused the sound. Knowing the source, I calm myself. I stand there listening and hear outside a car blow its horn. Until this point, Michael hasn’t stirred. It is as though he isn't really here. I move over towards him and he reaches his hand out so that our hands can touch.

For a moment, I think that he will leave but that touch seems to bring him back and we begin talking happily about a thousand different things. I must tell him all about Mrs. Masterson, who has such a warm heart and likes my pieces very much. I tell him about the encounter with the Sullivans and we laugh about the upset of Mr. Monroe who wasn't too fond of the figurine his wife had chosen for him. It's something I have need to say, but have no one to tell it too. It feels good and more so because it is Michael.

Once getting started I can't seem to stop and I talk about everything and tell him how I had driven downtown and walked around the shops on East Avenue.

Michael, with a puzzled look on his face says, "What do you mean, you drove?"

"I drove my car Michael."

"Your car?"

Then it dawns. He doesn't have any idea what a car is. Cars came around the late 1800s, 1885 to be precise. But before that they went by boat, carriages, or train. But mostly horse-drawn carriages.

I've been in a hansom, once, with mother in the Park; the driver sat up on top, and had a high hat."

I couldn't believe it and yet I knew it to be true. My head is spinning with the reality and yet Michael seems unperturbed.

That seems to be the end of that conversation as Michael moves to the next. He tells me that his friend Thornton is going away to boarding school. "I think perhaps I'll go with him," he said. "It's a church school, really, called St. Mary's, but it isn't Catholic. It's on a hill, and you see the lake; and Thornton says that he is looking forward to going. I don't want to go very much, but my aunt says I must, and anyway, Thornton's going."

“Are you having problems at home, Michael?”

“Oh, no, my Aunt and Uncle are great. They say that going to a boarding school is a practical alternative for wealthy people who find transportation difficult for their children. So being in a boarding school is easier. Then like an afterthought he adds, “I'll miss you, Taylor."

"I'll miss you, too, Michael," I said. “Michael, what is Thornton's last name?"

"His name is Thornton Bandero."

"And, your friend Christopher?"

"Christopher died?"

"I know, Michael, I was just wondering what his last name was."

"Oh, his name was Christopher Rodan."

I walked over to my desk and quickly jotted down the names so that I wouldn’t forget.

In such a short time, I have learned much and had my memory jogged on points I knew, but hadn’t thought about. This is Michael. This is the Michael whose parents died in 1864. I know it for a fact.

"Will you pose for me?", I ask.

"I was hoping you’d ask that," he answered. "Yes, I will."

"Will you come tomorrow, then?"

Michael turns away, but before he does I see a puzzled expression on his face. "I don’t know," he says. "I don't know if I can."

"The day after?"

He shakes his head. "I'll come as soon as I can," he answers; and that was all he would say.

We talk some more about my work which seems the safest subject between us and I try to answer all his questions about the commissions I receive, how many jobs I have done ... everything. His face lights up when he hears some of the commissions that people pay for my creations.

"You are rich?" he said. "When you do me, you will be even richer."

I laugh at that. It is said with such innocence because from what he has told me, I am sure his family was well off too. That and still sensing the child in him gave me joy.

"You must not forget me."

"Forget you?" I cried incredulously.

"Oh well," he said; " I guess you won't," he added contentedly. "Because maybe I'll be rich and famous too."

“I don’t think I care very much about being rich, Michael. I just want to sculpt and create it for the pleasure of others.”

He has been watching my face, and now surprises me asking, "You're not sad any more, are you, Taylor? I mean you were so sad the first time I saw you."

"No," I said, "I'm fine and I wasn’t said that day. I was scared that night I met you. I felt as though I were lost. ... "

Michael cowers down in his chair, and puts his hands up as though I am about to strike him. Suddenly he is that same little boy I saw that night in the gazebo. "No," he cried out, "Oh no! Don't ever say that, not ever again. And besides, you weren't lost, you were here, and here isn't lost. It can't be; it mustn't be."

I am in shock as I watch him quivering in the chair until turning to me almost piteously, "We can't both of us be lost."

I swear, we are no longer in my studio or at my home and as I look about there is nothing I recognize as being of my time. It lasts only a moment, and then it passes and we are back again, in my studio, with the lights on, and the grey snow outside, and my sculptures filling the room about me. It is the world I know, the world I see every day real and around me.

"No," I said, "I'm not lost. Why should I be? What a foolish way to talk."

Young Michael smiles up at me in a forlorn sort of way. "Yes," he says; "it's foolish. Don't let's talk like that anymore."

"Because," I said, "it scares a little boy like you?"

"Yes," he agrees gravely; "little boys like me."

"I have something for you," I said. 'Wait for me; I'll be right back."

“What is it?”

“You’ll see.”

I left the studio and went into the hall; to get one of the sketches of him that I had left in my portfolio. I could hear the snow hitting the skylight as I hurried back. “Michael,” I said.

The room is empty. I look in the sitting room, hurry into the kitchen and then back again into the foyer, but he is nowhere. I hadn’t heard him leave. I hadn’t heard the door open or close, but Michael is gone.

It isn't until later that I remember I hadn't even asked him where he lived.

It is a few days later that I could reach Samuel and give him the names of Michael's two friends and as expected he asked, “Taylor, did you find out where Michael lived?

I knew that question was coming and I gave a little sigh before saying, "No, I forgot. I got all caught up with his interest in my sketches and statues and just forgot."

"Well, don't worry about it. I will see what I can find out about the two boys and maybe someone will be able to tell us just where Michael and his folks are staying."

Chapter 16

"Taylor. Taylor."

I can hear the voice calling me but can't respond. I try, but somehow, I can't work my mouth.

"Taylor, wake up."

Oh, my, did I fall asleep I think as I force my eyes open and stare into the face of Dr. Paulson. I see his gray hair, his calm brown eyes as he leans in toward me.

"Taylor, can you hear me?"

I force myself to sit up and slowly I am awake.

"I don't understand, Dr. Paulson. Why do I fall asleep, if that is what I do, and if so, have I been talking at all?"

"Yes, you are talking and telling me what is happening to you."

"Good, that's good, but why do I feel this way."

"People react differently to psychotherapy. My aim is to improve your well-being and mental health. I can't explain this troublesome behavior in any way but to say that what you are sharing is so emotional and shocking to you it draws all your energy."

"So, it's normal?"

"Let's say, it's normal for you."

"Any clue of what is happening to me, doctor? I tell you that when I see Michael there are times when I feel I am no longer in the present, but then, it passes so quickly I question myself as to whether it happened or not."

Dr. Paulson is quiet before responding and I assume he is trying to formulate a 'sensible reply' to my question. "I would like to tell you I know exactly what you are feeling, but I can't. Not yet. It's still too early to say."

I know it is time to leave and get up to stand next to Dr. Paulson, who walks with me to the door.

"Taylor, progress will come once you have told me all of your story. We will explore your experience together and come up with a logical conclusion as to what is happening to you."

Dr. Paulson walks me to the door and we say our goodbyes.

Out on the street, feeling the warmth of the winter sun, it is easy to place the whole matter in the back of my mind. When I arrive home, Mildred sits me down to a full meal and keeps me company, listening to me talk about my work. As we chat, I sense something strange in the way she responds to me. I can't explain the feeling, but I think it is real.

The evening is growing longer and I want to ask her if she remembers Michael, but I am suddenly afraid to bring up his name so instead I ask about her niece's birthday party and how her children are doing.

I watch as Mildred cleans the kitchen and then walk with her to the front door, watching as she puts on her coat and boots, then we say our goodbyes. Shortly after she leaves, I am on my way to the studio where I manage to do some work and it makes me feel good inside. As much as I want to, I manage to avoid looking at the sketches of Michael making me feel in control. I am still capable of doing my job and that is very important for my psyche.

My mind is tired so I go to the kitchen and drink a glass of water before heading to the front door where I put on my coat and boots. I grab a knitted hat and go out for a walk.

It's cold outside, but the cold air clears my head and I walk a short distance until the snow becomes too deep to proceed. I stand there a moment gazing at the massive expanse of Lake Ontario until I feel the cold seeping into my boots and forcing me to return to the warmth of my home.

While Taylor recovers from the session, Dr. Sidney Paulson makes up his mind he must dig deeper and not limit even the remotest of possibilities if he wants to get answers. He has had many patients and all very interesting in themselves, and yet, this time he is finding it harder to do his job which is to not to be seduced by the stories, but to understand the suffering of the patient, in these stories, and to help to do what is necessary to find the harmony and balance in their lives.

Mental illness refers to a wide range of mental health conditions that affect the mood, thinking and behavior. From depression, anxiety disorders, schizophrenia, eating disorders and addictive behaviors, he has tried to apply them to Taylor. He has considered the fact that many people have mental health concerns from time to time. But a mental health concern becomes a mental illness when ongoing signs and symptoms cause frequent stress and affect the ability to function.

Of all the illnesses, he had to lean toward schizophrenia because this mental disorder being characterized as a failure to understand what is real seemed to fit the bill. The symptoms Taylor expressed were false beliefs, and unclear or confused thinking. Only the more he heard from her the more he had to admit that she didn't demonstrate any abnormal social behavior and in fact never said she heard voices, only that she saw this boy Michael. It just didn't ring true, but was it?

Dr. Paulson comes across the name of an individual that a colleague had used to help him understand some oddities in one of his cases. If anyone had told him he would be contemplating this move, he would have told them they were crazy, but now, Dr. Paulson decides to place a call to find out more.

"Dr. Wyatt, this is Dr. Paulson. We met at the World Summit on Psychology, Psychiatry & Psychotherapy, last October in San Francisco, California. Do you remember me."

There is a brief period of silence and then, "Yes, Dr. Paulson, I remember you. What can I do for you."

Dr. Paulson explains that he has been working with a patient and that he needs to consult. He asks if they can meet and Dr. Wyatt says that would be fine with him.

"What works for you?"

"I'm actually free now. Does that work for you?"

"Yes. I can be at your office in ten minutes."

"See you then."

Dr. Paulson disconnects the call and thinks he must feel exactly like Taylor did, having to share her secret. It's mind-boggling to tell someone something that you know can't be happening, but yet know that a side of your brain disagrees with you. He doesn't know what lead Dr. Wyatt to seek outside help beyond the fact that he thought it would help with a client. Maybe too he felt there was some reality to the issue.

In less than ten minutes Dr. Paulson entered Dr. Wyatt's office. Much like his own, the environment is staged for comfort. They greet each other and once seated in his inner office, Dr. Wyatt offers him a drink.

"That would be great. If you have it, a scotch and water will do me fine."

Dr. Wyatt walks across his office and lightly taps the side of a cabinet door. It springs open to reveal a bar. While he stands preparing the drinks, Dr. Paulson goes over the topic he needs to discuss. He reaches into his shirt pocket where he has made a list so that he covers each point with Dr. Wyatt.

When Dr. Wyatt returns, he takes a sip of his drink. "Perfect." He says.

"So, Dr. Paulson, how can I help you."

Thinking it best to start at the beginning Dr. Paulson shares what he legally can with Dr. Wyatt. No names are mentioned. When finished he adds, "Certain things she has shared makes me wonder if what she is saying is actually happening. The ideal of the past, the feeling that she is going back in time when he is around, and the notion that he is growing older; quickly. It just doesn't sound like something made up."

Dr. Wyatt is silent as he takes it all in. Finally, he speaks. "Well, that is quite a story. Quite a story to say the least." He pauses again. "But, I agree with you that the details make it ring true. I haven't met the patient so I can't say whether or not she is crazy, but I do feel she believes what is happening to her. I agree that you will benefit from talking with my friend.

Dr. Wyatt hands Dr. Paulson a piece of paper with the contact information. They say their goodbyes, then Dr. Wyatt says, "Dr. Paulson, keep me informed as to what happens, will you?"

"You bet."

It's Mildred's day off so I manage to get out the door early the next morning to run some errands. I needed more canvas and some chalks that were running low so I stop at my favor art supply house, pick out my items and spend more time browsing around before leaving. I manage to arrange for a delivery of a figurine to a client and when that is done, it is time for me to head downtown for my next session with Dr. Paulson.

Soon I am on the couch and relaxing and I easily picked up where I had left off.

For some reason, this session does not affect me as much as some of the others and I am aware of what I am saying and hear Dr. Paulson when he tells me the time is up.

As I prepare to leave I feel good and by the time I arrive home, my session with the doctor moves easily to the back of my mind.

I am slightly surprised when Samuel calls me to say he has some news. But then I remember I had asked him to see what he could find out about Michael's friends. So, when he asks me to meet him at Captain's Cove, I readily agree.

We sit at a table over in the corner and to anyone coming in, we appear to be two friends catching up with each other. We are two friends, but one is in shock and unable to believe what he is saying.

"So," I said, "tell me what you found out."

"I'm not sure you want to hear this, but here goes."

He starts out saying, this must be assumed we are talking of much later generations, but of course unless they too were famous there would be nothing easily found.

"So, here goes. Christopher Rodan could be a relative of the famous August Rodan. He was a famous sculptor of the 19th century."

"Yes, I know of him and his work. Actually, I recently had a customer compare my work to his. Strange, huh?"

"Yes, it is, but since you are aware of the name there is not much else I can tell you.

“What about Thornton."

"Just as interesting. Thornton Bandero could be a relative of Maria Magdalene, the famous actress known as Marlene Bandero. She married her director, Josef Bandero who transformed her into a cinema sex goddess They were of that middle-class aristocracy whose ancestors enjoyed not only wealth but position. Little Marlene gained a tremendous self-discipline from the severity of her early upbringing, but at the same time a strong-willed nature was being nurtured. She and her older sister Liza were taught proper etiquette and, from a governess, gained a workable knowledge of French and English. Not long after the Magdalenes moved to America, her father died. Their mother, having a fondness for military men, soon met and married Colonel Madison Porter who in the role of stepfather to the girls, won their immediate love and respect. "

"Porter noticed a musical talent in Marlene and soon she was taking both piano and violin lessons. In her late teens, she made remarkable strides in her violin studies, and by 1821 her mother, now a widow a second time since Colonel Porter, managed to enroll Marlene in a highly-acclaimed school of music."

"Wait a minute Samuel. Michael said that Thornton's parents were actors."

"Yes, I'm getting to that. I just thought you would like to know all the details so that when you talk with Michael he can tell you if these were the parents of his friends."

"How would he ... Never mind, continue."

"Anyway, Marlene's future looked bright as a concert artist but Marlene developed a nerve disease on her wrist which forced her to give up playing of the violin at once, or suffer serious consequences. After this disappointment, Marlene, already a movie fan like other girls her age, began to entertain the thought of becoming an actress. The rest is history. Marlene starred in *Madison Wilds, Simplicity Goddess, Madame She Devil, Hints of Class* and other box line draws."

I couldn't believe what I was hearing. Now that he had laid out the information, I realized I knew the actress and had seen some of her movies.

"So, tell me honestly Samuel, am I going crazy?"

"I know you too well to think that Taylor. I think you may have met this boy and that he is related to the Romans of music fame."

"Samuel, stop patronizing me. What are you really thinking!"

"I probably shouldn't tell you this, but I must. Taylor, I am sure I have identified the right families; the Rodans, Banderos and Romans. It is too much of a coincidence for so many facts to match for the families to be anyone but these, but…"

"Wait a minute, Samuel. You aren't saying these are later generations?"

"They have to be, yes, I guess I am saying that. I really don't know and it is possible, but ... "

"But what. What is it."

"Taylor, if my information is correct, Clara and Robert Roman had a son named Michael. I have not been able to find out when he was born, but they did have a son named Michael."

I could see the doubt on his face and the hesitation to say what he knew.

"August Rodan also had a son named Christopher and Umberto Bandero had a son named Thornton."

I don't know whether to be happy or sad, or maybe scared. Samuel must have read my facial expression. "Are you sure you want to hear this, Taylor?"

"Yes, just tell me as close as you can figure for the ages of Michael and his friends."

"Okay, but first I need to set a mark for the ages of

the parents at each of the children's birth which I don't know and am unsure I will be able to find out. but for argument sake, let's say that the parents had the child when they were 50."

"Fifty?"

"Yes, I know that is late, but let's go with it."

"Okay, if you say so Samuel."

"So, Christopher Rodan's, mother was born in 1801 and died in 1892. Now, if we were to say that she had Christopher when she was 50, Christopher today would be around 158 years old. As for Thornton Bandero's parents, I only know for sure that his father was born in 1804 and died 1889 so he at the very least would be 146 years old. And, if we assume this, we assume that your Michael is the child of the renowned pianists who were born in 1819 and 1810. They both died in 1864 and thus, Michael today would be 131 years old. "

"Cute, Samuel, very cute."

With humor apparent, he continues. "So, I guess that means that Michael is probably a great, great, great grandchild of the original Romans and really part of a future generation. We are also to assume that his parents, like the original Romans are concert pianists and they had a son and they named him Michael."

"Which all is possible," I said rather lamely.

"That's possible Taylor. Not only is it possible. It is the only explanation," Samuel said.

"So, what now?"

"Nothing, Taylor. Nothing. I can't begin to figure out where Michael lives from what I have uncovered. I just don't know."

"What about the school, I asked. Michael told me that he was thinking of going to St. Mary's boarding school."

Samuel thinks for a minute, looks at me and says, "Yes, I can check the school, but there are probably lots of them."

"He said that this St. Mary's, isn't Catholic. Could that help?"

“Yes, that will help since we don’t know where the school is. It will be a matter of checking into the names of students and finding a logical date when they might have been in attendance.”

“I’ll work on it too. Maybe the next time I see Michael he can give me a date or a location.”

Chapter 17

As far as the eye can see all is motionless and pleasing and giving a sense that it is all fixed and clear, never to end, and never to change. But change does come. In the darkness of the night the wind blows and the snow-laden clouds move in without a warning. In Rochester, it is called a nor easterner and because of Irondequoit's location near the lake, the effects can be devastating. For days, the air is full of winter sounds, the sounds we remember from our youth when we laughed and screamed as we slid down snow piles. And just as memorable is the sound the shovel makes as it hits the ice, or the snow blower motor as it whines and whirrs. Those sounds just like all the sounds heard year-round eventually go unnoticed as we grow accustom to them. After the storm, the city sparkles for a little while, then the snow turns black from the asphalt and the traffic, but soon it is gone, gathered in hard little hills and carted off in trucks or melts away from sidewalks and lawns.

The weather keeps me in and I work diligently on the sculpture commissioned by Mr. Masterson. When it is complete I brave the snow-covered streets and sidewalks to turn it over to them. They are happy, but I feel a little sad. Replicating the previous sculptor that I loved, was an easy project to complete and now it would be on to something new. With thoughts of Michael taking over my mind, it is getting harder and harder to be my creative self.

Most days now I spend in Dr. Paulson's office laying out my soul or else wandering the city letting my mind drift where it pleases. Often my desire to create a sculpture of Michael fills my head and my heart. Though I try to move thoughts of him aside, 5they keep coming back. I want so much to make a sculpture of Michael, and that makes me wonder when I will see him again. Strangely, I no longer think of him as a child. Since the last time I saw him, it is as though he is of no particular age, or at that point of being between ages when it is impossible to say that the child is a young man, or that the young man is yet a child.

Michael is draped in mystery that seems to penetrate my being as I try desperately not to analyze his existence. It is hard to force my mind to turn away from thinking of him until finally I just go with it, because I have come to believe that wherever in this world he actually belongs, in some way, for some reason, he belongs with me.

Even if I had known or understood, it would have made no difference. I can see that now. It was out of my hands from the moment we met. As much as it is beyond my power to bring spring or vanish the winter months. I could no more control the weather than I could control my destiny. And that it is. It is my destiny.

I believe that Michael is real and nothing is going to change that. Once upon a time, man would have laughed at the notion that there be such a thing as cellular phones and that one day people would carry this phone in their pocket or purse. Yet it has come to be that wireless phones are as commonplace as chicken soup. So, what may seem impossible may not be as impossible as it seems.

Each time I talk to Dr. Paulson I feel at peace because I am sharing the burden of my experience with him without judgement. The subject of my sharing has not changed since the first visit. It has always been about Michael. Now as I head to my appointment I know, just as Dr. Paulson will assume, he will hear more about Michael. Only I surprise both of us.

Just when I need cheering up and another focus my friend Annie Pierce, from Houston, Texas comes for a visit. She arrives one morning in a breathtaking if not seasonably appropriate, leather coat, her cheeks red from the cold and looking like she just stepped off the pages of Vogue. But the resemblance stops there. She carries a bundle of canvasses in a well-worn black leather case with a strap slung over her shoulder. Before we complete all the how-have-you-beens and you· look-greats, Annie has set up her drawings all around my studio.

Her unusual paintings can be threatening. They show violence in the world today in every shape and form. Now as I glance around the walls and the floor at these scenes of drama filling the room my pulse quickens.

We all encounter art we don't like, that upsets and infuriates us and we say it should not be allowed to exist. This question has been at the heart of the controversy that has split the art world. Annie being a free spirit artist captures the essence of today in her paintings and some of her choices are not well accepted.

Nevertheless, throughout history audiences have been offended and outraged by paintings that were socially, religiously or politically inappropriate. Artists used subject matters that were a taboo in social situations. Take for instance *The Trench Warfare*; a painting that portrays the effects of World War I by Otto Dix who is well known for painting horrid war paintings. Or *The Enigma of William Tell* by Salvador Dali that was called shocking, weird, offensive and lot other adjectives. This is one of the strangest paintings to hang in any art museum. Even Michelangelo has had disputes over his fresco painting, *The Last Judgment* that is on the altar wall of the Sistine Chapel.

So, it really boils down to sex, religion and politics when it comes to controversies related to paintings and that is Annie's forte. These paintings as background make my sculptures seem out of place. For my sculptures are more soothing, with most being colorless and discreet.

I can read her shock as she glances around the room at my work? She moves over to the easel, I think hoping to see some paintings, but only sees sketches of my creations and those I have yet to mold. She is not pleased with me because paintings and colors make up her world.

“What is this work you are doing. Taylor?” She cries “Statues and figurines! What has come over you?” Annie pauses to calm herself and then adds, "Not that you ever were on the way to being an important artist; but I always thought there was hope for you, at least.”

If it were anyone but Annie, her words would have hurt. But I can read between lines and know that she is aware I am successful, but not doing what she thinks success should emulate Her voice, like that of a high-pitched sea gull can be heard throughout the house and I find myself wondering what Mildred is thinking when she hears the screeching. She probably is recalling scenes from that old movie, “The Birds”, and running for cover.

Poor Annie, I never take her very seriously. For all her demonstrations of disappointment afford me joviality. I have long ago given up trying to understand her. But I am fond of Annie, for we had been children together; and I am delighted to see her.

She is a whirlwind of activity from the moment she enters my home. Her mind is a teapot of endless ideas that is only overshadowed by her love with color. She is like an untamed shrewd twirling, about the room.

Annie is as wild as her paintings but she is a happy woman who wants for naught. Though I doubt she has sold many or even a few of her paintings it is no matter to her. She sees herself as a genius. As for money, she inherited more than she could go through in one life time so she can afford to paint only for herself.

Annie has a saying that she does not hesitate to share with me once more. "Art should be mysterious and meaningful all at the same time."

"But Annie," I said, "though I love you to pieces, your drawings and the colors you use are full of violence with no calming elixir anywhere.”

Annie looks at me with her pretty almond shaped eyes as if I were. a silly little child. "Taylor, I don't believe you. I don't paint to please others, I paint to please me."

"But you must agree that a successful artist is one who sells paintings, right, " I tease.

"People aren't as stupid as you think, Taylor. They who have a creative spirit can understand my art."

"Do you think I have a creative spirit, Annie?"

"Oh, yes, but sculptures, Taylor. Why only sculptures when you have such an eye for color that is wasted on sculptures!"

"Sculpting is as old as human culture and has appeared in almost every civilization throughout the world," I say defensively. "Someone must be responsible for keeping this type of art alive. Why can't it be me?"

"Don't be mad, Taylor." "I just want to point out that you aren't using all your talents, is all. You do have the talent, so ... What the heck, I totally understand your artistic outlet." Seeing the unbelieving expression, I send her way, Annie adds, "I do, really I do and I approve."

I can't express how much pleasure Annie gives me by just being herself. I think that she feels the same about me. Annie brings the past back with her, the old, carefree and careless days in the wind and sun. The joy of traveling to Europe to develop our creativity and suffering the cold wintry days in the dorms feeling less than creative. Then there were the evenings in the little bistros followed by the early morning lessons at the Academy. It was a whirlwind of days of work and evenings of study, but it was all SQ wonderfully enchanting as we look back now.

There is so much I need to tell Annie about my work, my feelings, and hear the same from her so there will be many talks. There is also so much I want to show her and we find the days passing by as we go out to look at exhibits and then return home to sit and chat trying to catch up on each other's life accomplishments. I believe that the catch-up periods are the best for us both because we are always on either side of the coin when it comes to art appreciation.

Needless to say, Mildred takes an instant dislike to Annie. The very first night, after I respond to her timid knock she comes hurrying into the studio with a pale and grim expression and ask if she can leave for the day. It is so unlike Mildred's normal demeanor but I can sympathize. Standing there in the doorway with her hands folded across her stomach, and her eyes looking only at my face, I have all I can do to suppress the laughter threatening to overflow. "That's just fine, Mildred," I said trying not to let her hear the humor in my voice. "If we need anything, we can get it ourselves. If you want, you can take the week off as we'll be eating out a lot."

After thanking me and a stiff nod at Annie, Mildred hurried out the door. A short while later we hear her departing and then and only then do I allow myself to explode. I can hardly blame her, for we are quite a frightening twosome to those not privy to the type of friendship we built. We probably make more noise than these walls ever hear.

While I laugh, Annie just gives me one long, startled look and I am seeing something in her for the very first time. Annie wanted Mildred to like her! That is such a shocking revelation that I start to laugh again, pointing at her, but she stops me. "No, Taylor," she said, "you're wrong to laugh. That's a sweet woman and it hurts that she doesn't like me."

Seeing that it matters to Annie, I control myself. "I don't think she doesn't like you. I think she just isn't used to anyone as loud as you are, is all."

"Well, no matter, from now on I am going to whisper or at least speak in a low tone so I don't scare her."

And, for the most part, during the rest of her visit, Annie did try, though we weren't home that much as I wanted to show her the city.

We roam about the city with Annie, delighting in the fine weather that comes during her visit. I take her to the Eastman House and we go on the tour. When we finally work our way back home each evening it is very late.

"Taylor, I have so many ideas racing around in my head that I think I will break my wrist in trying to put all the images on paper."

"I know Annie. Each time I go someplace new I feel the same way."

At home, I pour us each a glass of wine and we drink it in the living room in front of the fire. Annie beams at me. "Here's to art," she says "And to friends," I add. We clink our glasses and take a sip, smiling over the brim.

Annie has a mischievous expression to her smile and I know something is coming. "Just the same," she says, "Different strokes for different folks. Art sometimes can only mean something to the artist who creates it."

I must smile at that and agree wholeheartedly.

That ends the session with the good doctor who says this was a welcome change with great input. When Dr. Paulson announces, my time is up, I have no problem hearing his voice. This session feels more like a conversation that I might have with a friend and the conversation came easy. It is different when I speak of Michael. Then it is a more troubled disclosure of events.

Dr. Paulson has found time to set up a meeting with Dr. Wyatt's contact and looks forward to what she has to say. Arriving at her home that serves as her office, he is taken aback. The building is located on West Ridge Road, a business sector, but it sets apart from the area, appearing to be on its own little island. Slowly he gets out of the car, looking around him as he makes his way to the door. As he is about to ring the bell, the door opens and he faces Madame Rosa.

She wears a scarf tied tightly encircling her head with wisps of gray hair escaping around the edges. She leans forward, shuffling instead of walking in front of him, guiding the way and stopping at a room on the left where she steps aside so that he can enter. As he takes a seat he can't help but stare at her face. It is a roadmap of wrinkles, deep and endlessly traveling around her facial features causing her eyes and her mouth to be mere slits. Now as she addresses him her mouth stretches into a horrific smile.

He is about to learn that her aged, chapped lips and her sagging skin encase a person who is far from being someone to fear.

Not wanting to stretch out this visit, I begin the conversation quickly. He tells her what his patient has shared with him, letting her know that this was just the start of what she has said and that it is still continuing.

Madame Rosa nods her head as she lets him continue uninterrupted. Finally, he feels he has presented what he could in the best way.

When she speaks, Dr. Paulson is startled at the clarity of her voice. "Dr. Paulson, Einstein once wrote that the most beautiful experience we can have is the mysterious. It is the fundamental emotion which stands at the cradle of true art and true science." I believe that what Einstein meant by "the mysterious" was a sense of awe, a sense that there are things larger than us, that we do not have all the answers at this moment and that we should be exhilarated rather than frightened."

It's his turn to nod as he listens.

"Dr. Paulson what do you believe?"

"What do you mean, exactly."

"Do you believe in the afterlife?"

"That people live after death?"

"The afterlife is the concept of a realm, in which an essential part of an individual's identity or consciousness continues to exist after the death of the body in contrast to the belief in oblivion after death."

"I can't say that I believe in it or disbelieve it really."

"What about reincarnation?"

"Not sure there is a difference, is there?"

"Yes, there is. Reincarnation is the belief that the dead go to a specific plane of existence after death, as determined by God, or other divine judgment, based on their actions or beliefs during life. "

He can only nod his head as he waits for her to explain what she is driving at.

"Reincarnation is the philosophical concept that an aspect of a living being starts a new life in a different physical body after each biological death. It is also called rebirth or transmigration. It is important that you keep an open mind, Dr. Paulson because what I am about to tell you, will depend on you being acceptable to what you do not know or can prove."

What she shares is startling and Dr. Paulson has trouble believing her.

Madame Rosa says, "I want you to listen to me and not judge until I finish."

Dr. Paulson nods his head and Madame Rosa says, "It is not well known that there exists a thing as Transitioners. They are rare, no one speaks of them, or no one wants to know of their existence. In any case, I think that this child man is a Transitioner." Dr. Paulson starts to interrupt and Madame Rosa lifts a finger to silence him.

"When someone goes before their time the Transitioner comes to help them complete their life. It may not be what they would know to do because they don't know the future…we do. So, they are as much in the dark as we. The Transitioners have a job of helping someone they are chosen to help and only that person, once they return in their new body. The way the Transitioner can return is by the death of a child who dies in the same manner as he did and at the moment the child passes over, the Transitioner will take over his body."

"Are you saying that the child will then live?"

"I don't know how it works exactly, but I don't think the child dies and then immediately lives again. I think the Transitioner uses the body and the person he once was lives. I can't be sure of that, it is just my theory."

"Well what's kind of weird is my client has told me, this little boy is growing rapidly. She can't decide on his age right now, but it is not still a five-year-old. So, this, uh, Transitioner is the person now and he has the characteristics of the person he was?"

He pauses. "Is that as confusing to you as it is to me."

"No, I understand what you are saying and I have no answer for you."

"Well, I need to ask you, are these, Transitioners dangerous?"

"They can be. I would need to know more to determine that; for instance, who was the child that he has come to replace, and also the connection between the child and your patient. Those are answers you must seek."

That ended their meeting and Madame Rosa says that he can call on her at any time. Dr. Paulson thanks her. He is careful to not let anyone see him leaving the building.

Chapter 18

Annie left for Houston. On the evening before she is to leave, I tell her about Michael; I guess in a way hoping she will be able to explain it or at least help me understand. After all, she has known me for some time. As I talk I watch her face and see her trying to believe me, but sense it is too weird to be happening, even for someone as open minded as Annie. I know it is and can understand her doubt so before she thinks I am off my rocker totally, I drop the matter and our conversation is less stressful.

The next morning, I drive Annie to the airport and stay to watch the plane taxi down the runway. I smile thinking, this mode of travel may have been invented just for Annie. She is always in a hurry, I cannot remember a time when Annie wasn't in a rush. She paints, talks, walks, and expresses her opinion quickly as though every phase of her existence is on a time schedule. Being around Annie can be tiring and though I miss her already, I appreciate my life returning to a slower pace.

When I return home, Mildred is in the midst of putting my studio back together. I stand in the doorway peering into the room that has taken on a more ruffled appearance and I can feel Annie. I smile watching Mildred as she leans down and picks up one of Annie's paintings she has left behind.

"Ms. Taylor, what would you like me to do with this?" she asks. In her hand is a painting of what I can only assume is a representation of a sunset. Splashes of light dominate the series of colors that are dark and dull, which appear to be effective in drawing the eyes toward the center of the picture where a bright yellow orb appears. As I look.at the painting I imagine that the likes of such a setting of the sun had to have last been seen during the age of dinosaurs and I know what happened to them. "Here, Mildred, I'll take that," I say.

Mildred gladly hands the painting over to me. “I just don't understand your friends' way of looking at the world."

"It does take some getting used to Mildred, I agree with that, but there is something special that Annie adds to her paintings."

Mildred looks at me with a quizzical expression. "Yes, and what might that be?” she says.

I stare at the painting in my hand, look at Mildred and can't hold back the laughter. "Well, I don't quite understand it myself, yet, but in time I will and then I'll share that with you."

When she moves to another part of the house I waste no time in hiding the last bit of evidence that Annie has been for a visit. I take one last look at the picture and then lovingly carry it across the room, placing it in the back of the closet that holds my art materials.

My life settles into a routine that I am more familiar with. The legacy that Annie leaves with me is the ability to return to my work, with deeper insight and emotions making the time with Annie well spent.

Chapter 19

As the weeks go by, the influence of Annie wears off and Michael again fills my thoughts and my dreams. Upon arriving home after the last session with Dr. Paulson, I cannot eat, nor can I work. I am so torn up inside over that visit with Michael because I feel so unsure that I will see him again. What if his memory of his parent's death is a sign of the end and he will no longer come to see me. I know I am just working myself into a frenzy but I can't seem to stop.

I continue to express my concerns, now more openly than before and though it is scares me to share such crazy notions, it calms my soul to let it out. Only at this session I have an epiphany that helps me accept what I can't explain.

I have been patient and now I want answers, even if they are based on a guess or a conclusion that is in line with some mental deficiency. I need to know so instead of sharing I start this session questioning.

"Dr. Paulson, sometimes you must believe what you cannot understand. It is done by educated people every day, trying to make sense of the here and now and those who peek into the future. Scientists must believe there is more out there or they wouldn't find themselves working on an invention of something that did not exist before. And psychics, psychics claim to see the future and what some have predicted has become reality. So that proves on either end of the spectrum humans accept the future though they can only really imagine it. This gives reason to consider what I am telling you as fact and not craziness."

I have rushed the words out my mouth so fast that my throat is tired. Now I sit waiting for his response. But, Dr. Paulson, as usual doesn't express an opinion, just lets me ramble on. To get some response that is exactly what I do.

"I wonder if these same people think about there being an ending to life itself. Would it prove true that life eventually comes to a total end, with scientific findings continuing until eventually there is no more to explore? Could that be? Or, is it possible that there is no ending and that when all else fails, we will be back at the beginning and reliving it again."

Silence again. "Please doc, tell me what you think."

I stare at Dr. Paulson as he lays down his pad and pencil, then uncrosses his legs, all the time looking at me. Finally, he says, "I really can't say either way, Taylor. I want you to tell me what you see and what you believe and not influence you either way. That's how it works."

Not the right answer and the results lead me to sulking through each day. I do not pick up a paintbrush, or charcoal. Nor have I molded anything into a creation of beauty. I barely have. the energy to get up each day and do the necessities of life. For, all intents and purposes my life is on hold and there is nothing I can do about it.

Dr. Paulson has listened to Taylor and each time she spoke he wants to tell her what he has learned, but that would be unprofessional. This has indeed been eye-opening for him as well as Taylor because neither one is able to accept what they feel is reality. Of course, Taylor has reached the point of believing that what is happening to her and to Michael is real and not a figment of her imagination. That is progress. On the other hand, the doctor is just beginning to grasp the reality of what she is experiencing and it frightens him. There is always a medical explanation, or there use to be. Now as he sits in his office reviewing Taylor's folder, trying to find a hint of something that might cause her allusions. He can find nothing until he comes across where she told him she was adopted.

It was during their first session and he had asked

Taylor about her childhood. She began by saying there was not much to tell and mentioned she was an only child; no brothers, no sisters. When he had asked if she missed having siblings she had replied, not really. Only after that she added there were times when she thought it would be fun, but her parents were very attentive to her and she liked getting all the attention. It was not until later in the session that she would say that she was adopted when she was a baby.

"Damn," Dr. Paulson said to himself. He had not asked about her real parents. He should have asked her that. He made a note. Dr. Paulson is as anxious as Taylor was for the next session

From the minute, I enter his office I can see that Dr. Paulson recognizes the change in me even before he speaks just as I recognize a change in him. He is dressed casually in gray pants and a blue shirt that is open at the neck. I notice that his shoulders stoop ever so slightly. It is probably the result of long hours spent in taking on the troubles of his clients. His left hand seemed to dangle uncomfortably at his side as though it searches for something to cling to, while his right-hand clutches the ever-present pad tightly as though expecting it to struggle for freedom. My eyes quickly scan his face noticing he looks drained, but when he realizes I am looking at him he manages a slight smile, points toward the session area and says, "Shall we."

I am ready to begin. I try not to hurry to the sofa but my legs do not get the message. Soon I am there, waiting as the doctor takes his seat before I allow myself to sit on the edge of the sofa. I pause and watch as the doctor crosses his legs and rests the pad on his thigh, then leans back and squirms into a comfortable position. I turn and allow my body to recline on the sofa, then I begin talking without any prompting. I forget that it is me who wanted answers because finally Michael has returned.

After all my worry and frustration Michael comes back. It has been a month since I last saw him and I immediately notice how much taller he has grown in that short space of time. He wears a long coat, unbuttoned and with its belt flapping as he moves quickly toward the house. I can see he is dressed in a uniform such as young men wear at boarding school. His white shirt is stiff with starch and his slacks have a sharp crease down the center of his long legs. I have been staring out the window of my studio when I see him hurrying up the front walk, so I walk to the door and swing it open before he even rings the bell. Michael comes bounding into the room full of energy, as he quickly slips out of his coat and I manage to catch it before it hits the floor. "Taylor" he cries, unable to contain himself.

I am totally taken aback, for if I have expected anything at all, it is certainly not so much cheeriness. There is nothing to remind me of the last time I had seen him; in fact, there is nothing of the little boy left at all. As I stare at him I can see he is on his way to being a full-grown man. My next thought is that I must finish my painting quickly, before it's too late.

He can barely contain himself as he stands there in the foyer and I couldn't help thinking it odd. I still am wrestling with the news of his last visit, yet he seems to have forgotten all of it.

Now as I observe him I am startled by the change. That cute little boy is now gone and in his place, is a tall, handsome man. He is close to six feet and muscular. His eyes that use to be brown are now green, but that can easily be accomplished with contacts. His clothing makes him seem elegant and intelligent.

Again, I can't quite place his age, but I assume he is still in school. When he appears to have calm somewhat, I can't keep from saying, "You've grown, Michael. And those clothes ... "

He looks down at himself, and laughs apologetically. "I know," he says. "Aren't they awful? They make us wear them at the school."

"Oh, of course, I almost forgot you mentioning you were going to boarding school. But I guess I imagined your plans would change after ... "

"Oh," he cries ignoring my discomfort; "of course you didn't know. I'm at boarding school now, with Thornton. My uncle sent me."

"Well, it looks as though it suits you."

We walk together to my studio. "I've been waiting for you Michael, wondering when you would come to see me again." Afraid he will leave, I quickly add, "Let's work on the portrait."

Michael says nothing. Instead he takes the lead and once in the studio he quickly settles in the chair, while I prepare my paints and position the easel where I will have the best light. I look at his clothing trying to determine what I should do.

Michael seems to catch on immediately to what I am struggling with.

"I'm sorry Taylor. I probably should have changed before coming, but there wasn't time. There is nothing I can do about it now, but I promise to remember and change the next time."

"No, it's all right, Michael. There is a lot I can do now and I can recall the clothing you wore from memory," I tell him.

By now, Michael knows me and seems puzzled.

"What is it, Michael?"

"Well," he said with a sulk, "aren't you glad to see me?

"Of course, I am Michael. It's just that I feel as

though I must hurry because we are running out of time. I don't know that it is true, I only know it is how I feel. So, you must forgive me if I forget to tell you."

"I understand, Taylor," is all Michael said.

It is very different from the first sitting and harder too. Michael is restless, and in high spirits; he wants to stop every few minutes, to talk or to just walk around. He has entered another phase of his life and it is so full he needs to share it with someone. He hops from subject to subject telling me about his new friends and what they do together, and then on to the activities he is involved in at the school.

"You can't imagine Taylor how wonderful life is. I am around my friends every day and we share everything. I never knew how much I missed being with other children. I am so happy now."

"I can see you are happy Michael, but you must sit still."

It is as though he hasn't heard me as he tells me about a new song he has learned and how he and his friends go for long walks and play tricks on the girls. I can sympathize with his excitement knowing this is probably the first time in his young life he is part of something and has a life of his own. So, I give him a break every now and then to share more.

"Taylor, do you know math and history?"

I must smile, "yes, Michael I took them in school."

"I like math and English he says calmly and the expression on his face speaks words he doesn’t share. Before I have a chance to say anything he is on to another subject. He tells me that he is sharing a room with Thornton and that they are now like brothers, they share everything they have with each other, including secrets. "Would you like me to tell you one of our secrets, Taylor?"

"Sure, if you want to tell me."

"Well, remember I told you Thornton's father had

done a sculpture of him. Well, he has that sculpture with him at school and it sits on his dresser, but only when he is sure no one will be coming in the room. I guess because he is older it embarrasses him to see his likeness sitting atop his dresser. It is a wonderful sculpture, though probably not as great as what you can do, but it is very good. It looks just like Thornton with the eyes dark and mysterious and the wavy hair. Yes, there's no mistaking that the sculpture is of Thornton."

I smile while I keep painting. Yes, Michael has changed since I have last seen him. He not only acts different, he is different. I even notice that he has filled out a little, no longer the frail little boy. The little boy I met is gone and in his place, is an older version that is enjoying life. I let him talk continuously, pausing when his expression changes drastically from the serene pose and listening, my fingers racing in tiny spurts over the canvas, trying at their best speed to keep up with my eyes; and my mind. Because this is to be special and I kept searching for what the eyes cannot see. For what I am painting is who Michael had been and who he is now at this moment sitting before me so much more grown than would seem possible. I also am trying desperately to capture the Michael he will blossom into in what I feel sure will happen in a short span of time.

I am truly working against time, and I feel myself trying to keep up.

I am swept away in my joy, watching the portrait come to life under each brush stroke, and stepping back to admire the growing strength and vitality apparent in the portrait. I am fortunate in a way that would seem impossible. I knew Michael at each stage of his life until now and because his maturity came so quickly I could easily recall each detail.

We stop to eat, although I would gladly have gone on without any nourishment and not missed it at all. "Isn't this fun?" he says as we sit down at the kitchen counter and of course, to him, it is and allowing myself to relax, I enjoy the moment too.

"Taylor, I tell my friends about you. Is that okay?"

"Sure, Michael, it's okay."

"I don't tell them everything, but I did tell them ... " he hesitated for a moment, "that you're very beautiful. I told them you were a great sculptor and that you allow me to come and see you whenever I like."

"Well, I'm flattered that you think so well of me."

Michael grinned adding shyly, "The girls loved that part of it," he declared. "They thought it was very Romantic."

"Good God," I said.

"Well, they did," he insisted. I could hear the laughter in his voice even though I knew he was embarrassed by telling me so much.

Silence falls between us now, a very pleasant kind of silence, the kind that can only be shared with someone who knows you well and that you care about deeply. I stare down at my plate, aware that I couldn't finish, then glance at Michael's plate. He manages to eat most of the food on the table and now sits back unable to take another bite.

I looked at his dear face and allow myself to think about how much he means to me and how I wish we could be together all the time, but then I come to my senses.

"Perhaps, if you've had enough to eat, we should be getting back to work."

His eyes travel to my face in panic. "You're not upset, are you, Taylor?" he falters. "I didn't mean to upset you."

"Of course, I'm not upset," I said, "it's just that we need to get back to the portrait if I am ever going to complete it. Okay?"

"Okay."

Michael gets up from the table, carefully pushing his

chair into place and follows me out of the kitchen. I can hear Mildred in the background clearing up our lunch as we step into the foyer and then everything is silent. We walk side by side, hands almost touching between us. In the studio, Michael takes his place quietly, but the silence does not last long. "Taylor," he says.

"Mm?"

"I want you to know that you are special to me and I want you to like me."

"I do like you Michael."

"Yes, I know you like me, but I want you to really like me."

"I really like you Michael, now please sit still."

That seems to suffice, but Michael couldn't sit still. He turns to telling me bits of other details about his school. I learn that they have the outfit he has worn to the studio, and a more complete outfit that includes a jacket and tie for Sundays. From there he goes on to tell me that he enjoys most of his subjects, except for history.

I have been silent, only half listening as I concentrate on my brush strokes. Now I ask, "Why don't you like history?"

He is silent for quite some time before finally answering me. "It makes me feel so sad." He pauses as if in deep thought and finally comes out with, "I only want to know about here and now. I think you feel that way too. Am I right Taylor?"

I am caught off guard by his remark and my brush stops in mid stroke. I don’t know if I should answer him, but somehow sense he knows how I will answer. "Perhaps," I agree. "Perhaps I like here and now most ... " my words trail off as I try to compose myself.

"Michael, please turn your head a little to the right for me now." In a queer, breathless voice he inquires,

"Taylor do you think. sometimes people know what lies ahead? I mean, they actually know what's going to happen to them?"

"Nonsense," I said.

"I don't know," he replies slowly. "I'm not so sure. Sometimes I feel sad about things that haven't happened. Perhaps they're things that are going to happen. Maybe somehow, we know it, and are afraid to admit it to ourselves."

Michael is quiet then adds, "Taylor, if you could see ahead do you think you would feel sorry for what was coming? Only because you are thinking ahead you wouldn't know for sure it was coming."

"Wow, that is some wild thinking you're doing. I say don't worry about something that hasn't happened. There is enough to worry about without making more problems for yourself."

"Oh," said Michael in a small voice. Even with the small amount of attention I could spare from my portrait, I could tell that I had hurt him. I was about to rectify the situation when Michael added, "All right, I won't talk anymore."

For the remainder of the time, he sat there silent and unsmiling, drawn back once more into himself, dreaming and distant. I want to clarify myself, but I am too busy to try to explain; and besides, it did the portrait good. The silence, stillness and the look on his face was the same as when we first began. When the light begins to fail, I put down my brush, and take a deep breath.

"I think I've got it, Michael," I said.

There is no answer. He seems to be in a world of his own. I go silently into the powder room off the studio to wash my hands and splash water on my face. I doubt if I am away for more than a minute or so. But when I get back, Michael is gone.

This time he left a note for me, on my easel that simply said, “Taylor dear I'll be back again someday. But not soon. In the spring or summer, I think. It was signed, Michael."

That ended the session. I could barely gather enough strength to leave Dr. Paulson's office. I felt drained and a little sad. I barely remember shaking the doctor’s hand and none of how I made it home. That sadness prevailed for some time afterwards and stayed on through each of my next appointments.

Dr. Paulson seems to ignore the change that has come over me. Just like I am ignoring a change I sense in him.

PETER NEWMAN

Chapter 20

After Dr. Paulson's session with Taylor he is ready to relax. This has not only been an odd revelation for Taylor, but for him as well, so when his wife Barbara calls to tell him she has set up a dinner party for Friday evening he is happy.

"So, who is coming," he asks.

"Well, Just Peter and Elizabeth along with Arnie and Vivian."

"That sounds great. I'll be sure to be home early to give you a hand." Before Barbara speaks, Sidney knows what she will say.

"That won't be necessary, I will have plenty of time to plan and get ready. Just allow yourself enough time to change and relax."

"I love you Barb."

"I know. I love you too."

Sidney Paulson has known Peter Newman and Elizabeth for quite some time; since their marriage. He had first met Peter when Peter had contacted him to interview a client of his whom he felt was not sane enough to stand trial. Sidney had done more than just label the client; he had done a thorough investigation into the client's history. That had taken a bit of proving since the insanity defense is looked down upon. But Peter, being the brilliant lawyer could take the information supplied by Sidney and cite past cases to mold them into a brilliant defense. Later Peter would tell Sidney he would not have won if it hadn't been for his expert review of the client. That had taken place almost ten years ago and in that time, they have met for consultation and socially. As impressed as Peter was of Sidney, the same was true the other way around.

Later, Sidney introduced Peter to his friends, Arnie and Vivian Masterson. Since they all were avid golfers, he was sure they would get along. They did. So, it came as no surprise that this would be the people that Barbara would invite for dinner. Sidney was aware that Barbara, Elizabeth and Vivian spent a lot of time together shopping and working on charity bazaars and their friendship matched that of their husbands.

Dinner is wonderful and the conversation flows freely. It is Arnie Masterson who turns the topic to children saying, "I remember when Vivian told me how she thought she had spoken to her child. I had tried to keep a straight face once I knew she wasn't joking. She really thought that our unborn child had spoken to her."

Everyone laughs except Sidney who says. "I think if my wife had told me that I would have been more understanding because I realize that there are things that happen that cannot be explained away with science. "

Barbara looks at him, puzzled. "Wow, where did that come from."

"That's not so wild," Sidney says, "There was the time that a client mentioned that he had a crazy experience. It was crazy not only to him, but to me when he told me about it. He was mentally sick so in my defense there was reason for doubt. Anyway, he had said that he was a twin. I said, "I see", though I did not. I had known him almost ten years. I knew his family as well and no one had ever mentioned that he had been a twin. Yet, now as I think about it, he might have been and the family decided against telling him that. So, I asked him if he and his twin were identical? To this he replied, "I think so".

"I don't understand what you're getting at Sidney. Explain." Peter said.

"Yes, sure. I must first tell you that as his story goes, his family had a tradition to help him understand the meaning of New Year's Eve. At the stroke of midnight, his father would take him to the door and have him open it to let in the New Year and it always made him happy to share that moment with his dad. The week before he met with me he told me he had been to visit his father and as they sat talking about the past, his dad had asked if he remembered what happened when he was about ten. He had shaken his head and his dad proceeded to tell me that on that year as usual they all sat waiting for midnight, looking at the front door. His Dad said he grabbed his hand and started across the floor to open the front door only something strange happened that his dad couldn't explain. At the stroke of twelve, there was a loud knock at the door and it opened by itself. They all rushed to see if anyone was there but the street was bare."

"My client added that he couldn't remember that day because he knew he wasn't there. That Christmas eve he spent with his mother, which he had been doing every other year since his parents' divorce. When he mentioned this to his dad, a strange look came over his face and before he turned his head away my client could see he was crying. It was at that moment he felt a connection to someone he had never met and before he knew what he was saying, he blurted out to his dad that it must have been Jim. His Dad said nothing nor did he need to as the look on his face told him everything. As a child, he had an imaginary playmate named Jim. That name meant a lot to him and somehow, he thought he might have known all along who this Jim was. He was his twin. Though his parents had never told him, he knew somehow that he had a twin who had died in the womb."

Everyone is silent until Peter says, "Come on, there are several earthly possibilities to explain what happened. It could have been the wind, a person running by and banging on all the doors or a loose hinge."

While Elizabeth, Vivian and Barbara cleared the table, Sidney looked across at Peter, sensing something was bothering him.

"Peter, what is?"

Peter has been remembering the day of the fire. It has been some time ago now, but though he thinks about Christine and Max, he has never thought about what happened that day at the hospital. He decides to tell them.

"This line of conversation has me remembering and well, I had forgotten about it until now. I guess it is because I couldn't explain it then and definitely couldn't explain it later so my mind just let it go." Peter pauses. "I need to tell someone this so why not my closest friends. I must begin at the beginning because I know you guys do not know that I was married before Elizabeth."

He could see the shocked expressions on their faces.

"No," Sidney says, "You never told me that."

"Well, I was. Her name was Christine and I loved her dearly. Um, we had a son, too." My friends visibly lean forward in their chairs trying to hear each word I speak. This is something none of them knew about me and they are curious.

"Go on."

By now the women have finished and catching a whiff of what is being said, eagerly sit down waiting with their husbands. He could feel Elizabeth squeeze his hand under the table, offering her support. He had told her all about his previous marriage and how it ended so abruptly.

Peter knows he must continue. "Well, Christine and my son, Max died in a fire. You probably read about the one that happened at FunScape over 20 years ago." The guest nod their heads. That fire was burned into the hearts of so many it has never been forgotten. "Well that was our fifth birthday party for our son, Max." Peter can literally hear the intake of breath from his friends.

"I was at work when it happened. By the time, I arrived it was a circus and when I finally identified Christine I was told she died instantly, but Max held on for several days."

I pause a moment as I remember that day. "When Christine's body was recovered, I am told she had laid over our son trying to protect him from the flames." Talking about it now, I can see it all so clearly and uncheck, tears well up in my eyes. At that moment, I feel my wife's arm around my shoulders and I can continue.

"Sorry, anyway, what I want to share with you is that Max didn't make it and on the evening in the hospital when Max passed, I saw something."

Now everyone in the room is sitting on the edge of their chair waiting for what I am about to say. I feel odd sharing this because I tend not to mention anything I can't explain. This I really can't explain.

"They have made major strides in understanding the principles of burn care over the last half century and maybe if this happened now, Max might have survived, but he was one of the last to be found in the building."

I must pause again and as I do, I turn and wink at Elizabeth.

"At first, I thought it was a nurse coming in to check on my son, but on closer observation what I saw was a little boy who was sporting an old style of trousers."

"They're called knickerbockers," Elizabeth says.

"Thanks, sweetie. They were wide leg pants fastened below the knee and he had on a matching vest and jacket. The jacket had a cutaway front with a single fastening at the neck, exposing the buttoned vest beneath."

"How can you remember all that," Vivian Masterson asks.

I think for a minute before responding. "When something as dramatic as what happened to my family takes place, you remember every minute detail for a very long time."

Vivian nods her head. "Please, go on."

"The little boy was standing by my son's bed and my first thought was he could infect my son so I needed to get the little boy out of the room. So, I try to go over to him, but I am unable to move. I try to call out to him, but no sound comes out my mouth. I feel pressure on me, and I absolutely can't move. I can't get to him or call out for help. It scares me not to be able to move, I am trying so hard to yell for a doctor, or pound my feet on the floor only to have no success. I literally sit paralyzed."

Now as I tell the story, I realize something for the first time. I let out a little laugh. "If that sounds crazy, there is something else that I just remembered now. As I look around the room it is like everything has changed."

"What do you mean, changed." It is Sidney Paulson who interrupts now.

"I don't know. It was like there was Max in his bed and there were other beds in the room too; only not as clearly present as that of Max. I guess I am saying it was like the room became a ward and the floors were wood planks instead of the tiles that had been there. The lighting too; wasn't like lights in hospital rooms today." I pause. "I guess it was as if I was in the past somewhere."

"Please, go on, Peter."

"So, I sit in this, for a lack of a better word, 'world' frozen and unable to move. I watch as this strange little boy climbs on Max's bed and then turns and looks right at me. I see him smile and then he moves directly over the top of Max and disappears."

I hear wonderment coming from my friends. "What do you mean disappeared. Disappeared how," Vivian asks.

I swallow and add, "Disappeared into my son's body."

"What?"

"I know. That is why I have kept it to myself because it is impossible. Yet, maybe not."

"You were married before and had a son?" Vivian says in what I see as an attempt to bring out something normal to the conversation.

"Yes," he was Vivian, but it never came up in conversation until now." Elizabeth responds. It was before we met you guys.

Arnie, who has been listening to all this says, "So, he was married before. That is not the point I'm interested in; well not quite interested. I have to tell you something that has bothered me for some time."

All eyes turn in Arnie's direction now.

"Recently I hired a sculptor to make some figurines for our fireplace. She came highly recommend and she does great work."

"Who is she?"

"Not that it matters, but her name is Taylor Bouchand. She has done other things for us and we have been pleased. Anyway, when she was getting out some sketches from her brief case, some drawings fell out and they were pictures of a little boy, dressed in 'old timey' clothes."

"What!"

"Yes, a little boy in old fashion clothes that she was sketching. They were good. I had reached down to pick them up for her, but couldn't help staring at them because they were so good. The expression she had captured on the little boy's face was charismatic and I told her that they were really good. She had replied that they were only sketches for now, but she planned on doing a painting and later a sculptor. They caught my interest, I would say."

"So, what happened?" I ask.

"Well, nothing, but it is what came to me later. I think I have seen that little boy in a painting before, only I can't place it."

"You think this woman, Taylor, copied a painting; maybe a famous one?"

"No, it's not like that, I'm sure. She wouldn't do something like that. It's just that…"

"I saw the sketches, too," Vivian adds, "But they didn't remind me of any other paintings I had seen." Vivian pauses, her mind going elsewhere as she turns to Peter. "I hope you don't mind me asking, but I wonder, do you have a picture of your little boy?"

Peter is at first taken aback, but knows that Vivian is just into children and that is the only reason she asks. She watches as Peter pulls out his wallet, then pulls out a locket, that he hands across to Vivian. "That's a picture of my son and my first wife, Christine."

Vivian carefully opens the locket while Barbara Paulson leans over to look too. "She's beautiful," Vivian says, "So are you Elizabeth," she adds. "Your son is so adorable…"

"What is it Vivian?" I ask noticing how she trails off.

"It's just that your son…"

"What about my son?"

Vivian hands the locket to her husband. Arnie looks at the picture and then looks over at Peter. "What she is having a problem saying is that your son Max is the little boy that is in the sketches done by Taylor."

I look at them, puzzled by what they are saying. "That's impossible. I don't know this woman Taylor, nor have I ever asked her to sketch my son.

"Let me see," Sidney Paulson says.

I watch as Arnie passes the locket to Sidney. Sidney looks at the picture, looks up and at Peter.

"What! You have seen the picture too!"

"No, no, but I have seen Christine, or rather the likeness of her. She is the exact likeness of one of my patients." He is reluctant at first to mention that Taylor Bouchand is his patient, but seeing the shock expressions around the table and wondering himself at the oddity of what is happening, he says, "Taylor Bouchand is a patient of mine. She could be Christine's double. That's how much they look alike."

The locket is passed around the table until it is back in Peter's hand. Everyone is quiet trying to figure out what has just happened, or what does it mean.

"Enough of this," Barbara says trying to bring some semblance of normalcy to the group. "I worked hard on this dessert so I would like to hear your comments."

Obediently the forks are lifted and sounds of appreciation are shared. Then Barbara turns to Vivian and says, "Tell everyone what you told me about learning you were pregnant.:

They laugh with Vivian and Arnie as they tell how surprise they were to find themselves pregnant since they had been trying without success for so long. Arnie said, "I told Vivian that it had to be the chocolate. You see, Vivian is always watching her weight and one day I came home to find her sitting in front of the television eating some special chocolate candy."

Vivian interrupts to add, "It wasn't just any chocolate. This chocolate is crafted in Tuscany by Cecilia Tessieri, the world's first female master chocolatier. It is not available everywhere, but my sister, who lives in New York City purchased it at Union Square, are you ready for this..."

Everyone nods.

"For $55.00 for a 17.5-ounce bar! It is not something you just pop in your mouth, you must sit and savor each morsel."

There is more laughter.

"Anyway, Arnie smiles at his wife. Shortly after that we were pregnant."

Soon the party breaks up and everyone leaves for home after helping Barbara carry the last of the dishes into the kitchen. It has been a long and very interesting evening. Barbara puts the dining room in order and then heads to the kitchen, while Sidney goes about making sure the doors are locked and the shades are drawn. He then heads to the kitchen to help Barbara finish cleaning up. They are both too tired to think about the odd conversations that began the evening so they go upstairs to bed.

Elizabeth and I drive home in silence, but once inside, I turn to her. "I hope the conversation didn't get so out of hand that it bothered you. Did it?"

"No, oh no, Peter. It didn't bother me at all. I know you loved your wife and your son, but I also know that you love me and our life."

I am quiet and it is like she knows exactly what I am thinking.

"Peter, I understand that you need to follow up on this…this strange development. I also want to know if there is anything happening here. What with Christine looking exactly like Sidney's patient and your son looking like the little boy in the painting that Arnie and Vivian saw. It is all so strange."

I look out beyond Elizabeth knowing that I need to see this woman Taylor and the sketches she has made. I need to know what is behind these strange coincidences and I am so happy that Elizabeth understands.

Chapter 21

All I can think of is why hadn't Christine told me she was adopted. We had a child together and would need to know family history. As I sat at my desk at work, I couldn't get it off my mind but I had to get to court so I set it aside.

I pulled out my client's file and studied the case that I knew like the back of my hand, but as any lawyer knows, there are no slam dunk cases. There is no case where the evidence is so overwhelming that any jury will give you a conviction. If I learned anything, in the courtroom you have to work for it.

I am representing Randall Williams, a very successful salesman, accused of murdering his live-in girlfriend, Felisha Markson. Not only is he being accused of murdering her, but of also torturing her to death.

Felisha was discovered dead in Williams's house and the Detectives say her body appeared to have more than 300 wounds and scratches. According to the lead Detective, Hamilton Scott, "someone beat this girl badly."

On examination of the crime scene photographs, one recoils at the apparent severity of Felisha's wounds--particularly around her face. Inside the house the bedroom was a wreck making it appear as though a fight had taken place in that room. There was a smashed closet door, blood smears on the wall inside the closet and on the bed. There were also several signs that someone had tried to clean up the mess.

According to a detective on the scene, Williams said that Felisha had taken a drug called GHB, a sexual stimulant and party drug. He also told police she had become upset and uncontrollable, and then died.

Within hours, police arrested Randall Williams and he immediately placed a call to my office. He was eventually charged with Miss Felisha's murder, and more unusually, her torture.

I can see it in their faces, the prosecution is over confident. I am prepared and because of that what happened next is a case study on how an apparent "slam dunk" case can fall apart.

The prosecution joined me in court and then watched their case fall apart. In their defense, Williams's had given me what I needed for his defense and I had taken the ball and ran. I argued strongly that there had been no murder at all.

I demonstrated that the huge number of injuries on the victim's body were self-inflicted. I put a recognized expert witness on the drug GHB on the stand and she showed jurors a series of home videos which she said illustrated the extreme loss of control a GHB user might exhibit.

She also said that Felisha's injuries were consistent with the kinds of self-inflicted wounds she had witness over the years. I followed her with a medical doctor who supported her views on the dangers of GHB.

And then the finale, my final key witness was a former medical examiner, Dr. Thomas Payton, who testified that a certain electrical heart signal, called pulseless electrical activity (PEA) was present in Felicia's heart when paramedics examined her after her death. Payton pronounced, that given the circumstances of Felisha's death, the only possible cause of this PEA was a drug overdose.

In this case, three strong defense expert witnesses shattered what prosecutors had believed to be an unshakeable case.

As I walk out the courtroom and back to my office I stop at the secretary's desk.

"Tamara, do you have a minute?"

"Sure boss. What's up."

"I need you to do something for me."

Before leaving the office, I make two calls, one to Elizabeth and the other to Christine's parents. I have kept in touch with Christine's parents, the Pryors so they aren't surprised by my call, "Sure, come on over Peter."

It's a short drive to the Pryor's home and Christine's mother opens the door before I even knock.

"Peter, it is so good to see you," she says giving me a hug. "Come in, come in."

Inside the Pryor's house is exactly as I remember it, giving me a sense of peace and comfort as I sit in one of the chairs by the fire.

"Peter, can I get you something to drink. I think you like red wine?"

"Yes, that would be nice."

I watch as Edna Pryor leaves the room and returns within minutes with two glasses of wine.

To make small talk I ask about her husband Vernon and about their sons. Edna assures me that all is going well. I can tell she senses something is on my mind so she gives me the nudge I need.

"Peter. What is bothering you? I can tell something is on your mind."

I clear my throat and finally say. "Yes, something is. I have been going over it in my brain and decided I must ask. Was Christine adopted?"

Edna is quiet for some time, then finally she looks at me. I see the tears in her eyes and want to say, forget it, but can't. I need to know. I wait and finally Edna says, "I can't see how it matters now, Peter. Why do you want to know? What difference does it make? Christine is dead."

"Please Edna," I plead.

I see her nod her head and finally she says, "Yes, Christine was adopted. We wanted a daughter and now she is gone. It didn't matter to us that she was adopted."

"It matters to me, Edna. I thought we had no secrets between us, and then I learn that she was adopted." Christine was adopted.

"She didn't tell you Peter because she didn't know. I never wanted to tell her and I could see no reason to. If anyone is at fault it is me." She looks directly at me and adds, "How did you find out?"

"I didn't, for sure, it was a hunch. Someone mentioned something to me that had me thinking is all. I don't mind that she was adopted."

I could see the relief that Edna felt and I allowed her to bathe in it before I broached the next question.

"Edna, what can you tell me about Christine's birth parents."

Her face goes slack, her mouth slightly open, and the color drains from her face as she stares wide-eyed at me. I wait patiently, giving her time to breath.

Edna lets out a sigh, opens her mouth to speak, but then snaps it shut.

"It's all right Edna. No matter what I will always love Christine."

Edna's voice is raspy, barely audible. "I don't know, Peter. I don't know."

"You don't know what, Edna?"

"I don't know anything about her birth parents. We never asked. We saw Christine, loved her and she was ours. We didn't want to think of her belonging to anyone else. Do you understand?"

I pause, knowing that what she says is true. "Yes, I can understand." I lower my head trying to figure out what my next step should be. I need something to go on if I want to pursue this further.

"Can you tell me what her last name was."

Edna pauses then says to me, "Wait a minute. I think I have something that might help you." She gets up and leaves the room. I hear her footsteps on the stairs and figure she is going to the attic. Christine and I had gone to the attic in this house to search for heirlooms to furnish our first home together. As I remember, it was organized, but full of stuff at the time, so I expect she will be a while.

I get up and look at the pictures on the piano in the far corner of the room. So many pictures of Christine at every age thinkable. I wonder if it is a good idea to keep the pictures out and then think about the locket that I still cling to. I return to my seat and lean back enjoying the warmth of the wine. It isn't long after I finish my wine that Edna returns. There is a look of embarrassment on her face.

"What is it Edna?"

She looks at me and says, "Don't judge me Peter, but I had a new birth certificate made for Christine so the real one was hidden in some old papers. I guess I must have thought it may be important someday. I guess I was right."

She hands me several papers. "You can have them Peter. I don't need them anymore."

I want to stay and console her, but I am afraid she may ask why I want this and I am not ready to share that with her. So, I give her a hug and thank her for the wine, then leave the house, feeling a bit optimistic. I know what I have is not a lot to go on, but it is a start.

The next morning, I can hardly wait to get to the office. I leave the house earlier than usual and take the quickest route downtown. In the parking garage I pause, take a deep breath and will myself to calm down. When I feel, I am back in control, I walk calmly into the building.

I don't see anyone from the office as I stand waiting for the elevator. When it comes, I climb in and press the button for my floor. I am not surprised that I am alone on my ride up as it is early. I think about what I have learned. It amazes me that I didn't know and the fact that Christine didn't know is even more shocking. How many times had I looked at her mother and father, wondering how they had created such a beautiful daughter. Edna and Vernon were plain looking people that you would walk by and hardly notice. Christine on the other hand was strikingly beautiful, causing passersby to stop and acknowledge her presence. I couldn't believe it never came up; that Christine hadn't wondered why she shared no personal traits with them or her brothers.

By the time the elevator doors open, I feel anxious again. I force myself to walk into the office controlling my feet that want to run. In my office, I place my briefcase on the desk and open it up and stare at the paper that lays on the top. I pick it up and hold it in my hands. This is Christine's real birth certificate. I look it over and read each word carefully. New York State Birth Certificate it says. Vital Record Information: Born in New York State in the City of Rochester, County of Monroe on September 20, 1982 at the Genesee Hospital.

I look below and see that the mother's full maiden name is Lily Powers and for father it states, unknown. For the name of the baby it says, Baby Girl Powers. If I am right, it should say Baby Girls Powers. I wonder about that.

This is what I must go on. I pause. Do I want to pursue this? Just what do I hope to accomplish by doing this. I shake my head in determination as I buzz for my secretary.

"Yes," Mr. Newman.

I look up and address Tamara. "Tamara, I have something to help in your search."

I hand her the paper and watch as she looks it over.

"I think for what you want, this is good enough. I can do an online public records search and go to the courthouse to search through public records, if need be. Since you just want to find if there is any connection between your wife and Taylor Bouchand, all I should need is the father and mother's names, and I can track the rest down." She looks at the paper, "Oh…"

"Yes, no father given."

"That's okay. I will work with what we have here."

"Thanks Tamara."

Before departing, Tamara goes over the legal briefs and court subpoenas she has completed, then reviews the court dates with me. I am pretty good at keeping my schedule in my head and know as soon as she leaves, I need to go to the courthouse. I close my briefcase and make sure I have everything, then head out the door.

In court that day, my mind is clear as I defend my client, not letting my personal matters take up space in my head, interfering with my ability to defend my client. It is not until the end of the day do I finally allow myself to think about Christine.

I want to wait, but I cannot put it off so with everything under control in the office, I pay a special visit to Sidney's office.

"Peter, what are you doing here?"

"Sidney, it's okay, no one saw me. I just can't wait any longer. I need you to tell me."

Sidney has expected this to happen since even he is anxious to figure out what is going on. After that evening conversation, he has a feeling that whatever is happening to Taylor lies in an explanation of the connections made that evening. But he must protect his patient.

"Peter, we can't stay here. Let's go get some coffee at the little café downstairs."

"Fine with me."

I can tell that Sidney is nervous as I follow him to the café and take a seat in the back corner of the room. I start to talk, but Sidney shushes me.

"Wait."

"We'll have two large Caffe Misto." Sidney says to the waitress.

"Anything else?"

"No, that will be all."

I turn to look at Sidney. "I come here often myself and with patients sometimes," he whispers and I get the message.

Chapter 22

I sort of knew that Sidney was not going to arrange a chance meeting for me to meet Taylor in his office, but I had to try. I was taken aback at first, but understood that this could put him in an awkward position. I wanted to discuss what I had found out too, but that would have to happen later.

I am anxious to see this woman who looks like my Christine. I love Elizabeth and the life we have built. It is just how all this happened it makes me think I need to talk with her and see if she can shed some light on the matter. Maybe she has. Maybe Sidney knows, but can't share what he knows with me.

It was two years after I lost my family that I even thought of dating and that was because I couldn't handle all the pushing from friends that I needed to get on with my life. I went through the female friends of friends until I figured that I could do it better on my own. So, I did.

On our first date, we met at a café and she wore an affinity pin on her blouse so that I would recognize her. The woman sitting across from me is so very different in appearance from Christine with her pale blonde hair and fair skin. As we talk I look at her nose that is small and slightly upturned while Christine's straight-edged nose was a striking feature that set off a kind of aural beauty and her hair had a deep brown base with honey color highlights. And her skin, Christine's skin was forever tan. I drank too much coffee and barely talked as I spent my time wondering about just where this would go. By the time our lunch was brought to the table, I nervously ate hoping I was using my best manners because I liked the woman sitting across from me and wanted her to like me. By the time, we parted outside of knowing her name, I hadn't gathered much information, but I knew I wanted to see her again. I decide to do better on the next date, if she agreed to seeing me again.

She did and this time we had sandwiches and walked through the park. We talked about life. We talked about books. We talked about one of our mutual passions: cheese. By the third date, Elizabeth shared.

"Peter, I don't know where this is going, but I like you. I am a romantic and I love wholeheartedly and generously. I want you to know that."

I could only smile at her, then as we said goodbye, I took the chance. I grabbed hold of both her hands and pulled her toward me. We kissed.

I was infatuated by her. Elizabeth was very different in appearance from Christine but had the same loving heart and personality. I couldn't wait to see her again and asked her out to dinner, since according to our society, dinner is more serious than lunch. I knew it and I am sure Elizabeth did too.

When I see her walking toward me I felt my heart fluttering, stomach jumping…the works. Elizabeth was beautiful. We sat shyly across from each other at the restaurant as though it was our first date and I was speechless again, but she put me at ease talking casually and asking questions to start a conversation. It was such a comfortable atmosphere and she was so easy to talk to that I found myself telling her about the death of my wife and son and how hard it was to come back from that and think of starting over.

Elizabeth's sympathy was genuine. Her sense of how hard it was for me to share this with her was evident in her expression and her words and after only a few months of dating, we knew.

We fell in love and there was no effort involved. It was simple and it keeps getting simpler. It was good and it keeps getting better. It was true love, different from that I shared with Christine, but wonderful in a different way. Years later, it still is as it continues to grow.

When my friends and family ask how we met, I tell them, "an online dating website", smiling at their surprise. When they ask, how long did it take before we found each other. I tell them two or three weeks.

Elizabeth told me that her friends were just as shocked at how rapidly our relationship happened and she would tell them no one would pass up meeting a man who wrote such an adorable profile.

Actually, I was surprised at the length of the profile. I had never done this before and thought I would just have to put in my name, interests and how to contact me. It went a lot deeper. I spent a lot of time developing it so to know it made a lasting impression made me feel good. I had written the truth and it said; I aspire to be the kind of person that Mister Rogers would be proud to call his "neighbor". Some days, I succeed. I like almond croissants, spice lattes and smartphone-free dinner parties. Professionally-speaking, I'm a good lawyer. I've been told I have a pretty epic smile and I believe in love. The forever kind. You should message me if you are curious & thoughtful, but not cynical. If you still believe in love, then I'm your man.

My belief is that when you say something that isn't true, you get something that isn't right. Being truthful is what it took to get the attention of Elizabeth and to have a second happily ever after.

I know that Elizabeth understands that this is a sort of closure that I must complete. It doesn't affect what we have and never will. After that dinner party with our friends, Elizabeth said, "Peter, I can't help thinking that this is not an accident. Think about it. Not one, but two of our friends have had contact with someone from you past. You can't just walk away from this without finding out what it all means."

"I love you Elizabeth and I know you know that, but you are right, I need to figure out what this is." At that moment, if it was possible, I loved her even more.

While I searched for answers, Dr. Paulson who has heard Taylor's story can't wrap his head around it as being true. He is a medical doctor and someone telling him of a little boy who came to her and who is now almost a grown man makes no sense at all. But he knows that Taylor is not crazy. He knows he must open his mind to all possibilities not only for Taylor's sake, but for his own.

TAYLOR BOUCHAND

Chapter 23

I think my biggest mistake was to go home and pick up the phone.

I should leave well enough alone. Even before I telephone the school, I know what the answer will be. "I'm sorry; there is no one here by that name." I don't ask the person on the other end of the line to go back over the files; because I know that they will not find anything no matter how many times they check.

So, there it is. I am perplexed by it all because I don't understand and the more I dig, the sadder I get. I can't help but wonder if I am going insane because I know that what I have come to believe, is impossible; yet I believe it to be true and that really frightens me. And now as I try to decipher it all I admit it is indeed terrifying, but the fact that my fears are undefined, that I do not know what I fear, make it all the worse. I admit to myself that nothing is scarier whether sleeping or awake than even a remote belief in the unknown.

Yet there is something more to it, this feeling I experience when leaving the doctor's office with the thoughts of Michael heightened is one of despondency. He is gone to where I do not know and as far as I know, no one can help me find him. There is nowhere I can even look for him.

I'm back to dragging myself out of bed each day and moping around the house feeling sorry for myself, but Mildred won't allow it to go on for long. She begins to spend more time in any room I choose to occupy. She chats away about her family and any bit of gossip she has heard. Though I want to be left to grief, I think she knows I cannot be rude to her so she continues to spark some life into my body. At first, I sit and drift off to a private place while she talks, but then after some time I start to listen and react to what she is saying.

Mildred continues to find time each day to spend with me. She not only suggests that I go for a walk, she joins me. When you're in a funk it is likely that your heart is in a fragile state and some extra attention helps. Mildred just opens her heart and extends her love by helping me look at the goodness in my life.

It doesn't happen overnight but eventually I begin to feel better. It is exactly what I need to pull me out of this depression and I have Mildred to thank for that.

"I don't know if you did this intentionally .... yes, I do," I laugh, "You did this intentionally and I appreciate it. Thank you, Mildred, for being you."

Mildred only smiles.

I go back to work; and there, before my easel again, I get a sense of who I am and what I am about. I begin to feel capable and worthy and little by little the sense of being helpless moves away, but the sense of loneliness remains.

Given the chance my work takes over my body and soul as I exert myself diligently on the second figurine of long stem calla lilies done in bronze for the Mathews. I call and set up an appointment to deliver the finished product, enjoying the ride out to their estate, but anxious to get back home as I have a backlog of projects to do.

Birds are not my thing, but like any artist the opportunity to do something different is always appealing so I take a commission to create a figurine of three white seagulls flying above a crag for a new client. I work diligently on the piece, even calling Mildred in at one point to get her opinion, which, as usual is very uplifting. I know she has a good eye and appreciates art, but I also know that some of her appreciation is because she also likes me.

It takes weeks to complete and get it just so. I stand back to admire the finished product. Only something is missing. I am not fully satisfied with the results. I walk around the figurine to view it from all angles, trying to pinpoint what is missing and then it comes to me.

Soon I am back at work carefully molding a couple of seashells within the crevices of the crag below the seagulls. With that addition, it now makes sense.

I call the client and set up an appointment for the next day to deliver their commission and that extra effort pays off. They are so happy with it that they give me a second commission.

Finally, it is time to work on the sculpture for the Masterson's. As I pull out my sketches I try not to think about the boy, but from the eyes of the Masterson's exactly what will appeal to them. In our discussions, the sketch they picked for a bronze sculpture was of a young man, perched on the top of a hill. He was to look thoughtful and serene and be placed in a time that was the present, but seemed to reflect the past, just like the sketches I did earlier. To most this may seem impossible, but for me it would come naturally. I work night and day on it.

The weather is moving ahead to the next season, but I at first am too involved to notice. With the coming of spring, the ice begins to melt from Lake Ontario heralding change while the sand moves freely on the shore and the buds begin to appear on the trees. Overhead the wild geese fly, freely giving the sensation that all is right with the world. Inspired by the arrival of good weather, I watch the graceful solitary seagull circling overhead and can feel the throb of universal life renewed and it inspires me even more.

That reminds me of one of my sessions with Dr. Paulson when we discussed my mood. He had said, most people experience a change in their mood and behavior with the change of the season. These seasonal changes, especially the "winter blues," or "February blahs, "at the onset of winter, may be a nuisance to some but real problematic for many others.

I had asked him if he thought I would see things

differently later and he had said that the seasons can cause changes not only in mood, but also in the energy level, sleeping, eating, social and sexual behavior. Winter with its darkness, cold, denuded trees, unfriendly winds, and lonely confinement, can cause depressed moods and other symptoms of depression. So, for those reasons, yes, he felt I would see things differently.

There may be some truth in what he says, but it doesn't account for my feeling of loneliness that is so painful I can feel it in the pressure behind my eyes and the heaviness in my chest. It doesn't get better; especially now as I finish the Masterson's sculpture.

Sure, it is a young man perched on a hill to the Masterson's but no matter how I try, I see it as Michael. I have created it from the drawings of Michael and it is the only three-dimensional image of him that I have. I admit to myself that is why I delay taking the finished sculpture to Mr. Masterson at once. I cannot bring myself to separate from it. I know that even while I am back to working I still am waiting for him to return.

One-day Mildred enters the studio and finds me talking to the sculpture of Michael. I don't have a clue as to what I was saying. She comes quietly up behind me, with a feather duster in her hand, and stands looking over my shoulder. "Well," she said; "well."

Aware of her presence I am startled at first, then I am overcome with embarrassment. Until that moment, I hadn't realized I had been talking out loud and wonder how many other times I have been conversing with the sculpture. In any case I now am disturbed at being found out and am about to make some lame excuse. But then I stop.

I am an artist, and most people will agree that creative people are apt to engage in odd activities. So, I have been talking out loud to myself; it is true though maybe

Mildred finds it quite natural for a woman like myself. I turn slowly around.

"Hello Mildred. Can I help you with something?"

"No, no Ms. Bouchard. I was just passing your studio door when I heard you talking. I thought maybe you were talking to me."

"Oh! Ms. Bouchard that's a beautiful sculpture," she says, seeing it for the first time. Though she has the run of the house, when I am working on a piece, it is usually draped until it is finished and Mildred is not one to snoop. She knows that if she wants to see one of my pieces, all she need do is ask. Now as she takes the image of Michael in, I watch her.

"Thank you, Mildred. Mildred?" "Yes Ms. Bouchard."

"So, what do you think. Is it a good replication," I ask?

Mildred, still in awe at the details of the sculpture says, "Yes, I think it is more like him than himself. It is magnificent."

Now, in my head I feel confident that Mildred knows who this is and so I walk across the room and uncover the finished portrait, step aside and let Mildred see. "The portrait is wonderful, too. It's so lifelike," she says.

I turn and uncharacteristically, give her a hug. "Thank you, Mildred that means a lot, to me."

Mildred is quiet, staring at the portrait, then says, "Excuse me for saying it Ms. Bouchard, but you have been working much too hard. I think a vacation away from here would do you a world of good. I hope you don't mind me saying this, but you look tired."

"You know Mildred, I think you are right. What I should do is take me a nice relaxing vacation and have a little fun. Yes, that is exactly what I should do."

I am seriously contemplating getting away, but before I have time to decide where I should go, I halt in dismay. For I realize that I can't leave. This studio is where he came to sit for his portrait and the kitchen was where he had joined me for lunch. He had told me that he loved to come back to this house. I can't leave. It is full of memories of him and I want to feel those memories around me. And besides, if I left for long, how would he ever find me again?

Mildred moves to the door, "you think about it. You can always leave me in charge of the house if you've a mind to," she says.

She closes the door gently behind her, and I turn slowly back into the room again. I must stay; I must tell Mildred that though I think her idea is a good one, I feel that I must stay and work. I go over to the sculpture of Michael and cover it back up with the sheet. I didn't want to look at it now as it just makes me sad.

Only that isn't enough, as I find myself thinking about very little else. All this happens in April and it is late May before I see him again. At least, I know now that I saw him; though at the time I wasn't sure. It was only for a moment; and I never got up close to him or talked with him.

The Memorial Art Gallery has an exhibition of Ramon Santiago's paintings, which is to be the biggest art exhibit of the year. Along with the Santiago paintings, several prominent local artists have provided paintings that will be for sale at the end of the exhibition. I am among them. For the opening of the exhibit, a black-tie affair was held with the artists, their guest and prominent dignitaries. After the gala, the following afternoon the exhibit was open to the public.

I enjoy spending time at the Museum to look at the paintings, see what other artists were presenting and envisioning their interpretations of what was being seen by the naked eye. Just as enjoyable was watching the visitors who moved along the halls, stopping now and then when a picture catches their eye. There are those who I sense have an eye for artistic viewing and others who haven't a clue. Both are equally entertaining to watch as I make my way through the exhibit.

The experience of seeing a work of art is subjective -- art exists to express an idea or emotion of the artist, and it elicits a personal reaction from each viewer. But a description of a visual work of art is most useful when it reaches beyond the purely personal to evoke a sense of the artwork for the reader.

The exhibit of Ramon Santiago is wonderful. Ramon was an American visual artist who was born in Rochester in 1943 and died in 2001. His works earned him international acclaim and an indisputable place in Rochester's art lexicon I watch as fans of Santiago recognize the look of some pieces, but not others. Clowns, portraits of women and human-animal subjects were hallmarks of his work. So, the still life of flowers is a rare departure. His art and figurative style, whether playful or serene, told dynamic stories. As I join others at the exhibit I can sense the whimsical element of his paintings.

I move on to view the Batiste Madalena exhibit and recall his story of being hired by the Eastman Theater in Rochester to create posters for display in its windows. Which he did, making them vibrant and alive as they captured the essence of a movie with a minimum of clutter. Only a few remain as many were tossed out. One of his greatest works was of the "Sermon of the Mount" a large painting done on the wall of the Irondequoit United Church of Christ and which still remains. At the exhibit, there is a picture of this painting for viewing.

I continue to enter the room where artist like myself

have added paintings and sculptures. There are framed miniatures, a wall-size paper collage, a two-story rearing wire stallion displayed in a grand atrium, sculpture of all types from many different artists include glazed, raku-fired, copper wire, fine porcelain, red clay, soapstone, alabaster, zebra wood and others of a mix of materials. The colors are muted for some and others are vivid.

I pause in front of Artist Nadine Winters Drawings and Prints, of landscapes of astonishing originality. It is true that no two artists viewing the same landscape will make the same drawing. There is always something unique in how they see it and then portray it.

I am impressed by the sculpture of a lute player done by one of the artists. He sits solemnly playing the lute, captured in bronze, but with so much feeling one can actually sense his playing.

Another artist has a portrait of a man seated cross-legged in a red lacquered chair with his shoes placed on a footrest. It draws my eye as the man is dressed in clothing that is similar to that of Michael when I first saw him.

As the day wears on I start seeing 'sold' notices appearing next to some of the art of local exhibitors and see it as a sign that I can respectfully prepare to leave. I work my way over to the area assigned for my charcoal sketches and pause, surprised. Several of these sketches have 'sold' signs on them. It had been a whim, my featuring the sketches created for replication of statues and the figurines. Normally I would have prepared paintings and if time allowed, a few sculptures. This I had expressed to the curator when I was approached, but he insisted that whatever I had he would like to include.

So, I had planned to do some paintings but time got away from me. Then I remembered a conversation I had with Annie.

"Taylor, these are just great and you keep them in the

closet?" Annie had said.

"They're sketches, Annie, just something to work from," I had responded.

"Well," Annie said, "they are too good to be sitting around collecting dust. They should be hanging on someone's wall for their enjoyment. That's what I think."

When we had the conversation, I hadn't thought too much of it. But later I did. I had been meaning to clean out the closets in the studio because they were becoming quite full, and when I happened upon the sketches I remembered what Annie had said. Now, it appears she was quite right.

After wandering around a bit and chatting with some of the artists, I worked my way back to the office at the rear of the gallery to collect for the sales.

"Ms. Bouchard." I was greeted by the office manager. "I can't tell you how much admiration has been coming your way for those wonderful sketches.

"Well thank you," I was getting quite a collection and couldn't think of what to do with them, so, here they are."

"Here they are indeed. But here they will not stay. I believe that we have a check for you. Wait right here."

While I waited Mr. Bachman, a Curator at the museum, entered the room. "Well hello Ms. Bouchard."

"Hello Mr. Bachman."

"I guess you've heard what a success those charcoals have made. Why haven't you showed them before?"

"Well, I didn't think of it till now. I usually make several each time I begin a sculpture or figurine. They help me to identify with the piece and are shown to the client to make a choice of what they would want. After that I usually just file them away."

"Well, I hope you aren't planning on 'just filing them away' in the future. I know how busy you are with the sculptures, but many customers have expressed an interest in these charcoals and I don't think it is just because of who did them. I think they really, really like them."

"That makes me feel good and maybe I will show them again at a future exhibit."

"Great. Ms. Bouchard, I was suggesting that you consider having your own exhibition here. Not of just your sketches, but your sculptures as well. I think that a lot of people would love to see your work in one location. I know that you create your sculptures and paintings for clients, but I know artists and so I know that you do some work for your own pleasure. These are the pieces you should share."

"I don't know, Mr. Bachman. It does sound interesting, but I have so much work I don't want to find myself in the position of saying, no to anyone." Seeing the disappointed look on his face, I add. "Tell you what Mr. Bachman. If you would like, we can discuss this further."

"Thank you, Ms. Bouchard, that is all I can ask. You have a wonderful day, won't you?"

"Yes, I will and you too Mr. Bachman."

The office manager handed me an envelope. "Here you are Ms. Bouchard. You will find the monies inside are for all the charcoals you supplied. Even though we have not sold them all, Mr. Bachman wants to display them and feels certain he can sell them, if you don't mind, that is."

How could I say no. As I left the office I couldn't help smiling and shaking my head. To me these charcoals were sketches, but to the customers and the museum they were very good charcoals. In fact, they were being looked upon as great pieces of art and were now in demand. I think at that moment I began to seriously think about doing more charcoals and paintings again.

The gallery was nearly empty by the time I returned. A few people were still standing in front of Santiago's

"Beauty and the Beast," but otherwise the big room was deserted. I decided to go over to look at the sketches and see how many remained to be sold.

Like all galleries, the room itself was only dimly lit; the pictures on the walls having their own personal lighting to reflect on the artists' creations and in so doing made the area itself seem shadowy and vague. I thought I heard someone behind me and I turned around to look, but there was no one there. When I turned around again, my breath caught in my throat and it seemed to me that my heart stopped beating.

There was somebody standing in front of a sprinkling of people by my sketches. As I tried to focus my eyes I move slowly ahead until I can get a better view of him. It is a young man and he is dressed in a uniform such as young men wear at boarding school; a stiff white shirt, and slacks with a sharp crease down the center of his long legs.

I cautiously move closer trying to see around the two individuals that block my view. I curse the darkness of the room as I continue to advance. And then he lifts his head and seems to be looking in my direction and I see his face. My heart pounds furiously as I recognize Michael. I hurry toward him, but my way is blocked. I deftly get around the person in my way and start forward again, but Michael is gone.

I want to cry as I frantically look around the museum, but I cannot see him anywhere. Sadly, I turn around to look behind me and see a couple at the door move aside as though to let someone pass. Perhaps it is Michael, I think and hurry forward.

The couple comes across the floor to me, smiling; but when they see my face, their expression changes. I recognize them. "Good heavens, Ms. Bouchard," the woman cried, "is anything the matter? You look like you've seen a ghost!"

I can only shake my head not trusting myself to say anything out loud. I pass by them without speaking, and stumble out of the door. I can feel them looking after me in bewilderment, but I must leave them as I cannot explain what has happened to me.

Once I am out the museum I take a deep breath and lean back against one of the pillars. When I straighten, I look around but there is no Michael.

Chapter 24

Spring settles in. The snow is gone and the sunshine is just long enough and often enough to dry out the lawns before the rainy winds of early spring arrived. Come, they did and they would not leave, it seemed. We were in a period of muddy yards, muddy puddles on the sidewalks, and muddy skies. There is something to say about the spring, beyond the flowers that manage to push their way into life. The rains make the grass greener and lusher than before and the buds on the tree give birth to new leaves, but the gloom and wetness lowers the spirits.

Thunder and lightning provide the symphony that awakens me most nights and I find myself sitting in the window seat, staring out at the bolts of light as they make a path through the dark sky.

Mildred is very busy these days, arranging for the window cleaners, drive way sealers, lawn care services and all the other needs to get the house and yards readied for the coming season. She is serious about having it all done right, since her theory is that what is not done in the proper fashion, will not be recoverable the following year. Taking care of all these arrangements and chores are jobs that Mildred asked to assume and I happily relinquished it all to her care.

I tend to stay in more, grouping my client visits into one or two trips. I find the rain annoying, especially since I must protect my paintings or sculptors as I try to hold them and an umbrella until I make it to a porch or covered door way. It can be pleasant to walk in the snow, but the rain is a different matter. Yet, I do enjoy the beauty of a thunderstorm with lightening. To the untrained eye, a thunder storm is just so much thunder and lightning, but from an artist point of view it is an elaborate laser show with dramatic sound effects and a downpour of tiny sparkling lights. So oftentimes as I watch the storm I am inspired to create what I see or what I can imagine.

Finally, we move into a time of weather transition when the rain comes less frequently and the clouds are fluffy and white. One day the grass in the yard smells sweet and fresh, and robins sing on the lawn while sea gulls strut on the beach. From then on, the sky is a lighter blue, the grass is green and the illumination from the sun finally provides warmth. We are in the true colors of spring and I begin to enter the start of a new phase of my life by setting up an appointment with Mr. Bachman, the Memorial Art Gallery Curator.

When first approached, about holding my own show at the gallery, I hesitated. I thought it was because I was afraid of work overload, but now I have had time to think and I know it was more about not having personal contact with each owner of my work. I have always met each client and talked to them about their aspirations for the finished project. I liked that. It was like a guarantee my work would be dear to the owner. The longer I thought about it, the more it felt right. If I want my work to be known, I must step out of my comfort zone.

So, when the day arrives I anxiously ready myself. I have taken time to create many charcoals that are new and not representative of a finalized painting or sculpture. Instead they are replicas of what I felt and saw throughout the day. It felt good to have this new-found freedom of expression and I can't wait to tell Annie all about it.

This is what I was missing; this free expression of my heart's desire. Now as I enter the studio I carefully gather up a few samples to take with me. I can't help smiling as I think; I have a collection. I have never had a collection.

I am still smiling when I step into the foyer and see Mildred standing there.

"Good morning Ms. Bouchard, how are you today?"

"Just fine Mildred, and you?"

"Wonderful," she says. "I was wondering how long you plan on being out. I have a noisy day scheduled with cleaners and all."

"I can't say for sure, but go ahead with your plans. I have a meeting and I plan on visiting several clients while I am out and then go over to Captain's Cove for lunch."

"Well that sounds like a full day. I think we can work with that."

I sit my portfolio of drawings down while I get a light jacket from the closet. I make sure the lock is on the door before closing it behind me. It is an amazing day that I step into. The smells, the warmth, the sound of the waves set my spirit free as I climb into my car and immediately open the windows. Finally, I am on my way.

The city streets and parks are teeming with life. People are running and walking along pathways, while others are mowing their lawns sending the sweet aroma of fresh cut grass through my window.

Each neighborhood I enter I see activity as though the world has been born anew. And it has, really, since no longer are we hampered by snow drifts, icy sidewalks or soaking rain. On days like this it is easy to believe summer is coming. I am happy, really happy as I make my way downtown and finally turn on University Avenue, minutes from my destination.

No matter how many times I see this building, it is still mesmerizing. The Museum is part of the University of Rochester and occupies the southern half of the University's former Prince Street campus. The main gallery was Inspired by the Tempio Malatestiano, a famous architecture in Italy and in 1926 an expansion doubled the floor and wall space and added the fountain court as a venue for live music performances. The fountain was designed by Gaston Lachaise and inspired by the Putto with Dolphin of the Palazzo Vecchio. With its success, in 1968 a wing was built to provide more configurable exhibit space. Each change was carefully made to blended seamlessly with the original structure.

The same holds true for the interior. I believe that the work on a building starts with an awareness of the emotional character. Buildings have a character drawn from the associations of their form and the materiality of their fabric. Obviously, one can never predict what someone's reaction to a building will be, but if it feels right to the builder it will usually feel right to those who enter.

Now as I walk down the cool dark halls of the museum I appreciate the architectural design that could give a sense of isolation or dread, but doesn't. To see a hallway in your dream, symbolizes the beginning of a path that you are taking in life or a journey into the unknown and self-exploration which is exactly what I am about to do. I walk on the tile floors hearing my heels penetrating the silence of the area until I arrive at the office door. I pause a moment, then enter the reception area which is charming, but full of modern furnishings, taking away from the history of the building. The office manager comes from behind a counter that tries to hide the computer and telephone on her desk. I smile at her.

"Good Morning."

"Good morning, Ms. Bouchard. Please have a seat and I will tell Mr. Bachman you have arrived."

I watch her as she moves soundlessly across the carpet and enters the door at the back of the room. It is a pleasant area, filled with warmth and beauty and I find it fitting. I watch the door open and behind the office manager I can see Mr. Bachman as he follows behind her. We shake hands and then he leads me to his office. The office manager returns with coffee. "Can I get you anything else?" she asks.

Mr. Bachman looks at me and I shake my head, no.

"Well then, I will leave you to it."

“Ms. Bouchard, I'm sure you are used to the way we set up for a showing. I usually like the sponsored artist to have the main lobby area for their portraits, but because yours will be charcoals, I think that we should use a different approach. The main gallery would appear too gauche to present charcoals. It works best with elaborate paintings with lots of color. Charcoals are subdued and are best presented in the wing. I’m sure you know the area.”

“Yes, I do. I think that will be perfect,” I say.

After going over a few more details, Mr. Bachman says, “Well, shall we go take a look?”

“Yes, let’s.”

I stand and watch Mr. Bachman as he steps from behind his desk. He walks over in front of me and opens the office door. I step through and soon we are on our way. We walk slowly to the display area, giving me a chance to admire the paintings and sculptors along the way until we are at the designated area.

Here the walls are covered with amber paint adding a false sense of sunlight without the reflection. There is personal lighting for each mounting area and spotlights on the wall directly across from the display area. I walk along the length of the room to get a view from all angles.

"I think this will be perfect, Mr. Bachman. You are right. It will work best for the charcoals."

"I thought you would like it, but I wanted to show it to you first and allow you to visualize the effect. I'm glad you agree. There is another suggestion ... if I may."

"Sure, what is it?"

"Well, if you have at least one painting that would work in the main display area and a few sculptures that we could display, well it just provides such an impressive introduction if the artist has a display in the main lobby too."

I pause for a moment, thinking. "I guess I can do

that. I have some paintings and sculptures we can use that I think will be appealing. Yes, let's do that."

I try to imagine the approach that Mr. Bachman suggests and as we move to the front area again, I envision the display that might serve the purpose.

"Do you have something, ah, a masterpiece; a unique or special attraction."

I hesitate, not wanting to share Michael, but then, I know it is perfect. "Yes, I believe I have something. It's a portrait of a young man that I consider my best work."

We start back toward the office and Mr. Bachman goes over a few more details with me concerning the delivery, framing and storage of the items for the exhibit. I show him the charcoals and paintings that I have brought with me.

"Exactly what I hoped. These are marvelous Ms. Bouchard and once they are framed we can expect to draw a tremendous number of potential buyers and art critics."

We talk a little more, then set a date for the exhibit and the length of time for the display. As he walks me to the entrance we settle on a second meeting date before I am on my way.

The traffic is light as I make my way to the home of my client, the Sullivan's. Elise and Paul Sullivan live in the Webster area, located approximately ,10 miles east of the city and like my home, the Sullivan residence is located along the shoreline of Lake Ontario. Their home sits amongst the rolling hills and, lakeshore meadows offering a spectacular view. It is in this area they have asked me to design a fountain to fit into the garden. I am anxious to show them the ideas I have come up with for their fountain.

They are out of doors when I pull up their long driveway and seem to be discussing something about the garden where they are standing, since Elise keeps pointing down in front of them. They are so engaged in the discussion that they do not know I am here until I almost stand behind them. It is Paul who is first aware of my presence and turns around quickly.

"Oh, Ms. Bouchard you gave me quite a scare. I didn't hear you drive up."

"Sorry. I didn't mean to sneak up on you,"

"Oh well, look at this will you. My wife insists on planting tulips and each year the deer come and eat them. For days, she frets because there are no buds on the stems, I guess hoping that the deer will tire of them and allow her to at least have a few hours to absorb their beauty."

"Paul, stop making fun of me. Ms. Bouchard, do come up on the porch. It is turning into a lovely day so I think we will sit outside and talk. Do you mind?"

Looking around me, I reply, "I would like nothing better. It seems to get more beautiful each time I come out here. You must really enjoy your home.

"Yes, we do, Ms. Bouchard, indeed we do," adds Paul. "But your area is also charming. Aren't you situated on Lakeshore Blvd; right on the lake?"

"You have such a great memory, Mr. Sullivan. Yes, I am."

I looked over at Mrs. Sullivan and can tell that she is anxious to get started. So, I stand up, turn around for permission, and getting it, place my portfolio on the wicker table. I unzip the edges and lay the three sketches out so that they can be viewed.

Mr. and Mrs. Sullivan come over and look closely at the designs, shuffling the sketches between them; their acceptance clearly written on their faces.

"Oh, Ms. Bouchard, these are lovely. Aren't they Paul."

"They really are. I don't know which I like better."

Paul looks up and asks, "Ms. Bouchard, you are going to have to help us make the choice. Which would you pick?"

I move across the porch and stand between them.

"Well, they will all look great, but then most anything would in this picturesque location, yet I lean toward the Angel because I know that when you drive up to the house and move slightly beyond the porch, you see the rise in the background where the fountain will stand. I can see the angel with her wings outspread appearing as though she beckons the visitors. I just think that would leave a good feeling with all who pull up to your home."

"Oh, Ms. Bouchard, that sounds so lovely. I can't wait to see how it looks. That's what I want Paul. I think Ms. Bouchard is right. The angel with the outspread wings would be ever so clever."

"Okay, Ms. Bouchard, you heard the boss. It will be the angel then. We sit for a while longer and finally I bid them goodbye. It is now after one o'clock so I decide to go to the Captain's Cove for a bite to eat and then on my way home, stop at the last client's house.

Leaving the Sullivans I start feeling different. I no longer am impressed by the weather as my attention is drawn to Michael. His portrait is my best work and so it must be the choice for the main gallery. I know that, but just thinking about him for a minute fills my heart and soul. I try my best to quiet my thoughts and by the time, I arrive at the Cove I feel I have succeeded.

The parking lot is almost empty. Most of the afternoon crowd has already departed and I will have the place almost to myself. I walk into the dimly lit foyer of the restaurant and look around while I wait for the hostess who seems to be busy elsewhere. There is a sprinkling of customers at tables and a few more over at the bar. As I look over at the bar, I recognize one to be my friend, Samuel so I walk over and tap him lightly on the shoulder.

"Hi Samuel," I say.

"Well hi, Taylor. It's been a while since you were in here."

"Yes, it has." I have a great idea. "Samuel, if you haven't eaten yet, would you like to join me in the dining room?"

"You know, I haven't eaten. Sure, I'd love to join you."

Together we walk over to the front of the restaurant and soon the waitress shows up to take us to a table. Once we sit down, we begin chatting about non-consequential things, both avoiding the subject of Michael until Samuel is talking about distances and it triggers me to say, "There is one thing about distance: that no matter how far away it is, it can be reached. It is over there, and one can drive to it. Distance always has a location such as it is north, among the pines, or east to the lake. It is never yesterday, or tomorrow. That is another, and a merciless distance where there is no way to get there."

As soon as I can control my tongue, I apologize. My voice is harsh and accusing, as if it is Samuel's fault he has not been able to find Michael.

Samuel looks at me with a worried expression, not knowing what to say. Finally, he finds his tongue.

"Taylor, please stop this."

It is like a dam has opened and there is no controlling my thoughts so even if I wanted to, I cannot. "I find that my memory has grown sharper; or else it is beginning to play tricks on me. It is not so much that I began to live in the past, as that the past began to take on more clarity, the actual form of the present, and to intrude itself into my thoughts. The present, on the contrary, seems to grow a little hazy at times, to begin to slip away from me if I don't check it so many things remind me of him. And then I will be detained by memory so urgent that what I remember seems almost more real to me than what is before me."

"Taylor," Samuel whispers, "you have got to snap out of it."

But I don't hear him. "Too much, *too* much to trigger the memory," I continued. "At nightfall, the voices of children, floating in through my mind, brings back to me another evening, on the boardwalk, and a child walking, saying, 'Do you *know the song I like best?'* Or on a sunny morning, beside the lake I'll suddenly find myself entranced and motionless, seeing in front of me not the blue water, but the white, shining ice and the skaters, feeling the cold wind on my cheeks again, and Michael's arm in mine, so firm and light. ... Or coming home in the afternoon, I'll hurry to the study with a beating heart, because he might be there-remembering so clearly the first time he came to see me, and then hearing him say, *'I thought maybe you wanted* me *to* come."

I can barely feel the tears as they flow down my cheeks freely. "Now Taylor, that's enough. Stop it right now or you will make yourself sick."

"I don't want very much, Samuel, or hope for very much-just to see him again, and to be with him once more. I try not to think about the future at all; how can I? Why we met, or how it had come about, I do not know. I believe that we were meant to be together and that the strands of his life are woven in with mine."

The waiter comes to the table and for a brief instance I think of something other than Michael as I order lunch.

"Samuel, what is it that makes a man and a woman know that they belong to each other? Is it chance and meeting? Or is it something deeper and stranger, something beyond meeting, something beyond chance and fortune?"

"I can't answer that Taylor. No one knows the answer."

"Well, what I think is that there are others, in other times of the world, whom we can love and who love us. I think that there is one soul among all others through endless generations who is the one that we must love and that love will never die."

"Taylor, you are talking crazy. This is a child you told me; a mere child."

"I know, Samuel, but..."

“Enough, Taylor.”

The way Samuel utters those words makes me stop talking and silence takes its place.

After that lunch, Samuel is scared for his friend Taylor. He can think of nothing to do to help her. He knows she is seeing a psychiatrist and that doesn’t seem to be helping much either. Now, as he thinks about Taylor's discussion he wonders if it is proper that he call the doctor and tell him about the conversation. Samuel is facing a dilemma and afraid of the consequences he decides not to make the call; at least not right now.

I have been putting it off so long that I begin to feel it is a part of me that I cannot let go. By May I reluctantly take the sculpture to Mr. Masterson, hating to give it up, but there is no help for it. Mr. Masterson doesn't say anything for a long while as he stares at the sculpture. At first, I think that he is disappointed, and my heart sinks, then quickly it is uplifted because if he doesn’t like it the sculpture will be mine; but then I see that he is very much moved.

He has grown a little pale; his eyes first widened, and then narrow; and he keeps stroking the palm of one hand with the fingers of the other. "Well," he says. "Well.

As much as I want the sculpture, I begin to feel elated by the effect it has on my client. Up till now, I doubt if I have really looked at the sculpture myself with any sort of critical eye. There, in my studio, it has been so much a part of me; because it really is. But here, in the spot where it is supposed to be, seeing it as Mr. Masterson is seeing it now, I can realize for the first time what I have created and I am proud. I am proud and at the same time humble.

After a while Mrs. Masterson comes in and joins us. She doesn’t say anything for a minute; and then she takes a long breath. "Well, Ms. Bouchard," she says in a strangely gentle voice, "that's it, all right."

Mr. Masterson clears his throat. "Yes," he says, "that's it. That’s what I meant. It's ... it's " He seemed unable to continue.

"I understand sir, I am so glad you are pleased and I hope it brings you as much joy as it did me to create it."

I must get out of there as quickly as possible or I think I will cry. I finish my business with the Masterson’s and leave with my heart empty and having to depress a desire to take the sculpture back, offer to do another, anything but let it go. But I know that would not be right and that the Masterson’s are the true owners now. As I drive down the road I keep telling myself it is not Michael, it is just a sculpture.

At the Masterson’s they continue to stare at the sculptor long after Taylor has left. Neither one wants to be the first to say what they are thinking. The features on this sculptor are those of Peter Newman’s son. He is older, but there is no doubt about it.

Chapter 25

It is in the bright spring sunshine, that Michael comes back to me. I have tried not to think about him or my feelings for him but I cannot help myself. I have come to terms with the fact that the emotions I have go far beyond that of a woman to a little boy. But this is not your average little boy, I tell myself. Nor is he still a little boy. I am beginning to believe that when Michael asked me to wait for him, he knew he would be aging quickly and able to catch up to me. Yet, still, I wonder about my feelings.

That day as he stands at my doorstep, I have not seen him come up the walk. It is when the doorbell rings and I peek out the side door window that I see him. I pause and stare at him through the window, his back to me as he faces the lake and this gives me time to familiarize myself with this Michael.

I judge him to be over six feet tall now. Slim of frame, but not fragile as his body fills out the brown tweed suit appealingly. His hair has a slight curl, but is far darker than I remember. I notice too that he is carrying what appears to be a briefcase or maybe it's a small suitcase.

At that moment, the man slowly turns and I catch the slight movement of his chin in silhouette. He's aware he is being watched. It may have been but a minute more that I peer at him, until seeing his dark brown eyes rest on my face. As I stare mesmerized his face illuminates with joy and I see the features of Michael clearly in this older version of him.

My hand goes to the door handle and I pull it open and I watch as Michael steps quickly into the foyer, moving forward until there is no space between us as he gathers me in his arms and kisses me soundly on the lips and it seems the most natural thing in the world for him to do.

He releases me and holds me out at arm's length, looking at me as I look back at him, smiling with neither of us saying a word. I cannot speak as I drink in all that is Michael. He has even managed to bring the sunny, sweet-smelling spring morning in with him.

His brown eyes never faltered as they searched my face as though studying every feature. Finally, I take a deep breath and say, "Michael, I've missed you."

"I know," he responds. "I've missed you, too." He drew back slightly and continues, "And it's been longer for me, much longer. I'm not in school anymore," he says.

This did not surprise me in the least. "I know," I said. "I know that." I lead Michael into the studio and watch as he turns slowly on his heels, and looks around the room with unpretentious joy. "How I've dreamed of this, Taylor," he says; "I can't tell you how many nights I've lain awake, thinking of this room

Again, I hear myself reply, "I know.".

"Do you?" he answers gently. " You can't know how it feels to be away ...," He pauses with a faraway expression on his face. "You only know how it can feel to be here and without me, but you are still here ... "The turn in his manner scares me and I am glad, though I do not know why, that he stopped before completing his thought.

"Michael, I have so much to tell you and show you, but I need to get it all sorted out in some order so I don't forget anything."

"Can we have some breakfast first. I'm starving."

"I don't think .... "

"Please Taylor, let's have breakfast."

"But Michael," I said, "if we have so little time ...

"We have a whole long day," he answered breathlessly. "And ..., and a little more."

Hesitantly I say, "Okay, let's go to the kitchen and I will fix us both something to eat."

As I move about the kitchen I feel his eyes on me and somehow, I manage to scramble some eggs, butter some toast and fix us coffee without dropping anything in the process.

“That smells so good, Taylor. I haven't had a good meal since the last time I was here," he adds admiringly.

As I carry the plates over to the island, I can’t help but wonder what Michael meant by us having a whole long day, and a little more. What exactly did a little more; mean?

"I finished the sculpture, Michael and I held on to it as long as I could, but I finally had to take it to its new home."

"Oh, but that's grand," he cries. "That's wonderful, Taylor. Aren’t you happy?"

"Yes, of course, I am," I try to say convincingly.

He is silent for a moment, and I can tell he is thinking about something. "Taylor," he says at last, "let's do something special to celebrate the completion of the sculpture."

"Sure, that sounds like fun. Then afterwards we could ...

He interrupts me, ""Please, Taylor, let’s just let the day take care of itself. Let's just look at it in small pieces so that it won’t go quickly.

"And then?" I asked hopefully.

He hesitates before adding, "I'm going to hurry, and then someday I’ll be as old as you."

"I'm thirty-six, Michael."

He nods his head. "I know that," and so, will I be soon."

"That’s not possible," But even as I say it, in my heart I know it is possible.

"I'm going to hurry, Taylor. I've got to."

While I am busy contemplating, this Michael seems to be lost in thought, his head bent, his eyes hidden under their long lashes. Then he raises his head and sits up with a smile on his face. "Let's go on a picnic, Taylor," he says.

"That is a great idea. Where would you like to go?"

"Somewhere near the lake, but not the beach. Let's go someplace private for the whole day"

It only takes me a moment to decide. There is Durand-Eastman Park that has a long stretch of Lake Ontario waterfront. It is my favorite place for a picnic. There is lush foliage and several small lakes with steep wooded hills that made it ideal for a secluded picnic venture.

"Yes, yes. That's what we'll do and I know the perfect spot."

Michael can hardly wait for me to finish my coffee and after clearing up the dishes and putting them in the sink for Mildred, I get out the picnic basket. Michael comes over to join me at the refrigerator and together we put fruit and cheese into the basket. Michael goes across to the pantry and comes out with crackers.

In the meantime, I have gotten out carrots and celery and we stand at the island cutting the veggies into strips before putting them into baggies and placing them in the basket.

“Wine?”

I look at Michael wonderingly, but then decide he’s probably old enough. “It’s in the wine fridge over there,” I say pointing across the kitchen. I get out the bottle opener, dishes, wine glasses and napkins while Michael surveys the wine cooler and finally makes a choice.

“I think we’re good to go.”

Michael smiles and follows me out the door, and with the picnic basket in hand, we walk over to the car and climb in. We are silent as we drive a few miles to the picnic spot and after parking the car we gather up our picnic basket along with a blanket that I had in the trunk and walk until we find a grassy area amongst the trees. It is isolated though it is near the edge of the Lake. All around us is nature, no picnic tables or grills so it seems private. Michael is anxious to check the area out so we climb a small hill, among some trees and though Michael is flushed and breathless, he is full of gaiety, running ahead of me, being the child, he once was such a short time ago.

I am out of breath trying to keep up with him until he finally slows down and we continue, waking side by side. At noon, we return to our picnic spot and sit together on the blanket in the sun. There are daffodils and some purple flowers growing in the grass and I watch as Michael picks a few to lay on the blanket. I unpack our picnic basket and we eat silently, enjoying just being together. Michael pours us each a glass of wine and we sip it, enjoying the sounds of the birds chirping and seeing the leaves flutter each time a slight breeze blows through the trees. It's magical.

When we can't eat another bite, I decide to see how much he will tell me. I explain to Michael that I asked my friend Samuel to see if he could find him for me, but he couldn't.

"Do you understand why, Taylor?" Michael said quietly.

Though I wasn't sure I understood, I said, "Yes, Michael, I do.

There is so much in his eyes that is left out of the words he speaks and again I hesitate to push for more. Silence falls between us, but it is a comfortable silence. The warmth of the sun and the wine makes me feel drowsy as I watch Michael pick up one of the purple flowers and hold it up to his nose inhaling the fresh fragrance. He then stares up at the sky above the trees as if seeing it for the first time. I am happy-happier than I have ever been before and unknown to me then, happier than I'll ever be again.

Michael rest his head on my stomach as I recline on the blanket. "What are you thinking, Michael? " I ask.

He answers slowly and gently, "I'm thinking how beautiful the world is, Taylor; and how it keeps on being beautiful-no matter what happens to us today or tomorrow."

"Tomorrow," I said. "But when is tomorrow, Michael?"

"Does it matter?"

"Yes, I think it does, at least it does to me."

"Well, then tomorrow is always. Today was tomorrow once and tomorrow will be today soon."

I understand what he means and grow silent, not sure what to say.

"Feel like a walk along the Lake, sleepy head," I ask. Michael turns to me and plants a kiss on my forehead

"Yes, lets walk for a bit."

We explore the woods and find a little brook with violets hidden among the ferns at the bank. I pick a few and made a tiny bouquet to take home. "This is to remember today," I say.

We continue walking until we find ourselves at the edge of the Lake. There we stand looking out in the distance. I feel a sense of nervousness about him and I wonder. He manages to shake it off and ask, "What is it, Michael?"

"It's nothing."

I have a story to tell you if you want to hear it.

"Sure, tell me."

"Well, do you know the story of the lady in the lake?"

I can tell by his expression he does not.

"There is a legend of a White Lady that exists in Durand Eastman Park. Some say the story was created to scare teens who come here seeking privacy, but in any case, the story is that the white lady was very protective of her daughter. She often warned her to never go near any men, telling her that they were hostile. Some say that her daughter followed her mother's wishes, and others say that she would sneak out to see boys in the night. On one of these nights, the daughter told her mother that she was going out for a walk along the shore, and would be back soon. When her daughter never returned, the woman was positive that her daughter had been raped or murdered. Every evening the neighbors would see her walking along the shores of the beach, calling her daughter's name. Other times they would see her walking in the forest with her German Shepard, looking for where her daughter was buried. The mother was always in a white dress. She grew so grief-stricken that she threw herself over a cliff into Lake Ontario, committing suicide. After that people would say that on foggy nights, or nights of the full moon, you can see her misty form looking for her daughter, with her German Shepard by her side. They also say that she takes a certain disliking to men, especially those who are hurtful towards woman. Some say that she even rattles their cars, and chases them toward the lake, but never harms the woman accompanying them."

Michael doesn't say anything as he continues to stare out across the water. I shiver as the air has cooled.

"Are you cold Taylor?" Michael asked.

"Just a little."

I feel Michael's arm go around my shoulders and he pulls me over closer to him, while he continues to look out beyond us. The sun begins to sink in the west, the sky ablaze with color and then the shadows fall around us as the air continues to grow chilly.

"I think we should think about going now," I said regretfully.

Michael nods and we start the walk back. Together we pick up the remains of our picnic and carry them to the car and soon we are on our way back home.

Chapter 26

The session is over.

"Taylor, so I have to ask you a question now."

I sit up and wait for Dr. Paulson to speak.

"First, how do you feel."

I think a minute. "I feel relaxed. I always feel better after telling you about Michael. I need to get it out and once I do I sometimes feel sad later, but eventually better."

"That is a signal that you are getting better. You are finally able to accept what has happened to you and not try and punish yourself. I think you know that all of this is a dream developed from your loneliness.

I couldn't believe what he had said to me. A dream! Hadn't I just told him there were two people who had seen Michael too. "It can't be a dream, doctor."

"Why not Taylor. It surely can't be real."

"But, Mildred saw him and so did Samuel. They both saw him. How do you explain that?"

Dr. Paulson hesitates for a moment before explaining what his theory is. "Taylor, it may be true that you think both Mildred and Samuel saw Michael or they said they saw Michael."

"I'm not sure I follow what you're saying," I said puzzled. "I need you to explain."

Not covering it up, I know he senses my frustration and finally says, "Okay, let's move over to my desk and I will attempt to explain to you what some of the possible reasons may be."

Dr. Paulson leads the way and I follow him across the room. When we are at his desk, he moves behind it to take a seat while I sit in the chair on the other side. He reaches down and I can hear papers being pushed about and then he raises his hands and lays several folders on his desk. I can only sit and wait.

Finally, Dr. Paulson speaks. "Taylor, we are dealing with hallucinations, or illusions. I am not sure which."

"Explain," please doctor.

"Well, hallucinations are false sense perceptions which can involve any or all of the senses. Hallucinating resembles true perceptions but do not correlate with actual external stimuli. They occur in schizophrenia, are common in functional and some organic psychoses and may appear in acute alcoholism and other forms of drug abuse. The main thing is that hallucinations are false sensory experiences. Most schizophrenic hallucinations are auditory, but some are visual or olfactory."

“I’m sorry, doctor, I am not schizophrenic, nor do I take drugs or drink to excess.”

“I know that Taylor.”

“So, what do you mean by illusions.”

"Think of illusions as comprising painting techniques whereby forms painted on flat planes are made to appear three-dimensional and to exist in deep space. The grapes in paintings have been said to seem so real that birds would peck at them. Illusions are no more than a method of fooling the eye. Illusions are systematic, characteristic errors in perception. They are discrepancies between the appearance of some measurable aspect of the world.”

Seeing my confusion, he continues. “Such as the size, distance, location, or shape of a visible object and the corresponding physical measures."

"But you are talking about something that is without motion."

"Illusions are also possible in the perception of movement, notably in the case of apparent movement, known as the phi phenomenon. In the phi phenomenon, successive stationary views of an object, even though they are in a different place in each view, are perceived as smooth, continuous motion."

"So, what you are saying is that I am seeing things and somehow I may have created the illusion for my friends?"

"I'm not sure Taylor. I can only say that most emotional disorders are the result of irrational beliefs or distorted perceptions of life events. Cognition is the filter through which people interpret experience and by which emotional reactions and behavior are determined. I will attempt to make you aware of the occurrence and irrationality of these distortions and to substitute more rational and realistic evaluations. I will help you become aware of your unrealistic assumptions and help you challenge them and then you guide the way to the cure."

"But Mildred saw him on one occasion and then Samuel saw him at another. How can that be?"

"We will try and find out Taylor, but you must be patient so that we find the real cause. It could be a group hallucination which I can't explain why, but has been known to happen."

"But I am not talking about a group," I cried out in frustration.

"Taylor, when there is more than one person participating in any given thing, it is a group."

"Oh," I said quietly.

"I am not trying to be evasive about this, Taylor, it is just that I think you are ready to explore why you think this is happening."

Dr. Paulson had played this discussion over and over

in his head, wondering if he should tell her what he had learned from a visit with a physic and talking with his friends who had somehow added credence to the impossible. He had thought better of it. There had to be a logical reason and until he found out what it was, it would be best to remain silent. He knows that Taylor is upset by his explanations of her phenomenon but he needs to prepare her to begin considering that this is some kind of illusion. It is his job as a psychiatrist to not fall into the illusions of his clients, but to use his training to guide them back to reality.

Chapter 27

As I leave Dr. Paulson's office that day, I know that I will not return. At first it had been comforting to tell Dr. Paulson all about Michael and how I felt when I was with him and when I was apart from him. I even hoped that the doctor would eventually be able to explain the aging process that seemed to be taking place, but now I realize that would never be.

I can't blame Dr. Paulson. If someone had come to me and shared such an incredible story, I would have my doubts about their sanity. Only, Dr. Paulson is a psychiatrist and incredible experiences are his forte. I guess I could have gone on with the sessions and accepted his inability to explain what was happening to me, but not now. I cannot listen to someone who believes that my seeing and believing in Michael's existence has implanted his image in the minds of not only myself, but in Mildred and Samuel. That on separate occasions when I have been with one of them, Michael has appeared to me and I have somehow incorporated my friend in a group hallucination. That, I cannot accept.

The next two weeks I speak to only Mildred. I work, refuse any calls or visitors in keeping to myself, for what purpose I can't explain. Mildred, being Mildred tries to encourage me.

"But Ms. Bouchard, what shall I say if they ask where you've gone or when you will be back?"

I think about that for a moment and then reply. "Tell anyone who asks that I did not give you that information."

Seeing she is not going to change my mind, Mildred says, "Very well, Ms. Bouchard, as you wish."

It is easy in a house the size of mine to keep to myself. After several attempts to cajole me into conversation, Mildred gives up, but makes it perfectly clear that she will call the doctor if she finds the food she left, uneaten. And so, I spend most of each day on the third floor of the house.

I watch television, read the paper, sort the mail, and listen to the radio. I manage to eat most of the meals that Mildred leaves, and those that I cannot eat, I send down the garbage disposal which will keep my lack of appetite secret. It is during this period that I come to terms with what I need to do. By the end of the second week I am feeling much better and that is when I receive an interesting correspondence.

The first letter began; "My Dear Ms. Bouchard. I am writing to remind you that your exhibit at the Memorial Art Gallery will be held on August 30, and that your presence will be important to the success of the show." The letter went on to say that he, Mr. Bachman had tried to reach me several times without success, and he wanted me to stop by to approve the layout and outline the prices for the items to be displayed. He also stated that he assumed that the Portrait of Michael was still to be considered unavailable for sale.

I have forgotten the discussion with Mr. Bachman and the agreement to hold a show. It wasn't like me at all to forget important engagements that concerned my work. But, this time I have. After reading the letter I pick up the phone and placed a call to Mr. Bachman.

After speaking briefly with his office manager, I am put through to his office.

"Ms. Bouchard. I was beginning to worry about you."

"No need, Mr. Bachman, I had some pressing business to attend to and now everything is back to normal. So, tell me, when will it be convenient for me to stop by?"

"Any time, Ms. Bouchard, today even if you are free.

I will make myself available when it is convenient for you. I only ask that you try and make it as soon as you can. The final arrangements need to be settled quickly since the show is only a few weeks away."

"I understand totally and I apologize for making you worry. I can be there this afternoon if you like. Say around two?"

"That will be perfectly fine. I will see you at two. When you arrive, just come to the office. We have diagrams drawn of the exhibit layout for your review and any additions or comments you might want to add can be completed right away."

After saying goodbye, I can't help smiling. It is indeed the perfect induction back into my life and it makes me feel good about myself. Just what the doctor would order!

The second letter is wonderful too. It is the first-time Michael has written to me. It is the first time I have seen his handwriting too and I touch the words gently as if afraid they will disappear. I turn the envelope over in my hand and notice there is no postage stamp nor a post office cancellation stamp. But it doesn't matter how the letter arrives, just that it does. I toss the envelope into the trash and read the letter.

The letter tells me about his feelings and nothing more. He ends it by saying "Goodbye, Taylor I'll be back again someday but not like before. Not ever again like before. Not until we can be together always."

I shiver as though a cold wind has entered my room and my hands are clammy, my fingers feel stiff from the cold. Then, as suddenly as the feeling has entered my body, it passes and I am left with the emptiness of knowing I will not see Michael soon. I sit holding the letter and turning it over and over in my hand until finally it dawns on me there is something I can do.

I lean over and dig through the trash can until I find

the envelope that the letter from Michael came in. I flip it over and read the return address. I now know the address of where he is staying and I know the name of the school.

I do a google search and come up with a phone number. I can begin a search on my own to find Michael now. I place the envelope in the draw of my desk in my bedroom and then go about readying myself for my appointment with Mr. Bachman.

"Hello Ms. Bouchard," Mr. Bachman states enthusiastically.

"Hello, Mr. Bachman. I guess I'm a trifle late but something came up and I needed to attend to it. Can we get started?"

Mr. Bachman has no problem with starting right away. The layout of the exhibit is done quite tastefully, and the location and dramatization planned for the display of the Portrait of Michael also meets with my approval. I confirm that the portrait is not for sale and review prices to be attached to the charcoals.

"Did you bring me anymore charcoals, Ms. Bouchard."

I nod my head, smiling to myself as I reach down to pick up my portfolio to display the additions for the exhibit. As I thought, Mr. Bachman is not only very pleased and glad to be able to add them to the show, but has a pleasant shock.

"My god," he exclaims, "these are wonderful!"

"I know we were going to show charcoals as you refer to them, but I thought a little color wouldn't hurt. These are some very early paintings that I did before I decided on sculpturing as my artistic outlet. They've been sitting around the studio for some time and I really have never shown them. I have no place to hang them, but I want them to be appreciated, so ... "

"Say no more, Ms. Bouchard. I will be glad to add another area for the display of these paintings. How many are there?"

"Twenty or so, I would guess."

"Good." Mr. Bachman pauses a moment then looking up replies, "I must move a thing or two, but I really see no problem. I don't know how soon this can be done, so I must call you to come in and see what we arrange."

"No, that won't be necessary. I liked what you did with the exhibit already and any changes I am sure will sit well with me. I leave the layout in your very capable hands."

I could see that I have embarrassed Mr. Bachman, but he quickly recovers. "Ms. Bouchard, I think this will be the best exhibit that this museum has had in some time. The charcoals in the back-exhibit hall will lead to the Portrait in the front lobby with a display of your paintings. Now we need to set names to the charcoals, these paintings and the portrait."

And so, we do. First, we assign a price that would provide an attractive sum for myself and a good percentage for the museum. Once we complete that, we move on to attaching names to the charcoals and the paintings. We are finally left with naming the portrait.

"Ms. Bouchard, do you have the portrait with you?"

"Yes, it is in the van. It will only take a minute for me to get it."

"No, Ms. Bouchard, sit tight." Mr. Bachman reaches for his phone and dials three numbers. I hear him talking briefly and then he hangs up. Soon a gentleman enters the room and addresses me.

"Excuse me, Ms. Bouchard, but if you will be so kind as to give me your keys and the place where you parked, I will bring the portrait."

I hand the gentleman the key and talk with Mr. Bachman until the portrait is delivered. Mr. Bachman then turns to me and says, "May I ... "

"Sure, of course."

I wait while Mr. Bachman lifts the covering, flipping it over to the back of the portrait and stands gazing at my creation.

"I am at a loss for words. This is truly magnificent. It has a modern enough look, but the young man seems to reflect a different time. I can't quite explain it."

"Thank you. It is my favorite and that and other reasons is why I will not part with it," I said keeping my tears in check.

"Well, Ms. Bouchard, what name shall we attach to the portrait?"

I think but a short while and then determine it will be what it must be. "It shall simply be called, *Playground In My Mind."*

“I like that. It's as mysterious as the painting.”

We are finally done with the business and in agreement of the date for the show as well. Even though there is plenty of time before the exhibit will be held, I understand the need to get all the pieces completed to have a successful showing.

"Mr. Bachman, I would like to ask for some advice."

"Sure, Ms. Bouchard. What is it?"

"Well, I know that at some point you have to find an artist or check on something that may relate to an exhibit. In any case, what I would like to know is how do you go about finding an individual or information on someone."

"Well, for starters I usually have a name and I then look through articles that may have been written concerning the artist. Or if I can place him or her at a specific showing,

I usually will call someone who may have a phone number or some other information to help me."

"What if the person is not well known, say, not famous. What would you do then?"

Mr. Bachman thought about the question for a moment before responding. "All I can do then is start with the name and check for information in the location that I heard of the individual or talk to someone who brought the name to my attention." Again, he paused and I could tell he wanted to ask me something, but instead, said, "That's all anyone can do."

"Well thank you Mr. Bachman for your time and for the opportunity of having the exhibit here at the museum."

"No, it is I that should thank you. It will be very beneficial for the museum and not only financially. I think that this show will bring more people to the museum and that is what we are always trying to do."

Before leaving, I inquire about the storage of the exhibit pieces prior to the show and am quite satisfied with their safety.

Once out on the street again, I climb into my van and head toward the Rundel Library located on State Street downtown. If there is any information to be found, it will be the best place to start. Besides, the newspaper office is around the corner and I can go there next. I have already exhausted searches on the internet with no success. Besides what I am looking to find is something, or someone who may or may not exist... I let out a sarcastic laugh.

I have a sense of urgency that will not allow me to take the time to think about the matter. I will start first with his parents and then see if I can discover a trail that would lead me to Michael. If not, I would make a trip to the school. Of course, I will not be able to ask anyone, but maybe I can check out the places he has mentioned and hopefully, I will see him again.

That is how I determined to begin the search. I need a starting point and Mr. Bachman has given it to me. Following his lead, I begin at the beginning.

I had first met Michael at the park on Lake Ontario. That would be the starting location which made perfect sense since he had mentioned his parents. "They are concert pianists and they are playing now at the Halstein Theater." That is what he had shared with me.

As I walk up the sidewalk to the entrance of the Library I remember what Samuel had said when I told him Michael's last name was Roman and that his parents were concert pianists who played at the Halstein Theater. Samuel had learned and shared, "Their names were Clara and Robert Roman."

By the time, I reach the front door, I know somehow that though Samuel had said it could not possibly be the son of these two individuals, but must be a future generation of Roman's and they had named their son Michael, I was more than certain he was wrong.

Once inside the vast space of the Library I go to the information desk where a nameplate displays the woman's name as Ms. Walker.

"Where might I find, information concerning famous concert pianists," Ms. Walker.

The lady seated behind the counter has a very pleasant face. She seems young for the job, but I soon learn she is perfect for the position. I watch as she picks up a pencil and writes down something on a sheet of paper, then smiling, hands it to me. I see that she has written several library departments on the sheet.

"I think that you will find everything in those three areas of the library. If not, just ask anyone behind the desk and they will point you to other locations I may have overlooked."

"Well thank you, Ms. Walker."

"Here, you might need this."

She hands me a floor plan of the library to assist me and I smile and thank her as I head for the first location on the piece of paper. The building is huge, but the directions and her notes help me tremendously. I gather up books and take them to a table where I can sit and search through them. I make notes, trying not to let what I learn upset me as I continue the process. Between the books and using the computers to locate archives of information, it is a very slow process, with no time to digest all that I find. I sit, I read, I take notes and by the time I finish in the first area on the sheet, I am exhausted, but feeling good about what I have amassed in my search.

I sit for a moment giving my eyes a rest, then plow through my notes seeing if I have missed anything. I am so engrossed that all sounds are filtered out around me until finally I hear someone calling out, "Miss, I'm sorry, but the library is about to close." I look up to see a woman standing patiently in front of me.

"Oh, what time is it?"

"It's after nine o'clock."

I can't believe it, but it must be so. I thank the woman and begin gathering up my collection and stashing them into my portfolio. I then relinquish my seat and walk through the echoing hallways until I am at the entrance doorway where I say, "Goodnight," before stepping out into the evening.

Chapter 28

That day provides me with more information. I hope that the copies and my notes might uncover clues that I would have overlooked since I wasn't totally sure exactly what I was looking for.

That first evening after visiting the library I spent devouring the information collected. I eat with papers all around me, thinking of nothing more than finding all I can to help me lay out a plan. Thus, becomes the pattern of my days to review what I have found, and go to the library at nine o'clock each morning to continue my research.

I look up information on my laptop now that I had an idea of what to put in the search engines. Each day that passes it becomes easier and easier; especially on the computer since mastering the Dewey Decimal System was not the easiest thing to do.

Until I started this, I had not realized how hard it can be to find information on anyone without running into charges. I started out believing that the information was free until finally reaching the point of possibly getting the information does the site ask for the money. It is the principle of the matter that has me going back to the Library where there is no charge.

During this period in my life I did little more. I used the excuse of my upcoming exhibit to hold customers at bay. I had completed the jobs that I had taken and now I wanted to give my full attention to the search for Michael.

It preys on me each day that what I am doing is ludicrous. I am trying to find someone who does not really exist. Yes, I face the truth in all this, but it does not stop me. Even the fact that Michael is capable of 'catching up' with me in age, I truly am believing now. What does that say about me, I wonder.

I think about the winter and remember that day we were ice skating. Even though it's freezing outside, people are out and about, bundled up and chattering among themselves while I enjoy the company of Michael. Then in the spring with the promise of the warmth of summer the days seem elegantly special as I share a picnic lunch in a clearing deep in the woods where sunlight filters through the overhead lattice of leaves and when the rainy days come they do not dampen my spirits because I see Michael.

Summer, my favorite season for walking alone on the beach in the summer twilight is not as special because Michael does not come. Instead the heat keeps me inside most days and nights I allow the summer to run its course.

Most times as I rush from home to the library and back again, I do not realize whether the day is pleasant or dreary. My mind is so focus on Michael that days are just days. So, I am surprised one morning when I look out my window and for the first time realize the season has changed again and it is fall. The leaves are turning gold and amber, and then drift to the ground. I watch the lawn service come and rake them into mounds before mowing the grass that seems to have a growth spurt. I can't believe that much time has passed without me.

I haven't really found much to help me in my quest so I can't stop. I look around the studio that is now full of papers and the peg board holds pictures and more papers as I try to lay out a trail. I must be close, I tell myself, because I feel as though there is nothing I don't know about the Romans, except how to find Michael in this time in history.

I move from the window in my studio and sit at the desk. A message pops up on my computer screen announcing that tomorrow is the day of my exhibit at the museum. It can't be possible, I think, but I know it is true. I must stop and change my mindset if I am to make the exhibit successful. I also need to get a good night's sleep. So, regretfully I put aside my research and concentrate on what I need to do.

I manage to get myself off and ready the next morning. The way it has been outlined, I am to put in not only an appearance, but be there for both the day and evening showings. Mr. Bachman has arranged two separate times during the day and two separate times during the evening when I would be available to talk with the patrons.

I tell myself that's not so bad. The exhibit is to be held for two consecutive days where I must appear and then my part will be over and I can return to my search. I have committed myself to this so I have no choice but to indulge those who would seek to steal precious moments of my time and because of the type of person I am, I must admit I will probably enjoy the opportunity.

This I tell myself as I make my way to the museum. It is like I become a different person once I leave my home and climb into the car. It is a beautiful day with the sun shining brightly enough to force me to put on my sunglasses and its warmth has me opening the windows. By the time I pull into the parking lot area, I feel good and it shows as the day progresses. I enjoy myself as I answer questions and move through the exhibit that is so tastefully done.

"So, Ms. Bouchand, you mentioned that a lot of these sketches were made to complete a sculpture."

"Yes, that's, right?"

Before the person can finish, someone else asks, "What types of sculpture are there?"

I think for a minute. "Well, there are many types, those that are created by adding material such as clay, wax, cardboard, paper, or other types of matter. Then there are those that are created out of stone, wood, metal and ice. It goes without saying, those of ice are temporary in nature."

That gets me a laugh before the next question is asked.

"Which do you do?"

"Well, I can do them all, but mostly I work with clay and wood."

The two individuals who have lead the discussion smile, thank me and then move on. I take the opportunity to get a drink of water and then return to my post. In a matter of minutes, I am again approached.

Ms. Bouchand, I am studying art and would like to know what steps you take in creating a sculpture."

"Now that is a question," I reply. "Well, first of all I am glad to have a chance to share with a budding sculpture. Would you like the sort version or the long version," I ask smiling.

"The long one, if you please."

"Okay, well for those who are not planning on becoming a sculptor, this may be a little boring so I won't be offended if you decide to break away."

No one moves so I begin. "First you should always draw out the shape. It doesn't have to be a great drawing, but it should clearly present the image you wish to capture. You need to draw the sculpture from many angles and make sure you include details."

As I talk, the crowd thickens and it gives me a sense of pride knowing that they are generally interested. I explain thoroughly the creation of a base for the sculpture and a support structure for parts of the sculpture that will require them.

"Then, you are finally ready to begin what you set out to do…create the sculpture."

They get the humor I try to portray as I pause

dramatically before continuing.

"So now you can start adding on your sculpting material. Start by creating the largest pieces of the sculpture and then go on to the smaller parts. Once that is done, add in details such as eyes and noses. Then step back and give it a look. Your hands have created it so this will allow you to see what you need to do in order to add texture."

"Excuse me, but what do you mean by texture."

"Oh, yes. Texture is what brings the sculpture to live. You may need to roughen a crag, or smooth a forehead." I walk over and point to the charcoal done for the bird above the crag of rocks as a demonstration. "Does that help?"

"Yes, the person says, I see."

"So, at this point you are done and you will need to bake your sculpture or allow it to dry, whichever is appropriate for the material you choose.

"This you do before you paint it?"

"Yes."

I can tell that I have made an impression as I answer questions and see smiles on faces. I shake so many hands of people praising my work. That first day I never leave the museum. There are so many people interested in the charcoals and interested in hearing what I can tell them about the life of an artist. It is indeed flattering.

The next day I am back early, ready and a bit excited as I hurry to the exhibit. Already there are several people there and I continue to answer questions and accept graciously the praise they give me for my work. It is on this afternoon that I must rush home to speak with Mildred and figure I will get a bite to eat while I am there.

I am a changed person. I smile more and feel deeply happy with my life as I make my way back to the museum. As I park my car and step out I ask myself, why hadn't I done this before. It is so uplifting and I can't wait to get back in side. Only there is a change this time as I think I see Michael and my whole world goes tipsy turvy.

I hurry up the stairs to the front door of the museum as if I am late for an appointment. Of course, there isn't a set time for me to be at the exhibit, but I am drawn by the warmth that comes my way as I talk and discuss the sketches. I open the grand door and entered the lobby of the museum and immediately I am overcome with a weird sensation. I am overcome with a heavy, dense feeling and my anxiety increases until I can barely breathe. As quickly as it comes, it passes, but scares me enough so that I need to recollect where I am and what I am doing.

"Ms. Bouchard, are you, all right?" Mr. Bachman is beside me with a worried expression on his face. I take a deep breath, forcing a smile before I turn to face him.

"Sure, Mr. Bachman, I'm fine, just fine. I was just thinking that I had forgotten something, but couldn't recall what it was." I give a little laugh and see that Mr. Bachman is satisfied with my explanation and the worried look disappears from his face.

"Well, I have someone who wants to talk with you, if you are ready."

"Sure, I'm ready," I said, and I really am.

I follow Mr. Bachman across the lobby and it is when we are halfway to the Portrait of Michael that the feeling comes over me again. This time I am able to control it, while I look hastily around me. It is but a brief glance, only I swear I see him. Standing off to the side of the portrait is a man, not such a young man, but a man that I know is Michael. He stands in profile gazing at the picture and I see him capture his lower lip in his mouth as though to hide its quivering.

I rush toward Michael, my heart doing flip flops in

my chest as I forget everything until Mr. Bachman calls out to me.

"Ms. Bouchard, there's no hurry," he says breathlessly trying to keep pace, "really, no hurry at all."

I only turn for a second to let Mr. Bachman know I hear him, but when I turn around again, Michael is gone. I scan the area, but know in my heart I won't see him.

Mr. Bachman catches up to me and says, "Wow, I didn't know women could walk so fast in heels."

"Yes, we can," I snap irritable, then pause to glance about, hoping, just hoping. "Sorry I took off like that Mr. Bachman."

"Oh, that's okay. I'm just glad you are enjoying all of this. It can be demanding to say the least, but like you have found, it can be very enjoyable too.

It all changes for me after that. I manage to smile and respond appropriately to questions, but my heart isn't in it any more. Just thinking that I saw Michael and then lost him, took the joy out of the day. I am caught in infinite sadness. It's a feeling as though there is no happiness in the world - as though joy has been sucked away, and you're left with this feeling as though nothing will ever get better.

I try, believe me I try to feel the joy I felt the first day, but it is lost to me. I talk to the people giving them mechanical answers to their questions that I don't feel passionate about enough to personalize. Yet the questions keep coming along with a flood of compliments, and I realize later that day by the amount of purchases made no one found fault with my changed attitude.

When the crowd thinned and more of the people were just looking at the drawings, I made my escape, planning to gather my things and go home. But I didn't. Instead I found myself standing off to the side, in the main display room, alone as I gaze at the Portrait of Michael.

I am impressed at how well I captured his image at an age I had only just imagined. He was handsome, yes, but the kindness in his eyes express his deeper feelings of compassion and innocence. How did I manage all of that, I wonder.

I did not see him approach as I continue to look at the picture of Michael. I wonder when I will see him again. I am so deep in thought it is not until I feel a light tap on my shoulder do I realize he is there. The touch startles me and my body jerks forward.

"Oh, Ms. Bouchard I am so sorry. I didn't mean to scare you."

I take a minute to collect myself, then turn to face the intruder. "No, it's all right. What can I do for you?" I manage to say this with a calmness I am not feeling.

"Well, Ms. Bouchard, my name is Peter Newman and I am very intrigued with the portrait."

I take a good look at the gentleman in front of me. He is dressed in a black suit with a white shirt and black bowtie. He is distinguished looking and if I had to guess, I would say this man is a lawyer. His suit, if not, looks tailor made to fit his trim body. He stands with his shoulders back and a slight smile on his face.

I look up and notice that his hair is parted on the side with fullness at the crown as the waves and curls try to surface. He notices I am critiquing him so I smile and say.

"Thank you, Mr. Newman."

Now it's his turn. Peter is used to thoroughly thinking a situation through before deciding upon a course of action, assessing and analyzing the matter carefully until he has a rational explanation. But this woman is a mirror image of Christine. Her hair is darker, her eyes accentuated more, but it is Christine's face.

"I. ... I."

"Yes," I say coaxingly.

Peter takes a breath and finally can speak.

"Ms. Bouchard, I know you don't intend to sell the portrait, at least that is what I've been told, but I want to explain why I have to have it."

"I don't understand." I step back a little as I see a strange look in his eyes and I begin to wonder if I'm safe here with him.

"Please, I need to talk to you. It's important. I am a friend of Sidney. I mean Dr. Paulson and he told me about you."

Seeing the surprise look on my face, he adds, "No, not about the sessions, just about how you look. It came up at a dinner party and after the discussion, I knew fate was trying to tell me something."

"I don't understand."

"You will, if you give me a chance to talk."

I feel less frightened, but still confused by this man. I look at him and finally decide I want to hear what he has to say.

"Give me a minute, please." I look at my cell and see it is almost closing time. "I need to check in with Mr. Bachman." I add. "Can you meet me out front and we can go somewhere to talk."

Peter grabs my hands and holds them. "Thank you Ms. Bouchand. Thank you very much."

He lets my hands go and turns and walks away. I watch him walk toward the front of the museum, then go to find Mr. Bachman. I first go to the exhibit, thinking he may still be there. He is not. I then turn around and start walking down the hallway away from the main lobby. It is then that I see Mr. Bachman heading in my direction.

"Everything went wonderfully well, Ms. Bouchand.

I can't thank you enough for giving the museum this opportunity to show your drawings."

"I enjoyed it very much, so thank you."

Mr. Bachman goes over some details with me and I wait until he finishes.

"Mr. Bachman, do you know a Peter Newman?"

"Yes, I do. He was here today. He's a well-respected lawyer in town." "Why do you ask?"

"Oh, no reason, I ran into him in the lobby and he asks to speak with me."

"Well, I wouldn't worry. He is very successful and may be interested in a purchase or two."

Well thanks again and I will be touch."

We shake hands and I walk confidently out of the museum to join Mr. Newman. I find him pacing back and forth on the steps of the museum entrance.

"Okay, we can go," I say.

"Great." We walk together down the stairs. "Do you know the Founder's Café? Pete asks.

"Yes, I like it. It's quiet there so we can talk.

We continue our way. I can feel his eyes on me as we walk side by side and it makes me a little uncomfortable. I wonder what it is he plans on telling me that he thinks will change my mind about selling the painting because there is nothing he can say that will make me want to give it up. But I can at least listen to him.

We arrive at the café and the waitress shows us to a table. Once we are seated, Peter says to me, "I need to tell you the whole story so please bear with me. It is important that I do it this way, or it won't make sense." I nod.

"It all started at a dinner party that I attended at the home of Dr. Paulson and his wife. It was myself, my wife and the Mastersons."

"I'm sorry to interrupt. You know the Mastersons?"

"Yes, I do and they play a part in this story too." Peter stares across the table at me as if trying to read my thoughts.

"It was during dinner that the conversation turned to odd experiences. It began with Arnie Masterson saying that Vivian told him once that their unborn child had spoken to her. Of course, we all laughed, except Sidney. Sidney Paulson said that if his wife told him something like that he wouldn't discount it, because he believes there are things that happen that cannot be explained away with science. Well Arnie is somewhat shocked so asks him to explain what he meant."

He has my interest; because after what Dr. Paulson said at our last visit, I would think he would be the last person to say something like that. Before Peter can continue, the waitress returns to our table.

"Can I take your order?"

I look up and reply, "I'll just have coffee."

"No, please, can we get a bite to eat?"

I smile at Peter, "Sure, no problem." I look over the menu and make a choice and then wait while Peter does the same. As soon as the waitress leaves the table, Peter continues.

"Anyway, Sidney says that he had a client that he had known the family personally for, I think, ten years. The client mentioned he had a twin, but Sidney was sure he didn't even have another sibling so he questioned why he thought this and the client said that the family had a tradition that at the stroke of midnight, his father would take him to the door and have him open it to let in the New Year. He then said that he had visited his father and as they sat talking about the past, his dad had asked if he remembered when he was ten and just as they went to open the door to let the New Year in, there was a knock and the door opened all by itself, but no one was there. My client knew he wasn't there that year as he spent it with his mother. He asked his father if maybe it had been Jim with him that year and by the look on his father's face he knew that all the years he felt like something was missing in his life, it was. He had a twin who had died in the womb."

"Oh," I say with surprise. "Wow."

At that point, the waitress returns with our food and while she places it in front of us, I look at Peter. "That is strange, to say the least, but what…"

"Give me a minute and it will become clear why I am telling you this."

The waitress leaves and I take a bite of my sandwich as I wait for Peter to resume.

"That got me to remember the fire. I lost my first wife, Christine and our son, Max in a fire on his fifth birthday."

"Oh, I am so sorry."

"It happened a long time ago, but thank you."

I can tell he needs a minute as I watch him take a bite of his sandwich before picking up where he left off.

"I had forgotten about what happened in the hospital until then. Max survived for a while and I was with him at the hospital, day and night. On the evening that Max succumb to his injuries I saw something."

Not aware I am doing it, I lean forward.

"At first, I thought it was a nurse coming in to check on my son, but on closer observation what I saw was a little boy who was dressed in old fashion attire. He couldn't be more than five years old himself."

I am on the edge of my seat when I say, "Oh my god!"

As if afraid he won't be able to finish, Peter rushes

on. "He stood by my son's hospital bed and worried he might infect my son who was badly burned, I tried to stop him, but I couldn't move. I literally couldn't get out my chair. And I couldn't speak, no matter how I tried."

I know the feeling and I want to tell him, but something holds me back.

"Two things happened after that. The room changed to the way a hospital room would probably have looked centuries ago and then the boy climbed up on the bed and laid over Max and then disappeared."

I can't believe what he is saying. Peter pauses and I can see he is fighting back tears as he drinks some water, then takes another bite of his sandwich. His head is down and I watch as he slowly lifts his face and I can see he is back in control.

"It's impossible," I manage to say, though I'm not so sure of that these days.

"I know it sounds crazy. But there is more."

"What more can there be?"

"Well, it is Arnie who next says that he hired a sculptor to make some figurines for his fireplace and that her name is Taylor Bouchand."

Peter sees me start to speak. "Please, let me finish. Anyway, he told me some sketches fell from your brief case and they were of a little boy dressed in old timey clothes and he loved the expression on the boy's face. Then his wife, Vivian, asked to see a picture of my son, Max and I hand her a locket I keep in my wallet. Inside is a picture of Christine and Max. Vivian says that the sketches are the exact likeness of my son, Max."

"I, don't understand?"

"That's not all," Peter says. "Then Sidney asks to see the locket and they hand it to him. Sidley looks at it and says that my first wife, Christine is the exact likeness of you."

"I don't believe it. How can that be?"

Peter pulls out the locket and passes it across the table to me. I am hesitant, afraid to open it because if I do, I will have to believe what he has told me. Finally, I get up enough nerve to push the latch and let the heart fall open. I look down at the picture inside and I faint.

When I open my eyes, the first face I see is Peter's. He stands over me as I look around wondering what happened.

"Take it easy miss. Don't sit up to fast," the waitress says.

I ignore her request and try to sit, wondering where I am.

"Are you all right Ms. Bouchand," Peter asks.

"Yes, I'm fine, really."

My mind works overtime and I remember I am at the Founder's Café with Peter Newman and we are sitting at a table having a bite to eat. Only now, as I look down, I am on a sofa and not at our table. Someone has moved me to a sofa in the lounge area.

I rub my forehead trying to remember and I do. Embarrassed, I manage to say, "Please I'm fine, let's go back to our table." What I really want is to just leave, but I have a feeling that is not an option.

I stand and Peter holds my arm as though he is afraid I will pass out again, but I really do feel fine. When we are back at our table, I manage to ask, "How long was I out?"

"Not long. Maybe five minutes or less. I'm so sorry Ms. Bouchand. I don't know what I expected, but not that you would faint. Please forgive me. Maybe I should stop there and tell you the rest later."

I look at Peter. "Are you crazy? How can you think I can wait to hear the rest? I need to know because a lot of what you said explains things that have been happening to me and I need to understand."

"I can't say that I have the answers, but there is one more thing I want to tell you."

"Go ahead. I can handle it. Please."

"Okay." Peter takes a drink of water and eats a little more. "I thought I knew everything about Christine, but obviously not. So, I went to see her parents with the suspicion that Christine was adopted. Her mother Edna was home and I got her to admit it. She also admitted that they had never told Christine she was adopted because they didn't think it mattered. In any case, she did give me a copy of Christine's real birth certificate which said that her mother's real name was Lily Warren and the father was unknown. For the name of the baby it says, Baby Girl Warren, but now I think that it should read, Baby Girls Warren. You are her double."

"I don't understand." I am silent, not knowing what to say or what to think, yet from my experience, I can't help believing that it happened. But that would mean that Michael had taken over his son's body and that was hard to swallow.

"Mr. Newman, I am so sorry, and I believe you ... " I saw he was about to ask a question and I knew what it would be so I quickly continued, "but don't ask me why because I don't think I can explain it."

"You have to tell me, please. Listen, I don't know what is happening, but I think that we are destined to meet and that somehow you can help in us solving this riddle."

"I don't know how I can help you, really."

"My god, I know it's crazy, but what possessed you to paint the same boy that I saw that day. I don't think it was a dream and I think you feel the same way. Please, you have to help me."

"Listen, Mr. Newman. I'm very tired so why don't we set up a time to meet later and then, who knows ... "

"Okay, when?"

" I don't have my calendar with me. Why don't I give you a ring and we can set up a date to meet?"

"I… Yes, that is fine."

He didn’t have to say it. I know he was afraid I would never call and then probably realized that as confused as he was, I must be too. I sat across from Peter and watched as he reached in his pocket and handed me his business card. On the back, he had written his home phone number and email address. I turned it over and then placed it in my purse for safe keeping.

“Thank you. Shall we go?”

Peter reaches in his wallet and lays a tip on the table and then taking the bill, we go to the cashier. It seems like forever as we wait for her to ring us up and I feel the eyes of the patrons on me. I can almost hear them saying, ‘hey that’s the woman who passed out’.

Finally, we are on our way out of the café and I tell myself it will be a while before I have the nerve to return to this place.

“Thank you for the dinner,” Mr. Newman.

“You are so welcome,” he says. “But please, call me Peter.”

“You can call me Taylor”

There is an awkward silence between us until I finally manage to say, “I don’t know what is happening, but I do think we are both a part of it.”

“I do too.”

Peter walked me to my car and as I sat there watching as he climbed into his, I realize I now have a missing part of the puzzle. Hopefully this information will bring me closer to finding Michael.

Chapter 29

The show is a bigger success than anticipated. Just about all of the charcoals were sold and there were several orders for more.

In the aftermath though, the big success story is the portrait of Michael. It seems that everyone is calling to set up an appointment to have their portraits done, which is not what I wanted but should have expected. I worked hard on my talk about portraits because it was the one I gave in front of Michaels.

I had stressed that portraits are effective and compelling when they tell us something about the person and that a good portrait is not just a visual representation of a person; it will also reveal something about the essence of the person. When asked what I hoped to achieve in a portrait I had pointed to the portrait of Michael saying that a strong portrait captivates viewers, draws them into the painting, and engages their attention. Such a portrait painting will cause the viewer to wonder about the subject of the portrait.

As I gave my talk and answered questions I witness an intense interest in those who stood around me and when someone asked the cost the spectators leaned forward together like a wave rushing to shore.

As for Mr. Bachman, he was full of praise and anxious to have another show scheduled as quickly as possible. It took some finesse to not make a commitment.

As for Peter Newman, I really meant to call him. The more I put it off, the easier it became to keep him waiting. It was just that I wanted to put the information he gave me to use before contacting him.

But then all is forgotten when Michael returns.

This morning, like many before I am up early. I find that the time just before the dawn has the most energy of all the hours of the day so I take my coffee and walk to the shore to watch the new day arrive. Nothing can be more inspiring to an artist than to watch the sky begin to lighten above the shore line while listening to the light splash of the water against the beach. I stand there watching the sun appear above the horizon and then slowly turn around.

I walk slowly up the path to my home and once inside, go about getting my thoughts together for the day when I feel a sensation come over me and I know its meaning before there is a knock on the door. I hurry to the foyer and without peeking to see who it is, I open the door.

He is older, much older than I could have imagined and yet he is still a little boy. The sun at his back reflects around his frame and I see him as he was on that first day we met, before it all changes. He looks at me and I see his eyes twinkle and a smile being born on his lips. All I can say is, "Hello, Michael."

"Hello, Taylor, I've missed you."

"Come into the living room, Michael and I'll get us some coffee."

"No, I can't stay. I'm not supposed to even be here now, but I had to tell you something. I had to tell you that I miss you and that I hate being away from you, but…"

"It doesn't matter, really, Michael why you're here. I'm just so glad to see you. Please come into the living room."

"No, I must go. I've been here too long already.

You only just arrived. "Don't go Michael, please."

"Taylor…"

"Tell me where you go when you leave me. I want to know where you are."

Michael ignores the question and says that he went to the see the exhibit at the museum and was touched by it. It had made him cry.

"I don't know why," he said. "It was a beautiful portrait you did of me and I wanted to stand there and admire it, but something was in my head and wouldn't go away. I saw the lake and on the horizon, was a sail boat, too far to determine its size or for identification, yet I felt that I knew it. Suddenly I wanted to come to you, but I couldn't; I had to go back. "

I reach out and grab his hand and turning it over, I run a finger down the length of his palm. "I thought I saw you, but I couldn't get to you, but Michael, please. You say that the place that you come from makes you sad and that makes me sad too."

There is a sad, forced smile on his face. "I don't want you to be sad. I'm being silly. Don't let's talk about it anymore. Let's say goodbye for now and I promise I will come back again. "

Michael gently pulls his hand away. Slowly, as though in a dream; he turns his face away from me as he moves toward the door. I stand there unable to move as he looks back at me and I see a sense of longing, of love, and of trust in his gaze. He reaches out and lays his hand lightly against my cheek, then turns and walks out the door, pulling it shut behind him.

I move slowly as my mind churns in wonderment. And then I remember what is preying on my mind. That day of the exhibit when I entered the lobby I was overcome with a sensation as though I was a swimmer fighting my way to the surface for air. I had felt that and it had scared me. Michael had talked of a boat on the horizon that he felt somehow connected to and it had scared him even though he did not know why. I go into the dining room and out the sliding glass doors, hurrying toward the shore line.

The lake is sparkling with the brilliancy of a sea of diamonds as I hurry down the path to the beach to stand and stare out at the horizon, thinking. Finally, I lean down to take off my sandals and walk on the sand, feeling it ooze through my toes, scrubbing gently against the sides of my feet as I advance.

"Don't drown yourself in the lake," a voice speaks from behind me.

I turn quickly around and see Peter Newman. Slowly I compose myself, "Why would I want to drown myself in the lake?"

"I don't know," he said, "Sometimes when we are scared we do funny things. Personally, I don't trust the water and try to stay clear of it."

"Why, Mr. Newman, you don't look like the scared type," I said teasingly. "Besides, you're tough and I don't think the lake wants you."

Even I feel as though I am not the one saying the words. It is so unlike me. I look at Peter and see the strange expression on his face. I watch the red start to creep up to his hairline. "It's the tough ones that drown the easiest," he said and I know this is not like him either.

"Touché," is my only reply as I watch Peter close the distance from me until he stands at my side.

"Your housekeeper told me you were out here."

I didn't respond, instead I start walking again, and Peter keeps pace with me.

"Ms. Bouchard, you can't run away from this. Something is happening and it seems to have caught us both up in it. I know it and I think you know it too."

"I think we should be on first name basis, Peter; especially if we are going to discuss what I think you wish to discuss."

"Fine with me, Taylor," he said, "I need to get to the bottom of this as it is driving me insane. Please tell me what you know and then maybe we can help each other understand this, ah, situation."

We continue to stroll until we are finally at the dock and that feeling of drowning comes over me again. There in the water is my sail boat. I can only stare at it watching as it rolls back and forth with the waves coming to the shore. It seems to be beckoning to me. I snap my head around and look at Peter.

"Let's go in and talk. Mind you, I am not saying that there is a connection between what happened to you and what is happening to me. I just think that it might help us both to share what we know and what we think, and then maybe we can at least move on."

Peter follows closely as we make our way up the path and into my house where I show him to the den. Sitting in the quiet, Peter relaxes. Mildred arrives with a tray of coffee and bagels that she sits on the coffee table. I smile and thank her and soon we are alone.

I watch Peter as he fixes his coffee and pours a cup for me. "How do you take it."

"Black. Thank you."

Once seated again, Peter begins by saying. "I have told you my story and I know how weird it may seem, but it did happen. Just the evening before all this happened Taylor, Max was ... "He pauses mid-sentence.

"What is it Peter," I said, knowing the look of remembrance since I had been there so many times before.

"I'm not sure, but I vaguely remember his prayers that night and I think ... " He paused again. "No, I know what I heard!" he added adamantly.

"What was it. Please tell me."

More as though he was repeating it for himself than

for Taylor, Peter began:"

"Now I lay me down to sleep. I pray the Lord my soul to keep If I should die before I wake I pray the Lord my soul to take. God Bless, Mama, Papa, ... "

A look of sheer surprise came over Peter's face, and then he adds, “And God Bless Michael."

My breath catches in my throat as I hear the ending. The same prayer did not seem strange since it was a very popular one to teach children, but...

"It can't be, Peter." It must be a friend from school, or an uncle or something."

Peter didn't respond right away as he is trying to remember each little friend of Max, the relatives on his wife's side and his and then slowly his head turns until he looks directly at Taylor. "No, there is no Michael."

For a long time, we sit there staring at each other and not saying a word. I know that I'd see Michael again and I want to tell Peter, but I do not. Finally, I ask half in earnest, "You think someone is trying to tell us something?"

Peter responds, "That's exactly what I am thinking, only what?"

“I hadn't remembered until just now what I told you. I need to show you something though.”

Peter gets up and opens his wallet. He pulls out the locket and hands it to me. I stare up at him, afraid to open in again.

“Please, Taylor, open it.”

Slowly I press the little latch on the side and the pendant opens. Inside, staring up at me is my face. It is my face even though the hair is blonder there is no doubt in my mind. I watch as Peter paces the room unable to accept any more than me what he has said. But we must accept it and we must figure out what it means. Only now we are so caught up in our own thoughts we cannot share what we are thinking or feeling. When Mildred enters the study, she sees Mr. Newman leaning against the pane of the windows facing the lake while I stare at my hands in my lap.

Mildred clears her throat. "Ms. Bouchard, you have a call." As though coming out of a daze, I am startled when I turn to face her.

"Thank you, Mildred."

I watch Mildred leave and I get up and go over to pick up the landline extension in the room.

Peter turns around and watches Taylor who seems to be listening to the caller. Her mood is one of surprise as she stands silently for some time with the receiver at her ear, "Thank you very much," she finally says before placing the receiver back on the table.

Sensing that I am being watched I look over at Peter.

"This seems appropriate. That was Mr. Bachman, the curator at the Memorial Art Gallery. It seems that someone else is interested in purchasing the Portrait of Michael. He was calling to tell me to expect a call from a Mr. Roman."

"So, what did you say?"

"I said, thank you, but that is not the point?"

"I don't understand, Taylor, why isn't that the point?"

"The point is that Michael's last name is Roman."

PETER NEWMAN

Chapter 30

After meeting with Taylor, I am surer than ever that something is happening and it is happening to us both. I don't know if we are to do anything about it, but I know that if we want answers we can't' just let it go.

I consider what I know that is somewhat sane and I come up with the fact that Christine and Taylor are twins. That is all I can say rings true. The rest must be explained in another way. I put in a call to Sidney.

"Hello Amy"

"Hello Mr. Newman. How can I help you?

"I need to speak to Dr. Paulson. Is he available?"

"Let me see."

I can hear the click as I am put on hold. While I wait, I try to figure out what I will say.

"Mr. Newman, here's Dr. Paulson."

"Hi Peter, what can I do for you."

"We need to talk. You tell me what works best for you, Sidney and I will be there."

The line is silent and I can just see Sidney trying to figure out what to do. Should he sit down with me or should he figure a way to blow me off. Finally, he speaks.

"Okay, lets meet at the house. We can talk in my office and we can join the women for dinner, if Elizabeth is free. I'll call my wife, Barbara as soon as I hear from you. Say about six, if that works for you."

"That's fine. I'll get right back to you.

I call Elizabeth, knowing she will say yes and then I call Sidney back.

"Great, Barbara is looking forward to seeing

Elizabeth again."

As soon as he hangs up the phone, Sidney is sure he knows what Peter wants to discuss. It may be time for him to tell Peter about his visit with Madame Rosa. Whatever is happening here, Sidney knows that it won't go away.

Knowing that I may have some information soon, I feel better as I make my way to the court room, my mind already changing course.

By the time I enter the courtroom my mind is clear with my only thoughts being how to defend my client, Matthew Anderson who is accused of killing his step-grandmother in Victor

Matthew Anderson, talks frankly with me during his first-degree murder trial in Circuit Court Judge Wanda Berger's courtroom. He faces life in prison or death by lethal injection.

Mr. Anderson, who has been listening intently and taking notes during the trail, lowers his head and stares at his yellow legal pad as Victor's Sheriff's Detective Lydia Evans describes finding the body of 66-year-old Leah Tomlinson — Anderson's step-grandmother — face down in her living room.

She says the charge to Anderson, 28, is first-degree murder of Tomlinson.

When asked, my client pleads not guilty.

Looking gaunt and chewing gum, he stands before Circuit Court Judge Wanda Berger dressed in a light gray shirt, dark slacks and a blue tie. Occasionally whispering to me, he otherwise remains stone-faced through the proceedings.

Assistant State Attorneys Manuel Jones and Harold Lewis call 14 witnesses during preliminary testimony in the trial. According to authorities, Matthew stole a red and white pickup truck and drove it to Tomlinson's home in Webster, where Anderson once lived. Authorities say he killed Tomlinson, who had worked for the Victor Tax Collector's office for more than 30 years prior to her retirement, and he then stole her Subaru, heading across several states before returning home. Tomlinson's car was later found in Pittsford, prompting police to go to her home, where they found her body.

At the end of the day, the State testimony is to continue through the week, after which I will present my case in defense of Mr. Anderson.

With the day over, I hurry home to shower and dress for dinner at the Paulson's. When I enter, Elizabeth greets me with a glass of wine in her hand. We spend a few minutes catching up on each other's day and then I go to change.

In the shower, I go over in my head what I have already shared with Elizabeth. Elizabeth is just as puzzled by it all as Taylor was in hearing it for the first time. Elizabeth asks what Taylor had added and is not surprised when she hears that she says nothing but that she agreed to meet again.

"My Peter, that was a lot to throw at her at once. You should have done it in spurts. I would have fainted too. Poor woman."

She was right and I know it, but I tell her I don't think we have a lot of time to figure it all out. I don't know why I feel this way, but that is the truth. Now as I think about it, I know that I am going to tell Sidney of my visit with Taylor and what I shared with her. Hopefully he will have more to add to the story.

Chapter 31

We sit in Sidney's home office with the door shut. He pours me a drink and once we are settled, I start by telling him I have had a visit with Taylor and shared everything with her.

"How did you manage that?"

"Well, I read in the paper she was having a showing at the Memorial Art Gallery and I made a point of being there."

"So, how did you handle the connection of me in the conversation."

"I told her we were all friends having dinner and the subject came up and that you noticed that my Christine and she looked like twins."

Sidney thought about that for a moment and then said, "Good. That doesn't sound like I broke any doctor, client privileges." He adds, "So what did she have to say."

"Well, that's it. It was as Elizabeth informed me later, way too much to share with her all at once. She fainted in the café. So afterwards she said she'd call me and we could talk again.

Sidney looks at me. "So, what are you hoping to hear from me."

"I don't know. I just have a feeling that you, like me, didn't just let it go. I think you might have found out something helpful. Am I right."

Sidney doesn't speak right away, but finally he says, "Yes, I couldn't just let it go. I want to help Taylor. I know she isn't crazy. Hell, you met her. Does she seem crazy to you.?"

"No, not at all. She is troubled though, and I think you know why." Seeing the look on Sidney's face, I add. "I know, you can't tell me that, but there must be something you can share."

We drink in silence and finally Sidney opens up.

"Okay, I did something I never do, but it is something I can share with you. Here goes. But first, promise you won't judge me."

"Oh, come on Sidney! After what we have all shared. As weird as it is, nothing can be shocking. But put your mind at ease, I will not judge."

I went to see a psyche named, Madame Rosa. What she told me was seditious. She said that it is not well known that there exist things called Transitioners. She said that Transitioners are rare and no one speaks of them, or no one wants to know of their existence. In any case, she said from what I told her she thinks that this child-man is a Transitioner. She explained that when someone goes before their time the Transitioner comes to help them complete their life. She said that how they go about it may not be what would be, because they don't know the future…we do. Transitioners have a job of helping someone they are chosen to help and only that person, once they return in their new body. "

"Wait a minute Sidney. You believe her?"

"It's not a matter of belief, it is a matter of finding something that 'fits' what we are experiencing here. The way the Transitioner can return is by the death of a child who dies in the same manner as he did and at the moment the child passes over, the Transitioner will take over his body."

"Oh, my God!" This is all I can manage to say.

"She didn't say how it works exactly, but I don't think the child dies and then immediately lives again. I think the transition will take some time."

"Let me get this straight. You're saying that this Michael is my Max."

"I guess. I don't know. But I must share just one thing that Taylor told me and you can't repeat it. If she wants you to know, let her tell you."

"Okay. You have my word. What is it?"

"Well she told me this little boy is growing rapidly. I mean like he was a boy one day and then a young man the next time she sees him."

"Wow."

"Yes, wow. Afraid for Taylor's safety, I asked if these Transitioners are dangerous and Madame Rosa said that they can be. It would have to do with who the child was that he replaced and also the connection between the child and the person he appears to."

"I don't get it."

"All I know from what Madame Rosa said is that when someone goes before their time they come to help them complete their life. The Transitioners, if it is your son, had to die in a fire and returned at the age that Max was when he passed."

"So, how long will this Michael live?"

"Don't know. After talking with her I did a little research. I needed to add some credence to what she told me. Transitioners have been known about for centuries all around the world, but not always called that. I have read about them In Cornwall, Germany, Ireland, The Isle of Man, Scotland, England, Poland, Scandinavia, Spain and Wales and I am sure there are other cases that I have yet to uncover. People tell the story of what you are experiencing in many, many parts of the world and what explains this is that a Transitioner is someone who goes before their time and the way they can return is by the death of another child who dies in the same manner as he, which for Michael was by fire. "

"Is that it?"

"Well, there is just one more thing. The reason of

who they present themselves to is someone who is related to the child who passed away."

That ends our conversation. We have a wonderful dinner talking about upcoming vacations, newsy interludes throughout the week—safe topics. While in the back of my mind and I am sure Sidney's the wheels are turning trying to make sense of the mystery that seems to be our responsibility to solve.

Nothing did we share at that time with our wives as we ate dinner. As Elizabeth and Barbara chatted away, it seemed to me that they had either forgotten or now passed over the strange conversation at our last dinner party.

How did they do that, I wonder and then when I look at Sidney, I know how. Both have heard strange happenings from us. I have had clients who thought they had seen the devil and Sidney has probably had similar experiences. We live through it and our wives here about it. So, to them, it is just one more strange happening. But not to us, not until we fully understand it all.

I had one dilemma still. Should I tell Taylor Bouchand what I know. What I learned from people I know and trust is one thing, but now there is a Madame Rosa in the midst and her information connects the dots.

"Peter! Peter."

I finally realize someone is calling my name. "Yes, I say frazzled.

"Where were you?" Sidney's wife asks.

"Nowhere, just thinking. So, what is it?"

Chapter 32

When we say goodbye to our friends, I see a worried expression on Elizabeth's face. I know I will have to tell her something or she will continue to worry, trying to accept my privacy. We've been married long enough for her to know that sometimes the stress of my job can get to me when I have a case that I take to heart, no matter how I try. So that is the excuse I give her. Fortunately, I have many to pull from.

"I don't want you to worry Elizabeth."

"I'm not, really. I know it has to do with Christine and your son and you need answers."

"Yes, it does." To take her mind off in another direction I start. "You know the young woman I told you about that ask me to be her lawyer."

"Maddie something?"

"Yes. Well, she tells me something that has me wondering what I should do. She's only eighteen, you know and I don't want to ruin her life."

Worriedly, Elizabeth says, "What did she say, honey."

"She wants me to represent her for the murder of her mother. She tells me that when she's home she keeps seeing things out of the corners of her eyes. No one in her family sees them and they call her crazy. She hears her mother and father whispering and she knows they are talking about her. And when she sleeps at night people whisper to her through the walls and she can't understand what they are saying. She can't sleep well or thoroughly. She tried taking a knife to bed with her and locking herself in her room, but she is still too scared to sleep. So, one night when she forgot to lock her door, her mother came to check on her, but it wasn't really her mother that she saw standing there. She ran and jumped on her and stabbed her repeatedly."

"Oh, Peter, that is awful. Just awful. So, what are you going to do?"

"I don't know. I don't want to have her committed, but that is what will happen unless I can figure something out. I don't want her put in prison either. "

I hate myself for picking out such a dramatic situation, but it is the best I can do on short notice. This is a client and it is what she told me, and I am worried about her. So, it isn't a lie, just a side step.

"Can we talk about something pleasant," I say smiling at my wife as we stand on our front steps.

"Sure, we can do that, or we could just…"

I turn the key in the lock and turn around, lifting my Elizabeth up in my arms. I carry her across the threshold and wait while she kicks the door closed. I put her down and hug her tightly, giving her a long kiss, then while I lock the door, she hurries up the stairs.

I follow her, forgetting everything except that I want to be with my wife.

TAYLOR BOUCHAND

Chapter 33

It is all too much. I have enough to deal with trying to figure out Michael and how it is all possible. Now I must deal with the fact that there is a reason he came to me and that reason means that there is yet another problem. Not only is Michael, really, a little boy, but he is my NEPHEW!

I have been alone for so long and I have accepted that. Now I find out that I may or may not have a sister who is possibly my twin. It doesn't make sense. My parents were always open with me and if I had been adopted they would have told me. Wouldn't they? I walk around the studio like a caged animal trying to make sense of it all. I pause thinking that I need to start somewhere so why not find out about myself.

It had always been my mother that I turned to when I wanted something, but she died long ago. I was sixteen when she passed, old enough that she should have told me if I was adopted. Why didn't she?

Maybe it is all a mistake. They say everyone has a double. Maybe Christine is my double and not my twin… That's possible. That makes it better all the way around, only I don't believe it. I stop and stare out the window trying to decide what I can do. How can I make sense of all this? A tear runs down my cheek and I quickly wipe it away. "Crying is not going to solve anything," I say out loud. "Stop it and think."

It may be the sternness that I use that makes me think about my father. He was always a wonderful father but he was the disciplinarian and as such he hated confrontations. If I were to ask him if I was adopted, it could go two ways. One, he would tell me the truth, or if it wasn't the truth, he would be hurt. I am all he has since he didn't marry after mom died. Can I do this to him?

I put the matter aside and work on a project that I

need to finish by the end of the week. I try, but my mind keeps coming back to all this and I make the call.

I am happy when the receptionist answers and says that dad is in the operating room and will have to call me later. Now all I can do is wait.

The remainder of the day I work, finalizing most of the jobs I have put off. I call and drive to clients for the rest of the day and it keeps my head clear. When I return home, there is a call from my dad. It doesn't surprise me that he has left a message on my land line because he refuses to call my cell; saying that if I am not home, I could be driving and he is not going to be the one that causes me to have an accident. I have told him repeatedly that I don't answer the phone when I'm driving, but he doesn't listen.

I go into the kitchen and make myself a cup of tea first before making the call. I wait thinking about what I will say. When he answers, I am ready.

"Hi dad, it's me. I wonder if you are free for dinner."

He says he is. I start to pick a place to meet, but stop, thinking this is not the type of thing to discuss in public, and besides, he may have something at the house he can give me once I hit him with the bombshell.

"Why don't I come over and I'll fix you a home cooked meal. Sound good?"

He likes the idea and I set up a time. I know he likes eating at home so he'll have something in the fridge I can use to whip up something to eat with no problem. I do like to cook but I don't get many chances since Mildred does most of the meal planning, so it will be a welcome change.

I am about to hurt my father, is all I can think about and that thought drudges up a memory of the time I last upset him. It was when I took my mother's pendant and was wearing it around my neck when they returned from an evening out. My father grabbed me by my upper arms and I saw something unexplainable in his eyes when he told me I was not to touch that necklace, ever. Now as I think about it, that was weird. Their reaction was so out of character for them. I tried hard to remember the pendant, but all I could remember was what my father said. My mother, didn't say a word. All she did was take the necklace off me and go upstairs without even saying good night to me. She didn't come to my room later to tuck me in either.

Why hadn't I questioned their actions before. Was I being ridiculous now, thinking there is something to this. I was should have known better than to put the pendant on, but I was old enough for them to tell me why they were so upset. It wasn't like I went out of the house with it. I was in my pajamas and just wanted to wear it. I decide to ask about that necklace once I have my answer to my first question. With that I start getting ready.

On the drive to my dad's house I am nervous and a little apprehensive, but I must remain strong. I must get answers I tell myself. I must know the truth. By the time, I pull into the drive way, my mind is set. I get out of the car and walk determinedly up to his front door and ring the bell. In a few minutes, my father is framed in the doorway.

"Hi dad. It's so good to see you."

"Likewise, pumpkin. Likewise."

I step inside and am on my way to the kitchen, hearing my dad close and lock the door, then call out. "Want a glass of wine?"

"Yes, that would be wonderful."

My father joins me in the kitchen, a glass of wine for each of us in his hands. He places one glass near me and the other he takes with him as he sits on one of the stools at the island. I can feel his eyes on me as I roam about the kitchen to see what I have to work with.

"How hungry are you dad. Do you want a big salad, or something more substantial like chicken parm along with that salad?"

Dad is quiet thinking. "Well, from the sudden call and the worried expression I saw on your face at the door. I think I need to pick the more substantial choice."

I am not surprised. My dad always could read me, but I doubt if he has any idea how big this discussion will be. I continue gathering the items I will need for our meal. We chat back and forth about non-consequential things since I know there is not much about his job he can share. Being a doctor, he never did come home and say, "Guess what happened today?" Instead, he might say what he did but without giving it any substance so that it is like he played the game operation and took out a liver.

Finally, the food is ready and my glass is empty. Dad fills the glasses and helps me carry the food into the dining room. Even now that he is alone, he still insists on eating in the dining room. He often would say that eating at the island was like eating at a diner counter and he just wasn't into that.

When we are finally seated, I look at my dad. He's tall, with hair that is jet black and caramel colored skin. I remember the first time we went to see his family and I realized that they were African-American; not that it mattered. Later as I got older, dad would always tell me to remember that I had the gift of being a part of two worlds. I saw that as meaning I didn't have to worry like the other girls of burning when they tried to get a tan. I tanned easily.

Yes, I did feel I fit in as my father's child more so than my mother. Mom was beautiful with long curly brown hair and eyes a brilliant blue. She was willowy with high cheekbones and a smile that lit up her whole face. Now as I look up over my father's head and stare at the portrait of my mother behind him, I am amazed that I hadn't notice how differ we were, or for that matter how different I was from my dad. How did I miss it?

"Taylor, this is good, really good. Thank you for fixing dinner for us. I like this."

"Me too dad."

We continue eating until my dad pushes back his chair and says, "That's enough. I can't eat another bite. Can I get you some more wine," he asks as he gets up to carry his plate into the kitchen.

"Yes, I can use another glass," I say as I follow carrying my dish with me. While he pours us wine, I go about cleaning up the kitchen, putting everything away and our dirty dishes into the dishwasher.

"So, Taylor, where do you want to talk."

I look at him. "I adore you dad."

"Taylor!"

"Okay, let's go into the Livingroom."

We walk side by side into the Livingroom. I take the big winged back chair near the window and he plops down in his favorite spot on the sofa. He crosses his legs and I watch as he allows the upper leg to swing back and forth. I prepare myself.

"Dad. I do have something I need to ask you. I recently found out something that has me wondering if I am adopted."

I see my dad lean forward, his legs uncross as he stares at me and I want to take it back. He doesn't say a word. No denial, no acceptance. I can't stand the silence that is now between us, but I am afraid to say anything. I must let him tell me one way or the other. Finally, he gets up from the sofa and walks over to stand by the window, and without turning to face me he says, "Who told you that?"

I can't see his face which would help me in answering him. So, I tell him it doesn't matter, then add, "Is it true?"

Dad turns to face me and says, "No, yes, not really that simple."

Now I am the one on edge. "What does that mean?"

My dad turns toward me and I can see tears filling his eyes. Taylor, come sit beside me on the sofa."

I get up and we walk across to the sofa and sit down. I wait patiently. Finally, he tells me the story.

"Your mom and I were on our way home one evening and she said it was going to rain and I laughed at her, disagreeing totally. She laughed as she told me to wait and see. I do recall how much I loved to hear her laugh." He looks over at me and tries to smile.

"I remember your mom saying that she had told me so; that we should take the car because it was going to rain. But stubborn me had us walking to a small café down the street from our apartment."

I look at my dad in profile and know he is smiling by the slight increase in his cheek definition. He clears his throat and continues.

"Well, we were sitting in the café near a window when suddenly the sky opened up and the rain came down in buckets. Your mom started laughing and said, "It's not going to rain, is it?"

Anyway, we stayed warm and dry in the café as long as we dared, watching as other people came in waiting to be seated. We finally motioned for the waitress, paid our bill and relinquished our seats. Your mother was always full of surprises and when I was about to step out into the deluge, she pulled me back. I turned and watched as she reached into that big satchel purse she carried and came out with a little; and I mean little umbrella. She opened it up knowing that it was impossible for even one person to stay dry under it. She smiled up at me and said, "Shall we?"

"Any way, we hurried out into the rain. It was warm out so it wasn't all that unpleasant as we made our way toward home. We were almost past the edge of the café wall when we saw her. This tiny little woman, carrying something in her arms. She was soaking wet, her hair plastered to her head and she was shaking as she made her way to us."

"She yelled out to us to stop, knowing that the usual reaction would be to pretend we didn't see her and keep going, but she didn't know your mother. No, your mom would never have ignored her. She stopped. So, I stopped and walked with her as she shortened the distance to this woman. When we drew closer, we could hear crying, baby crying sounds coming from the bundle she carried."

Dad paused and I reached over and grabbed his hand. I squeezed it and he turned to look at me. "I'm all right pumpkin."

"So, the woman said to us. Please, take my baby. Yes, that is what she said. Your mother said, sure she would and reached out and the woman handed her the baby. Up close it was not really a woman. She looked to be around fourteen; at the most sixteen years of age. We though she just wanted your mom to hold her for a minute, but she then said to us, 'She's yours.' Afterward, she ran. She took off and ran. We stood there dumbfounded unable to believe what had just happened. We looked around and saw we were the only ones on the street. No one had seen what had happened. We didn't have her name or an address. Of course, an address was the most unlikely, so we headed home. When we got there, we pushed back the blanket and there you were, crying your eyes out, all wet and turning red."

Dad stopped and took a sip of his wine. He looked at me and said. "What were we to do. We didn't know who to call or what to say. Later when your mom and I talked, she said that they would take you and put you in the system and who knows what would happen. You see, Taylor, after we got married and waited three years for a baby, we knew it was not meant to be. But now, someone had changed that for us. Don't look a gift horse in the mouth. Isn't that the way the saying goes? Well anyway, we saw this as a gift."

"Dad, but how…"

"How did we get away with it?" I nod.

"It was easy back then before all the forensics and stuff. I had my Bachelor's degree, and was in medical school. I had met your mom and she was done with college. We married and then it was on to rotations, residencies and exams for me until finally I completed medical school. We were in the process of discussing together what I should specialize in and you can now guess why I chose pediatrics. Lucky for us, I was able to train here in Rochester."

"What? I mean, you were not living in Rochester when this happened?"

"No, we were not and don't ask where, please. In any case, once we settled in, it was very easy. Here we were two young adults, transplanted and in need of a birth certificate that we lost during the move. We filled out the papers and soon had a birth certificate for our little girl who we named Taylor."

"That's it Taylor. That's the story. We loved you as our own and you were ours. That's why we never told you."

Dad paused and then turned toward me and said. "So, I don't understand how anyone could tell you since no one knew the story. We never told anyone and we never had close friends until much later in life. How did you find out?"

I got up and reached for his glass. I carried them out into the kitchen and poured us each a fresh glass of wine. I walked slowly back into the Livingroom and sat back down. Carefully I told him what I knew.

"Wow, I don't believe it!" Have you seen this woman Christine? Do you know her story?"

"Wait a minute, Dad. No, I haven't seen her in person because she died some time ago. But I saw the picture of her that her husband carries and it is like looking in the mirror. If we are not twins, we are related."

Dad is trying to absorb all of this. "So, do you know where they lived and their story of how they got their baby. Was she adopted or is she their child."

"Okay, brace yourself. Christine was adopted; I think legally. They had her birth certificate."

"Yes, so, what does it say."

"Mother, Lily Warner, father, unknown. Then below it says baby girl Warner."

"That's it?"

"Yes, that's it. But it probably should have said, baby girls Warner."

Neither of us speaks, caught up in our own thoughts. Finally, my dad says, "So the girl's name was Lily."

I nod, realizing that we are both accepting this now. I give us a minute to enjoy our wine and then ask the final question. "Dad, remember the pendant that mom always wore. Can you tell me about it? I think there is a story behind that too."

Dad stares out into the distance and then turns to me and says. "Yes, that pendant had belonged to your real mother, this woman named Lily Warner. She had offered it to your mother as a present she would give her if she would take the baby." He paused and added, "Yes, that is what was said. Take the baby and that baby was you. Your mom wore it not because it was something she loved. She wore it as a reminder to never turn her back on someone in need because you don't know what special gift can be offered, meaning you."

Your mom stared at it for a long time and then turned to me and said, "I think we ought to keep this. I agreed."

"Why did she want to keep it?"

"It spoke words to her. She told me to her it was proof that even though this child gave her baby to strangers, there was some good in her. She cared."

"Was there something in it?" I ask hesitantly.

Talking more to himself than to me he says, "Yes, what we thought were two pictures of you with the girl Lily, but now I think it was only one of you."

Chapter 34

So now I know. I expect to feel different, but I don't, I just feel like me. My parents are still my parents. The only difference is out there somewhere could be my birth mother. I let out a little laugh. A birth mother and a twin. "Wow"

For the first time in weeks I think about Dr. Paulson. I hadn't realized until just know that it is because of him, I am able to face this. All those questions that I felt had nothing to do with my problem, did. As he tried to understand me, he helped me to understand myself. So, "Good job doc!"

I spend most of the day in front of the computer hoping to find out more about this woman Lily Warner, but when I put the name in the search box, it comes up with lots of Lily Warners. That's all I have except of course she had twins. "Oh, why not," I type *Lily Warner with twins* and wait. I laugh at all the choices I get again. This is hopeless and I know it so I continue gathering information on the Romans.

I have so much to work with now that I have spoken with Peter and I go from one site to another, sending pages of data to the printer. I stare at screens until my eyes will no longer focus and my fingers tire and I know it is time to stop. I stand up and am about to stretch when I hear myself say, "Time is running out. I know it is."

What does that mean, I wonder?

This is getting to me and I need to get out of the house so I force myself to take a break and leave. I go to Captain's Cove and as I had hoped, Samuel is there.

"Well Taylor, where have you been keeping yourself. The word is that you were on vacation."

"Well, I sort of was, but it was not the relaxing type of vacation that you are thinking of. I just had to sort out a lot of stuff. Samuel something has happened."

His interest peaks, Samuel leans forward and listens as I tell him about Peter Newman and the story he shared with me and before he has time to say a word I tell him the story of my birth.

It takes a while for it to sink in and Samuel is silent staring through me. "You think somebody has told you about the 'real' connection here. Well, what did he tell you, really? That's what I want to know."

"I thought it was clear," I said. "You must see a connection."

"Not to me," said Samuel. "I'm still trying to figure it out, but what I know for sure is that whatever is happening is going to be explainable in a logical way. For now, what you must remember is that they're dead, making it all past and done with."

"Is it? I'm not so sure."

"Good God, Taylor, it's the past so put it behind you."

"The past isn't behind us, Samuel. I am beginning to sense that the past is all around us. I think that for some unknown reason the past at some point must, or needs to return to the present because of something that was left unfinished or undone."

Samuel starts to interrupt, but I hold up my finger to silence him. "I know this sounds crazy, but you met Michael and saw him and know he exist, but he really doesn't. Well, not in the sense that you or I exist," I smile at him across the table. "I'm only beginning to think about things like that," I said.

Samuel is silent wanting to correct her, but afraid that would put her over the edge. He instead says, "If you haven't eaten, why don't we take our minds off the past and think about the needs of the present."

I must smile at that and agree he is right. I am hungry and with pleasure we plunge into a more satisfying topic of conversation for the rest of the meal. He asks about the exhibit and I tell him how successful the outcome had been. Samuel lightens the mood and soon has me laughing.

As I prepare to leave, Samuel joins me and we go out into the parking lot together where he hesitantly asks, "Is Michael coming to see you again, Taylor?"

I answer almost without thinking. "Yes," I said. "Someday."

Samuel nods his head thoughtfully. "Good," he said. "

We then said our goodbyes and I head toward home, glad for the walk and time to clear my head.

I feel lonely again as I wonder where Michael is, and what he is doing at this very moment. Then I wonder if there is anything he can do in that far-off place. By the time, I reach home night has fallen and I walk around the side of the house to reach the beach. The sun is beginning its descent and hangs low on the horizon making a silver road on the lake's surface.

It's crazy but I know he will not return until we can be together always, he said as much. “Hurry,” I said to him, in my heart.

I hesitated a moment longer to watch the sun disappear and then went into the house to find Mildred standing at the back door.

"I was about to leave when I saw you out there Ms.," she said.

"It's beautiful, isn't it Mildred. No matter how many times I see it, I still am amazed at the beauty of the setting sun."

"It is that," she said.

Then for no apparent reason, I turn to Mildred and say, "Do you think God is trying to tell me something? " I ask.

Without missing a beat, Mildred replies, "I wouldn't put it past Him," she said.

"But what is it?"

She shakes her head. "I wouldn't know,"

I watch Mildred as she walks away, leaving me to ponder the thoughts in my head. Finally, I go into the house, check to make sure all the doors and windows are locked and then make my way upstairs. Surprisingly, I fall instantly to sleep.

I come down to breakfast the next morning feeling quite like my old self. The moment I cross the foyer and breathe the warm, sunny fragrance of fresh squeezed oranges and eggs I feel at peace. Once seated at the table I look out the window at the glassy surface of the lake all still and shining, bluer than a bluebird's wing. I go to the window, and draw in a deep breath. This was going to be a day of revelations if I have my way.

Mildred must have heard me about as she comes around the corner of the kitchen. "Mildred, have you eaten yet?"

"No, Miss, I will have something later."

"If you don't mind, I'd like you to join me," I said.

Mildred nods her head and then goes to get another place setting and fixes her plate. There is no need for words as we enjoy the beauty of the day as it comes through the windows.

Done eating and just enjoying our coffee, I ask.

"Mildred, what did you think of Michael."

There is a funny expression on her face, but she recovers quickly. "I don't know." She looks down into her coffee. "Oh my, look at the time," she says. I had best get to work."

I let out a sigh. After a bit, I manage to get up and go to the office to use the computer.

As I sit waiting, I think about Samuel and how he had reacted to what I told him. He didn't want to hear such crazy notions and it is probably because he knows there is something about Michael that is strange and different, only he won't admit it; not just yet anyway. I have admitted it and I admitted it out loud so now there is only one alternative and that is to confront the reality.

Inside the house is quiet and cool as I get up and stand by the window thinking now about the phone call. Mr. Bachman had mentioned that a Mr. Roman was interested in the portrait and that the gentleman would be calling. Could this be a coincident? Clara and Robert Roman were the parents of Michael, but they died in 1864 during the fire at the Halstein Theater. It had to be a coincidence or maybe someone from a later generation of Romans, which seems more reasonable.

But, I conclude, I am willing to believe Michael is real so how can I convince myself that this Mr. Roman is not. Suddenly I can't wait for the call, I have to meet this Mr. Roman as soon as possible so I call the museum.

"Hello Ms. Bouchard, I'm sorry, but Mr. Bachman is out right now.

Can I leave him a message?"

I hesitated and finally say, "Yes, tell him I would like him to call me as soon as possible."

"Is anything wrong, Ms. Bouchard?"

"No, I just need to speak with him."

I hang up the phone and stand wondering what to do next. Dr. Paulson enters my head and I wonder if maybe I have been too hasty in severing our relationship. I could use someone who is trained to listen and put sense to all that I now know. I pick up the extension but then put it down again. I need someone who believes in the existence of Michael, not someone who is trying to help me realize that it is all a dream. I know he has heard most of what I know, but I can bet he is trying to make it all make sense.

So, I hang around the house waiting for a call, until I think I will go crazy. I finally step out on the deck behind the house and look out at the lake thinking about Michael and remembering the day he told me he was going to the finishing school in France. How well I remember my visit to France some time ago, with the old weedy, fishy smell rising from the tide; the gulls circling and crying, out in the harbor; and the beach covered with sun worshipers. It was not that much different from the shores of Lake Ontario with boats gliding across the blue water, kicking up a little foam at their bows. Just as the sunset gave me pleasure here, I spent endless hours watching the slowly and peaceful sky and water deepen as the sun reached the horizon, not to return until the start of a new day. And I wondered, where, just where did it go?

Chapter 35

The fall drains away, but Michael does not return. By September the mums are in full bloom and Mildred always has a fresh bunch on the table in the dining room and on the one in the foyer, which she says is her way of preserving the life and extending the season.

As the season progresses, there are only a few diehards on the beach now that the days are cooler and the evenings could be downright chilly. A few, but not many still walk the boardwalk and some venture out on the pier, while still others are walking along the roadways. When I do go out I usually drive to the Erie Canal and see the reeds standing tall along the edges and now and again I will see people rollerblading or walking along the pedestrian paths that runs along its banks.

In the afternoons when I return the sun slants lower through the pines around the sides of my house and during the day the bluebirds, pigeons and sea gulls sweep nervously through the air knowing that a change is about to take place and the gaggle of geese flying southward in their V formation is becoming an all *too* familiar sight against the sky.

I decide to take my sailboat out one last time before putting it in drydock for the winter. The 42' Catalina MK II was a gift to myself several years ago and since that time I have managed to take her out quite frequently, but only going long distance when I can encourage a friend to join me. I call her Alana. I need distance to take my mind off Michael and an overnight sail will do me good so I call Samuel, who loves sailing as much as I do and he readily accepts my invitation.

The Alana, was never intended to be a high-performance sail boat as the prime criteria was sea worthiness and a comfortable, livable interior for long distance coastal and off shore cruising. I love the boat and manage most summers to spend a lot of time on her.

As I want to take off early in the morning I spend the rest of the day making sure the Alana is ready for sailing. I keep her moored in the boat house most of the summer and into the early fall only this year she has not been on the water much, as I have been *too* involved with other things. I feel she needs to sail as much as I need to get away from shore.

I clean the inside myself; making sure that the master cabin and its private head are clean and have what I will need for the trip, then checking both rear cabins and heads to assure either one is ready for Samuel. I add a few male necessities that Samuel might forget. Then it is on to give the main salon the once over.

Back in the house I go to the storage area and get out my box of supplies for the sailboat, making sure they are cleaned and ready to put on board. I check all the safety supplies, the lights and my maps, though I am familiar with the route we plan on taking. Then it is on to the grocery store to pick up the food, wine and beer. By the time I finish the preparations I am tired and ready for a good night's sleep.

The day chosen for our sail proves to be a safe one. It takes a good bit of navigating to get out of the boathouse as the tide and wind both have to be right. Samuel constitutes my crew; and he sits forward, ducking the boom when we come about, and handles the jib sheets. We have a steady 20 knot breeze and higher gusts as we sail away.

Lake Ontario gives us options and I like that. It may be the smallest of the Great Lakes, but it doesn't seem small when you try to look across it. It is the outlet to the Atlantic if you travel down the Saint Lawrence. I have managed to sail most of its 193-mile length and 53-mile width; and stayed at many of the state parks along its shore. Now as we head out we need to make a choice. If we go north we can anchor on the shores of Ontario, Canada, but Samuel and I settle on going eastward along the southern shore toward the Niagara River and Sodus, New York.

It always amazes me how it feels out on the water. It is a world by itself, in the glimmering sun, a world of never-ending blue and today with a steady wind we can relax and enjoy the wind gliding us across the lake surface.

"Taylor, this is a good idea. The weather is perfect."

"Yes, Samuel, it is. I am so glad you accepted my invitation."

"It's been some time since we sailed together and I love being on the Alana. It really is sad the way you keep her anchored for so long. If she were mine I would have her out every day."

I smile at Samuel. I like that Samuel and I have a solid relationship. We are an unlikely twosome; him being a private detective and me an artist but we have a lot of qualities in common. We both have a sense of humor, similar interests to some degree at least, good communication skills, and a strong desire to help each other work out conflicts and problems together. And, yes, we are both single and not looking to change that anytime soon. I remember when I introduced him to Annie, hoping to spark up an interest between my two friends. Samuel was polite but later told me that I should not do that again. I respected that and the trust between us was back in harmony.

For most of the trip we are silent, enjoying the sights along the way. We toss out the anchor at several points so that I can make a sketch of the area and Samuel tries his hand at fishing. All to soon it is time to go ashore.

We anchor that night near Oswego, New York, and while Samuel builds a fire at the shores edge. I bring a picnic basket of goodies and two canvas chairs to shore so that we can eat without having to go into town. We dine on a tomato and cucumber salad, fresh corn on the cob, red potatoes and red snapper that I had seasoned ahead of time.

After we eat, we walk around gathering wood for the fire and soon the fire is blazing, providing much needed heat against the coolness of the evening. We sit on the canvas chairs drinking wine while we stare into the flames reveling in the quiet.

We talk in the firelight; with the shadows in the woods behind us, the pale sky above full of stars, and the sailboat rocking quietly at its anchor, on the tide. In a, roundabout way I tell Samuel what is on my mind.

“We think that we are the only ones here in the universe. We also make ourselves believe that when we are gone, we're gone but can we be so sure? I think about that a lot lately."

Samuel looks at me without responding.

“Think about all we believe, like dinosaurs. They exist no more and we never saw them, but we don't doubt they existed."

“Yes, but...” he changes his thought in mid-sentence. “I do agree there is much that we are willing to accept without being able to experience it.”

A comfortable silence falls between us. This is what friendship is all about; being able to share logic and the unknown comfortably without fear that what is said will sound crazy. Samuel is the only man that I can really be laid back and open with.

Samuel yawns. "What say we put this fire out and climb back on board and get some sleep."

"I think that is a good idea."

While I go about gathering up our belongs and carrying them to the sailboat, Samuel is busy dousing the fire with water. Once on board, we go below and stow away the items then I have another wine, while Samuel opts for a beer.

“Okay,” that’s it for me. I get up and head to my sleeping quarters and I hear Samuel as he makes his way behind me. “Which room should I take,” he asks.

“Your choice,” I prepared them both.

Under his breath, I hear the gaiety in his voice, “Should have known….”

That night, I dream of Michael: I dream of our meeting, long ago. I see him as the child, walking down the long empty row of benches on the walkway in the park, and I hear him say as he had said then, "I wish you'd wait for me to grow up, but you won't, I guess." And in my dream, I remember him repeating the child's prayer. *Now I lay me down to sleep. I pray the Lord my soul will keep ....* And I remember pieces of the song he sang as he played with his jacks. It was words that I caught only snatches of, but it had to do with a boy named Michael.

I wake with a sense of alarm, with a feeling that something is wrong. I hurry above board and immediately feel that the wind is stronger, a bit too strong. I look up at the sky, unaware that Samuel has joined me, and I see threatening clouds overhead. “We've got to get home," he says.

We hurry back down to get dressed then meet on deck preparing to leave. Out on the water, the wind seems even stronger. It is a little aft of us, and I let the sail take all it can. It is something of a job to hold her steady. We are in a hurry so we turn on the motor to get us home quickly.

"Don't worry," Samuel says comforting. "This is a big boat and can withstand a little storm."

Though not quite visible I think the sun is up, hidden behind the thick clouds. I grip the boat's edge for balance as it bobs up and down. Buoys are ahead and I keep my hand on the tiller while Samuel holds the main sheet just behind the cleat. With each gust of wind, the boat heels obediently and I hear gurgling water an inch closer to my back. The lake heaves to only a foot away from the boat's side, then sinks, then heaves again as though it is doing deep breathing lessons.

The first of the big swells hammers the side but we see it coming and are prepared. Alana heels crazily in the growing darkness of the storm and I shove the tiller hard to starboard. Samuel rips the main sheet from its cleat and lets it go. The boom sweeps across the lee of the cockpit like a scythe, as the boat sweeps across the water that pours over the coaming and onto the empty seat.

The haze deepens very slowly, but the clouds increase appearing to be at different levels, moving rapidly. They turn a different tone of white, too, like cotton gone a little dusty. Samuel has made the main sheet fast, but I wonder if the sail will hold. "Samuel," I call out to him, cupping my mouth, "hadn't we better reef the sail?"

It's hard to see him, but I catch his nod. I manage to bring the boat up into the wind. My fingers are trembling as I cup my mouth again. "We'd better get out of here," I say.

The boat goes off with a rush, and I try to head up a little to windward, to get some shelter from the shore. The waves are running a good deal higher now, and breaking at the crests; I put all my weight on the tiller to hold her steady. I am feeling decidedly uneasy, not able to really judge the strength of the wind, but I can feel it is blowing hard. And there is a strange sound to it, from somewhere far away.

My arms and hands are aching from holding the tiller, and my legs are tired from bracing myself against the sides. I call to Samuel to come aft and take over, while I go forward to bail some of the water that has come in, mostly over the stern. We manage to safely switch positions.

The waves seem higher as Alana tilts up at the stern, hangs for a moment on a crest, and then rushes down the slope after it. Samuel fights to keep the boat straight. Each time the tip of the boom hits the water, I think we're going over. My throat is dry, my eyes blinded at times and I keep listening to the wind. It isn't like anything I'd ever heard before.

I assume we have been at it over an hour when suddenly the storm breaks loose in torrential rains that push and shove us in all directions. There is little time to be afraid as we work together to keep the boat upright. I am thankful that we are trained to handle such a situation and even happier that we can recall those teachings.

Silence rules until finally the worse is over and we find ourselves in view of the dock and my boathouse. Standing on the pier is Mildred. I look at Samuel, "She must have been watching for us."

"Yep, and she looks frightened."

Mildred observes as I climb out of the sailboat and gratefully plant my feet on the deck, while Samuel goes below to gather his belongings before joining us. Our clothes are soak and wet and our hands bleeding and sore, but we are safe now. "It was such a nice day yesterday and last night the stars were out and the wind calm. Who would have thought."

"Come on inside, I've made a fire, and I got out the brandy. You are both soaked and should change into something dry."

We follow Mildred into the house and while I go upstairs to change, Mildred takes Samuel to the guest bedroom suite where he manages to find something dry to put on in his overnight bag. By the time I return, Samuel is sitting before the fire in the family room where Mildred has brought a tray with hot coffee and pastries.

"Come have a coffee," Samuel says. I feel him watching me as I walk across the room to pour a cup of coffee, add a little brandy and then sit in the chair directly across from him. I wrap my hands around the mug and bring it up to my lips and feel it warm me all the way down as we sit in front of the fire. Soon Mildred joins us.

"I don't know how it was out there on the lake, but here I could feel the house shake every now and then, and I heard the windows rattle. I wondered if you two were okay out there on the lake. I was more than a little worried."

"It's a good boat Mildred and big enough to handle such a storm, but thank you for caring." I said.

Suddenly I feel shaky. My legs tremble, and my teeth chatter. When it passes, I manage to say, "I'm sorry Samuel. I swear the report didn't mention any bad weather coming our way. "

Samuel looks at me, and nods his head. "I know Taylor, how thorough you are. Any way I like a challenge now and then. Makes life interesting."

Later after Samuel has left for home, I start drifting in the chair and though it couldn't be much past three in the afternoon I tell Mildred I was going up to bed.

In my room, I take a shower and put on a long cotton nightie then brush my teeth. I find antiseptic in the medicine cabinet and apply it to my hands. The bleeding had stopped almost immediately after arriving home, but my hands are still tender. As I climb into the bed I pull the covers up to my neck and finally admit how scared I was. "Thank you, God, for looking after me and Samuel."

I sleep soundly and if I dream I don't remember. The next morning, I wake to see sunshine coming through my bedroom window. I stretch, enjoying the warmth then get up to shower, wash my hair, and when I am done, I feel refreshed.

Downstairs I go into the kitchen where I greet Mildred, pour myself a cup of coffee and carry it with me to the studio. Mildred is used to this and doesn't heed my progress.

I work most of the day and enjoy the solitude so

much that I am not aware of the day passing into the afternoon until Mildred pops her head in to ask if I am hungry. I am, but I don't want to stop so I tell her, no. The next point at which I am aware of time passing is when Mildred quietly enters the studio with a tray that holds a bowl of salad and a plate of rolls. She doesn't say a thing as she sits it down on the table and slips silently out the room.

My body aches from being in the same position for so long. I stretch and stand up in front of the easel, realizing that I am losing light. It is definitely time to stop. I walk over and pick up the salad bowl, carrying it with me as I survey the picture I have been working on. I look at it from all angles making sure I can see and feel depth and reality in the image that appears on the canvas and I think it is good, quite good.

The picture is of a sailboat far out at sea so that it appears to be swallowed up by the tossing of the waves. Above the boat the sky is dark and seems to be moving menacingly overhead, while on board two small figures fight for control of the boat. I like it and though it is not the type of picture people sought after, I imagine it hanging in the museum as a display of creativity with color. I am certain that will be the destiny of the painting, but that isn't so bad. I can afford to use my talents for just pleasure.

That night when I go up to bed I recall that feeling I had at the museum. That feeling when I entered the lobby and was overcome with a sensation as though I was a swimmer fighting my way to the surface for air. It had scared me, that sense of drowning and I begin to wonder if maybe it had been a premonition of what Samuel and I had gone through on the boat or was it something yet to happen. I wondered if there was a meaning to it.

Chapter 36

It is three months before I receive a call from Mr. Roman asking when it would be convenient for us to get together. During that period of waiting I have not been idle, but instead have continued my research, realizing that the facts I am uncovering may not be facts that are absolutely connected to Michael, but it doesn't matter. I can feel it in my heart that I am on the right trail and my biographical sketch is opening the door of knowledge I need.

At several points during my research I want to call Peter Newman. On one hand, I told myself I owe him an explanation of how I had come to paint the portrait of Michael, but then on the other hand, I didn't want to have him thinking I believe what he has told me about his son dying and my Michael taking over his body. That disturbs me more than anything else. I need to have that explained in a logical way and I need this not to be my Michael because that would mean he is related to me.

Yet, I am curious. Is Michael's physical appearance that of his own or is his physical appearance that of Peter's son, Max? I believe it is that of Max since talking with Peter and knowing how his friends saw this to be true. But now, what about now. Is this still Max or is it Michael as he would be? It's too confusing to think about.

It all seems so crazy and unbelievable, but, I am beginning to think there is something to his story. I have even figured out a way to tie it all together and that scares me. If I were to ask Peter when it was that this son and wife died, ask him to tell me the exact day, date and time, and that happened to somehow overlay exactly to the exact day, date and time that I first saw Michael, well then, I would have to consider it creditable, wouldn't I? Yet, I know that there could still be a connection between the incidents even if it were not to be exactly on the date...

It could be a mere coincidence if I learn that Michael appeared to me after the date of Max's death. I am not well versed enough to know if this is something that happens at exactly the same time, and since I don't know what Michael is, I haven't a clue how to proceed.

But keeping Peter at bay is like a safety net. I love Michael. I know this to be true. I want to know, but then again, I don't and I fear that Peter can bring truth to it all, which terrifies me.

On several occasions, I am tempted to call Samuel and get his opinion on all of this, but something holds me back. It is the same when I think about calling Annie. I know that besides having in common the fact that they both have seen Michael, they also both are extremely worried about me lately and I just don't have the heart to add more reason for them to worry.

This is the state I am in when I receive the call. The call that could tie it all together.

As I listen to the voice on the other end of the telephone, I find myself wondering if there is a way of telling whether I am talking to a ghost. Is there a phone line from here to the great beyond? Even though I chuckle, I seriously worry about my sanity.

"Ms. Bouchand, are you still there?" the voice asks, shaking me out of my reverie.

"Yes, Mr. Roman. I am here. I was just wondering what you would like to see me about?"

"The portrait," came the reply.

Of course, I remind myself, the portrait. Mr. Roman is calling because he wants to see the portrait. I knew that. What I don't know and what I can't ask is the why behind the reason that he wants to see the portrait again.

"Ms. Bouchand?"

"Yes, I'm here. I was just checking to see when we could meet," I lie. "I am free this afternoon if you want to meet that soon. Does that fit into your schedule?"

"This afternoon would be fine."

The voice on the phone I find very pleasant and something tells me that he will be nice. I have seen pictures of Michael's parents and know what they looked like. What I didn't know is beyond being successful pianist, what made up the rest of their personality. This I would like to know.

"Stop it Taylor," I whisper "Stop thinking this is Michael's parents. That would be impossible."

"Ms. Bouchand?"

"Yes, I'm here. I need your address. Please tell me where you live and I will come by around two, two- thirty, if that is convenient."

There is a pause on the other end of the line now as I wait for Mr. Roman to supply me with an address or directions. In anticipation, I get out a pad and a pencil to write down the information.

"Well, I think it would be best if I came to your studio ... If you don't mind, that is? I would like to see the painting again, that is if you still have it and it is in your studio."

He wants to come here, I say to myself. Is that because he doesn't have a residence that I can come to? I reprimand myself again as I listen to Mr. Roman and hear a sense of urgency as well as hope. This man is anxious to see the portrait, but not only that, I bet he is hoping that he can convince me to sell it to him.

"Mr. Roman, are you aware that I do not intend to sell the portrait? If you are hoping to buy it, I must tell you, it is not for sale."

Mr. Roman confirms that he is indeed aware that I had told Mr. Bachman that the picture was not for sale, but he still wants to meet with me.

I'm not sure now what to do. I hesitate to invite the man to my home, but what else can I do. I give Mr. Roman directions and verify the time before hanging up.

I go speak to Mildred, letting her know that we will have a guest that afternoon, then I go about organizing the studio. I place other charcoals and paintings I have done on the display wall in the studio so that Mr. Roman might see them. I then carefully take the portrait of Michael put it on an easel and place a white sheet over the painting.

It is not that I want to be dramatic, but more a way of steering Mr. Roman's attention to the other paintings which hopefully would appeal to him and take his mind off the portrait of Michael. It is just a theory, but one I think best to pursue to keep the client happy, plus it allows me to concentrate on something other than the visit. I then spend the time trying to be productive, but can't help thinking about the impending meeting.

The doorbell rings at precisely 2:30 p.m. and Mildred goes to the foyer to open the door letting the visitor in. I hear her asking if she can take his hat, and smiling to myself I think, because he of course would be wearing one. Everyone wore one back in his day.

I wait nervously in the studio, I hear the light banter and then footsteps walking down the foyer until they stop directly outside the studio door. There is a light rap and then the door knob turns, followed by the motion of the door being pulled outward to reveal the figures of my housekeeper and the visitor and it is then too late to hide my surprise.

Framed in the doorway is yet another grown up version of Michael. Mr. Roman stands over six feet. He is trim and has no sign of gray in his dark brown hair that he wears in a neat, businesslike cut. His eyes are deep-set and a rich brown as are his eyebrows that are full above them. He wears a white dress shirt with the top two buttons open and the collar starched stiffly so that it stands up covering most of his neck. His nose is average length and size, emphasized by a thick black mustache covering his upper lip. He wears tan pleated pants with a black belt and a black suitcoat.

All of this I take in as he stands at an angle in the doorway with his hands in his pocket and only a slight visible smile pushing up the corners of his mouth. I know I am staring but I cannot help it because I am sure that I see the past standing in the future. The silence is broken when Mr. Roman speaks. His words soft spoken and melodious.

"Ms. Bouchard, I am Robert Roman.

It is in the way he says his name or the way he presents his hand as he walks toward me, whichever the case I feel my eyes close as I strive to regain control and stop the pounding in my chest. Only it won't stop. Then everything goes black.

I don't know how long I am out. I wake up to find myself stretched out on the sofa in my studio. My eyes rest on the worried face of Mildred as she presses a cool washcloth to my forehead. It takes a moment before I realize I fainted and then my face flushes with embarrassment.

"I'm all right now, Mildred," I say slowly moving up into a seated position. I didn't dare look around at first as I try to compose myself.

"I'm sorry, I gave you such a fright, Ms. Bouchard. Are you all right now?"

There is genuine concern in Mr. Roman's voice and when I finally dare to look up, I can see he is indeed worried. "Oh, no, I'm just fine." Quickly I wrack my brain for an excuse and come up with one. "I feel so silly. I was just putting the last picture up and I must have moved too quickly. I was just dizzy from the motion, that's all."

It seemed believable and soon I stand and face my visitor.

"Hello Mr. Roman, I am Taylor Bouchard. Mildred, that will be all for now, unless Mr. Roman would care for something to drink."

"If you don't mind, I could use a cold glass of water."

I look in Mildred's direction and see her nod before turning around and leaving me alone with Mr. Roman.

"Mr. Ro ... "

"Please, call me Robert."

"Thank you. Please call me Taylor."

It is as though I know him and he knows me and yet, we have only met. It's a strange sensation that works its way through my whole body until I

Need to lean back against the wall for support. His voice is enchanting.

"Robert, I have several of my paintings over there on the wall.   Would you like to look at them?"

He doesn't reply, but stands where he is looking at me as though sending me a message. And I know; I know that there is nothing that would interest him besides the portrait of Michael. I watch as his eyes drift from my face and over to the easel with its covered treasure. Neither of us speak. It isn't necessary as we both walk toward the easel in such a natural, unexplainable unison. I am the first to reach the easel and carefully I remove the sheet and let it fall softly to the floor and where once the room had belonged to us, it now is penetrated by the appearance of Michael

Silence fills the room as we stand staring at the portrait, I as though seeing it for the first time and Robert as though he is connected to it. We are so engrossed that Mildred entering and putting a pitcher of water and two water glasses on the round table near the door goes unnoticed. We continue to stand only slightly apart gazing at Michael until finally Robert speaks.

"I must ask you this and I must have a true answer. Please, Taylor, where is he?"

"What? I don't..."

"Please, I know he has come to you and I need to find him."

"I am so sorry, but I really don't know where he is or where he came from. All I know is that he was here."

Robert Roman moves closer to the portrait as though trying see behind him or through him, allowing the silence to veil the room again.

Finally, he draws his eyes away and turned towards me.

"That is Michael," he said matter-of-factly. He cannot rest and I need to tell him that I forgive him and that everything is all right. Do you understand, Taylor, he needs to know it's, all right."

No, I don't understand and I am afraid to ask what he means. I can't even ask why he is here. He died. Robert and Clara Roman had died on November 15, 1864, but yet Robert is standing here in my studio on December 5, 2017. It is not possible, or is it.

"Ms. Bouchard, I would like to share something with you if you will allow me."

I thought about that and though I want to say I don't want to hear what he has to tell me, I find myself saying, "yes".

Mr. Roman waits a moment as though trying to put it all together in his head before sharing it with me and then he begins.

"Close in importance to the basic human needs for food, shelter, and companionship comes the urge to create an orderly world governed by dependable rules and to develop a reassuring structure of beliefs. There has never been, nor is there likely to be, a shortage of authorities ready to find reasonable explanations for all observed phenomena and to provide solutions for the mysteries of the universe. Yet there are events that seem to say that our rules, our beliefs, even our common sense, may sometimes let us down. This is such an experience that I share with you now. "

I sit on the sofa and Robert sits on the other end.

"Taylor, I know why you fainted and that is because you could see Michael in me. Let me first tell you that I am not Michael and I am not his father. The Robert who was his father was my great, great, great grandfather." He pauses and smiles. "I guess since we are talking about a little boy, Michael who would be almost two centuries old, that is not so far fetch to believe."

I find myself relieved to know that I am not in the presence of another ghost. For some reason that would be one ghost too many for me to handle. A giggle slips out. "Sorry."

I relax more and looking at Robert, I realize that he is not done explaining.

"I am telling this to you since you have been chosen by Michael and you need to know how this is happening. I'm not sure about the 'why'. In any case, the way I understand it is that Michael's death was not to be." He takes a long drink of his water.

"I don't know if you know about his parents, but let me tell you that his parents, Robert and Clara Roman were pianist and scheduled to play at the Halstein Theater in Rochester. Robert studied at the Royal Northern College of Music where his fellow students included composers Sir Peter Maxwell Davies and Sir Harrison Birtwistle. Robert was twenty-five when he entered the famous International Tchaikovsky Piano Competition, where he won joint first prize with Russian pianist Vladimir Ashkenazy. Robert was renowned as an interpreter of late-Romantic repertoire and made dozens of recordings."

"Michael's mother Clara was also a pianist, giving her first concert at age 8. At 24, she won the International Chopin Piano Competition, which gave her international renown. Today, she is acknowledged as not only one of the best female pianists, but one of the best pianists in the history of the art".

"I tell you this so that you know a little more about Michael. He is the son of not only famous, but well-known parents who travelled the world. I have been researching this for many years and I can tell you that Michael is what some call a Transitioner."

I start to interrupt, but Robert silences me.

"I need to add some credence to what I am about to share so bear with me. Transitioners have been known about for centuries all around the world, but not always called that. I have heard about them in Cornwall, Germany, Ireland, The Isle of Man, Scotland, England, Poland, Scandinavia, Spain and Wales and I am sure there are other cases that I have yet to uncover. People tell the story of what you are experiencing in many, many parts of the world and what explains this is that a Transitioner is a child who goes before their time and the way they can return is by the death of another child who dies in the same manner as they did, which for Michael was by fire."

I am silent waiting for him to tell me more. When he doesn't, I ask, "Please, Mr. Roman; Robert. Please tell me; why me?"

"Well, Taylor, the reason for who they present themselves to is someone who is related to the child who passed away."

"I don't know why, really. Only Michael can answer that question or possibly the parents of the child whose body he claimed. You would need to find that out first. But, can you tell me about the first time you saw Michael. "

I told him everything from the beginning in the park to the last time he came to me here. Robert listened closely, taking in my every word and when I finished he said. "Thank you, Taylor. This will help. Michael has returned many times to many people and I am trying to find out when it stops, or if it ever will."

Robert stood up and I follow suit. "Well, that's all I can tell you and I thank you for letting me see the portrait."

"Will I see you again. What if I call you when Michael comes again, or just to ask questions. I feel like I'm going crazy."

"I understand Taylor, truly I do. I am constantly on the go so it will be hard to reach me as I am also a concert pianist. I guess it runs in the family. But, here is my card."

I take the card from his hand and look up into his face. Just like that, he reaches out and hugs me and it feels right. When he releases me, I smile at him and then walk him to the foyer. He touches my shoulder, turns and walks out the door.

Chapter 37

There is nothing coming up on the internet to help me that I don't already know so off to the Library I go. I haven't a clue what I am looking for, just that there is something bugging me and it is that feeling I am running out of time. I am unsure what it means, but I have to figure it out.

I begin first by gathering books on anything that I remotely think might help and take them to the table. I start reading and jotting down what I want and where I can find it. New births are always reported by the hospitals or professionals who deliver the child, while coroners offices assign death certificates. Marriage licenses are kept as a matter of public record. These three types of documents will be extremely helpful. I know that as far back as I am going and because the individuals I am researching are not all renown this won't be easy. I run across the following information.

In general, vital records weren't kept in the United States until the early 1900s. Vital records usually contain the full name of the individual involved in the event, the date of the event, and the county, state, or town where the event took place. Many vital records contain much more information. For example, birth records usually have the parent's full names, the name of the baby, the date of the birth, and county where the birth took place, marriage records often record the names and birthplaces of everyone's parents. Divorce records usually list the names of the couple's children. Death certificates often mention where the individual will be buried, and give the name of the individual who reported the death.

I read through all the instructions given for requesting this information and that it may take time to obtain. The more I think about it, the more I am certain that won't do.

I give up knowing that the best way to get this information is from Peter Newman and Robert Roman. Maybe they don't know all the answers, but they are my only source to check.

I start with Peter who is unable to hide his surprise that I have called. We talk and he agrees to come to my house. Want I want to talk to him about is not something to discuss in public. With the date set, I then call Robert Roman and he is happy to sit down with me. With it set up, I relax.

I am shocked when the doorbell rings and I open it to find Michael standing there. My eyes feast on his image that is now that of a grown man. My first instinct is to grab hold of him and never let him go, but something in his demeaner stops me.

"Hello, Taylor. It is so good to see you."

"Me too," I say, me too." I smile, adding. "Come in, please."

Michael hesitates before saying, "Can we go somewhere and get something to eat."

"Sure, let me grab a jacket." I start to ask him to come in and wait, but I can tell he doesn't want to, so I leave the door open and pray as I walk away, 'please don't let him disappear, please'. When I return, Michael is still there.

We walk side my side, not saying a word until we reach a diner. We sit at a table near the window and watch the people who come in and out.

"Taylor, I'll be right back," Michael says.

Don't, I start to say, afraid he is going to leave, but instead of heading toward the door, he goes down the hallway toward the bathrooms. I relax.

The waitress comes to the table and I am pretty sure what Michael will want so I place our order. I stare out the window until I am aware that Michael is back. I look at him and say, "I placed our order. Hopefully it's what you wanted."

"Whatever you ordered is fine, Taylor, just fine."

Shortly after Michael returns our breakfast is on the table and I dive in wholeheartedly. I ordered plain buttermilk pancakes for me and Michael has blueberry. They taste divine. I sip my coffee.

I don't know what to say. Michael seems so distracted as he sits across from me. When our food arrives, we eat. Michael smiles at me and grabs my hand and the waitress comes to refill our coffee cup, giving me a strange look. Michael releases my hand and I notice that he barely touches his food.

"Michael, do you want something else?"

"No, Taylor, I'm just not hungry."

When the waitress comes to clear the table, I ask for the check and she disappears and returns with it. "Was everything all right," she asks.

"Yes, everything was fine." I hand her my credit card and she leaves again.

Michael is quiet throughout the exchange and my worry grows, wondering what is on his mind. When the waitress returns, I take my copy of the receipt and put the credit card in my purse, quickly and ignore the change that falls out onto the table.

When we are outside I ask, "Michael, what is it. What is bothering you?"

He doesn't speak right away and when he does he says, "I'm tired Taylor, very tired."

"Are you not sleeping," I ask.

When he speaks, he doesn't answer my question, but instead says, "I'm sorry Taylor, but I have to go. I am so sorry. I just had to see you again."

"Why do you have to go. Where do you go."

All aspects of his face droop downward, indicating defeat. I sense he is giving up and it scares me. I move closer wanting to hold him, but he steps backwards.

"Bye Taylor," is all he says as he turns and walks away.

I am shocked, unable to move at first and then slowly I manage to take a step forward. One minute I was sitting across the table from him and the next I am standing here alone with Michael nowhere in sight.

I stumble forward, looking down at the ground not want to make eye contact with anyone. Michael had been sitting right here beside me. I had talked to him, touched him, heard him clear as a bell.

This just can't be what I think it is. It can't, I realize because plenty of people saw me with Michael. At that moment, I need validation of some sort so I go back into the bagel shop and try to find the woman who had taken our order. I finally see her. She is in the midst of taking another table's order, but I can't wait.

"Miss," I say interrupting her. "Do you remember me?"

"I never forget a three-cent tip," she mutters.

Not sure what she means by that, I ignore it and ask, "How many people were at my table?"

I follow her to the cash register." Is this a trick question? You were by yourself. Even though you ordered enough to feed half the kids in Africa."

I open my mouth to point out that I only ordered one meal for myself, and Michael had ordered his own. But then it dawns on me that wasn't true. I ordered for him while he was in the restroom.

Adamantly I add, "I was with a man in his thirties—his hair was dark and he was wearing white linen pants and a dusty blue short sleeve shirt."

"Look, Miss," The waitress says, I saw only you. You ordered two meals, for sure, but you were alone."

"He was in the bathroom."

"Maybe, but he never came back to join you. I tell you I only saw you."

I leave the café and start walking. My head buzzes as it fills with the sound of everything I know, everything I believe, being challenged.

Were there really such things as spirits and ghost and as the research I have done states, that the former has made it smoothly to the next plane of existence. The latter had something anchoring it to this world.

I still needed to verify this situation. Was it real or not.

By the time I reach the house, I have made a decision.

I barely take the time to take off my jacket and hang it in the closet before I go in search of Mildred. I find her in the laundry room. "Mildred, can I talk to you?"

She is startled, not hearing me approach and when she is back in control she says, "Sure, Miss. What is it?"

I take a deep breath and say, "Mildred. The boy in the picture, the one we were looking at together. Have you ever seen him here?"

There is a puzzled expression on her face and I'm not sure which way she is going to answer.

"No, Miss. Should I have seen him here?"

I try again. "Did you maybe see me with a young man. A young man who looked like the boy in the picture, only older?"

Without saying it, I already know the answer. "No."

"What is it Miss. Can I help you with something?"

I give her a weak smile. "No Mildred. Thank you though."

I walk out of the laundry room feeling dejected. I thought for sure Mildred had seen him, but now as I think back, each time he came to the door, I answered it, not Mildred. And, that time in the studio as she talked about Michael. I was talking about the real Michael and she was talking about the portrait and the sculpture.

There is one more chance. One more chance that Michael is real.

I pick up the extension and dial Samuel's number. He picks up on the first ring. "Hi Taylor."

"I hate when you do that Samuel."

"I know, that's why I do it," he says fondly. "What's on your mind."

"I have to ask you something and I want an honest answer."

"Sure, go ahead."

I stand there with my nose and forehead scrunched up. I raise one eyebrow higher than the other and purse my lips together. I am confused. Do I really want to know what Samuel will say?

Pull yourself together, I tell myself.

"Okay, Samuel, have you ever seen me with Michael."

There is silence on the other end of the line and with each passing minute I grow more anxious until I can't wait. "Please Samuel. Tell me."

"I'm sorry, Taylor. The answer is, no, I haven't seen Michael. I didn't know how to tell you or what to do. I know you have been seeing a psychiatrist so I thought that it would all blow over. That you would be all right again. Every time you mentioned him I shrunk away from responding, not knowing what else to do. Do I say, Taylor, there is no one with you, or should I say, sure, I see Michael. I took the cowards way out and just said nothing."

Now it is my turn to be silent. I try to imagine this from his standpoint and wonder what I would do if the shoe was on the other foot. I probably would have done just as he did; just as Mildred had done also.

There is nothing more I can say or ask at this point. "Samuel, thank you."

"You're welcome Taylor. I wish I could be of more help to you. I don't know what you are going through, but you are a strong person and will figure it out. I know you will."

I disconnect the call and put the phone down. I could call Annie, but what would be the use of that. She would say the same thing, that she hasn't seen Michael.

It would be so easy to believe he does not exist if he came to me in dreams, but I have been fully awake every single time. So, it is not a dream.

Knowing how I feel I realize that Peter must feel something like I do. I need to tell him what I know so that maybe he can be at peace. That's what I tell myself. The truth of the matter is that Peter believes as I do and I need to talk with someone who doesn't think I'm losing my mind.

PETER NEWMAN

Chapter 38

Too much time has passed and I haven't heard from Taylor. I am worried about her and wonder if she is trying to find a way to accept what is happening to her because that's what I'm doing. When I'm not working on a case, I begin reviewing old ones that had gone cold or rang of something unexplainable.

One of the things I was taught in law school is that I'd never be able to think the same again - that being a lawyer is something that's part of who I am as an individual now. The more I read it has me concluding that admitting this to a lawyer only happens if a person is looking to get off on an insanity plea, but for Sidney, his patients are willing and open about this because they are seeking help. They tell him about their hallucinations because he is not judgmental and because they know him and trust him.

So, what do I do. I tell myself I am a lawyer so I know how to do research on even the oddest of situations and this calls for research. I need to look for precedents first which means I must start at the beginning. I sit pondering this, not wanting to admit it to myself until finally I accept what my mind and my heart is telling me. What I witnessed should be classified and the classifications are either miracle, a supernatural phenomenon, or a hallucination.

I spend hours trying to determine exactly the classification because this is not happening to a stranger. It happened to me and is happening to me again. I read information on many online sites. I read on one site that a miracle is a divine operation that transcends what is normally perceived as natural law and the Merriam-Webster Dictionary which says that a miracle is an extraordinary event manifesting divine intervention in human affairs.

I am satisfied that these definitions are accurate when I come across one that goes a step further and says that such an event might be attributed to a supernatural being. I sit up straight in my chair and push it back so that I can stand and walk around a bit. I look at my watch and realize that I have been at it for over three hours now, but I must continue. I sit back down and type, 'supernatural' press enter and wait. The consensus gives the word basically the same definition as miracle. I type 'supernatural being or phenomena'. This time I get a definition stating that it is all that cannot be explained by science such as ghosts, gods, or other types of spirits and other non-material beings, or things beyond nature.

I want to stop now, but I must go on. I type, 'hallucinations' and press enter. I read several discussion posts and sites dealing with the terminology. Hallucinations are explained as frightening events of seeing, hearing or smelling something that no one else seems to experience but is convincingly real. The event is produced by the same neural pathways as actual perception.

I read on. Millions of people hallucinate but are quiet about them, not wanting to believe it is happening to them. "I can relate to that."

Medical sites present their findings of hallucinations as being caused by migraines, seizures, fevers, or delirium. "Hm," I say to myself as I read, 'hallucinations' can be caused by interactions between medications.

I lean back in my chair and feel lucky that at least I have several people I trust sharing in this experience. I am not alone and I can imagine that Taylor was alone with this knowledge for quite a while. "What must that have been like for her."

I rub my eyes and read further and come across something inspirational. I read it out loud. "But hallucinations can have a positive and comforting role, too — this is especially true with bereavement hallucinations, seeing the face or hearing the voice of one's deceased spouse, siblings, parents or child — and may play an important part in the mourning process."

I smile feeling assured enough to type, 'Bereavement hallucinations' in the search engine. I pick one of the sites and read that bereavement hallucinations frequently occur in the first year or two of bereavement, when they are most "needed." I stop there because it has been a long time; too long for me to be seeing my wife and my child again.

Suddenly I look up as it hits me like a ton of bricks. "They haven't appeared to me. This is not happening, really, too me. It is happening to Taylor."

What does this mean. The only logical solution I come up with is that I and the others have been drawn in to help Taylor get through this. "So how can I help?" I ask myself.

The phone rings and I practically jump out of my chair. It rings again and I come to my senses, pick it up and say, "Yes?"

"Peter. It's me, Elizabeth."

I look at my watch. "Oh, Elizabeth. I am so sorry. It is late. I just got so caught up I lost track of time."

"That's okay, honey. I just want you to know I left dinner in the fridge. I'm tired so I'll see you in the morning."

"Love you baby."

"Love you too."

I disconnect the call and suddenly know what I must do next.

I look at my calendar and see I have a light day tomorrow. As much as I want to continue, I know I need sleep. I get up from my chair, logout of the computer and turn off the lights as I make my way to the elevator. As I step out into the hall, I lock the door of the office behind me.

Soon I am out of the building and climb into my car. There is no one in the garage box office as I make my way out onto the street and head toward home.

Chapter 39

The next morning, I am refreshed and anxious to get to work. I have a quick cup of coffee with Elizabeth and kiss her goodbye before we both head out the door. In the garage I pause and say, "I'll be home early tonight and we can go out to dinner."

"I'd like that a lot." She smiles and climbs into her car.

I wait until she is on her way and I follow suit.

As I head to work I keep an eye on my speedometer as I know I am anxious to get to the office. The traffic is light and I manage to make most of the lights on the main street as I plough along, humming at first, then singing out loud the words to the song, 'Playground in my mind."

I arrive at the garage and say hello to the attendant before pulling into my parking space. I grab my briefcase and hurry into the office building in time to catch an elevator that has just arrived.

Soon I am walking through the doors and heading toward my office and once inside I turn on the computer, wait a few seconds and then login. While it is going through its changes, I go for a cup of coffee, chat with one of the paralegals for a minute and then head over to the secretary's desk. I take my first sips while checking with her on my calendar and just as I thought, most of the day belongs to me.

Back in my office I sit and begin. All the cases of the office are in files online and I begin searching through case records for those that cover a disappearance or death of children.

I came across the case of the Betlems who on a bright summer day in 1961, their three children vanished without a trace from a South Carolina beach. It happened almost 50 years ago. The Betlem children were in route to a popular suburban seaside beach for a day's swim. Jane, the oldest at age 12, was responsible for her younger siblings, Anna, age 5, and Grant, age 4.

The siblings boarded a public bus at 10:00 A.M. for a five-minute ride to the beach—a trip they made many times before. Their mother Nancy spent the morning with her friend, while her husband Jim was at work. Nancy told her children to return home by 2:00 P.M. for lunch.

When the scheduled time came and went, Nancy assumed her children simply missed the bus. But when the next bus arrived and the children were nowhere to be seen, the mother grew concerned. She called the police soon thereafter. The following day, the Betlem children were officially declared missing.

According to eyewitnesses, the three children left the beach around 10:15 A.M. They were then seen at 11:00 A.M. by an elderly woman who spotted them playing under a sprinkler. But someone else was also present: a lean, blond man in a blue bathing suit. He was first lying belly down, watching the Betlem children play. Fifteen minutes later, the mystery man was playing with them.

At around 11:45 A.M. the children were seen buying snacks at a cafe. This would be the first clue that something was amiss—the children hadn't left the house with that much money. Someone must've given it to them.

The disappearance of the Betlem children stunned this upscale resort area, and triggered one of the largest missing persons investigations in the nation's history. Drowning was ruled out, as all their belongings were also missing. An appeal from Jim Betlem was broadcast on national TV. Authorities followed every lead, but every lead led to nowhere.

Even a paranormal investigator was called in for assistance. His visit caused a media circus. The parapsychologist claimed his sixth sense led him to a warehouse where he believed the bodies were buried. The warehouse's owners, reluctant at first to participate, finally agreed to have the area search. An excavation commenced, but no bodies were found. With not enough evidence to support their theory, that the Betlems murdered their children, the case went cold. And that's where the story ended.

I next read the story of Melinda Peters. On the morning of February 14, 2000, her parents went to wake their 5-year old daughter, only to discover she was not in her bed. Even though Melinda shared a room with her brother, he had no idea what happened to her. Witnesses later reported seeing a girl matching Melinda's description walking down the highway at around 4:00 a.m., so it seems she may have sneaked out on her own. Melinda was currently studying a fantasy book in school about children who go on adventures after running away, which could have inspired her actions. Things got even more bizarre once Melinda's belongings started turning up.

Three days after she disappeared, Melinda's pencil, marker and hair bow were found in the doorway of a tool shed approximately one mile from her home. A year-and-a-half later, Melinda's book bag was found 26 miles away. It contained more of her belongings and had been double-wrapped in plastic trash bags. This has led authorities to suspect foul play, but there are still no answers about why Melinda would leave her home in the middle of the night, who she might have crossed paths with, or what ultimately happened to her. That concluded this story.

In March of 2000, 5-year old Leah Roberts was found missing from Daycare. In checking the area, they found that Leah had managed to take her back pack with her but no one saw her leave. On March 18, a jeep was discovered abandoned on a back road in Washington. The vehicle had crashed over an embankment and while it's likely the driver would have been injured in an accident like that, there was no sign of any blood. What was later identified by her mother, all of Leah's belongings including the clothes she was wearing that day were scattered throughout the scene, but there was no trace of Leah.

One week later, police received a call from a man claiming he saw a little girl matching Leah's description walking down the road miles away from the crash scene. The caller said she looked disoriented, but he inexplicably hung up before giving any more details. This has been the only known sighting of Leah Roberts since her disappearance, but there's no other indication about what may have happened to her.

There were so many stories of missing children and I wonder if something that is explainable happened to them or was it something more than that. I feel silly thinking this, but I need to take off the legal hat now and see behind the story. In each of these situations there was a 5-year-old involved. I get up and walk around the office wondering if that has something to do with it. I sit back down and begin again.

I remember a case I had of a woman who murdered her little girl. I recommended that she be examined by a psychiatrist. The report came back that she was sane enough to stand trial and she was given life without parole. Now as I think about it, I wonder. Harriet had told me that ever since she moved into their new house 3 years ago she noticed strange things happening. Very subtle but noticeable things. She was woken by tapping or knocking on their second story window. It scared her so that she went to grab her five-year-old daughter to save her, only when she lifted her daughter up, she felt strange, different, not like her daughter at all. At first, she ignored the sensation but then she started hearing voices in the house and each time she turned, the only person in the room was her daughter. It was when objects started falling randomly and she barely got out of the way, that she was beyond scared. She looked at her daughter standing there smiling and knew it was her and she snapped. She went to the kitchen and got a knife and killed her. I quickly searched through the files for the daughters age, but couldn't find it.

Am I crazy or is there something here that supports what I feel in my heart to be true. I believe that my little boy Max lives in this thing called Michael.

Chapter 40

Finally, Taylor calls.

Mildred opens the door when I ring and says, "Come in Mr. Newman. Taylor is expecting you."

"Good morning Mildred."

Mildred leads me toward the studio, but just as she reaches out to open the door, Taylor opens it from the other side.

I can tell by her expression that she has been going through much the same thing as I have and I feel for her.

"Thank you, Mildred," she says and then turning toward me adds, "Peter, it's so nice out, I thought we could sit on the patio. Is that all right with you?"

"You must be reading my mind."

I follow her to the side patio which gives us a view of the lake. Mildred brings out a tray of coffee and pastries. Taylor smiles at her and when she leaves, she turns to me and says, "I am so sorry I haven't gotten back to you, but this is hard for me."

"I know. So, what have you learned?"

Taylor takes a sip of her coffee and then begins. She tells me that until just a few days ago, she didn't know that others could not see Michael. She thought that for sure Mildred had seen him, but when she asked her outright, she admitted she hadn't seen anyone with me besides Mr. Roman and yourself and some other friends, but no Michael.

I ponder this. "I'm so sorry Taylor, really. I know finding that out had to, well, blow your mind." I decide to keep nothing back as I add, "I wonder if I could see him."

Taylor looks at me. "I wonder if you can too. I wish there was a way to reach him so that we could find out, but I can't so I guess we won't know the answer; at least not now."

I look out at the lake and sip my coffee.

"Peter, there is more. I actually found out for sure that it is true, I was adopted, well sort of."

"What do you mean?"

"Well, unlike Christine, I was handed to my parents by my birth mother; but not legally adopted."

I listen as Taylor tells me the story of how her parents were given her and what little she knew beyond that. She told me about the pendant necklace and the pictures in it. "Now my parents know that it wasn't two pictures of me, but me and my twin."

I am silent, waiting. "Is that all," I ask.

"Yes, Peter, that is all."

It's my turn. I need to share what I have found out with her, even if it will sound crazy. It can't sound crazier than the Transitioner story I told her earlier.

"Until we met and my friends shared all of this with me, I was a non-believer. I have had so many clients who either faked insanity so they wouldn't go to jail, or were crazy I thought because of the outlandish stories they told me. Now I wonder if what they said was true."

"Taylor, this has all had me wondering and I went back over past cases feeling as though I made light of some things I was told because they were unbelievable. Now, I don't know. Know I am starting to believe more about things I don't understand."

"I know what you mean, Peter. If someone had told me this had happened to them, I would not have believed them, but know…."

There is silence. We drink our coffee and stare out at the lake. I wonder to myself if there is reason to be afraid of Michael, or if he is just my sweet little boy.

"Peter, I want to explain something to you."

I turn to face Taylor. "Okay, I'm listening."

"I am embarrassed to say this because it is wrong, but from the moment I saw Michael I have loved him. Granted he was only five when I first met him, but there was something about him that wasn't five. Anyway, I did not think of him as a child. I can see him so vividly sitting in the gazebo, playing with jacks."

"Jacks?"

"Yes, you know where you throw the ball up and try to pick up as many of the six-point metal knobs. I believe some people call the game knucklebones." I look at him and see that Peter understands. Any way, he was playing that game, dressed in his old fashion clothes and singing a song." I smile remembering.

"What song was he singing," I asked.

"It was cute; a very old song. I don't know what it is called, but it goes…and I began singing. "When this old world gets me down, and there's no love to be found, I close my eyes and soon I find, I'm in a playground in my mind, Where the children laugh and the children play, and we sing a song all day. My name is Michael, I got a nickel, I got a nickel, shiny and new, I'm gonna buy me all kinds of candy, That's what I'm gonna do",

I can't help it and find myself singing along with her. "See the little children, living in a world that I left behind, Happy little children, In the playground in my mind. Oh, the wonders that I find, In the playground in my mind, In a world that used to be, Close your eyes and follow me, Where the children laugh and the children play, And we sing a song all day…

Taylor smiles and then we laugh together as the song continues to replay in my head.

"Taylor, I have to tell you. That was our song. Christine, Max and I sang that song all the time."

Taylor looks at me surprised. "You know it too. I know it only because I heard it once or twice on the radio or something."

"It's called, 'Playground In My Mind' and it was recorded by Clint Holmes in 1972."

I can't believe this, but I now am positive that this Michael is my Max reincarnated. "How old was Michael the last time you saw him."

"I'm not exactly sure, but I think he was in his thirties. Weird huh?"

"Nothing seems weird to me anymore, nothing."

"Okay, I have something else to share with you Peter."

I nod, not saying a word.

"I think that Michael is going to die soon. I don't know why I think this, but I do. I want to figure out how so that I can avoid it happening, but I don't know what to avoid."

I think for a minute. "Do you think he will die in a fire, like my Max," I ask.

Taylor ponders this, "No. I don't think so. I think that, as you said, is how a Transitioner can enter the body of someone. The age and the method of death of the body they enter has to be the same. But, I think that once the Transitioner enters the new body, their death is another story."

I contemplate this. "Taylor, that is impossible to find out. You are talking about two people who have died and one has returned through the other. The death of both has taken place and at the same age. So, with the new life, what happens in the future cannot be known." I pause. "It's an unknown for sure."

Taylor looks at me quizzically. "You of all people should know that in this situation, there is an answer and it is probably staring us in the face. We need to just think."

I feel her pain and know that she believes what she is saying because she doesn't want to give up Michael. So, I remain silent.

"Peter, for now, please think about what scared Max or any hints he may have made."

"You think the answer lies with my five-year-old son? He never even had a chance to think about death and being frighten of anything."

Taylor looks at me. "You're right, Peter. I know that whatever it is, is only known by Michael and I'm not sure he knows for a fact. He is aging so fast and he seems to be unhappy where before he wanted to 'catch up' with me. Now it is as if he is aware that something is going to happen. I feel it too. I think it is going to happen soon and that is why I am trying so hard to figure it out."

"Taylor, you need to give yourself a break. This is too much, way too much."

She doesn't say anything for a long time as we just sit and stare at the lake. When she does speak, she surprises me.

"I do need a break. I have been threatening to go on vacation for some time now but have put it off because I was waiting for Michael; thinking he would come to me only at my home. But that is not true. I think he can find me wherever I go."

"Where are you planning on going?"

"I plan on going to Atrani, Italy. It is a city on the Amalfi Coast in the province of Salerno in the Campania region of south-western Italy. It is actually located to the east of Amalfi, just about several minutes' drive down the coast. I've been there before when I visited my friend, Annie and found it to be breathtaking. It is situated between sheer cliffs and the turquoise crystalline sea, near the so-called Valley of the Dragon. The village used to be summer residence of noble families of Amalfi and till this day it remains quiet and picturesque. There are winding streets that remain largely unchanged. To get to Annie I can walk through the nearby tunnel and I'll emerge in another town, the larger, and more famous, Amalfi where Annie lives."

"How long will you be gone?"

"I don't know, but I promise if I find out anything, I will let you know."

"Can you get the internet there."

"Good question. I know they have WIFI so I can get email, but I'm not sure about the internet. Probably in Amalfi."

"What's your email address," I ask.

Taylor gives me her email address and I give her mine. We continue to sit outside for a bit longer and then say our goodbyes.

"Take care Taylor."

"You too Peter."

TAYLOR BOUCHAND

Chapter 41

I take a United flight at 3:41 pm from Rochester and have a little over an hour layover in Newark, New Jersey. The airport is busy, but I manage to get a sandwich to tie me over. From there I board a plan for Zurich Switzerland where I face an almost four-hour layover. It's not so bad as I manage to catch up on my reading and actually finish my book "Gwendy's Button box" before boarding a plane headed to Naples, Italy. In the early afternoon of the following day I arrive in Naples Italy, exhausted and ready for a good night sleep in a real bed. I am so glad I sprung for a luxury hotel.

I wait patiently for my luggage and then hurry outside to catch a taxi to take me to the Vesuvio, the only 5 Star Deluxe Hotel on the sea front of Naples. In a half hour, we are pulling up in front of the Grand Hotel Vesuvio and as I stand on the sidewalk in front, waiting for my luggage to be unloaded and then transported into the hotel, I can't wait to get inside. I pay the taxi driver and thank him then hurry into the hotel.

I stand there admiring the architectural design. It is even more gorgeous than the pictures I found on the internet. A bell hop comes up to where I stand.

"Posso aiutarla?"

I turn and smile at him and noticing that I am English he repeats, "Can I help you?"

I let out a sigh of relief. "Yes, I'm checking in. Sorry, my Italian is not very good."

"No problem miss." I trail behind him as he takes me to check in and then continues with me to my room.

"Here we are, miss."

I step forward and open the door, then wait as the bell hop brings in my luggage and while he settles it on the luggage stand, I reach in my purse and hand him a tip, saying, "Grazie".

I follow him to the door. "There is a buffet breakfast for our guest," he says and then he is gone, I allow myself to appreciate the room. From its marble floors to its pale yellow striped walls it gives me a sense of relaxation. I check out the bath and then return to the front room to step out the French doors and take in the view from my patio.

"No exaggeration here," I exclaim, looking down at the Gulf of Naples in all its azure Mediterranean splendor. Boats rocked in the enclosed harbor below, beside an imposing fortress that juts out into the water and I can make out the ruins at Herculaneum, Pompeii, and Vesuvius that frame the gulf. It is like looking at a painting, life size and with movement. It's so beautiful and I have only this one evening to enjoy it. It's hard to pull myself away from this view, but I know I must. So, I turn and a little half-heartedly reenter my lovely room.

I do like the coolness of the marble floor as I walk barefoot in my room, gathering what I need to take with me to the bath. When I step inside the bathroom a feeling of calmness overtakes me. It is like entering a spa where I would like to linger, only know if I do I will lose time that I could put to better use. I look longingly at the soaker tub, but settle on a shower. And what a shower it is. There are water jets that I turn on so they can gently attack my body, taking away all the aches and stiffness from my long travel. It is wonderfully energizing. When I step out, I am hungry and ready to sit down to a good meal so I hurry myself along, grabbing a simple sundress, underclothes and shoes. I dress and then go about arranging my hair and reapplying my makeup.

I am finally ready and do a double take in the mirror, twirling around, admiring the summer flock I have chosen. It makes me feel beautiful. I move closer to the mirror and am happy with what I see. "You're ready," I say to my vision in the mirror, laughing. I grab my purse and I am out the door.

When making my hotel reservation I also made a dinner reservation, knowing that the ninth floor Caruso Roof Garden restaurant was a popular dining area and I didn't want to miss out on its excellent Italian cuisine. I check in with the maître d and soon I am shown to my table that as promised is near the window so that I can take in the view.

My Italian is less than serviceable and I hear no one speaking English, but I needed fear. Once seated I am able to order a glass of wine speaking in English and enjoy it while I sit taking in by the window view, forgetting about everything until I hear someone clearing their throat. I look up and the waiter stands near my table. "Miss, my name is Abramo and I will be your cameriere tonight. Would you like to place your order now.?"

I can hear his accent, but his English is superb. I am grateful and I tell him so.

"What would you suggest, I ask."

He graciously offers a choice of spaghetti alle vongole.

I agree to his recommendation and in minutes I am enjoying the best meal I have ever had. It is wonderful and I take my time so that I can really relish its unique flavor. This is an expensive hotel and I would not usually spend such a sum for accommodations, but I did and I will make sure that I participate in all that I can before I leave.

No one rushes me. I order another glass of wine and sip it slowly as I stare out at the view. When I resign myself to finally taking leave of the restaurant I am tired from my trip, only now I am too full to go to my room and sleep so I decide to take a walk.

Downstairs in the ingresso, I approach the reception.

"Scusa," I say, "Lei parla inglese per favore?"

"Yes, I speak English. What can I do for you?"

Letting out a sigh of relief I ask, "Can you tell me what would be the best scenic short walk to take."

Without hesitation, the front desk person who's name tag identifies her as Ms. Felicita says, "Yes, let me see, you can easily visit Piazza Cavour, Castel dell'Ovo & Piazza Bellini," she says, pointing at a map that miraculously appears in her hand. "And the hotel is opposite the Castel dell'Ovo in the historic quarter of Santa Lucia," if that interest you."

"That sounds promising. I think I want to go to the beach area."

"Well the port for boats to Capri, Sardinia and other destinations is 15 minutes' walk away and the hotel is a 17-minute walk from the beach." As she replies, she reaches across the desk to hand me a map.

"Grazie."

I walk toward the beach, not sure how far I will get as I set out, just enjoying the views. People are strolling up and down the esplanade. Behind me tiers of whitewashed buildings covered the steep slope. Even at this hour, the streets are packed. Cars and motorcycles nose through the narrow lanes, surrounded by pedestrians, many of them carrying open bottles of wine. I feel carefree and happy, not aware of how far I have gone until I pause to enjoy the view in front of me. It's a panoramic sunset across the Bay of Naples. With the skyline of Napoli just visible on the far left. The volcano, Mount Vesuvius holding center stage and Pompeii is to the right of Vesuvio and on the far right is the beginning of the Sorrentine Peninsula with Meta which is just out of view of the beach.

It is breathtaking and I stand amongst others who are talking in Italian, but I can tell they are expressing the beauty of the sight in front of us. It is not long before I turn around and head back to the hotel feeling confident I will sleep well.

I do sleep well and wake early. I go through my morning rituals, pack and then make a call and find out about breakfast. I am told it starts at ten o'clock. "Oh, no, that's a little late for me," I say.

"No worry. If you like we can send up a tray of fresh coffee with steamed milk, croissants and jams if you like."

"Grazie. That would be very nice. Grazie."

"It's no problem Miss."

By the time the food arrives, I am all packed and ready.

"Can I send someone to take your luggage down to the lobby, Miss."

"Sì, grazie,"

In a matter of minutes, there is a knock on the door. I can immediately tell that the bellhop doesn't speak English as he nods at me, then walks over to gather my luggage. I hand him a tip and smile.

I go out and sit on the balcony to enjoy my continental breakfast. The air is a little cool, but I don't mind it. It is just so nice to relax like this; especially with the day I have ahead of me. When I finish eating, I reluctantly go back inside. I check to be sure I haven't missed anything in the room and then at the door I turn around and say, "Goodbye, my room, parting is going to be such sorrow." I laugh at myself and then I am ready for the last leg of my trip.

I take a taxi to the Napoli Centrale. The train takes me through Pompeli and Nocera Inferiore and although there are several old churches and convents I see, as we pass through the town I can tell it is primarily modern in appearance. It takes about 15 minutes before we pull into the Vietri sul Mare, a town and commune in the province of Salerno, situated just west of Salerno. I have a choice of transportation. I can take a bus from here or go into Salerno and take the ferry. I opt to take the ferry. Soon I am on my way again. Three hours later I arrive in Atrani.

As soon as I get off the ferry I place a call to Annie. Thinking ahead, I am glad I setup up an international package with my provider so I wouldn't run into any problems using my cell.

"I'm so glad you're here. We are going to have so much fun Taylor. Sit tight. I'm on my way."

There is a bench on the platform and I sit with my luggage enjoying the warmth of the day while I wait for Annie.

"Wake up Taylor," she says jokingly, leaning down close to my ear.

I jump. "You startled me, Annie," I say laughing.

"Come on, let's not waste a minute. I am anxious to get out on the water.

We drive back to her place, talking non-stop as we try to catch up on what we've been up to since we last saw each other. When we arrive at Annie's, she helps me with my luggage and orders me to change. I do. "Hurry Taylor or all the good sailboats will be taken."

"Okay, okay, I say," walking into the front room. "I'm ready." Soon we are out the door.

We go a short distance to the sea where Annie gets a boat and soon we are out on the water. We spend the day exploring the Amalfi Coast with Annie pointing out the sites. "The Amalfi Coast is the perfect combination of wild nature and ancient fishing villages and its picturesquely nestled between the sea and rocky cliffs," she says. What this translates to is that it is something worth painting.

We sail by the town of Positano with its houses clustered along the hillside, seemingly climbing down to the water and I remark on its beauty. Annie slows the boat down so that we can enjoy the view, then we are off again at Annie speed.

"Well, Taylor are you hungry."

"You bet."

We steer into shore and anchor the sailboat before climbing up a steep incline to an even steeper path that takes us to a little outdoor café.

"So, Taylor, did you see a spot you want to paint?"

"A spot. You must be kidding. There are so many sceneries I would love to paint or sketch."

"So, you plan on staying a month, right? That will give us a lot of time and places to paint."

I smile at Annie, knowing that she enjoys having me here, especially because she wants to influence me to paint more. In this area with this scenery, she will win me over.

It has been a long day for me as I haven't quite caught up to the time change. When we finally head back to port to the rental place, I am drained and ready to sit back and do nothing. Annie is still bursting with energy, hardly able to contain herself as we wait while they check over the sailboat and give us the okay before we can be on our way.

When we arrive at Annie's I say, "Annie, if I am to be worth anything tomorrow, I need some sleep."

"I'm so sorry, Taylor. Here I am rushing you about when I know how much time it takes to get here."

"That's okay."

"Tell you what. We can talk while I fix us something to eat and then I'll let you get some rest."

I nod, smiling as Annie starts talking right away about her plans for my vacation. I hear a word here and there, but my mind is exhausted and can't follow her rapid chatter. She continues to talk while we eat and after drinking a glass of wine I am done for. I turn in knowing I fall asleep immediately.

Chapter 42

Each day blends smoothly into the next. When Annie and I aren't painting we are at festivals and parties. Where I am a loner, Annie is sociable.

During our young years I wondered what Annie saw in me. When we first started hanging out together she would take me to meet her other friends who were fun loving and always on the go. I would try to fit in but most times I would get a drink and move to the sidelines and watch the interacting. There was so much laughter and, yes, drinking and I wanted to be a part of it, even dreamed of waking one day and being a totally different person, but that never happened. I finally resigned myself to being who I was and Anne still called me a friend.

Eventually the time comes when I felt at ease going out on my own to paint. It was fun going with Annie, but painting is a personal thing that comes from within so you need to pick the spot and you need to let your mind take it all in so that your creative juices take over. Annie knew this too.

One morning over breakfast I announce, "Hey, Annie, how about we do our own thing today."

After all this time, I can read Annie and at that moment it was like she let out a sigh of relief.

"Oh, come on, Annie. I expect you to understand, but you could have been a little disappointed."

Annie smiles. "I was trying to let it be your decision, but I was afraid you would never let go. I mean it in the most endearing way, but you know why.""

"Yes, I do. We need to go where we feel inspired to paint, not just stop anywhere. I know that was what we were doing."

"And one more thing, Annie…"

"Don't say it. I already know. You don't need to be dragged to my social events" There is a pouty expression on her face. "Do you think I thought you were enjoying yourself. Taylor, one of the things I like most about you is how comfortable you are with yourself. I never learned how to do that which is probably why I love painting because that is the only time I allow myself to be secluded."

"Was it that obvious? Did your friends…"

Annie interrupts me again. "No, they didn't say anything. They were all too busy with themselves to notice anyone else."

We start laughing and can't stop as Annie mimics her friends who I know she adores.

"There is something about each of them that I am drawn too. For sure I like how easily they laugh and entertain each other."

I try to hold it in but the snicker comes out.

Annie smirks but can't fake it for long and again we laugh together.

Finally, I get serious. "Annie, I know what you mean and it is endearing. You like valuable pieces of their personality and together they bring the personality you want. That's not a bad thing."

It doesn't surprise me how many people know Annie and how many invites she gets. Annie turns none of them down. "It will be good for you Taylor," she would say each time I begged out of going. But Annie wouldn't take 'no' for an answer and I would find myself getting dressed to spend the evening with this one or the next. The funny thing is that I enjoyed her friends who were very nice. Most of them knew each other so I eventually felt like I knew them. That was good, but later after they all had asked and heard the story of how Annie and I met, and I had shared that I was an artist like Annie there was little left to talk about.

From that point on Annie and I would have breakfast together and then go our separate ways. Each evening we would come together and either watch TV or I would read while Annie went out to be with friends. It was a comfortable arrangement for both of us.

One day it rained from morning to night. Annie and I had breakfast together and waited, but soon realized this was it for the day. I made the best of it by going out on her patio and sketching the view from my vantage point. I became so absorb in the project I didn't hear Annie coming up behind me.

"Wow, that's great."

I turned; "Do you think it would be better in color?"

Without hesitation she said, "Yes." Keep sketching and I will bring your paints."

It is great. Annie sets up an easel at the center and I continued from the left edge, adding color to the sketch and watching it come alive with the rain dancing over the landscape and the sky ominous above.

That evening Annie's friends join us and I find myself delighting in them. There is still the halo of energetic fun, but it seems less intense. They listen more and I find myself keeping up my side of the conversation. When Annie's friend, Thomas arrives, he comes in chanting a poem.

"*The day is cold, and dark, and dreary; It rains, and the wind is never weary; The vine still clings to the moldering wall. But at every gust the dead leaves fall, And the day is dark and dreary. My life is cold, and dark, and dreary; It rains, and the wind is never weary; My thoughts still cling to the moldering Past, But the hopes of youth fall thick in the blast and the days are dark and dreary. Be still, sad heart! and cease repining; Behind the clouds is the sun still shining; Thy fate is the common fate of all, into each life some rain must fall, some days must be dark and dreary.*"

Someone yells out triumphantly, "The Rainy Day by Henry Wadsworth Longfellow"

"Right," Thomas says as he continues a slow walk around the room. So, what is he trying to say?"

There are several responses to his question, but one catches all of our attention.

"“I think it tells the story of a man who is experiencing depression. He is depressed because he is no longer young, yet he continues to dwell on the past instead of looking to the future. Eventually he realizes he is not alone, that everyone has regretful moments in life, and they learn to deal with them and move on. By the end of the poem he expresses hope knowing that like others, he must learn to accept and move on."

At that moment, I realize what keeping isolated has caused me. To read and watch alone I have but one opinion, but now as these friends talk and express their point of views, I know I have stifled myself. I don't want that anymore. I smile as I get up to fill my wine glass and at every opportunity I add to the conversations that are now filling the rooms of Annie's house. That evening when we say 'goodbye' to the last visitor, I am exhausted, but happy and one look at Annie and I see she notices the change.

I feel a change in myself that shows in my paintings. I paint not to just capture what my eyes see, but with added emotion. As I study the painting I did the night before, the colors make all my senses drowsy. I focus on each area seeing the pale sand-yellow, the bright green, and the faded blue of water and I remember the moment. I take in the sky deepening off to violet in the distance. The birds singing their songs while others search the lawns, or dart like minnows in and out of the trees. Yes, in the stillness of the painting I can hear the sounds of the day.

By June the Orange-Tree Flowers are in bloom. In Italy, the garden is reserved for vegetables and flowers are grown on the balcony so seeing flowers growing freely is a rarity. So, I paint them. On balconies and porches there are Oleanders, Bougainvillea, Jasmine, Crocus, Cyclamen, Bluebell, Violets, Periwinkles, and many others that I do not know the name of, all sharing space in the flower pot and I paint them.

After the rain, the earth smells fresh and the air carries the scent of the foliage. I decide to not start the day painting, but to go down for a swim. When I get to the beach the water is swift and fresh, and the little green crabs flee away from me in the shallows. Some children are there already, playing in an old hulk drawn up on the shore. One, with hair the color of hay, is playing that he is a pirate. He has his sister armed with a cap pistol and they shoot at invisible enemies.

I think about home where all summer the children play on the beach near my home. They are happy and friendly enjoying each wave as it sweeps in across the sand. The younger children would turn their backs to the lake, and run sensibly away. When the water, edged with foam, draws back again, they go running after it, with an air of driving the lake before' them. But at the next wave, they flee as before, with shrill alarm, and fresh surprise.

Now I watch these children. The sun warms their small brown legs, and they collect with enthusiasm bits of clam shell, sand dollars, and colored stones worn by the tide. The larger children plunge into the waves like little dolphins and with them I follow suit. The water is clear and cold, but I find it refreshing.

Time stands still and the weeks slip by, one after another until soon it is time to think about going home. I have been happy here and I don’t want to leave only I know I must so I decide to make the most of the time remaining.

PETER NEWMAN

Chapter 43

Life is back to normal for me. After having a long talk with Elizabeth, I realize that dwelling on all this was leading nowhere and I needed to focus on my work and, yes, my life now.

"Hey Peter, can I see you for a minute," David Carradine asked as I walked by his office door.

"Sure," what's up?"

"I have a case I want you to consider. I know it's not your norm, but I trust you to handle it for me."

I go into his office and take a seat. "Tell me about it."

David takes a moment and then begins.

"Warren Abella and his wife Faye, live in the town of Hamlin in Monroe County. They have two young children, Faye was pregnant with a third, at the time of the tragedy."

"On June 24, Abella took his wife to Hamlin Beach for a day trip. At 6.30 pm they climbed into their car prepared to drive home but Faye, a good swimmer who had her hands full with the children did not get a chance to swim so she wanted to have one last dip. Her husband pulled over and so, they exited the car, telling their children they would be right back and went to the water."

"What happened next depends on who's version you believe. Police maintained that Abella told them that waves knocked he and his wife over twice and that Faye was dragged under. Abella grabbed the shoulder strap of her swim suit, but it broke and she disappeared underwater. "

"A passerby saw the unattended children in the car and called 911, but later in talking to the police they said they didn't see anything."

"Now here's where it gets touchy. The story about the strap of her swimsuit ripping loose, Abella later denies telling the police when the detectives claim that when her body was found later that night her shoulder straps were intact."

"Faye's family and friends are suspicions of murder; especially after several things came to light. Suspicion rose first because he immediately put in a claim for her insurance and that lead to a family member doing a search on his phone and their computer."

"What they found out was Abella had gone to prison for rape and emails confirmed that he had a mistress who he promised to marry."

"I know this is all circumstantial but the fact that Abella staggered out of the surf to report his wife Faye missing, didn't add up. But the fact that no one saw what actually happened will make it hard to charge him with murder."

"Finally, you won't believe this, but there was the email from a work colleague of his that said, *if you want to get rid of your wife, the easiest way is to take her swimming and hold her under. Then feel sorry and start to cry.*"

"Want to give it a try."

"Yes, I do."

This is just what I need. Murder cases are fascinating if you remember that all information you obtain is not always reliable and factual. A client can be innocent but what is presented points to guilty until all the facts are known. I begin with the case of record on the rape charge for Mr. Abello. I go through court records requesting copies on the rape case from the clerk of the court in which the case was heard. I assign paralegals to check for published documents that may uncover details on this case or any other case concerning Mr. Abello.

I participate eagerly in the legwork, going through arrest records and interview the detectives who worked on the case pending and the previous rape arrest. I pay attention to the fact he has a mistress and find out all the details I can and have her interviewed, as well as people who know her. I seek out facts, angles and people connections that wouldn't be covered in the normal course of business by official sources. And it all comes together. I am ready to face the jury and get my client, Abello set free.

It is cases that require detail investigation that separates lawyers into categories of being a good lawyer or a bad lawyer. It's not about the win, but how you go about doing it. I know that David saw this as a case impossible to win. That's why he turned it over to me. He is in for a surprise. After months of investigation and three days in court the jury takes ninety minutes to bring back their verdict of 'not guilty'.

Chapter 44

It's my birthday and my wife makes sure I know it.

"Peter, why don't we have friends over for dinner on your birthday?'

"I don't know Elizabeth. Why not have a quiet dinner alone?"

"Because you have friends who want to share the day with you. But, if you're not up to it…"

"Am I up to it?" I ask. "Are you?"

"Yes, darling, I want you to celebrate your life and having a birthday is the best time to do that. Are you in?"

"Yes, I am, but you have to let me help."

Elizabeth gives me one of her charming smiles. The one that works from her mouth up to her eyes and makes her so endearing. "Yes, my love, you can help, but I am hiring a party planner and they pretty much take care of everything. But if you want to help you can help with the furniture arranging."

It is fun. We spent the next month working on the plans together and she makes me feel as though I am a big help. Each evening we talk about one issue or another, but she will not let me in on exactly who is coming. That is to be a surprise until the day arrives.

The evening of the party, as previously arranged, I arrive late. As I pull up in front of our house, there are lines of cars, some that I recognize, but others I do not know.

When I walk inside I cannot believe what Elizabeth has done. As I step over the threshold a lei is put over my head and those who stand in the area, are wearing the same. As much as I felt I was helping, I now realize that there was a lot that Elizabeth was doing that I was not aware of because that is only the beginning.

Handmade wooden spirit houses, candles and fresh flowers sat atop tables throughout the house. Gone is our traditional dining room table and in its place, there are several low tables surrounded by Thai mattress and triangle cushions. Above are strings of colorful lanterns hanging from the ceiling. It is like I have been transported into a home in Thailand.

As I follow Elizabeth she leads me to the patio where other guests are in conversation together. Just like the house has been transformed, the outside follows suit. Here there are beautiful handmade Thai lanterns adding that little bit of pizzazz to the patio and gardens as they are hanging around the area. There are handmade Thai floating water lanterns on the pool with floating flowers giving it a tropical feel. A waitress offers me a traditional Thai beer and Elizabeth whispers in my ear. "There is iced tea and mojitos if you're interested."

"You outdid yourself, honey. I never expected all of this. In all our conversations, I had no idea this would be the result."

"I know, and there is more."

I wander around thanking my friends for coming. My mind is so full of the moment I can't think of anything beyond this evening.

"Are you having a good time?" I ask. The answer is always "Yes."

Some people say, "Happy Birthday," and I thank them.

A gong sounded and someone said, "Dinner is served."

People began milling into the house to take a seat in the Thai styled dining room. Elizabeth has arranged a Thai-Style Tapas Dinner, my favorite.

It makes a stunning sight, laid out in a lavish, colorful spread. There is green papaya salad, stir-fried clams with Thai chili jam and basil, Thai-style marinated flank steak and herb salad, chicken satay, and Thai shrimp cakes with sweet chili sauce. For dessert, there is banana-coconut-sesame cake and champagne.

There is laughter, light banter with soft lighting and music. From the heart's perspective of this evening, the thought that everything is exactly as it should be, is completely true. In my heart, everything is divine perfection, not a single atom is out of place. Everything comes and goes at the precise moment it is meant to and I don't want the evening to end.

But it does. Too soon it grows late and we say good night to the last couple. I stand with my arm around Elizabeth as we wait while the party planners gathered up all their belongings and then help transform our home to its normal state

"It's kind of sad to see it all go," I said.

"Yes, it is." Elizabeth murmured.

I walked around locking doors and windows while Elizabeth goes upstairs. I pause in the dining room and lean over to pick up a brightly colored feather that floats to the floor, making me smile. I carry it with me upstairs.

Elizabeth finishes in the bathroom. I reach out and pull her into my arms.

"Thank you honey. It was amazing."

"You are so welcome."

I go into the bathroom and get ready for bed. When I return to our bedroom, Elizabeth is already asleep. I climbed into bed with my wife and I dream.

The following morning when I turn over the sunlight streaming through the window wakes me. I sit up and look around the room feeling as though something is wrong. Then it all comes back to me.

"I know how Michael will die." I said out loud.

Elizabeth still caught in the throbs of sleep said, "Huh,"

I leaned over and kiss her cheek. “Sorry,” I whisper, “Go back to sleep.” Then, my next thought is I must tell Taylor.

TAYLOR BOUCHAND

Chapter 45

By late June I am back home feeling rested and energetic to get back to my life only the weather is a little flakey as a wind comes whistling in from the lake, driving the rain almost level before it calms. It blows hard for three days causing doors to warp and stick and even my bureau drawers won't open. Mildred says, "Miss, maybe we need to keep a fire burning in the fireplace to keep the house air dry. What do you think?"

"I think, nothing is going to help, but you can try."

I keep busy in my studio since it is impossible to plan on working outside and even to make deliveries, but I have to admit it gets quite warm inside with the warmth of the weather outside and keeping a fire going until finally the wind swings around to the west and the sun comes out. It is summer again.

I do a good deal of sculpturing and I finish a canvas of the Amalfi Coast and dock at Positano. As I sit looking at the canvas I think of Annie and miss her. The distance between us has changed our friendship in many ways and I worry that someday our friendship will just disappear.

This makes me sad. I sit staring off into the distance before finally shaking the feeling of loneliness off and picking up my paintbrush. I work with a fury of passion as if I am afraid the visions of Amalfi will vanish.

I start another canvas. This will be of the coastline in Amalfi. Each day I work outside and fine joy in painting sceneries. I paint the old building in Ravello; the empty structure that stood lonely above the sea and I can't help but think how proud Annie would be that I am doing more paintings.

As if in disagreement, the breeze picks up again and the lake grows darker so that I must put away my paints and sculpt. At first, I haven't any idea of what I want to make, so I take a walk along the beach and find the perfect pieces of driftwood. It is linear shaped and will work well for the base of my sailboat. With the driftwood in hand, I am ready to begin. I gather the equipment I will need so that once I begin I won't have to stop my creativity and search for supplies.

I glue together pieces of driftwood until I am happy with the shape. Then I carefully drill a hole and then place a dowel into it. That will be the base to hold the mast. Then it is on to putting in the eye screws at the front and back to hold the sail in place.

It is so much fun that I am unaware of anything but what I am creating. I lay out the material for the sail and cut it to form two sails.

Mildred comes into the studio and ask if I would like some lunch.

I look up and smile. "No, not right now. I'll get something later." I then return to finish my work. Carefully I attach the sail sections to the mast at the top and then the bottom. I pause for a moment to decide the next move and then am back to work as I attach the sail to the eye screws in the bow and stem of the boat. I step back and look at it and feel good.

The day has gone and it is late when I finally decide to stop. I go into the kitchen and get a drink of water. I know that Mildred has left a dinner for me, and I search the fridge to find it. I put the dish into the microwave and while it heats I pour myself a glass of wine. The buzzer sounds and I take out my meal and settle with it at the island.

It tastes good and the wine relaxes me so that by the time I finish I am ready for bed. That night I dream.

Everything is quiet and dark. The water comes in in long swells out of the darkness and boats head out into the swells. The eastern sky turns grey, and then pink as the dawn arrives. The stars pale out, while tones of blue begin to show in the sky. Far out from shore, I see a fishing boat drawing the nets up as they go. Below the fish swim backwards and forwards under the boat like shadows. Then the nets are raised until they break water in a rush of silver, and the fishermen begin scooping the captured fish into the boat over the sides. The sun rises and the boats head to shore.

I wake up remembering my dream and wondering what possessed me to dream about fishing boats. I get up and stretch as I look out at the new day ahead of me. By the time I come out of the shower I know that the sculpture of a sailboat may have led to that dream. During these last few days my mind and my work has been about the lake or water in general so why not fishing boats. I let out a chuckle and then get dressed.

Chapter 46

I don't want to be alone. For the past few weeks I have spent nothing but time with myself and now I want company. I call Samuel.

"Samuel, I hope I'm not intruding but I wonder if you would like to go sailing with me."

There is silence on the other end and then finally Samuel speaks. "I would love to, but I can't today. Maybe tomorrow."

"That's okay. I'll get back to you."

I try to resign myself to waiting one more day, but I don't want to. I start feeling sorry for myself because I want to go out on the sailboat, but have no one to go with me. "I could go out alone..." That would work, except I want someone to talk with.

By noon I am still wondering what to do when I receive a call from Peter.

"Hello, Peter, I am glad you called."

"I'm glad I caught you home."

"I've been away on vacation but I'm back now and feeling good."

Peter hesitates for a moment wondering if he should tell her about his dream, but over the last few weeks, the dream seems less important now so he decides to let her enjoy her new-found happiness.

"So, what are you up to, Taylor."

I tilt my head to the side, thinking and then pose the question. "Peter, do you like sailing?"

"Matter of fact I do. I'm a pretty good sailor too."

"Well, if you have time, would you like to go sailing

with me. You can bring your wife with you and we could make a day of it. I just need a change of scenery and sailing relaxes me. What do you say?"

"Well, I am free, but I will have to check with Elizabeth. Can I call you back?"

"Sure. The sooner the better. You know how the weather can change."

I disconnect and wait. In the meantime, I go into the kitchen. Mildred is there straightening up. "Mildred, can you help me pack a picnic for possibly three or two people. I have asked Peter and his wife to go sailing with me."

"Sure Miss, I will be glad to. I'm happy you are giving yourself some time for fun. You have done nothing but work since you came home."

"I know, Mildred. I wanted to capture the images of Amalfi before I forgot them."

Together we pack crackers, cheese and fruit. Then Mildred gathers supplies to make little tea sandwiches while I get a bottle of white and red wine. When I bring the bottles to the counter, the phone rings. I pick it up. It's Peter.

"Hello, Peter."

"Jeez, I can't tell you how it bothers me that when a person calls, their name appears so that there is no surprising a body."

I laugh. "It used to bother me too, but I like being able to know whose calling. Saves me a lot of rushing when it's an annoying telemarketer call."

"Yes, me too. Have to admit that. Anyway, I can go sailing with you, but Elizabeth can't make it. She said to tell you she is sorry because she really wants to meet you and that I am to bring you around, if possible, when we return from sailing."

"That would be nice. Thank you."

"Well, I'll see you in about fifteen minutes,"

I disconnect and then thank Mildred for her help. I carry the picnic basket to the foyer and grab a light jacket from the closet as it can get cool out on the boat. I run upstairs to get some sunscreen and make sure I have Chapstick in my bag and by the time I return, Peter is at the door.

Mildred lets him in. "Thanks for coming with me. I want to sail away from shore and don't like to go out too far alone. So, thank you."

"No problem. I enjoy sailing and I would either be doing this or out on the golf course. Besides this will give us a chance to talk."

In the still, warm afternoon we set out. The empty shore curves away endlessly to the south under the summer sun, with a light breeze stirring the grasses on the dunes, and occasionally we can hear shouts of children as they play along the shore. We start out in silence taking care of the sails and I am happy to see that Peter is well versed in handling a sailboat. Every now and then we smile at each other, just enjoying the quiet companionship and the sights along the way.

The day has grown exceedingly hot and humid and even the breeze doesn't add comfort from the sun. So, after an hour we put down anchor. "Peter, did you bring your suit?"

"Never sail without it."

"Well, what about a swim before we eat. "

"Let's do it."

We stand on deck, striping off our clothes. Like me, Peter has worn his suit under his shorts and in no time, we're ready. I watch as Peter does a perfect dive off the edge of the boat, then I jump up and then down so that my feet break the surface of the water before my body submerges.

The water feels cold, but from pass experiences I know that feeling will be temporary. By the time Peter swims over to join me, the water temp feels just right.

"Want to swim a lap around the boat," Peter asks.

"You're on."

Soon we are splashing about as we try to beat each other back to the starting point. I had thought about having a relaxing swim, but now I am caught up in the challenge of beating my new-found friend. The once calm waters are now parted by arms pressing it back while legs kick through the surface repeatedly until we are back where we started, breathing heavy and feeling exhilarated.

We scull water to float in an upright position with our heads above water and with our arms extended sideways at shoulder. We quickly perform sweeping movements of our arms and kick our feet.

"Had enough?" Peter asks.

"Quite enough."

Peter continues to tread water while I climb up the ladder. As soon as my feet touch the deck, I hurry down below and bring up a couple towels so that we can dry off. When I return, Peter stands, shaking the water out of his hair. I hand him a towel.

"Dry off some and then join me below."

I hurry toward the bow of the boat and take the stairs down to the lower level. As I move about I realize that I feel comfortable with Peter and think maybe I might be ready to tell him about Michael.

Peter joins me below and without a word, begins helping me get the items out of the lunch basket and arrange them on the small table. There is Grilled Chicken with Creamy Lemon-Pepper Orzo, a Cucumber and Tomato Salad, a tub of Roasted Shrimp Salad, followed by a fruit salad for dessert with navel orange, grapefruit, clementines, fresh berries, and banana encased in a tasty honey vanilla bean sauce. Mildred has packed a couple bottles of fruit infused water that we will enjoy with our lunch. There are two bottles of wine; a Sauvignon Blanc and a Pinot Gris.

I see a smile appear on Peter's face.

I smile. "What is it?"

"Nothing, really. This is just great," Peter says.

"Glad you approve. I always feel hungry when I'm out on the boat and my housekeeper, Mildred would not let me out the door without packing a lunch. I don't know if it's the weather or the work to keep afloat, but I do appreciate having a good lunch."

"I think it's a little of both."

"Taylor, I…"

"I know what you are going to say, Peter, but can we hold off on that conversation. I am not ready to talk about it, just yet."

"Sure, of course."

I hate saying this to him, but suddenly I don't want to share my time with Michael with him. It seems selfish even to me, especially since he has told me of his experience. I look over at Peter and smile. He smiles back, making me feel as though he understands. A pleasant silence falls between us. We have not known each other long, but I feel as though I can trust Peter. We eat our lunch with Peter commenting on the food and the choice of wine.

"Thank you. It is very good, isn't it…" my reply is cut short when Peter says, "Whoa, the boat is really rocking now."

I walk over to the porthole and peer out. I am disturbed by what I see. The once pale blue sky is now threatening and the smooth surface of the lake is hemorrhaging with white frothy foam. Peter joins me at the porthole, looking over my shoulder to see the rain splashing against the window and obscuring the view of the off-shore cabins. We are caught in a gray mist that lights up as bolts of lightning travel to earth. The claps of thunder, the lightening show and the pelting rain mesmerize us until we finally come to our senses.

"Come on, Peter." I scream out loud so that he can hear me. We both hurry topside.

The sky was hidden above a dark thick layer of clouds, but far off in the distance, just before the navy-blue water line was a peek at the sky as it was before. As the boat tilted, the water near the boat was filled with white waves trying their best to make it onboard, bringing me back to the reality of the moment.

Moving like a drunken sailor, I went to open the box where the life vests were stored and took out one for each of us.

"Here, Peter, put this on."

I toss one to him and then take a moment to hook my vest. "Peter, come help me," I yell.

We go below and while I make sure that all hatches, portholes and doorways are closed to prevent flooding. Peter checks that bilges are clear of water.

"Peter, turn on the navigation lights. The switch is over there," I point with one hand while pressing the other against the wall to keep upright. I go about making sure that all gear and other loose objects are safely stored and that done, we hurry back on deck.

It is so overcast I can't see even a foot in front of me. "Peter, I think it will be best if we head to the nearest shoreline."

"I agree," his words barely audible as he wipes water from his eyes.

"Okay, I said, I grab the navigation map that I keep

in a plastic sheaf and together we made a decision on which way to go.

"Want me to steer," Peter asked.

I nodded my head, confident that he knows what he is doing and besides he is stronger than I and strength would play a major role in our safety.

I watch Peter as he makes his way to the stern, and commands the tiller. He navigates the boat toward shore heading the bow of the boat to approach the waves at a 45-degree angle. I hang on to the port side, watching and ready to assist, silently praying that the engine won't die.

Above us the sky is menacing, and the wind howls, swirling around us and making it hard to stand on deck.

"This doesn't look good." I say, my voice barely audible competing against the sounds of the wind and the claps of thunder.

I act as lookout trying to alert him if the water level drops too low as we sail toward land. "Look over there. I see something that looks like a pier. Do you see it?"

I watch Peter as he shades his eyes from the downpour. "Yes, I think it is. Let's head in that direction."

Peter yells over to me and I catch part of what he says, "… safely reach the harbor and dock."

I yell, "Okay."

The waves are steeper, identifying any shallow areas, but making it difficult to control the boat so we keep alert with Peter fighting the waves that slap against the sides, making it hard to steer. Finally, we reach the shore, pulling up along the dock. As soon as I can, with the boat bobbing I carefully step over the side. While Peter takes down the sails and ties them off I prepare the proper lines to the stern, fore and aft and the fender ties. I struggle against the wind and pelting rain and am thankful when Peter can assist me.

"Do you know who's dock this is?"

“No, I don’t. Hope their friendly and don’t mind the intrusion.”

“Not like we have a choice.” We look at each other and burst out laughing.

With the boat tied safely up and our feet on dry land we relax a little. I look around and see a man wearing a yellow slicker long raincoat, the hood up and hiding most of his face, standing a foot away from us. “Hello, saw you coming in. My name is Bill,” he says, his voice floating away on the wind. “This is going to get worse, come with me.”

If I had been alone I might have been a little leery of following this man but because Peter is with me and we really have no other alternative, we gratefully follow along.

Bill takes us to his golf cart and we climb in. We can hear the sand pit against the cart whenever we cross an exposed place in the road, and once or twice the cart swerves sharply in a sudden gust forcing us to cling tightly to each other. Bill bounces along in front of us toward the north side of the lake until finally he stops.

“This is my place,” he says. “Go on up and make yourself at home, I’ll be back.”

His house sits back and up high from the water edge and as we start up the path I am aware of the strength of the wind as I lean into it while the rain falls in sheets, making it hard to see in front of me. Several times I slip on the wet rocks, but Peter supports my arm and keeps me from going down.

Plodding slowly along there is no letup in the wind or the rain, but the path keeps us heading in the right direction until we stand at the entrance to the house.

“Well that was an experience,” I say.

“Yes, it was.”

"I'm glad we're here,"

I see Peter's face and he is trying his best to smile. "Hope the house is sturdy."

Right then a branch from a tree down near the water's edge suddenly snaps and sails a few yards up the slope toward us.

"Come on," I said; "let's go in."

The front door won't open so we go around the back way, to get out of the direct force of the wind. There we manage to open the door and the wind sweeps us through the entrance. It takes both of us to lean back against it to force it closed.

We stand side by side and I hear Peter as he breathes freely. I do the same. I stand up straight and look around and notice the chill and stillness of the house being accentuated by the sounds of the storm on the other side of the walls.

Peter walks across the room to the fire place. There he stoops down and starts working on a fire. He's good at it and soon has a blaze going. I explore a little and find the kitchen. "He said make ourselves at home" I whisper seeing a bottle of wine in the fridge. I pour us each a glass and leave the bottle on the counter. As I head back to the front room, I feel the house shake and the sound of the windows rattling as I hand Peter a glass of wine.

"I wonder if my boat is safe. She's like a part of me, you know. I have had her so long," I said.

"I wouldn't worry, Taylor. She's a sturdy boat and we tied her up tight. "

"Instead of worrying about the boat, I guess I should think how lucky we are that we were able to make it to shore and that our new-found friend, Bill was neighborly enough to let us stay here." I said.

Peter nods his head.

Outside the rain continues, relentlessly pounding against the house and angling just so that it causes a fair-sized puddle to grow just inside the door. I hurry down the hallway and find the bathroom, just across from the kitchen. There I locate some towels and bring them back with me to put in front of the doorway.

I stand there a moment, listening to the rain outside. "Sounds like the wind is gaining momentum."

"Yes, it does seem that way."

At that moment, the house shakes dramatically Though the rain has slowed, the wind seems to be getting stronger all the time; once or twice it shakes the house so hard I think the walls will cave in. There is nothing to do so we sit, warming ourselves and drinking the wine. After a bit, Peter gets up and looks out the window. "Maybe we should see if we can help our host," he says.

"Yes, let's do."

There is a closet at the front door and I open it to find two windbreakers. I hand one to Peter and I put on the other one. They don't fit well, but they will keep us dry.

We go out the back way, and it takes the same amount of strength for us to close the door after us as it did when we arrived. We walk close to the building to the front of the house, and when we turn the corner, the wind tears the air right out of our months.

"Boy," said Peter, holding his hands in front of his face, "I'm glad I'm not out on the lake now."

I try to see the lake, but it is lost in a gray smother of rain and spray and blowing sand. I see that near us telephone poles are down, and I point at them. And then the big elm behind the house falls.

It goes over slowly, with a sort of sigh, taking a lot of ground with it. Peter doesn't say anything, but his eyes have a wild look in them. He grabs my arm, and points at the barn near Bill's house. We watch as the old barn sags over on its side, then the wind worries it along toward the lake. We see Bill as he moves quickly out of the way.

"We ought to go over and help him," I shout, with my mouth close to Peter's ear. He makes a gesture of helplessness. "How are we going to get there?" he shouts back.

He is right. We crouch together with our arms wrapped around one of the straining pines. We are pretty high above the water where we are, and I don't think the lake will reach this far. I barely have the thought when I see the wave coming toward us but it doesn't look very high-just a line of brown foam, with branches and sand in it, but it scares me just the same. It passes below us, and then there is just water, moving fast.

A moment later, I see him.

He is below me, and a little to the east, trying to get up the slope from the lake. He seems tired; and the wind is worrying him. While I watch, he loses his balance, and half falls; and then he begins to slip backward toward the water again. Another wave is coming from the east; I can see it coming.

I don't know how I get down the hill to him, against the wind, but I do. I get my arm around him just in time, and pull him up out of the way; the crest goes by almost a foot below us.

He lays back against me, white and spent, with closed eyes. "I am afraid I wouldn't get here, darling," he says.

I hold him close. Even then, with that mad flood below us, I think we'll make it all right. I put my face down against his; his cheeks are deathly cold. He lifts his hands slowly, as though they are a great weight, and puts his arms around my neck. "I had to get back to you, Taylor," he says.

"We'll have to hurry, Michael," I tell him, trying

desperately to pull him along, up the slope, but he is like a dead weight, he seems to have no strength left at all. He smiles at me piteously, and shakes his head. "You go. Taylor," he says; "I can't make it."

I try to lift him, then, but he is too heavy for me; I can't find a foothold on the slippery ground. The water is higher, now, almost at our feet; a dark ripple washes in over my ankles. "Michael," I cry, "for God's sake ... "

"Let me look at you," he whispers. He holds my face in his hands, and looks at me for a moment with wide, dark eyes. "It's been a long time, darling," he says.

I don't want to talk, I want to get out of here, I want to get him up the slope away from the water.

"Michael," I cry; "please ... "

His arms tightened around me for a moment. "Hold me close, Taylor," he says.

I hold him close, but my mind is in a panic. I can't lift him, I can't get him away, and the ground where we are laying is beginning to give. "Peter," I shout as loudly as I can; "Peter."

It is then I see it coming.

It comes in from the bay, a great brown wave, sweeping up the hill. There is no escape from it; we can't climb above it. Well, I think, we'll go together, anyhow.

Bending over, I kiss him full on the lips. "Yes, Michael," I said; "we're together now."

"Taylor," he whispers "

"I know," I said.

And then the wave hits us. I try to hold on to him, to go out with him, but it tears us apart. I feel him whirl out of my arms; the water draws me under, and rolls me over and over then pushes me upward.

Then something crashes into me, and that is all I know.

Peter finds me sprawled in a tree half in and half out of the water, and drags me back to safety. How he manages to carry me up the slope and back to the house in that wind, I don't know. He lays me on the sofa and Bill brings him a blanket to put over me while he tries to get me to drink some hot tea.

Peter sits beside me all that night. He tells me later that he had to hold me down, that I kept trying to get back to the lake. I don't remember much about it, it was all dark for me and all I remember is the dark.

It is a week before I can travel, but it makes no difference, because the roads are out, and we couldn't have gotten through, anyway. I lay on the sofa in this strange house and eat what Peter brings me, and try not to think about what has happened. When the weather permits, Bill drives us home and Mildred who was beside herself with worry, helps me up to bed.

Peter brings back the news from outside. He tells me that there hasn't been as much damage as we might have thought. Even Bill's home had escaped major damage and he had safely brought my boat back to my house.

I tell no one what I have been through because I can tell from their conversations they do not know I was trying to save Michael. I am sure they only saw me struggling my way to safety.

It's hard and each night when I am alone, I cry myself to sleep. It seems so unfair for it to end this way and harder because no one mourns the loss of Michael. I stay in bed recovering from the shock of what has transpired longer than necessary because I am afraid to face the reality of never seeing Michael again.

But the day comes when I know I must return to my life. It is a bright autumn day, deep blue and sun-yellow in the streets, and the buildings rising clear and sharp against the sky. Mr. Bachman is waiting for me at the gallery. "'We worried about you, Taylor," he said. "Miss Lily and I ... we couldn't get any news for a long while."

"I'm so sorry you had to worry, but I am doing fine now."

We are in Mr. Bachman's office having a cup of tea and discussing future endeavors. I am less anxious to consider another show, but Mr. Bachman thinks it would be a good idea. I tell him I will give it some thought and get back to him.

The days run together without hope. Yet I get up, spend time in the studio and make the rounds to my clients. It is hard to go forward, but I know I must. During one of Peter's visits to check on me, he says, "Taylor, you look good. How do you feel?"

I smile and say, "I feel good. Really I do."

"Well, then, I have something to tell you."

"What is it Peter."

He takes a deep breath. "I had a dream sometime back and in that dream, Michael drowned" He pauses. "It was shortly after talking with you about Michael and I guess I had him on my mind. In any case in my dream it was so very similar to what happened to us. There was a storm, a vicious storm that you were caught in with Michael and something happened and you tried desperately to save him, but you couldn't. I woke from that dream and my first thought was to tell you or warn you. Then you called and invited me out on the boat and I was going to tell you but then we were caught in that storm and I never got a chance."

I looked at Peter, knowing from his expression he didn't know. He didn't see Michael. He only saw me. No one knew Michael existed and no one knew that he had died. No one was looking for his body because no one reported him missing.

There were tears in his eyes as he finished his story and I began to understand what he was trying to tell me really had nothing to do with Michael.

"I am so sorry, Peter."

"Why are you sorry for me?"

"Because you wanted to tell me and didn't get a chance to."

"It wouldn't matter, except now I think that it was meant as a warning for us and had nothing to do with anybody or anything else. I shouldn't have let us go out on the boat."

"You shouldn't blame yourself, it was an accident and you couldn't know." I paused before adding, "Besides, I had a dream about water too."

PETER NEWMAN

Chapter 47

I hadn't worn that old overcoat in some time now. It sat in the back of the hall closet in a plastic bag, forgotten. I don't know what made me think of it just then, but thinking of it I remembered.

As I walked over to the closet, I opened the door wide and stepped inside so that I could locate the coat, stuck way in the back. My hands grabbed hold of the plastic bag and then worked their way up to the hanger. I carefully lifted it off the bar and worked it to the front.

I stood there with the coat in my hand for some time, as a flood of memories came forward. Even after such a long time, there was still a faint smell of smoke on the fabric of the coat. I shook my head, trying to let go of the past and bring myself forward again.

Carefully I managed to get the coat out of the plastic and watched as the plastic drifted to the floor while I reached inside the pockets of the coat until I found what I was looking for.

I released the coat and watched it fall on top of the plastic. Then carrying my find, I walked across the room and sat down on the window seat, looking at the gift I had in my hand. I had forgotten about this gift I wanted to give my son. How could I have forgotten about it?

I now remembered how I had brought the CD home and taken it out of the suit jacket and placed it in the safety of my coat, this coat. I stared at the contents, allowing the tears to fall until I finally was able to get up and go over and place the CD into the player. The room filled with music and I sang along.

www.ingramcontent.com/pod-product-compliance
Lightning Source LLC
Chambersburg PA
CBHW030822310726
48980CB00006B/594/J

* 9 7 8 1 9 2 8 6 1 3 3 9 8 *